Seven Lives

Seven Lives

Johanna Kirwan

Fire & Feather
Publishing

First published 2025 by Fire & Feather Publishing
www.fireandfeather.com

ISBN 978-1-918128-00-0 (HC)

ISBN 978-1-918128-01-7 (SC)

ISBN 978-1-918128-02-4 (ebook – Kindle)

ISBN 978-1-918128-03-1 (ebook – ePub)

Interior Design & Illustrations by Janet Levrel

Contents

"What counts in life is not the mere fact that we have lived. It is what difference we have made to the lives of others that will determine the significance of the life we lead."

Nelson Mandela, speech at the 90th birthday celebration of Walter Sisulu, Walter Sisulu Hall, Randburg, Johannesburg, South Africa, 18 May 2002.

Foreword

On Shifting Ground

There are seven stories here, seven women—seven paths—traced across shifting lines of countries, contracts, and consequences. They share something that quietly binds them. Each believed, at one time or another, in the possibility of change. Each encountered the word 'development' not as a theory, but as a threshold.

To really make a difference, to live in another country for work, is to become someone else, again and again. You unlearn your morning rituals. You forget how silence is interpreted. You change your tone. Your clothes. The way you greet, the way you eat, the way you explain where you're from. You leave behind friends, family, lovers—sometimes without knowing you have left them for good. You adapt because you must. And then, just as you begin to belong, you pack up and do it all over again.

After a while, you stop noticing the shifts. You become fluent in change. A different version of yourself for each setting, each assignment, each city. It's not performance, exactly—it's instinct. Protection. A chameleonic kind of survival. You blend in so well, you forget what standing out ever felt like. Until one day, you're not sure which version of yourself is the real one or if a real one still exists.

Over the course of thirty years, the ground shifted. The work that once felt clear—development, assistance, help—became tangled in politics, power, and paradox. At twenty-two, you think you bring something the world needs. But the older you get, the more you see that the knowledge, the resilience, the actual expertise—it's already there, in the countries. You are not the answer. And that realization is humbling, disorienting, and liberating. If you are not there to give, then what are you there to do?

Billions of dollars have flowed through the development sector—some of it lifesaving, some of it well spent. However, for every success story, there are duplications, contradictions, and failures that often go unspoken. Western consultants fly in and out, diagnosing problems in places they barely know. Projects are designed in distant capitals, delivered through acronyms and log frames, and measured in short-term outputs. The language is technical. The posture is often paternal. And too frequently, what is offered as assistance ends up reinforcing the very power imbalances it claims to challenge.

And then there is the question of gender. A partner, a wife, and a quiet infrastructure of support often accompany a man in this work. A woman, especially one who chooses to do this alone, is expected to carry everything herself. She is praised for her strength, even as that strength slowly isolates her. She is admired for her ambition, even as it comes at the cost of her connection. The longer she stays, the more she trades intimacy for independence, roots for reach. To rise in this world—to reach a point where you can truly shape decisions, not just deliver them—is often to walk a path so narrow it barely leaves space for a personal life.

But these stories are not case studies. They are not meant to explain development assistance or to measure impact. Instead, they are fragments of what it means to step into a culture not your own—to arrive as a stranger, to start from nothing, to try and listen before speaking. They are stories of watching, stumbling, learning, and changing.

What does it mean to try to support something you don't fully understand? What does it cost to keep trying? These women won't give you answers, but if you care about international development, they may leave you with better questions.

Johanna Kirwan,
August 2025

Prologue

Big Hopes and Ideas

1979

Nancy parked her moped in the car park outside the conference hall. She took off her rain-soaked anorak and stuffed it down the back compartment of the moped. She examined her jeans, pleased that the cycle clips had spared the cuffs from any serious wet spots. It had taken her three hours to navigate the route from her parents' home in Cricklewood to Brighton, weaving in and out of back roads. She shook herself down and tried to look more presentable. It was a cold March morning, and she really should have worn a jacket over her bell-bottom jeans and t-shirt.

Nancy took a breath and walked into the building. She followed a corridor, bare aside from a flurry of pictures of old souls on the wall. The Institute of Development Studies (IDS) was renowned for its expertise. She was excited about the two-week course she was starting today, her first training to prepare for two years of volunteering outside of England. And the best and worst thing, she didn't even know where she'd be sent. She was shortlisted for Nepal and Sierra Leone. She really didn't know much about development, but she knew she wanted to work overseas, anywhere she might be needed. Her desk job for the British government in Watford had been interesting enough, but after a few years she'd spent there, she couldn't wait to hand in her notice and start her travels. It wasn't that she was zealously religious and wished to save the world. But she'd been feeling she needed satisfaction in her work. She wasn't born for a life behind a desk in Watford.

Nancy stepped nervously into the conference room at the end of the corridor. She closed the door quietly, trying to make as little noise as possible as she entered. The room was already full; she knew that about fifty participants had signed up. Nancy looked down at her scuffed sneakers. She should have dressed more smartly, but it was too late now. She stuffed her large duffel bag with all her papers under her arm and looked around. They were serving hot drinks on the side of the room, so she made herself a coffee with milk and took a few of the cookies from the side plate. Nancy had put on weight since leaving university, and her jeans felt tight. She swallowed the cookies quickly with a few gulps of coffee and looked around furtively. Most of the participants were eager young men in suits, standing in small circles and making big gestures. Two young women were talking at one of the bistro-style tables, and Nancy walked over.

"Hi, I'm Nancy," she said in what she thought was too high-pitched a voice. One of the women turned around and smiled brightly.

"Oh, hi, I'm Lisa, and this is Marie Louise," Lisa said as if she were already at home here. "I'm from Dublin, and Marie Louise is from Paris. You sound British?"

Nancy nodded, hoping her expression didn't appear too apologetic to the Irish girl. Lisa didn't seem to notice. She was short and petite, but she stood straight and with a lifted chin. Marie Louise greeted Nancy with a French accent.

"I am so tired after traveling here from Paris last evening. It was a long trip." She was taller, standing at about 5 feet 7 inches, with dark hair and a slim build.

"So, are you starting to work in international development work as well?" Nancy asked them since they looked to be about her age, in their early twenties.

"I just completed my degree at the Sorbonne," Marie Louise said. "I don't want to travel right now, but I'm keen to learn more about this field and how to seek consultancies. I studied energy and environment for my bachelor's."

Nancy started to feel more at ease. She noticed that both women were wearing suits. Lisa's didn't look particularly expensive, but Marie Louise was wearing a beautiful navy silk suit with a colorful scarf.

They made their way into the auditorium for the first lecture from a well-respected development expert. The expert argued in his presentation that traditional international development practices often exclude the poor, marginalized, and powerless— the "last" in society. He called for a radical shift in development practice, reversing roles, methods, and mindsets so that the voices of "the poor" were prioritized in planning effective interventions. Nancy was impressed. She noticed Marie Louise was falling asleep. Lisa took furious notes and nodded a few times. The speech was followed by a short film of Cambodia focusing on the Khmer Rouge and the years of famine and forced labor. At one point, Nancy had to look away from the pictures of those children with bloated bellies, tears streaming down her face.

During the break, the three of them made their way outside to the courtyard. Four other young women were seated at a table, talking rather animatedly. At least a few more women were present, Nancy thought. She noticed that one of them was slightly overweight like herself, but she was extraordinarily beautiful. The woman turned around and stood up.

"Hi, I'm Rebecca." She sounded American. Next to her sat a woman wearing a green sari with a denim jacket over it. She got up from her seat more slowly to shake their hand.

"I'm Geeta. I'm studying at St Mary's in London, civil engineering." Geeta was striking, slim, and she had a kind face.

"Hi, I'm going out as a volunteer to Asia or Africa in the next few months," Nancy said in a low voice as if she wasn't sure if any of them were really interested.

Nancy looked over at the third woman, who was rather sharp-looking, thin, and was fiddling with a book as she introduced herself. "I'm Anna," she said as she looked back down at her book, and Nancy could see it was Robert Chambers' famous development book, *Putting the Last First*. Anna glanced back up quickly. "Sorry, I don't mean to be rude, but we only have a few days here, and I want to learn as much as possible!"

Nancy noticed that a tall woman was walking directly over to join them at the table. "Hi, I'm Patricia! Do you mind if I join you?" Patricia was elegant, in a midi black skirt with a white blouse, carrying her jacket. She pulled a chair from a nearby table and pushed herself into a space between Geeta and Nancy. "So, are you all going on overseas assignments soon?" she asked.

Nancy answered first to get it over with as quickly as possible. "I'm volunteering, either in Nepal or Sierra Leone, building water supply systems."

"How interesting," Geeta replied. "I trained as an engineer, so that's something I might consider. I might work in India after I finish at St Mary's. There are certainly enough problems in water supply there that I could help with, especially in the north of the country."

Nancy noticed that two of the girls rarely looked up: Anna, who was still too busy reading her book, and Rebecca, who kept glancing at each of the girls and then quickly looking away. Nancy thought that she might be very shy. She considered herself shy as well, but she was good in small groups.

"Rebecca, why are you at the conference?" Nancy asked her, trying to coax her into relaxing a little. Usually, Americans were not quite as shy as this, she thought. Rebecca gave her only short glances when she answered.

"I'm considering working overseas. I'm not sure. I'm visiting a friend in Oxfordshire; we studied together at Johns Hopkins in Baltimore. She mentioned this Institute, and I booked it. But I'm not that sure I want to live overseas, far from my family. They live in a small town about forty minutes from Baltimore." She glanced at Nancy. "Thanks for asking."

Anna looked up and spoke. "I'm interning in New York for the United Nations Development Program (UNDP) for the summer." She looked straight back down at her book and continued reading, then glanced at her watch.

"You will love New York," Rebecca said, almost whispering. "Good theatres, classical music concerts and operas." Nancy smiled at Rebecca and thought she wouldn't mind some of that herself. She had always longed to visit New York.

Nancy then looked at Patricia, who seemed distant. "And yourself, Patricia?"

Patricia sat up. "I've known since I was a child that I would work overseas. I can't imagine a life without travel and working overseas. It's not an adventure for me, it's a need," Patricia replied. Nancy thought that was an odd thing to say for someone in their early twenties.

"And where are you going?" Nancy asked her.

"I'm already working overseas in Thailand, on the border with Cambodia," Patricia answered.

"That must be challenging. I've read that there are hundreds of thousands of Cambodians in camps on the border," Geeta commented.

A few days later, the women had spent all their breaks together. On the last day, they met for dinner at a cheap restaurant near the sea, a low-key place that Nancy had found. Nancy arrived first, looking as smart as she could in a flowered wrap-around skirt with a t-shirt and sandals. She sat and waited for the others, looking out at the sea. The conference had excited her about her future, and now she was praying she would be sent by the voluntary service to leave as soon as possible. She thought back to her interview in London. She had dressed as smartly as possible in a skirt and blouse, which she borrowed from her housemate. Her housemate had said to her, "You know the problem with some people is, they talk about these things, going overseas, and all that, but they never do it... I'm sure you won't be one of them."

Her words had stuck with Nancy.

When everyone had arrived, a young waitress walked up to the women and pointed at the menu on the wall. Everyone made their order rather quickly as they knew they had little time left together. Lisa talked first: "So are you keen to work in Asia, Africa, or the Middle East?" she asked the other women.

"I'm hoping for Nepal," Nancy said.

"Why?" Geeta asked her.

"I guess I'm a romantic. Who wouldn't want to go to the land of the Himalayas? The other choice, Sierra Leone, would be tougher. I would rather start with an easier country. And I've always been interested in Buddhism," Nancy responded.

"I hope you get it," Geeta answered. Nancy thought Geeta was probably wondering if this rather rotund, jolly girl was tough enough to go halfway around the world and live in a country far poorer than even India.

"Well, I think I would want to go to the poorest regions and those countries most in need. I don't care which region, but I guess the need is greatest in sub-Saharan Africa," Lisa said.

"Don't you think that's a bit idealistic?" Patricia said. "I mean, we heard a lot this week about the dangers of deceiving oneself that development programs actually alleviate poverty..."

"Well, emergency assistance by the likes of Médecins Sans Frontières (MSF) and other agencies does save lives. You can't argue with that," Lisa responded.

"I'm not," Patricia replied. "But you mentioned one of the best agencies out there. They have suffered, losing staff in various countries and going where many agencies are too scared to travel."

"Patricia, you seem to have more experience than we have from working in Thailand. What do you consider the best agencies to work with?" Rebecca asked from the second table.

"I don't know yet. I'm working with a reputable NGO on the border. Still, there are far too many agencies where expatriates live in nice houses, employ servants on low wages, send their children to the best schools, and rarely interact with any locals. And they make decisions about where roads and schools are built, often with hardly any locals involved," Patricia continued.

Anna looked up from reading what appeared to be a new book. "I read that in Nepal, the road route in the west of the country was determined by the Canadians with hardly any consultation with the Nepalese Government." Anna returned her eyes downwards, and Nancy glanced over at the cover: Small is *Beautiful: A Study of Economics as if People Mattered* by E. Schumacher.

"Is that good?" Nancy asked Anna.

"Yes, it's all about the danger of top-down development approaches," Anna responded.

"A good book, but Schumacher is arguing for less sophisticated technologies for developing countries; what he calls "intermediate options". Let's see if India and other countries will settle for less than industrialized country options," Patricia responded.

Nancy looked over at Patricia, curious about her rather more knowledgeable comment. She thought that she was likely a few years older than the others and certainly more experienced.

"What do you see yourself doing then over the coming years?" Nancy asked Patricia.

Patricia looked out the window at the sea across the road as the tide was coming in. "All I hope is that I can make a difference in some lives. Not excessive, just enough to say, I lived a life of service..."

Nancy wondered if that would be enough for her. She wasn't sure.

After the girls finished their meal, they laughed as they all raised their glasses of wine in a toast to each other. They then left the restaurant, crossed the street to the sea, and walked together on the pebbles as the tide wet their feet. Everyone made pledges to keep in touch on their journeys. But they wouldn't see each other again as a group for decades.

Nancy sat on the beach a while longer after the others left, looking into the distance.

Part One

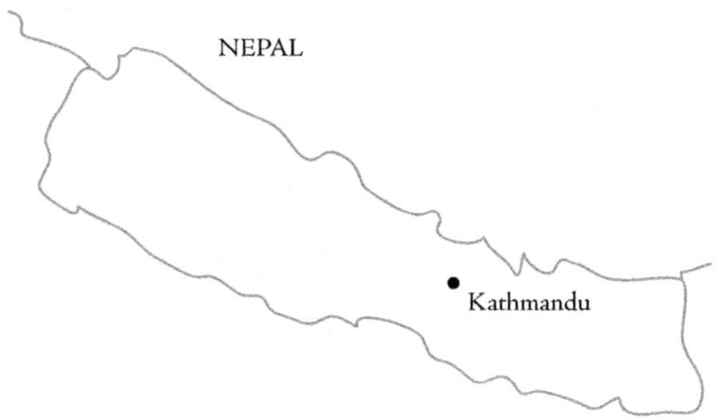

Nepal (1979–84)

Nancy

Naivety

Chapter 1 · Arrival in Kathmandu

Nancy was studying a gecko crawling up the side of the poorly painted wall in her lodge in Thamel, Kathmandu. It was around six o'clock in the evening; the sunset sky was firelit, and the faint sound of rickshaw bells rang through the open window. The gecko moved slowly, hesitated, and then jumped on the mosquito near it before moving on to the next one. The night air was warm and dry, and Nancy was basking in the first few days of her new life in Asia.

She decided to leave her room and walk around the lodge and into the streets of Thamel as the sun was fading. The smells were unique to her; wood and incense burning, oriental spices from the food cooking in local shops, including garlic, mustard, and cinnamon, but many she couldn't recognize. The smell of wet mud and cow dung from the unpaved roads, and smells that were more repugnant from raw sewage strewn on the back streets. She stopped at a stall, full of second-hand books, and bought a few for one rupee each. The narrow streets teemed with backpackers: arriving, leaving, searching for places to eat. Nepalese children were everywhere, playing in the streets while their mothers cooked and sold street food. No one noticed Nancy. In the 1970s, Kathmandu was an international destination for travelers, and the somewhat overweight, dirty blonde-haired woman weaved through the back streets with few people taking any notice of her.

Luckily, the dust that had filled the September air earlier had settled in the valley by this time. During the day, it had clogged her sinuses and made her sneeze constantly. All her life, she had suffered from sinus attacks, and she was somewhat concerned if this would be a significant problem for her living here. Nancy had read that, according to Nepalese folklore, Kathmandu Valley was once a large lake that had existed for thousands of years. Now, all that was left was dust from the basin. The Indus Valley population had lived by the lake around 2500 BC, and the Dravidian people had been there over a thousand years earlier. As she walked, Nancy wondered what this busy, dusty valley must have looked like when the Tibeto-Burmans and the Indo-Aryans settled here centuries ago, an ever-evolving mix of Buddhism and Hindu heritage.

She walked along the cobbled paths to Hanuman Dhoka palace, a temple complex about ten minutes from her hotel. Kathmandu was full of temples, but this one was the most important. The buildings dated back to the sixteenth century. The Palace was named after the monkey god, Hanuman. It was now a tourist attraction, but she read on the plaque at the entrance that the royal family had lived in this palace until 1886. The wooden carvings around the building had survived; they were well-worn but still intricate. Nancy took photos with her Olympus camera, which she had bought especially for her two-year stay. She stood in a line, taking pictures beside five other tourists, capturing the same shot. She didn't mind being mistaken for a tourist.

Ten days ago, Nancy had flown in from London with seven other volunteers to help rural communities in the Nepalese hills construct water supply and sanitation systems. After spending the first few nights in Kathmandu, she would head to orientation and language training near Dhulikhel, on the edge of the Kathmandu valley. Nancy was a little scared of what the coming months and years might bring in this entirely new environment. However, when they had landed in New Delhi and had been there ten hours in transit, she had felt comfortable with the smells, bustle, and strangeness of a new continent. She felt quite at home when she arrived at Tribhuvan airport, which consisted of only one room with a baggage carousel.

Walking around Hanuman Dhoka Palace and the surrounding streets, Nancy noticed that the two-story buildings were primarily made of brick with wooden window frames and doors. Like the palace, the woodwork was beautifully carved, a local skill developed over centuries. The houses in this area of Kathmandu were terraced, and most of the buildings sold wares or had food shops on the ground floor. Nancy was always fascinated by buildings and sometimes wondered why she had trained as an engineer rather than as an architect. However, as an engineer, she had considered that she stood a better chance of securing a job overseas.

There was little drainage on the narrow streets of cobblestones, and when it rained, everyone had to wade through countless pools of water. There were dogs, cats, and goats milling along the paths, and in some places, she could see chickens kept in the houses downstairs. Nancy knew that rabies was present in Nepal, so when one of the local dogs sitting in the middle of the path came towards her, she stepped back in fear. She made a mental note not to pet any dogs as she walked along, despite her love for animals.

Nancy had never been interested in climbing, preferring gentle walks in the Peak or the Lake District. In preparation for her volunteering assignment, she had read many books about mountaineers, including those by Peter Boardman, Reinhold Messner, Doug Scott, and Dougal Haston. She was both mesmerized and appalled by the heights and risks they took to climb Everest and other peaks in the Himalayas. Due to her fear of heights, it reminded her of reading horror stories.

She stopped at one of the trekking shops to hire a sleeping bag for two months for her village language training, which she would commence next week. All the volunteers knew that they could hire sleeping bags and trekking boots, and she had saved the 20 kg of luggage she was allocated for essential items, including face cream and shampoo, to bring for her two years of volunteering, as these were extremely expensive to procure locally. She slowly returned to her lodge, stopping to examine local souvenirs in Nepali and Thai jewelry shops, nestled alongside the hiking shops selling trekking gear.

She entered the hotel reception, a spartan room with a single bench, where she greeted the man at the counter. He was checking in four tourists with enormous backpacks. He looked up at Nancy, acknowledged her, and returned to his mayhem. She had been told that the Nepalese seldom lost their temper and were extremely polite.

As she climbed the stairs to the first floor, she could hear her colleagues in the corridor deciding whether to try the local Khukri rum. Abigail was a tall, stocky woman, highly intelligent and opinionated, who had recently graduated from Oxford University with a degree in engineering. Nancy thought she would be the closest to the other female engineer in the group.

However, they had run out of conversation after a few minutes. Abigail came from a very middle-class, educated background and had been expected to attend university. In contrast, Nancy was the first member of her family to attend university. Her parents had left school early, growing up in rural Ireland, and they had emigrated to the UK in their early thirties, striving for a better life for their children.

Patrick was a tall, introverted, and overwhelmingly kind forester raised in Reading, outside of London. Nancy liked Patrick for his empathy, consideration of their group, and enthusiasm for the country. He was open to all experiences and never complained once. She also liked him because Patrick had to work for his achievements. Nothing came easily to him, and she could relate to that.

Nancy sat at the table on the veranda with the others and drank the rum too quickly. One other woman in the group, Moira, a pharmacist with whom Nancy had bonded, came and sat beside her to watch over her as she soaked up the drink. Moira came from a similar background to Nancy; she was introverted and wisely intelligent.

Nancy got up from the table and walked over to the rail to look out over the narrow streets of Thamel, which, in the early hours of the evening, was still full of tourists on their way out for dinner or to a local restaurant for dal bhat, rice, and lentils. They were likely also seeking the cafés that many mountaineers frequented, where Tongba and Raksi were readily available. Tongba was a fermented millet drink usually served in a wooden container and drunk through a straw. Raksi, a strong drink, clear like vodka or gin, was traditionally served in a dirty glass with alcohol strong enough to kill every contaminant.

Kathmandu and Nepal were renowned for their hippy trails. From the mid-1960s, hordes of hippies searching for Shangri-La bussed or hitchhiked through Turkey, Iran, Afghanistan, Pakistan, and India before arriving at the end of the road in Kathmandu. They came in tens of thousands, preaching peace, and high as a kite, most of the time experimenting on drugs and seeking 'enlightenment' through Buddhist teachings. Nancy wasn't interested in experimenting with drugs. She had grown up in

London, educated in the heart of the city, where drugs were passed along in the back row of her school occasionally, and she had never been enticed to try them. That wasn't where she was interested in getting her highs. Nancy was determined to travel. She knew the best route was finding a suitable job, and she wasn't going to sabotage her plans in any manner.

Nancy walked back to the table where the others were sitting. They were discussing the next stage of their training and hardly noticed her as she sat down. Abigail was impatient to start work since they had already been in the country for over a week.

"I just don't understand why we can't start our language training now in the village and why we must start in Kathmandu. We need to move to the type of villages where we'll work so we can pick up the language quickly!"

"Relax! There is plenty of time. Didn't you read the notes? We're here for two years." Noel responded. Noel was a twenty-two-year-old forester. He and Patrick were to be posted remotely together. Nancy would soon discover that you could never be quite sure if Noel were honest or if he would sell your soul to the highest bidder.

"Abigail, there is plenty of time for work. You should try to enjoy the time we have now to learn Nepali," Moira added.

For Abigail, this was a mission, and she was a high achiever. She was here to help people living in poverty. She had done extensive research on Nepal and, unlike Nancy, had specifically requested to work in this country. Noel came over to join them. He was 6 feet tall, with blond hair and a reasonably attractive demeanor. You could tell that Abigail was already falling head over heels for him. Noel merely had to open his mouth to comment on anything, and she would fall over with laughter. Nancy was not so readily impressed. She was also inexperienced in relationships, and good-looking men unnerved her somewhat.

Nancy was sure that Noel's clever mind was devising some plan to slip away from the others so he could explore the streets by himself tonight and learn more from the local population about how this city ticked. She would have loved to go with him, but she was sure he would leave her stranded in some dark, lonely alleyway while he drank with the locals.

Lionel and Mike sat in a corner, exchanging hard-luck stories. Mike was the only one who lost his luggage enroute when his rucksack was sent to Khartoum instead of Kathmandu. He was a landscape architect, but like the others, he would turn his hand to building village water supplies. Lionel was extremely polite and funny, but he found adjusting to his new environment to be challenging. As the youngest of the group by a few months and the most vulnerable, he missed his parents somewhat terribly, particularly his mother, and was taking more time to adjust to this new culture. Nancy felt that she understood Lionel since she had led a sheltered life herself.

She took another glass of the thick, sickly-sweet Khukri rum from the bottle still on the table and remembered that today was her twenty-third birthday. She could hardly believe that less than a week ago, she had bid farewell to her parents and sister at Heathrow, leaving her world with a rucksack, a few souvenirs, and tear-drenched cards from her parents. Nancy had led a protected life in London until she was eighteen, when she left for university in the Midlands. She had had great difficulties adapting to life away from her family, and her studies had suffered. She majored in civil engineering within a class of eighty men and five women. After experiencing a Catholic school education, to say the environment was intimidating would be a gross understatement. However, Nancy battled through the difficulties, making good friends with her fellow female students, mindlessly falling in love with a second-year student who was hell-bent on writing a book on concrete, dropping out of love with him after he fell for a history student, and faced a major identity crisis in her second year. As one of her senior lecturers noted years later when they met: "Nancy, you never really found your place at university and floundered most of your time."

As Nancy continued to sip at her rum, she considered why this new Asian environment was easier for her to adapt to than for some of her fellow volunteers. She had only traveled outside the UK to a few European countries. The agency had given her two options: Sierra Leone or Nepal, and the final decision was made only two months before her departure. The joy she felt when the Boeing 747 took off at Heathrow for Delhi was euphoric. She was sure she was where she was supposed to be; that this was her life's destiny. She would have had difficulty describing that mission if pushed. Nancy was religious in a quiet and undisciplined manner. Seeking a life where she could benefit others was essential to her, but not quite in the same manner as Abigail, since she did not envisage herself as dedicating her life, or even a few years, to a mission. However, in many ways, Nancy's perspective was somewhat naive in her desire to "serve a purpose".

After three rounds of rum, the lads were getting louder and rowdier on the veranda. Noel had left to wander the streets, and Pat was singing a Scottish ballad. Lionel had gotten up to vomit into the sink in the toilet at the back of the veranda. The rum proved too strong, and the group, still suffering from jet lag and culture shock, started stumbling back to their rooms.

Nancy left the others on the veranda to return to her room and collapsed onto her bed, thinking she should set a better example regarding behavior since she was a few months older than the others. In many ways, she felt much older than the others, and she wondered why she had always felt old, even as a child. She had always been more comfortable talking to adults than to other children. At university, her closest friend had been a woman in her eighties whom she visited after her lectures, to help her with shopping and other tasks. Buddhist monks that she met while trekking later in her stay in Nepal described Nancy as "an old soul," but upon her arrival in Asia, she had little understanding of the concept.

The gecko was still in killer modus operandi on the wall below the window, consuming more mosquitoes.

Chapter 2 · Intensive Language Training

Two weeks later, the team of volunteers and their language teachers traveled to the hills two hours outside of Pokhara, the principal town in the Western region of Nepal. The cars stopped on the highway, and the volunteers and language trainers trekked up the hill for about thirty minutes to reach the village. The walk was steep and quite hot at 80°F. Nancy was at least 30 pounds overweight, and although she was a good walker, this was a steep incline. She stopped a few times to drink water from her flask and pretended that she was admiring the scenery. Abigail forged ahead of the crowd, and Nancy wondered why she hadn't even broken into a run to demonstrate how fit she was. The foresters were also ahead of the crowd.

Walking in Nepal required stamina rather than being very fit. Most of the middle hills were undulating, and you would frequently walk downhill for an hour only to walk uphill for another two. On this day, the walk was only one hour long, which was relatively short compared to the average trek in the hills of Nepal. Nancy stopped at the top of the path to admire the view of the bright green rice terraces in the mountains, which were remarkably beautiful. The fields were scattered with women collecting the shoots for replanting. She did not want to miss anything. Moira joined her to take some pictures.

Nancy had come to Nepal to oversee the construction of village water supply systems. In the late 1970s, rural Nepal had low coverage rates of clean water in the hills, with approximately 25% of the population having access to it. Most systems were gravity-flow supply systems, where natural springs were capped in the upper elevations, led by gravity to a reservoir and then down to a series of tapstands within the village. These systems were efficient, compact, and easy to design and construct. The real challenge was the isolation. While constructing the system, one had to live in rural and remote villages and work closely with the villagers who provided labor. On average, it took around four to six months to construct the water system. However, issues like water rights or supplies taking too long to arrive could easily disrupt the timeline. In the case of water rights, if a landowner were not happy with the distribution of tapstands, they would refuse access for the pipeline trenches to be excavated on their land or cut the pipe after it was laid. A significant challenge was obtaining supplies and equipment for the villages. Carrying bags of cement and pipes into these communities required porters to carry heavy loads up and down hills, sometimes for three to five days, and even longer in the Far-Western region of the country. Ensuring that supplies and equipment were delivered promptly and that cash was available to pay the porters was virtually impossible.

Another major challenge was the caste system. Invariably, access to the improved water supply service was the right of any higher-caste Brahmin or Chhetri within the village. Lower castes were frequently prohibited from using the same tapstand as the higher castes and, therefore, had to continue to seek water from unsafe sources. The government and donors had to ensure this did not occur, with the poorest, low-caste communities having equitable access to clean water.

The caste system was still prevalent in Nepal, particularly in the middle hills and Terai plains, where Nancy would be assigned to work. Caste affected many aspects of life, including family, food, dress, occupations, and culture, and determined a person's way of life. Several rules were in place regarding the types of food and drink people accepted and from which caste. All food was divided into two categories: kachcha and pukka. Kachcha referred to any food cooked using water, while pukka referred to all food cooked in ghee. Generally, a person did not eat kachcha food unless it had been prepared by someone from the same caste, since sharing a kachcha meal implied intimacy and approval.

Most Nepalese volunteers were from the United States, the United Kingdom, Germany, or the Netherlands. However, there were also quite a few Japanese volunteers who were particularly impressive, as, lacking English in most cases, they quickly picked up the Nepali language within weeks. Volunteers were very convenient to deploy during the construction period, as they did not have families like expatriate engineers, and they all learned Nepali quickly. Living in a village for six months or so was challenging for most new volunteers, knowing full well that when you started, you could barely speak Nepali to ask for food or any support. One was virtually isolated. For Westerners, accustomed to a higher standard of living, it was akin to living in the fourteenth century, with no running water, no toilets, and no electricity; you were lucky if the villagers provided a bed. Some volunteers slept on the front porch since the house where they stayed had no space, and it was cooler. A typical Nepali rural house was rudimentary, with hardly any furniture. People sat on the ground to eat and drink. And, of course, rarely were they sitting around relaxing during the day.

The women barely had time to themselves, working from early morning, cooking for families, caring for infants, and then working out in the fields, mostly on other people's land, and less frequently, perhaps on their own land. The crops grown varied by region but were predominantly rice, maize, wheat, barley, and millet, with agriculture and tourism as the mainstays of the economy. When women went to collect water, they might walk an hour or two to reach the source, meet up, and talk to other women. They couldn't use the precious drinking water they carried to wash clothes, so they walked to local streams and rivers to clean themselves and their clothes. In the 1970s, the average number of children per female was five to six, with one child dying under the age of five in any family as a result of ill health or malnutrition. It was a tough life for any woman living in the rural areas.

The men had more time to socialize, engage in local village politics, sit under the trees drinking chai (tea), and review what was happening locally. The men would also work in the fields, but it was a far easier existence.

During their language training, each volunteer stayed in a different house with a family in the Gurung village. The Gurungs, whose ancestors had come from Tibet about two hundred years ago, initially had no caste system but developed their own structured system over time. However, they comprised only about two percent of Nepal's population. The purpose of the volunteers' training was to immerse themselves in the Nepali language and to rely on themselves rather than on each other. They would then come together for four hours daily for formal, structured Nepali lessons. Most of the team was making good progress in language training. They had spent two weeks prior within the Kathmandu valley in a town named Dhulikhel, where they had studied for eight hours each day, surrounded by views of the Himalayas and beautiful countryside. The locals were wonderfully gracious, and the team had grown accustomed to their daily meals of dal bhat, followed by sweet local desserts.

As they sat in the open air with their Nepali teachers, learning a new verb structure, shouting could be heard across the nearby hill. One of the younger men was brandishing a knife and screaming in a local dialect, so that with their basic Nepali, it was impossible to understand what he was saying. An older man was standing across from him, clutching a kukri (Nepalese blade knife) that was lethally sharp.

"That's the father and son from the house where I am staying!" Mike shouted.

"Everyone, stand back, please!" the teacher instructed.

"The father had fought for the British Gurkha army many years ago, and the son was still enlisted with the Indian army. I don't know what's going on, though! They don't talk to each other at the house," Mike said.

The Gurkhas were predominantly recruited from the hills, from the Gurung, Magar, and Rai tribes, because they were renowned for their formidable fighting skills. The relationship between the Gurkhas and the British army dated back to the nineteenth century, when the British East India Company encountered fierce resistance during the Anglo-Nepalese War (1814–1816). Nancy had heard of the Gurkha army but was unfamiliar with its skills until she arrived in Nepal.

"Why did the son not join the Gurkha army?" Nancy asked.

The teacher replied, "there are strict physical requirements to join the Gurkhas, and the son may have failed the physical exam regarding his weight and height."

"The father and son were really nice to me at the house. It's sad to see how much they hate each other," Mike added.

The father lunged at the son, nicking him on his chest with the blade, and the son responded by running at his father with his knife.

At this point, both the teachers and Mike got up and tried to intervene between the two parties, but there was a danger of being caught between the two and being accidentally stabbed. Eventually, after the teachers pulled both men back and they calmed down, the son collapsed onto the ground, crying into his hands. The father stormed off to his house, cursing his son and the foreigners who had invaded his village.

"Well, that isn't the picture we are presented with of life in a rural village in Nepal!" Mike stated. "If we hadn't intervened, one of them would have been killed. What's surprising is that most of the other villagers just watched as it played out."

"Yes, well, it's probable that would happen. At best, relations between India and Nepal are tenuous, which is playing out in the tension between father and son," Nancy said.

"Well, that was quite frightening. I, for one, was quite scared that they would turn on us," Lionel said.

"I was scared they would turn on me as we tried to stop the fight," Mike stated.

"The worst thing is that the nearest hospital is in Pokhara, a two-hour drive away. If either were severely injured, they would be dead by the time they reached it," Moira said.

The Nepali lesson resumed in a somewhat subdued manner. Nancy was quite unsettled by the experience. She had not felt threatened by either man, but she had felt their raw anger. What if this happened in her village when she was alone?

In the evening, the team sat together, outside, drinking Tongba, deciding that this was another night to become mindlessly inebriated and seriously consider if they had made the right decision to enter this strange culture that seemed impossible for any of them to understand. This wasn't quite the picture of assistance she had envisaged in the UK before her arrival. She had developed a vision of underdeveloped villages, where people welcomed them with open arms. She knew this was a rather rosy image, but the possibility of something going awry during her assignment was now becoming more real. Nancy left the others after one Tongba. She didn't want a headache the next day, and she wanted a clear head to think about what had occurred today, and any safeguards she needed if she was to last two years in this country. She was certainly sure that she didn't wish to be assigned to a remote region, where it would be difficult to call for support, if required.

Chapter 3 · Living in a Village

Nancy settled into her life with her Nepalese family in Dashinkali, a small village one hour from Kathmandu. She had been selected to work on a sanitation project, one of the first of its kind in the country, at a school that required toilets with a septic tank system. She had requested this assignment as she was fully aware that no other volunteer was working on sanitation, and it would allow her to develop a specialization that would be unique for future work opportunities. At that time, sanitation coverage in Nepal was less than 1% in rural areas, and nationwide it was only 2%. As someone aptly phrased it, in Nepal, you looked up at the Himalayas and fawned at their beauty for fear of looking down at the excrement around you. Diarrheal diseases among infants and under-five-year-olds were rampant, as were worm infections due to poor sanitation and hygiene practices, and this contributed significantly to the high child mortality rates. Nancy knew this was the right path for her to pursue, but the challenge in Nepal at that time was daunting, and even the aid agencies could not see a clear path forward to support this initiative, as there was no interest on behalf of the government.

Nepal is divided into three horizontal geographical regions: the Himalayas in the north, the central hilly region, and the Terai (or jungle region) in the south. In 1972, Nepal was divided into four vertical regions for development purposes: Eastern, Central (which includes Kathmandu), Western, and Far Western. The Far-Western region was, by far, the most underdeveloped region, and primarily male volunteers were assigned there. However, a few female American Peace Corps volunteers worked there as teachers. Later, in 1982, King Birendra divided the Far-Western region into Mid-Western and Far-Western development regions since this area required the most development assistance. Nancy was glad that she had been assigned to the central region. This was the softer landing she had been hoping for, as she was more concerned with developing her professional rather than her survival skills. She wanted a challenge in her work, but not so much in her living conditions. However, even living in a rural village at the edge of the Kathmandu Valley was a challenge for a Westerner.

Nancy might have been experiencing culture shock due to the basic living conditions she was facing, but she was also fascinated by living in a culture so different from her own. The owner of the house, Gorka Bahadur, was the local shaman, or Jhākri[1], who communicated with the spirit world for healing purposes, using herbs and beating drums to address illnesses within the village. He was about forty-five years old, but he looked much older. He had five children, the youngest of whom was eight months old. He was only about 5 feet 5 inches tall, stocky, with a very kind face. His wife was about ten years younger than he was. She said little but worked intensely for most of the day and was incredibly kind to Nancy. Their children played outside the house, fascinated by the rather plump foreigner.

"So, Nancy, you are welcome to anything in my house, and my wife will cook and clean for you for the duration of your stay," Gorka Bahadur told her.

"That is very kind of you, Gorka Bahadur. But if you like, I could cook for myself?" Nancy replied.

Gorka Bahadur burst into laughter at her response.

"Nancy, have you ever cooked rice on a wood stove? I've read about your country, and I am well aware that you've a wide range of kitchen equipment you've become dependent upon. I would be worried that you would burn my house down," and again he laughed. Nancy felt somewhat inadequate after his comments, but after watching his wife, Kamala, cooking and toiling in the dark, sooty, and smoky kitchen, she realized how right he was.

After a few weeks, Nancy had settled into the village and her work. She was tired and hungry after having built the base for the school tapstands that day with her host, who also worked as the local mason, local development leader, and the real innovator within the village. Luckily, Gorka Bahadur understood English reasonably well, although his spoken English was weak. He was a Gurung, and many of his people were local shamans or faith

---

1 Jhākri shamanism or dhaamee is practiced among numerous ethnic groups of Nepal and Northeast India. Belief in spirits is prevalent, hence also the fear of spirit possession.

healers. However, Nancy was still barely able to communicate in Nepali. Languages had never been her forte, and she had twice failed her French 'O' level. Kamala tried to ask her in Nepali if she was pleased with the day's work. However, Nancy's language still being so rudimentary, she perhaps caught only one word. So, Nancy pointed to the food and her mouth, trying to convey that the meal was indeed delicious. After a few months, Nancy and Gorka Bahadur would take walks, talking about Nepal, politics, the afterlife, his life as a shaman, and many other topics that would have been impossible to believe if you had been a fly on the wall during her early days in the village.

In the morning and evening, Kamala served food to Nancy, her husband, and the children. After everyone had finished, she made herself a small meal and sat by herself to eat. Nancy noticed how thin and frail she was, and assumed she didn't eat much herself, but her plate was loaded with rice, vegetables, and some meat. Her leanness was likely due to her heavy workload and the limited time she had to rest or attend to her own needs. Their house was relatively better off than many, and they ate meat at least twice a week, accompanied by lentils, rice, and vegetables. Many poorer households could afford meat only every few months. If there was a festival, then animals were slaughtered, shared, and eaten together. Dashinkali was a fifteen-minute walk from a village with a revered Hindu temple, dedicated to the goddess Kali, and an important pilgrimage site for devotees. Goats and chickens were killed there, especially during 'Desai' (or 'Dashain'), the longest and most significant festival in Nepal, which is celebrated over two weeks as a time for spiritual cleansing and renewal. During this period, devotees seek blessings to ward off misfortune and invite prosperity. Nancy, in her first year, really did not understand nor enjoy the festival. However, during her later time in Nepal, she came to love the family celebrations and the happiness they evoked in the Nepalese.

The school where she worked was located beside a leper village in the valley. Many of them would visit the local tea shop, where Gorka Bahadur and she would buy a sweet, spiced glass of tea.[2] Most of the lepers were not badly affected, but many had lost fingers, and their hands were severely marked. All were receiving treatment at the local mission hospital to prevent the disease from spreading further. Nancy was not scared at all by them. She was also aware that it wasn't an easily transmitted disease, and most people caught it over a prolonged period when exposed to a carrier. She could not envisage her life being so different from the year when she had been living in Watford after her graduation. She had worked for a government office where the superficial conversations had focused on irrelevant information, such as which local pubs were the best for beer. Now she was sitting with people suffering from such terrible afflictions that she had only vaguely read about.

Later that evening, Nancy walked over to the local tapstand, about ten minutes from the house, where she had learned how, after sunset, one could take a bath nearly fully clothed very discreetly, and this was now her nightly excursion. She wore a maxi skirt pulled up above her chest, which provided good coverage for her bathing. About five other women were at the tap, either collecting water or washing themselves, and they tried to engage her in conversation.

"You are very old to be unmarried," one of the women said to her in Nepali, pointing at her ring finger. "You will have great difficulties in finding a husband at your age," she added.

Misinterpreting their questions, Nancy responded in her basic Nepali: "I don't like rings, so I don't wear them."

Blank looks were exchanged all around. Although Nepal did not share many Western customs, wedding rings were standard in most Nepalese weddings. Traditionally, the bride and groom would exchange a ring made of grass at the beginning of the ceremony, before presenting the actual wedding rings. Nancy loved her evenings at the tap and sitting outside afterwards on the hill beside the house where she could look down on the Kathmandu valley and contemplate the life she had left behind.

---

2 In 1979, Nepal was in a transitional phase for leprosy control, moving from older, isolation-based practices toward community-based treatment and rehabilitation. All patients diagnosed received drug treatment.

Frequently, Nancy felt a little isolated as she was the only expatriate in the area, and the village was a one-hour bus ride away from Kathmandu. Most of the other team members she had trained with lived far more remotely. She didn't really miss the others at all. She was close to Moira, who was stationed in Kathmandu, so they would often meet up and eat together. Moira was assigned as a pharmacist to a hospital in Kathmandu, but she was always busy, as there were a limited number of pharmacists. If she was not working at the pharmacy, she was training local pharmacists.

Noel and Patrick were based in the Western region and heavily engaged in reforestation programs. Mike and Lionel had been assigned to villages near Pokhara, a beautiful tourist venue about an hour's drive from Kathmandu. This was a godsend, as they had great difficulty adjusting to life in Nepal. Abigail, trying to prove she was the toughest of all, took on an assignment in the Far Western region. Believing she was the most resilient was a fallacy, but the organization was convinced. She was placed in a remote village three days' walk from the nearest road, with little food to eat, and was residing with a family that was already pressed for room, so she slept on their porch. Nancy heard tales of Abigail's adventures from people she met on their travels. Whenever the team met up in Kathmandu, which was infrequently, Abigail expressed her homesickness and complained of her loneliness. She was somewhat scornful of Nancy, who had acquired such a plum assignment near Kathmandu and did not suffer her hardships. However, Nancy was not embarrassed as she was not here on a hardship quest. She considered that Abigail was on a volunteer mission, where one speaks the language perfectly, lives under basic conditions, endures hardships willingly, and then returns home to live a conventional life.

Over the coming months spent in her village, Nancy would learn many lessons; how to understand that other cultures are equally important as one's own, that organic intelligence far surpasses the realms of that acquired through education, and that it was possible to love a country of which one had no real comprehension, and where honest communication went far beyond learning to speak their language. She had never had such an honest and open working relationship as she had with Gorka Bahadur, despite their language difficulties, with his stilted English and her beginner's Nepali.

At the house, Nancy often heard Gorka Bahadur banging the drums. It took a while to realize why he was hitting them, and then she would see a group conferring with him outside the house to communicate with someone recently deceased. He was also eminently practical. People conferred with Gorka Bahadur to request his support when anything needed to be done. He had pushed the government to install a water supply system, which was one of the first hydraulic ram systems. This system differed from the standard gravity flow water supply system in that it pumped water uphill using the gravitational power of falling water to transport a smaller portion of that water uphill. It required no fuel or electricity, only water pressure, and water could be lifted to elevations of up to 400 feet, depending upon the quantity and velocity of flow at the source. Gorka Bahadur ensured the system was well-maintained, and if any parts were needed, he would walk into Kathmandu and purchase them. If necessary, he paid with his own money and later collected revenue from the villagers. For him, the caste system was not something that he ever dwelt upon. He helped anyone who required his support and often assisted the poorest families within his village. He owned a modest amount of land and could support his family through its crops and his masonry skills. He did not charge for his work as a shaman, but the villagers would bring him food and gifts in return. He was one of the most respected people in the village.

One night, they walked through the village, returning home from the project site as they often worked late into the evening.

"Do you not get scared of contacting those who have passed away?" Nancy asked.

"Why would I fear the dead?" Gorka Bahadur replied. "They can't hurt me. Never fear the dead. Keep your fear for the living," he stressed.

Gorka Bahadur had initiated the construction of the taps and latrines at the school. When he told her this, she was truly amazed that he had placed such importance on sanitation, given its low priority in Nepal.

"I'm really surprised that you know so much about the importance of sanitation as a public health priority. How did you learn this?"

"I read everything I can. To me, it's essential that we do everything possible to develop our village. If schools in Europe have water and sanitation, why can't we?" he responded.

"I wish more people in this country thought like you do," she replied.

"I am sure there are many people who would love to do more for their people, but they don't have access to either information or money. I am near enough to Kathmandu to pester the government, and I will do it repeatedly until they get so tired of hearing me, they have to help," he told her.

Gorka Bahadur had consistently pushed the Ministry in Kathmandu to approve the project and lobbied for a volunteer to be assigned. And that was how Nancy was assigned to the village. He had offered accommodation for the volunteer. Nancy shared her large room with rats since grain was also stored there. At night, she would hear the shuffling and often wonder if they would eventually make their way to her bed. This was one of the nightmares that she frequently had, and she would have preferred a smaller room, without cohabiting with the grain and rats.

Nancy sat out on the veranda one day, her water bottle by her side, as she had to treat the water before drinking it. Kamala always brought her over an old piece of material to sit on when she went outside. Even though everyone at the house and village made her feel very welcome, this was the most isolated she had ever felt. For the first few months living in the village, she was most probably suffering from low-grade depression, combined with culture shock. It didn't help that she couldn't afford to talk to her family in London frequently, and the last time she had spoken to them was now three months ago when she had traveled to Kathmandu. Making an international phone call was quite a laborious task. She would go to the post office, submit the number and pre-pay, and then wait thirty minutes for a booth to take the call, as only three phones were available for international calls. The cost was nearly one month's salary as a volunteer. Since working in the village, she had not been spending much money, so her treats to herself were phone calls or meals with friends while in Kathmandu.

Nancy was finishing up the construction of the septic tank at the school, working with the Kathmandu government office. Then, one day, during construction and cement laying, Gorka Bahadur informed her that she appeared to have made a grave error in her design. She promptly dismissed his concerns, telling him she was convinced she was doing everything right, as most overly confident expatriates assume. She then realized one of the most important lessons she carried with her for decades. Local expertise and knowledge are far more critical and relevant than structured learning. Gorka Bahadur was correct; they had to shift the construction site for the septic tank due to the soil conditions, and construction materials were wasted in the process. Local expertise, such as his, was invaluable, and Nancy needed to engage him fully in the planning, design, and construction stages, as he knew the land far better than she did. At many stages of her career, she reflected on her time with Gorka Bahadur and the immense amount she had learned while living in his village. He was that classic example of Gramsci's concept of organic intelligence, which states that organic intellectuals are essential to the development of a new social class.[3] Gorka Bahadur was more concerned about the conditions of his fellow men than for himself. He truly was a selfless man.

3 "Antonio Gramsci"; Stanford Encyclopedia of Philosophy, 2023.

Chapter 4 · Illness

One morning, Nancy woke up and knew something was seriously wrong with her. For the past few days, she had been under the weather and had trouble walking down the stone path from the village to the school. That morning, she was frailer and could not even get out of bed. She took out the local medical guidebook, *Where There Is No Doctor*, to try to diagnose her symptoms.[4] The whites of her eyes had turned yellow, and her stools were off-white. According to the book, she most likely had the symptoms of hepatitis A, a disease contracted by drinking contaminated water. Two weeks earlier, Nancy had visited Lionel in Pokhara and had stopped at Fewa Lake to share a few drinks with other development workers. She remembered distinctly having a lassi, a drink made from yogurt mixed with water, and at the time, she had misgivings that she could become ill, as the water was unlikely to have been chlorinated. However, it was easy to make mistakes and consume something contaminated. Diarrhea was a way of life in Nepal, but you tried to avoid the more severe illnesses, such as typhoid or hepatitis.

Becoming more convinced that she was seriously ill, Nancy packed a small bag with some money and her passport. She bid farewell to the family and took a bus back to Kathmandu to seek medical attention. The path to the bus stop took twenty minutes to walk. After five minutes, she was unable to walk any further. She had never felt so physically weak before and decided the best way to proceed was to take a few steps, rest, and then try again. By the time she reached the bus stop, Nancy was crawling on all fours, much to the bewilderment of the villagers waiting at the bus stop. Luckily, the bus arrived within twenty minutes, and she found her way to the back, where she promptly fell asleep until she entered the city.

Whenever she was in Kathmandu, Nancy stayed in a two-bedroom apartment that she shared with an American Peace Corps volunteer

4 *Where There Is No Doctor: A Village Health Care Handbook*, Werner, D., Thuman, C., & Maxwell, J. (1970), Palo Alto, Calif: Hesperian Foundation.

named Susan, who was quite the opposite of Nancy: highly confident, very assertive, and an extrovert. Susan often invited friends and locals for drinks in the evening, while Nancy wished to read or study plans for her project. They had met early on and decided to seek a place together to cut costs. Sue was not at the apartment when Nancy arrived, having been assisted there by a few of the other bus passengers. She collapsed onto her bed and fell asleep.

"Wake up, Nancy! Are you OK?" Nancy opened her eyes to see Susan standing beside her bed. Susan was a few years older than Nancy. She was an attractive, tall woman, a little overweight, but she carried herself with great confidence, far more than Nancy, who tended to be self-conscious.

Nancy weakly opened her eyes and stared up at Sue.

"What time is it?" she asked her.

"Seven in the evening. What time did you get here? You look terrible!" Susan responded.

"I think I have hepatitis," Nancy whispered.

"How do you know? When did you arrive back here?" Susan asked again.

"This morning, I looked it up in my book. I need to see a doctor," Nancy said.

"Hang on, and I will call your manager at the volunteer office and tell him to send someone over. It's too late now, so they need to come tomorrow morning. Can you eat?" Susan asked.

"No. I'll throw up. I can drink water, though," she whispered.

"How did you get this? You must have drunk contaminated water. At the Peace Corps, we are ingrained to drink only treated water."

Nancy was too embarrassed to tell Susan she had drunk a lassi in Pokhara. Even her office, less strict than the Peace Corps, warned them never to drink anything mixed with water unless they added a chlorine tablet. She had brutally learned her lesson.

"Do you want to get up for a while and sit in the lounge?" Susan asked.

"I don't have the energy. I think I'll go back to sleep," Nancy responded.

Susan said, "I need to meet Mickey this evening, but I can ask him to come here, as I don't want to leave you alone. Nancy, I am pretty sure

Mickey is seeing someone else, but I don't want to ask him in case he breaks up with me."

"If he is, I doubt it's serious. Mickey is enjoying his time here, and he's such an entertaining guy," Nancy replied.

Mickey was also a Peace Corps volunteer and often visited the apartment and enjoyed talking to the "English lady". Nancy always felt more at ease with American than British men. She wasn't sure why this was, but she suspected it was due to feeling more self-conscious around her fellow citizens.

Mickey looked rather dissolute, but he was an interesting character. Sue consistently lamented over Mickey, stating he was openly dating other people and that she was sure she was falling in love. Compared to Susan, Nancy had far less experience in dating men, and she certainly was not seeking a regular boyfriend in Nepal. She was pretty happy to be commitment-free. However, having someone to care about her while she was sick would have been nice.

Sue brought water to Nancy and left it on her side table. She put out the light and drew the curtains. Nancy did not wake up until 11 o'clock the following day. Susan had already left for work, and Nancy found a note from her director under her door, asking her to take a cab to the office, where they would arrange for her to see a doctor.

Nancy got out of bed feeling a little stronger than she had the day before, after a good night's rest. She went to the kitchen to make tea, but still couldn't eat anything. She dressed and walked down the stairs to get a cab to her office. The streets were hot and dusty as she passed the bazaar shops and jostled her way through the motorized rickshaws and bicycles. Luckily, she only had to walk for about five minutes before a cab drove down the road. She kept the receipt to give to her office. The doctor confirmed that, indeed, she had contracted hepatitis A. After Nancy returned to the office, she went to talk to her manager. Robin was a young man in his mid-twenties who had previously volunteered in Malaysia and was now assigned to Nepal before returning to the UK to pursue his master's degree.

"Well, Nancy, this is a serious disease that requires a lot of rest. You're not much good to us if you can't work," he told her rather bluntly. "You need to find somewhere in the country where you can rest up for four to six weeks. Otherwise, we will need to send you home, and we can't afford to bring you back."

"Well, I could ask the Mary Knoll mission. Moira is good friends with them, and I attend their mass when I am in town. They might help me," she replied.

"We could pay them a small sum, if they agreed to this. Your project is a flagship one for the agency since there is so little sanitation in Nepal, and we'd like you to complete your work in Dashinkali and then work on national sanitation planning, as we previously discussed."

"I don't want to go back," Nancy said weakly as her energy level was now low after the morning visit to the doctor's office. I will ask Moira to go with me tomorrow to Mary Knoll to see if I can stay there for a month or so."

Nancy took a cab back to the apartment, went to her room, collapsed onto the bed, and fell asleep immediately.

The Mary Knoll Order had a large residence in Kathmandu, and since Nancy attended their services with Moira when she could, they readily agreed to let her stay with them for four weeks to recover. The next day, Nancy packed a few things to bring to the Order, with Sister Agnes assigned as her prime caregiver. Her agency agreed to pay a fee to Mary Knoll to cover the costs.

Mary Knoll was more progressive than most Catholic orders. Its nuns wore conservative but western clothes, and its priests were more liberal. They combined their development work with their roles as Catholic priests and nuns, assisting in health and education projects. Father Joe, the most popular priest, frequently traveled around town on his motorbike, visiting families in need and providing Mass services. Nancy was raised by agnostic parents, but religion was a quiet priority for her.

Nancy could not recall much from her time at Mary Knoll, as she slept for twelve hours or more most days. She had never felt so exhausted in her life. Sister Agnes prepared soups for her and spoke with her for a few minutes each day to update her on what was happening in the world. A few people visited, but she couldn't remember many of the details. She mostly read books or listened to Nepali language tapes. She wrote to her family and friends back in the UK on aerograms, which were cheap and arrived quickly, and briefed them on her health status.

After a few weeks, she felt like she was beginning to return to the world with her full faculties. She realized this when she started to look forward to her meals and no longer felt the need to eat merely to maintain her strength.

"Well, Nancy, it's been a pleasure having you here at the Mission. You were brave to stay here and battle your illness, rather than leave," Sister Agnes told her. "Have you thought about what comes next, after you complete your assignment here in a year or so?" she asked her.

"I think I would like to stay here even longer." Nancy's response surprised even herself. She had no idea how she would be able to stay in the country after her two-year volunteer assignment ended.

"That's a good idea if you can. Two years is a very short time to make an impact, and if you remain, you can certainly help move the government on the sanitation issue." The Mary Knoll brothers supported several water and sanitation projects in the country and were well aware of the challenges.

Nancy now saw clearly that she did not wish to leave Nepal at the end of her two-year assignment, but she would seek other employment. She envisioned spending at least four years in Nepal to gain overseas experience and establish her career in development.

When Nancy was a little stronger, she visited her mentor, Hashem Asadi, an Iranian civil engineer at the Ministry of Local Development. He had left Iran after the Shah's demise, with whom he was close, and had left most of his estate and money in Tehran. Hashem had been educated in the UK and had married an English woman whose mother was concerned (as he expressed it) that she was marrying a man with a "fruity accent". He was a warm, supportive, and welcoming man who guided Nancy professionally and peppered most of their conversations with personal anecdotes that often had her doubled over in laughter. Nancy entered his office and discussed her options for remaining employed in Nepal. Hashem mentioned a few agencies that she should investigate, and he also agreed to contact people to see if any opportunities were available. Nancy had met a few people from the UN since the project she was assigned to was affiliated with the United Nations Rural Development Organization. She decided to pursue that path and asked if Hashem would help.

Back at the apartment, Susan had organized a large party, and most of Nancy's team had come in from the field. Somehow, during that evening, while Nancy was still recovering and Sue was dancing up a storm on the rooftop, one of the British volunteers, Noel, got into a fight on the stairs with an American Peace Corps volunteer. She knew at this point that she was fully recovered from hepatitis, as she used great strength in pulling the two men apart. Luckily, Noel calmed down, and she was able to assure him the incident would not be reported to Robin at the office. She got herself a juice and walked up the three flights of stairs to the rooftop with ease, contemplating what the coming years would bring.

Nancy returned to the village the following week to complete the work with Gorka Bahadur. Over the next month, she finished the project and bid farewell to everyone there. She felt conflicted about leaving Gorka Bahadar and his family, as she had become attached to them, but she was pleased to move on to the next challenge. Gorka Bahadar walked with her to the road and bid her farewell as she felt the tears streaming down her cheeks. She returned to his village again in 1985, when she was conducting a national survey for her master's degree, and even after only five years, he looked considerably older. Nancy knew that Gorka Bahadur would not live long past fifty years. The average life span for a Nepalese at that time was around that age, and he had worked harder than most. She knew she would never forget his influence or the lessons he had taught her.

Chapter 5 · The Nepalese Language Teacher

Nancy had now been in Nepal for nearly two years. She had just returned to Kathmandu from a one-month mission to the Eastern region for the Ministry of Local Development, where she conducted an assessment of sanitation and hygiene. After Susan left Nepal, Nancy had to move out of their apartment in Kathmandu and rent a smaller place while she completed her volunteer assignment. She found a one-bedroom ground-floor apartment near the Ministry of Local Development. After she had finished her village assignment, the Ministry appointed her as a national sanitation adviser to assist Hashem, her mentor. The apartment was clean, but the path to the house was a nightmare during the monsoon, as it became muddy and smelly. Nancy would reach her door with at least four inches of mud on her feet and legs.

She had been taking Nepali language classes from Jaghan for the past few weeks. Her office had hired him to help further advance her language skills. He usually came over to the house to conduct their lessons as it was the most convenient with his schedule. Jaghan was approximately 5 feet 8 inches tall, taller than most Nepalese men. He was a Brahmin and related tales of how the caste system impacted him. He was unusually handsome, with penetrating blue eyes. After a month or so of lessons, Jaghan suggested they start dating, but Nancy was somewhat reluctant. She did not see any future with him, and there was something about him that she considered somewhat rudderless. He was traditionally Nepalese in many ways, with his belief in his status as a high-caste Brahmin, yet he longed for a Western life and was eager to live in the United States. He also taught Peace Corps volunteers, and their local slang name for him was 'John Doe'. The irony of the name was lost on Jaghan. Nancy could imagine that the volunteers considered Jaghan too Western with his smart suits and designer shoes, craving for the elements of a life they had all been glad to leave behind.

She did agree that they could go out together after their classes to eat or drink Tongba. Nancy was attracted to him, but she assumed this was due to his looks rather than a strong chemistry between them. One day, after eating a meal together in town, they returned to the house. It was still monsoon, so they were both drenched when they arrived. Nancy did not want Jaghan to accompany her back as she knew it would be difficult to ask him to leave. He was too pushy for her, and his style was so different from her own. He was an extrovert who loved attention. Nancy was still somewhat overweight, and her dress style was to wear long skirts with flowing blouses, which was both culturally suitable and meant that she never really needed to worry about losing weight, as her figure was suitably disguised.

Jaghan entered the house and immediately threw himself onto Nancy rather clumsily. He pushed her into the bedroom, muttering "please" under his breath at least four or five times. She pushed him away but did not wish to be impolite, although she was surprised that he lunged at her with quite such force. She liked Jaghan, but she didn't want to sleep with him. Jaghan pushed her further inside the apartment, into the bedroom, and onto the bed. She tried to free herself and get off the bed, but Jaghan was almost pleading with her to let him enter her, as he was kissing her hair and ears. Jaghan pushed up her skirt and pulled down her panties.

Nancy was too shocked to intervene, and she didn't wish to scream and make a scene. He tried to have intercourse with her, but he was unable. He pulled himself off the bed, apologized, and dashed out of the house. Nancy was somewhat stunned. She blamed herself for allowing him into the house so late at night. She thought that she had asked for this to happen. She only met Jaghan once again at a Peace Corps function a few months later. He pretended not to have seen her, and she also decided to ignore him. The episode with him had shaken her somewhat, much more than she wished to admit to herself, affecting both her confidence with men and her self-respect. Nancy also felt that perhaps she had treated Jaghan poorly by not seeking a relationship with him. Years later, reflecting on this episode, she was appalled that she hadn't realized Jaghan was at fault and not herself.

Chapter 6 · Working with the United Nations

It was now March 1982, and Nancy had been in Nepal for two and a half years. She had just returned to Kathmandu from a holiday in the UK to spend time with her family, who were overjoyed to see her. She settled back into her apartment in Lazimpath, north of Kathmandu, in the city. The locality was known for its residences, restaurants, and high-end shops. Once she started her contract with the UN Rural Development Office (UNRD), she rented a two-bedroom apartment near her office. Determined to avoid joining the expatriate jet set, she opted for a Yamaha bike over a car, which proved perfect for navigating city traffic. It was also ideal for escape trips on the Ring Road to unwind after a hard day at the office. It was amazing to see the number of people on that road, on their motorbikes, practicing the same trick. In the apartment above hers was another British woman, Sue Slater, an artist renowned for her portraits of Nepalese tribes. Sue often stopped by for a cup of tea after work to catch up on work woes and to relay the local gossip within the Valley. One day, Sue hurried in looking rather flustered.

"I just bumped into Haruto! He's come back for a month to conduct an assessment for the Japanese International Cooperation Agency," she said, almost breathless.

"Did he tell you he was coming?" Nancy asked her.

"No. I had no idea. I didn't think he would ever come back here again after he married," she replied.

About twenty years ago, Sue had fallen deeply in love with a Japanese volunteer, Haruto. They were living together when his eldest brother committed suicide, so he immediately returned to Japan, took over family responsibilities, and married. She had never fully recovered from this, so there was always an aura of profound sadness about her, despite her cheerful nature.

"Did you agree to see him again?" Nancy asked her.

"Yes, I'll meet him for dinner tonight, but really, this isn't good. He now has two young children, and I don't want to get sucked into an affair with him," she said.

Sue made the last statement as if she had no choice in the matter, Nancy thought. She was somewhat conservative when it came to involvement with married men. She had never allowed that to happen to her. However, she knew it must be tough for Sue as they had been involved before he was married. She loved Sue as a friend, so she was never going to judge her, but she was worried that she would be hurt again, as he was only in Nepal for a month.

Sue went on to discuss the latest news from the Nepalese Royal family and developments in the country, while Nancy had been away. At that time, the Royal Prince was studying at the British Budhanilkantha School and was being groomed to succeed the present King Birendra. The prince studying at the school was considered bad luck according to Sue, since the statue of the reincarnation of Vishnu was located nearby at the temple, and the Nepalese believed that the King was a reincarnation of Vishnu. Whether she agreed with Sue or not, Nancy thought back to Sue's words when she learned that the Crown Prince had killed both of his parents and his siblings in June 2001.[5]

Nancy was also working in Lazimpath, about one mile from her residence. In the early 1980s, Kathmandu still retained its magic and charisma. She loved walking through the crowded streets of Thamel in the evenings after work, and she and Sue often went together to buy food or meet other friends there. There was heavy traffic, but the infrastructure had yet to spread across the valley to the extent of the present-day city, and it was easy to escape to lush green fields and views of the mountains within about five minutes.

That day, after breakfast with Sue, Nancy walked to the office. Craig, her boss, was already there. Craig was a very kind, brilliant British man who never interfered in her work but would gently guide her back if she strayed too far off track. Later that day, she was flying to Nepalgunj and then to

5 Eyewitness reports confirmed that Crown Prince Dipendra was the gunman. A detailed investigation was impossible as the 'Tribhuvan Sadan' (the building where the massacre occurred) was demolished by the Gyanendra government, which made Gyanendra the most unpopular king.

Doti to view an education project in the Midwestern region. Nancy was traveling by herself but would meet up with technicians upon her arrival in Doti. She packed her things, collected some key documents, and made her way to the car. When Nancy arrived at the airport, the check-in process was swift as she boarded the Royal Nepal Airlines plane to Nepalgunj. The flight took about two hours, and upon arrival, it was hot and dry. Nepalgunj is on the southern Terai strip, and temperatures in the 1980s were frequently around 90-100 degrees. Tourists seldom visited, and there were only a few decent hotels or shops. Since Nancy had a few minutes, she left the airport to visit a bazaar shop and buy some fruit and other essentials. She asked the shopkeeper for some rice, as it wasn't visible on the shelf. He swatted his hand across the rice container, and the black coating of flies ascended, exposing the rice. She decided against the purchase.

A few people were at the airport, and she waited an hour before her flight arrived, which was to take her to the airport nearest to Doti, Silgadi. Nancy loved most of Nepal, but the Mid- and Far-Western regions always scared her due to their remoteness. If the rural village she had lived in, in the Kathmandu Valley, was akin to the fourteenth century, then Far-Western villages were like stepping back into the tenth century, since most were remote, requiring three to four days of walking, with no electricity and scarce food. There was certainly no opportunity to purchase Western goods, which were available in the Eastern and Central regions. Often, Nancy would be surprised to have walked for three to four hours in the East, only to see a Coca-Cola sign over the local tea shop. There was no chance of this in the Far West.

She boarded the plane for Silgadi, noting there were no other expatriates. It was a short flight, landing within forty minutes. A technician met her at the airport, and they set off walking uphill for Doti, a twenty-kilometer walk. Luckily, the kind technician had taken her rucksack, leaving her to walk freely. They chatted about the region on the way up, as her language skills were now fluent, but the trek uphill was exhausting. After two years, Nancy had learned to pace herself as she frequently trekked with technicians. However, the sun was intense on this day, and there was little shade.

When they arrived in Doti, Nancy made her way to meet the director, who was running the SETI (Education for Rural Development in the Seti zone) education project for one of the UN agencies. She was keen to learn about the work, as the project had been successful according to everything she had read. She was impressed that the project had been mentioned positively by local women on the footpath coming up to Doti. The villages of the Seti zone could only be reached on foot and were rarely visited by other expatriates. In the region, they faced food scarcity, contaminated water, lack of hygiene, and health care was virtually unavailable, and most people were illiterate. The project's purpose was to provide children with basic primary education, but it also included literacy lessons for women and support for community development. The region was a shock to Nancy, as the level of poverty and hardship was immediately apparent.

As she walked around the town, she saw that the children were incredibly thin and dirty. There were few shops, and any items sold were basic supplies, including rice, flour, soap, and locally produced washing powder. The houses were very spartan, made of stone with mud plastering and grass roofs. She walked past a home on the opposite side of the road from where she was staying and glanced inside. There, she saw chickens downstairs and about four young children, including an infant, lying on a soiled mattress across from them. At least two of the children were crying very loudly, and Nancy could not see where the mother was. It was challenging to understand why there was so little progress despite the development programs that had commenced in Nepal in the 1950s. It certainly challenged the belief that development assistance was making a significant impact. It was difficult to get an accurate picture of development issues in Nepal unless you traveled to the more remote regions and saw directly for yourself how underdeveloped they were. This helped a lot in designing projects that were practical and based on local needs.

The few days in Doti passed quickly, with visits to villages where schools had been built and attendance at women's literacy classes. Nancy was exhausted by the end of the trip, but she had been able to collect excellent information to share with other staff in Kathmandu. When it was time to leave, Nancy walked down the hill with her guide, wondering what she would be like when she was old, as her knees were already in trouble at twenty-five. The old, sleepy town of Silgadi welcomed them as they stopped at a tea shop for chai, which, after the walk, was very welcome. Nancy saw a woman walking past, statuesque in height, with blonde hair and quite beautiful. Since she spoke fluent Nepali, she surmised that this was a Peace Corps volunteer. Nancy made her way over to her.

"Hi, do you live near here?" Nancy asked her.

The Peace Corps volunteer responded, "my village is up that mountain, about three hours away. I've lived in Nepal's Far-Western region for one year, teaching mathematics."

"Are there many volunteers here? It seems very remote," Nancy said.

"Quite a few. There are about ten of us in the Doti District. Most of us teach, but a couple are building water supplies. I am on my way to Kathmandu for a month," she responded.

"How long has it been since you were in Kathmandu?" Nancy asked.

"I rarely go, but this is one of those times since the Peace Corps organizes various events where volunteers can fly in to get some rest, especially those assigned to more remote areas. The last time I was in Kathmandu was six months ago," the volunteer responded.

Nancy discovered the volunteer was named Anne, and they hit it off immediately. They went to the tea shop to talk further. Anne was very attached to her village, where she taught, assisted in local development projects, and helped the women learn to read and write. Anne opened up more at the tea shop.

"So, don't you get lonely here?" Nancy asked her.

Anne responded, "it was terrible at first, and I felt pretty vulnerable, but now I'm close to my family, and they are very protective."

When Anne was talking to the shopkeeper, Nancy noticed that her Nepali was far more advanced than her own, most likely because she had communicated for months without using English.

Nancy replied, "I was stationed in the Kathmandu Valley as a volunteer, so it was much easier."

Anne tried not to look at her scornfully.

"Where do you come from in the States?" Nancy added.

"I was born in California and attended Pomona College near Los Angeles. My parents live in Santa Barbara. Dad is a doctor, and Mum is a teacher," Anne said.

"Why leave California for Nepal?" Nancy asked her.

"I wanted to work for the Peace Corps for a long time, back home. They chose Nepal. I would have worked anywhere in Asia," Anne responded. "The biggest problem I have is that my boyfriend is also a teacher, but he's stationed even further west. He also teaches math. We don't see each other except when we are both in Kathmandu."

"Well, at least that's something you'll have in common after you leave here," Nancy said.

"The Peace Corps doesn't mind if we have relationships with each other, but it strongly discourages relationships with locals," Anne stated.

"I understand that. If a local woman has a relationship with a foreigner, she's considered unclean and is unable to marry any Nepalese man," Nancy said. She thought back to her relationship with Jaghan, but she had not taken advantage of him in any way; it was he who had initiated the involvement. The dynamics for men, however, were very different. There were quite a few mixed marriages that she had observed in Kathmandu of Nepalese men with Western women.

"Some Peace Corps guys do have local girlfriends, though, and a few marry them," Anne said.

As Nancy and Anne continued to bond over tea, they realized that although their backgrounds differed vastly, their perspectives were similar.

They made their way up the dirt track to the local airport, where the plane would fly out late in the afternoon. When they reached the airstrip, they were informed that the flight had been cancelled for the day due to rain in Nepalgunj, and it was expected to arrive the next day. They negotiated rooms at a local inn for the night. That was the easy part; the more difficult part was finding something to eat. The area was impoverished, with limited availability of meat, lentils, and vegetables. The women were able to arrange for a plate of fried potatoes and onions and considered themselves lucky.

After dinner, they went for a short walk before retiring to their rooms to sleep. The roosters woke them up at 4:00 AM with their crowing. They quickly got dressed, had some tea, and returned to the airport for the latest news, but there would be no flight that day, and none were expected for the coming few days. At this point, Nancy tried to send a message to her office, but there was only one telephone at the airport, and the queue was horrendous. She anticipated that the office would know she was stranded.

After four days of no flights, the strain was beginning to take its toll on both Nancy and Anne, who were growing somewhat tired of the fried potatoes and onions. The villagers would laugh each time they returned from the airport, looking forlorn. On the fifth day, when they made their way up to the tarmac, they could see a plane about to land. After the pilot brought the aircraft to a stop on the narrow strip, Nancy rushed up to him to find out if any further planes were coming since this one would already be full of people who had been waiting longer than they. She did not see that the plane's propeller was still running, and she was about to walk straight into it when a young child violently pushed her out of its path.

"Do you realize that child saved your life?" Anne screamed at her.

Nancy hadn't even noticed. She looked back at the propeller, which was still running. She appeared shaken as she noticed her hands trembling.

A plane eventually arrived two days later, and Anne and Nancy were able to fly out after the forced 'holiday' in Silgadi. An hour after they took off, the aircraft arrived in Surkhet, where ten more people boarded. One man, an American, Nancy assumed, wore a broad hat. He must have been about 6 feet tall, around twenty-five years old, with blonde hair escaping from under the brim. Nancy did notice that he was extremely good-looking and walked with an air of confidence. He strolled quickly down the aisle and sat beside an old Nepalese lady carrying a sack of potatoes. Eventually, two hours later, they arrived in Kathmandu. Anne and Nancy were somewhat overwhelmed by being back in the capital. For Anne, it had been six months since she had been in Kathmandu. For Nancy, it was only two weeks, but it felt a lot longer due to their recent isolation in the region.

Both women made their way out of the airport. Nancy did vaguely look around to see if the good-looking American was also searching for a cab into town, but she didn't see him anywhere. A car from the UN agency was outside waiting for her, and she gave Anne a lift to her hotel, agreeing to meet up later in the week. Elated that she had arrived back at her home in Lazimpath, Nancy collapsed on her sofa, poured herself a large glass of red wine, and contemplated the lessons she had learned from being stranded in the Far West without any creature comforts for two weeks. She further contemplated the rather good-looking American who was on the plane and whether she would ever see him again.

Chapter 7 · Falling in Love

It was July 1983, and Nancy was trekking with Martin, the good-looking volunteer who had been on the plane returning from the Far-Western region when she had been stranded in Silgadi. They had now been seeing each other for nearly a year. Martin was a Peace Corps volunteer assigned to the Mid-Western region in Surkhet, where he supported the construction of water supply systems. They had started going out after they met at the Marine Club in Lazimpath. The club, which featured a bar and dancing, was frequented by many volunteers on Friday evenings at the invitation of the Marines. It was a fun place to meet friends and new people. Nancy had not gone to the bar much as a volunteer, but now, since she lived nearby, she sometimes walked up there with friends. That night, she had arrived there with other Peace Corps volunteers who had eaten dinner at her house. As she looked up at the bar, she recognized the American volunteer who had been on the flight, getting on at Surkhet. He had a beer in his hand as he was talking to some of the Marines. Her eyes caught his, and he stared back at her. After about ten minutes, he came over and asked her to dance.

"So, are you a Peace Corps volunteer?" he asked her.

"No, listen to my accent," she answered. She would tease him a little before telling him who she was.

"So, you could be British," he said. "So, a British volunteer?"

"Close, but no," she answered." I work for the UN in water and sanitation."

"Funny, so do I!" he replied. "I build water systems! So maybe I know you, as I work with many of the UN engineers."

"My name is Nancy Cody," she answered.

"Oh, I have heard of you from my technicians. You're the lady who trains in sanitation! They love you, and the training!" he told her quite excitedly.

After about fifteen minutes of dancing, they went up to the bar and got a drink.

"So would you like to have dinner now?" Martin asked her.

"No, thank you. I came with others and will leave now. I'll see you around," she told him.

A week later, Martin visited her office and met with Craig and several other engineers. He breezed into her office and introduced himself again, in case she had forgotten him. She laughed to herself. They talked for about twenty minutes, and then he left after she answered a call. The following Friday, she was at the Marine Club again, and she saw Martin at the bar with friends. He came up to her, but this time he did not ask for a dance; he asked her if she would go to lunch with him the next day. Nancy suggested dinner instead, and that he should pick her up from her apartment in Lazimpath. Their relationship started that evening after their dinner at a nearby restaurant. There was a powerful attraction between them. It wasn't as if they were very similar, since they weren't at all, but they were drawn to each other in some intense way.

Martin was two years younger than Nancy, at twenty-four, and only a year out of college when he arrived in Nepal. He had been raised in upstate New York, and his family could certainly be classified as upper-middle class. His perspective was that of a conservative American, and Nancy often found that difficult to tolerate. However, Martin was her first serious relationship, and she felt she should have a high tolerance for their differences. She had fallen in love with him the second time they met, about four months after their initial encounter, as Martin had returned to Surkhet a week after they first met. They had bumped into each other in Thamel. She knew he was coming back to town, but she wasn't sure when. They went Tongba drinking with other volunteers, but it was clear to the others that Nancy and Martin were deeply engrossed with each other, and it was best to leave them alone. She wasn't sure what it was about him that made it easy to fall in love, but he was a free spirit, and she certainly considered herself one. With Martin assigned to the Midwest region and Nancy working in Kathmandu, it was a challenge for them to meet. But that summer, they spent most of their time traveling to the east, visiting projects, and spending time together in Kathmandu. Martin was the son of a renowned professor of social policy at a New York upstate university who was internationally famous within academia. Nancy had met his parents when they came to Kathmandu. His father was dominant and charismatic, with an exuberant personality.

Nancy liked him due to his brilliance, but she could see how he could be overbearing. His mother was much quieter. She did not work, although, from Nancy's perspective, she seemed both intelligent and powerful in her own right. She was very different from Nancy's mother, as her influence over her son did not extend to her directing him in any way. Whereas the father was consistently referring to when Martin would return and study for his master's degree, his mother did not comment at all but looked over at her son with a great depth of understanding. Martin frequently told Nancy that he thought he would fall far short of his father's career achievements. She couldn't understand why he would limit himself in his vision of success when he was still so young.

They decided to trek together to Kala Patthar, a seven-day walk from Lukla, the airstrip nearest Mount Everest. The trip was Martin's idea, as he wanted to trek in the Everest region, and he thought it would be a good opportunity for them to get to know each other better. Nancy was excited as this was the first holiday that they had taken together, and it was a test of whether they could tolerate each other for an extended period. She was a little nervous that the trip might fissure the relationship since both were strong-minded, intelligent, and sometimes intolerant of each other's opinions. Whenever they were together, there was an ease of conversation. Martin was very knowledgeable, most likely due to his father's influence. She thoroughly enjoyed their conversations, and laughing was a large part of their enjoyment in each other's company.

The ascent of Kala Patthar was very popular among trekkers, as it provided the most accessible view of Everest without requiring a climb to its summit, at an altitude of 18,500 feet. Nancy still suffered from a great fear of heights. Sometimes, while crossing rope bridges, she had to use all her willpower not to look down and lose her nerve to cross. They were traveling with Mickey, a Peace Corps volunteer who had dated Susan, Nancy's former roommate, in Kathmandu. Susan had left to work in China, so Mickey was dating a tourist, who intended to stay in Nepal for a year, partly for pleasure and partly for Mickey. Nancy enjoyed Mickey's company since he was sharp, intelligent, funny, and relaxed. Luckily, Martin also liked Mickey a lot and looked up to him in some ways since he was a little older and, like Martin, had a successful father who worked for National Geographic magazine.

The trek up to Kala Patthar was a relatively easy climb, beginning at Gorakshep, the former base camp for Everest. It took eight days to reach there from Lukla, and then it was a two to three-hour steep climb to the top. Mickey and his friend decided to stop at Gorakshep and walk back to Namche Bazaar, a laid-back, colorful town about an hour's walk from Lukla airport, teeming with guesthouses, restaurants, and trekking shops. Martin and Nancy stopped at Thyangboche, a beautiful Tibetan monastery located at 12,000 feet and felt the calm and peace emanating from the monks as they prayed. One of them passed a white scarf to Nancy and blessed them for a safe trek.

The view of the snowcapped peaks of Everest, Lhotse, Nuptse, Pumori, and Ama Dablam (according to the guidebook that Martin had brought with him) was incredible. You could also see the Khumbu icefall on the slopes of Everest, the deadliest part of the ascent. Nancy knew this was a special moment. She felt even more in love with the country and its wonders. Martin and Nancy were silent on the way down the mountain, returning to Namche Bazaar, both struck by the beauty they had seen. At the lodge, they bumped into friends of Nancy's, David, the head of an NGO, and his wife. The four sat on the floor for dinner together and proceeded to drink Tongba while laughing about their experiences working in Nepal. When they returned to their room, they talked for a while.

Martin asked: "He's pretty young to be the head of a large NGO, isn't he?"

"He's very knowledgeable and highly respected. Age is not an issue. He started working in development when he was twenty-two, same as me," Nancy responded.

"He seems to have gone further than you, though," Martin responded. "Why do you think that is?"

"Well, he's a man. It's easier!" Nancy responded. Nancy thought about Martin's question and realized that she didn't have the confidence that David had. He was very self-assured and never questioned himself, unlike Nancy, who frequently did. And yet, he had never learned the language nor spent as much time in the field as Nancy had.

Nancy was also unsure if she wanted to follow David's career model. She desired to learn as she progressed, and if she stayed in development, she didn't only wish to ascend the career ladder, she wanted to make a difference.

Martin and Nancy searched the numerous lodges until they found Mickey and joined him for drinks. When he returned to the US, Mickey intended to be a photographer for National Geographic. He had clear aspirations, but Nancy wasn't sure he would achieve them. Mickey loved the easy life.

"Found you! What are you doing here?" Martin asked Mickey.

"The Rakshi is the best, and the food is also excellent," Mickey said.

"How long do you have in the country now, Mickey?" Nancy asked him.

"About six months. Then it's straight back to D.C. and some further studies. I can't say I'm overly enthusiastic. I wonder if that Buddhist monastery up there, Thyangboche, might take me as a monk for a few years. I saw a few foreigners living with them," he responded.

Martin laughed, but he wasn't sure if Mickey was joking. Nancy was sure he was not. Mickey was the type who could easily decide to stay at a monastery and develop his spiritual side. Martin was more conventional. As intelligent as he was, he would not veer too far off the traditional path in terms of his career development and personal life.

Mickey had fewer hang-ups than Martin and wasn't overthinking the next steps in developing his career. Mickey could have stayed in Nepal for years, not working, just trekking and enjoying the country. His Nepali was fluent; on the trek, he would talk for minutes with anyone who passed. Nancy loved his enthusiasm for everything in Nepal, as he truly loved the country. They sat and talked about the trek, planning their return to Lukla airport before they flew out two days later. She considered why she had fallen for someone like Martin instead of Mickey. Mickey was just as intelligent and self-confident, and clearly, there was an attraction between them that had been there since he started dating Susan. However, Mickey was five years older than Martin. He would most likely settle down and get married earlier. Nancy wasn't interested in settling down any time soon.

Chapter 8 · Disenchantment

Nancy stopped in Biratnagar in the Eastern Terai to meet her close friend, Chandra, a Nepalese from Kathmandu whom she had met while volunteering in the region. Martin had returned to Surkhet, and she would travel there the following month for work and to see him. Chandra was a bright man who spoke English atrociously, but they had forged a close bond. He was about to get married, so they were celebrating his upcoming nuptials. It was an arranged marriage, as Chandra's family was quite traditional, but he had agreed to meet his wife-to-be and liked her. Nancy and Chandra drank Rakshi and ate rice and sheep's brains. It was months later that Nancy decided to become a vegetarian. She wondered if it was partially linked to that meal.

The next morning, she made her way to the Indian border through Biratnagar with a UNRD driver and car. She had been informed that one of the six projects she had started was stalled due to Indian supplies and equipment being prohibited from entering Nepal at the border. Nancy had been given a one-million-dollar budget by her supervisor, Craig, and she had developed six projects supporting sanitation within different development regions.

The next day, she set off with one of the UNRD engineers based in Biratnagar to determine why the supplies were stopped. Apparently, the agency had been asked to pay baksheesh to the customs officers. Ultimately, the aim was to produce the products in Nepal; however, during the project's development, it was quicker and cheaper to import from India and then find a local manufacturer to replicate the sanitary pans. Nancy was unable to successfully negotiate with the Nepalese guards at the border to allow the shipment to enter. She called the relevant government department to help her with the negotiation, but they refused to intervene, which made her somewhat suspicious. She did not intend to ask her boss if additional funds could be made available to cover the extra charges. After careful consideration and much disillusionment, Nancy decided the project should be stopped. There was no point in continuing with a department that was not open to considering new options. Indeed, with sanitation coverage of less than two percent in the country, innovation and new opportunities were vital for expansion.

She rang Craig to seek his opinion before she made her final decision.

"Hi Craig, I am afraid things have gotten complicated in Biratnagar. The customs office refuses to release the pans unless we pay them a considerable surcharge, and the government has refused to intervene. However, the rules clearly show that we are only due to pay ten percent, not a hundred percent surcharge."

"Well, what do you want to do? The problem is that if you pursue a project that the government is not supporting, they will make it difficult at every step for you," Craig said.

"I know. Well, there are five other projects to support. I can focus my energy on those, I think. Shall I close this project for now and review it later?" Nancy responded.

"That must be your call. I won't tell you to drop the project. However, if you make that decision, I will support it," Craig said.

Nancy returned to her room and wrote an email to the department, stating that she was seriously reviewing the project due to the border importation problems. No further cash advances would be made at present, and the agency would conduct an audit to settle accounts. Sitting on the bed, she cried and decided she would never be quite so naive as to trust a counterpart when they agreed to a project in name only. She also realized her errors in not ensuring that her counterparts were entirely on board with her ideas and vision. Years later, she would recognize that any expatriate-designed project without full government engagement and local participation was bound for failure.

As she took the plane back to Kathmandu from Biratnagar airport, she wondered if she would ever be quite that naive again. She was a very trusting person, and perhaps she needed to be more careful in where she placed that trust. She sat back and thought of Martin, wondering if maybe she was putting too much trust in him. She knew she wasn't ready to settle down, but she also knew she wanted to continue the relationship. Both of them wanted to study for master's degrees. Perhaps they could study together somewhere.

Chapter 9 · Travel to the Mid-Western Region

Nancy traveled to Surkhet in August to conduct a three-week training with technicians and to meet up with Martin. She loved the water and sanitation technicians, who were such hardworking and enthusiastic individuals. Many were former Gurkha soldiers, and they were highly regarded within their villages. However, sometimes, tempers would flare over Tongba and Raksi in the evening, and fighting would break out between the technicians. Nancy sometimes saw a Khukuri knife in their belts and thought back to her first encounter with that knife in the fight between the father and son during her language training in the Western region.

Nancy was somewhat of a legend among the technicians, as she was hardly a typical Nepalese woman, and most expatriates they worked with were men. She was training the technicians at the local university. While there, she saw Martin in the evenings, walking over to the room he rented from a family. It was good to see him after four months, although she had been very busy and so had he, constructing a water supply system outside the town in a rural village. His room was basic with a bed on the floor and a small table. Every evening, she would walk back with him to his room, where they would eat and talk for hours. He then accompanied her back to the training center where she was staying, as she needed to be present for breakfast with the technicians each morning.

Martin and Nancy worked during the day with other staff in planning sessions and conducting the training. They enjoyed working together, and Martin was respectful to her in front of the technicians, not indicating there was any intimacy between them. Nancy didn't wish anyone to know they had a relationship, as Nepalese culture was quite conservative. However, most of the team was already aware, and they didn't treat her any differently.

One day, they accompanied the technicians on a visit to a nearby village to inspect the system and discuss hygiene with the villagers. Since it was July, the grass was full of leeches, and they had to stop every ten minutes or so to pull them off their legs and feet. It was essential to pull them off carefully, or the head of the leech could cause a nasty septic wound if it remained in the leg or foot. Usually, heating it with a match was the best method, as it would fall off quickly. After each of them had pulled off about five leeches, they came to a river.

"This river is much larger than usual due to the monsoon," Martin warned her before she crossed. Nancy stepped out slowly into the water. After a few steps, she lost her footing and fell. She tried to get back up, but she could feel the strong current of the water start to sweep her away. Martin reached out for her arm and missed, and she began to feel herself being quickly pulled downstream. At that point, one of the technicians gripped her sleeve while another took the other arm. The sleeve tore away from her shalwar kameez, but the second technician still kept a firm grip on the other arm. As Nancy flailed around in the water, Martin looked on helplessly, as he had just steadied himself from falling over. After a few more seconds, the technicians pulled her over to the riverbank, where she sat trembling as she realized that, like a cat, this was another life she had just lost, and if the technician had not kept a firm grip on her arm, she would have been swept away by the river. Martin sat down beside her on the ground and handed her the water bottle.

"I'm sorry that I couldn't hold on to you," he said. "I had too much trouble keeping myself vertical and not going under." Nancy looked over at Martin and stared at him rather blankly. She wasn't thinking about him at all, as she was still trembling from what had happened and seriously reflecting on her fear of water.

The next day, after the river incident, they arrived at the village where they would spend the night before continuing the trek to the town where the water supply was being constructed. Martin and Nancy walked up to a nearby hilltop, sat, and watched the clouds over the valley below.

"Those clouds are something. They are moving in quickly. I would define that as a cirrocumulus cloud. Or maybe it's a stratocumulus?" Martin stated.

"What's the difference?" Nancy asked. Martin was quite knowledgeable on many subjects, likely due to having been raised by a university professor.

"Cirrus clouds are wispy, and stratus clouds are like a veil drawn over the valley," he responded.

It was a truly scenic place, surrounded by lush green hills. Nepal had a beauty that was unique and raw. A few women approached where they sat, squatting down to smoke beedis (local tobacco rolled in leaves). They asked questions about Nancy's age and whether she was married. She approached the ladies, squatted herself, and smoked a beedi. Sitting with rural women in the hills was a treat for Nancy, as this was something she could only do as a volunteer and had little time for in her job with UNRD. She loved their warmth, honesty, and curiosity about her as a foreigner. The women would frequently ask her why she still had no children at the age of twenty-six and if she wasn't too old to get married now. She enjoyed their humor and jokes. To them, she was an anomaly, but there was no animosity. She always wore appropriate clothing, either a shalwar kameez or a sari, in a respectful manner. She was respectful of their customs, having learned this while living with Gorka Bahadur's family in Dashinkali. He would often discreetly correct her if she sat inappropriately at village meetings or used the wrong form of greeting for a village elder. She still missed him and his family.

After chatting for a few minutes in her fluent Nepali, she left them and returned to Martin.

Martin got out the 'water' bottle, a neat mixture of Drambuie and water. They had prepared it before they left to help them sleep on the route, as they would most likely be sleeping on balconies in their bags, fighting off bedbugs.

"It doesn't get much better than this in terms of beauty. Martin, do you believe in God?" she asked him.

"No. I was raised by an atheist, so I guess I never really thought about it. I believe that we are reduced to dust when we leave the earth. That's it," Martin responded.

"I've always believed my life has a purpose. I find it impossible not to believe in something greater than this world. When I was at school, this Jesuit priest visited us for a retreat, and I asked him about his beliefs. He had studied astronomy at university. He told me, 'This universe is so complex and wondrous that I can't believe it exists without a greater power having created it,'" Nancy stated.

"You're fortunate—I can't believe in anything beyond this life. I believe in living a good life according to one's moral standards, but not because you believe in retribution for dark deeds," Martin said.

"I am not talking about simplistic beliefs about heaven and hell. I am referring to something beyond our comprehension regarding beliefs, something that guides our actions and leads to a better world," she replied.

"But why would that exist? Why would any greater power be concerned about the menial tasks we complete here on earth?" Martin said.

"But what if there are other worlds like this one? And if there was a big bang that created this universe. Why not even another universe? And why do our actions matter? I don't know. But I firmly believe that our actions do count," Nancy replied.

Nancy knew Martin considered her somewhat naïve, as he had already accumulated far more life experience than her, despite being two years younger. He already had experienced two serious relationships, and he had been exposed to a far more worldly environment through his family.

The technicians accompanying them had gone ahead to the village to purchase food and arrange accommodations for the night. Nancy and Martin continued talking for a few hours on the hilltop, sipping their 'water' bottle. By now, they were more than a little tipsy. They spoke of Martin's family life and upbringing in contrast to Nancy's. They discussed books that Martin had read and that he wanted her to read, and they imagined where they would be ten years from then. They connected on that mountain top in a way they would remember well beyond their time in Nepal.

Chapter 10 · Departure

Nancy was preparing to leave Nepal. Her boss had spoken with her, and they had agreed that it was time for her to pursue a master's degree in public health. She was reluctant to leave, but since her trip to Surkhet and her time with Martin, she had been distracted. She knew she was deeply in love with him, but she wasn't sure how they would navigate a future. Nancy intended to travel for three to four months before returning home to the UK. She had been accepted by the London School of Hygiene and Tropical Medicine to study for a master's in public health the following September, and she needed time to settle back in the UK. She had no idea where Martin would come into her plans. She did not envisage that her life would ever be secondary to a partner. She had always felt that she had some purpose that she had to fulfil in terms of her work, and that her life, although it would be interesting, would not be an easy ride. However, the idea of parting and not seeing Martin again was painful to consider. She was set to leave Nepal in late January, but before she left, she arranged to fly out to see him.

Nancy arrived at the airport in Surkhet in December 1983, and Martin was there to greet her. It was a warm day in the hills, but the evenings would be cold, as Surkhet is located at an elevation of 3000 feet. Even at the airport when he greeted her, she sensed that Martin was withdrawing from her, now that he knew she was leaving. Martin took her to the local Save the Children office to meet the new doctor, Sebastian, an Irish citizen with a fantastic lilt and a wicked sense of humor. Over the next two weeks, Sebastian often reminded her there was a life beyond Nepal and Martin.

Nancy and Martin walked around the hills surrounding the valley and visited some villages where Martin was building water supply systems. Most of the services were already in place, including a spring-capped intake, a compact reservoir tank constructed above the village, and several tapstands serving around thirty houses. A few tapstands remained to be completed with stone masonry and cement pointing. However, the villagers were well on their way to celebrating the arrival of clean water and no longer having to trek for one hour uphill to collect it. Martin excelled at his job, earning the confidence of the government technicians and elders within the village. There was something very pure about helping to construct water supply services in villages in Nepal. These remote areas were usually untouched by external assistance, and there was little disillusionment with development projects, as they desperately needed the support. Villagers were willing to provide labor to support the construction and welcomed expatriate support with enthusiasm. The villagers knew that the government fell short of meeting their expectations, so foreign assistance was welcome.

Martin and Nancy walked back from the village to Surkhet, walking up and downhill for about ninety minutes.

"I have been accepted for a master's program in London, and it starts in September," she told him.

"Well, not a surprise. You're very bright," he replied.

"Do you think I should accept the offer?" she asked him.

"It's not for me to say whether you should accept or not," he replied. Nancy remained silent as they walked along. Martin was also very quiet until they entered Surkhet, and they discussed trivial matters, such as where they would eat that evening. They dined with some of Martin's Peace Corps colleagues. Nancy always had a more profound feeling of culture shock sitting with a group of Americans compared to being with her Nepalese colleagues, as she found many of them rather loud.

After dancing their hearts out most of the night, Martin and Nancy returned to his lodgings. It would only be a few days before she returned to Kathmandu and traveled to China, where she was to meet Sue, the former Peace Corps volunteer who had now settled in Chengdu as a teacher. She also intended to visit Malaysia, Thailand, and Hong Kong before she returned home. Martin and Nancy talked, but the conversation erupted into an argument.

"Martin, could we try to see if it works? Would you be willing to come to the UK on your leave and meet me there?" she asked him.

"Our lives are too different. You're British, and I'm American. I don't want to live in the UK," he answered.

"Neither do I!" she responded.

He responded, "but you're going there now, and I don't know what will happen to me."

"You have a fixed idea of how a partner should behave. You don't want an independent woman. You want someone who follows you and whose career is subservient to yours!" Nancy shouted at him as tears began to well up in her eyes.

"I'm not sure what I want, but I know that I just don't see this working out—not right now," he quietly responded.

"I need to do this course in the UK. I could study in the States, but I need this time with my family. I've been away for four years, and it's unfair to them," she cried.

"I see that, but it makes it impossible for us. I love you and will always love you, but I don't see this working out," Martin said.

"I don't know what that means. You say you love me and always will, yet you don't want to make this work. I just don't understand. I don't understand why you're so adamant," she cried.

They cried together into the night, hugging and arguing further. Later, as she tried to sleep while crying, Nancy thought Martin was too young, at twenty-four, to commit to someone who did not even live in the same country. Life had to be straightforward for Martin.

Nancy made her rounds the next day and said goodbye to Sebastian and the others. She then packed, ready for her departure. Martin tried to be his usual upbeat self at the airport as he bid farewell to Nancy. He hugged her as she walked off towards the plane, and she started to feel excited for the next phase of her life. As she looked back, she saw his face was drawn and he looked upset. She wasn't sure if she would ever see him again, and that was painful for her. She cried silently on the plane to Kathmandu.

A week later, Nancy left Kathmandu for Hong Kong. Saying goodbye to Nepal was even more painful than saying goodbye to Martin. She felt a deep connection to the country. She had arrived as a young volunteer with little knowledge of working in another culture, and she was leaving as someone more worldly, tolerant, and infinitely more confident in her abilities. Compared to the naive volunteer who had arrived more than four years ago, she was leaving as a more assured and confident woman who knew that she would go on to live an interesting life. Nancy walked down to Thamel for the last time and met Moira and Sue Slater for a meal.

Chapter 11 · Traveling in Asia

Nancy traveled by road to Hat Yai, near the border, after spending a week touring Malaysia. She had flown to Kuala Lumpur from Beijing after spending six weeks traveling in China. It had been a fascinating trip, and Nancy found the visit the best way to take her mind off Nepal and Martin. She was worried as her period was now four weeks late. She found a hotel and booked a room for the night before leaving for Bangkok the next day. She was now starting to panic as to what she would do if she were pregnant. She would be studying in London and having a child while doing this would be extremely difficult. Nancy wasn't even sure she wanted children, and at twenty-six, she considered herself too young to raise a child alone. All these thoughts were flitting through her brain at a rapid pace. She also thought that Martin might think she was trying to trap him if she had the child. And where would she raise the child? She didn't wish to remain in the UK and didn't see herself staying with her parents to do that.

Nancy left the hotel and walked to a Catholic church about twenty minutes away. Luckily, only one or two people were in the church, which was very quiet. She kneeled and prayed for an hour.

The following day, she boarded the bus for Bangkok. It was a thirteen-hour journey, so she bought food and water for the trip and settled into her seat. Her mind was still racing about the consequences she would face if she were pregnant. She had decided that she might need to terminate the pregnancy. After about seven hours, the bus made another stop on the road at a garage with restrooms. Nancy went into the toilet and saw that she was bleeding heavily. She had felt something, but she wasn't sure what it was. Now, she was sure she was having an early miscarriage. Feeling somewhat numb, she entered the shop to purchase sanitary pads, as most foreign goods were readily available in Thailand.

By the time she reached Bangkok and checked into a hotel, the discharge was very heavy, and she felt weak. She had three days before her flight to London, and she slept for the next twenty-four hours. After she got up, she prayed in a way that she had not for a long time, since she felt such an immense relief that she was not pregnant. She realized that she was angry with Martin. She had used birth control pills, but she had also suffered from diarrhea during her visit to Surkhet, which might have interfered with their efficacy. She knew that she wasn't able to commit to a child at this time, nor was she ready to commit to Martin. She felt the shift since she had been the one trying to push Martin for a commitment. Now she realized that she was the one who wasn't ready either. If she had wanted a commitment, she could have negotiated to stay longer in Nepal and remain there until Martin had finished his assignment with the Peace Corps. She hadn't done so and had left for her career development. Nancy knew that she had too many things she wanted to do and places she wished to visit.

Chapter 12 · Back Home in London

Nancy had been back in London for about two months. She sat on the bed upstairs in the front bedroom, which her mother had kindly prepared for her return. Her parents were happy to have her back after four and a half years away, but she felt strangely out of place in her own culture, as if she were a foreigner visiting the country. When she returned from Nepal, her mother was concerned about her dress and habits, commenting that she "smelled of Asia," and Nancy wasn't sure what she meant by that. Her friends noticed the difference. She was more confident, but she was also far more determined.

She was losing weight since she wasn't happy with her return to a British diet of mashed potatoes, cabbage, and too many eggs. Her poor mother never knew what to cook for her. She had become a vegetarian, and her family were heavy meat eaters. Her mother tried her best but was never the greatest cook, and her meals were not very attractive to Nancy. It was now June, and the weather was still rainy and cold. Most British people would have considered it warm, but she had the electric heater on in her room. She was due to start her master's degree in late September, so she had four months to wait, and she wasn't sure what she would do with her time. She certainly didn't want to stay at home every day. She had savings from her assignment in Nepal, so money wasn't the issue; instead, it was her fear of boredom. Her friend Sheila had arranged a few weeks' work for her at the Consumer Association in London, and she had been bored silly with processing questionnaires and interpreting answers. She managed to complete the assignment for the sake of her friend and was at least paid for the task.

The worst thing was the physical pain that she felt in her chest. This had only started after a month or so back home. It was like an ache, and she wasn't sure why. She knew she missed Martin, but didn't think it was only because of him. Her mother knocked on the door and entered with a tray of food.

"Nancy, you're not eating enough. You need to eat more. Make sure you eat these sandwiches. Do come down when you feel rested, as Dad wants to see you," her mother said.

Nancy looked at the sandwiches with oodles of butter her mother spread on them, three thick slices of cheese, and salad cream oozing out of the crusts. She placed them to the side and drank her tea. She further considered why she felt so sad. She didn't regret leaving Nepal, as she needed to study, and the London School of Hygiene and Tropical Medicine was one of the top global centers for learning in public health. It wasn't that she saw any future in Nepal, and she felt that she had done her best to help the country. However, she realized that she had adapted and changed considerably to be able to function there. She had changed her customs, learned the language, worn Nepalese clothing, and suppressed some of her more Western traits by being far less blunt and direct in her communication style to do her job. It was too difficult to change back, and she wasn't sure she wanted to. Nancy knew that part of the reason she had loved her assignment was that she had escaped all expectations for her life. She didn't have to find a 9–5 job; she didn't have to find a suitable man and get married; she didn't have to buy a semi-detached house and scrape together the mortgage each month. She had led an exciting and unpredictable life in Nepal, free from cultural expectations, and she had been happy to escape these norms. Now she was back, and her parents expected her to settle here, get married, and give them the wonderful grandchildren they had always hoped for.

Nancy left the sandwiches. She carried the tray downstairs, washed her dishes, and entered the lounge to sit with her father.

Part Two

South Sudan (1985–86)

Lisa

Decisions

Chapter 1 · Welcome to Juba!

Lisa had arrived at Wilson Airport in Nairobi by taxi. It was a hot August day, with little wind. The airport was a small runway, primarily used for military planes, and few people were there at 6:00 AM. She was tired, having come from London only a few days ago, and although she had rested in Nairobi, she was still jet-lagged and exhausted. Wilson Airport was a small facility used primarily for military and private charter flights. However, most flights to southern Sudan departed from here, as only small planes could land at Juba Airport. It was tranquil with few people around. Lisa was also hungry, having left her hotel without eating or even a cup of coffee.

Lisa walked toward a small plane parked near the hangar. She approached someone she assumed was her pilot, who was walking toward her. As she got nearer, she was shocked to see that the pilot appeared to be in his early to mid-twenties.

"Greetings. I believe you are taking me to Juba this morning?" Lisa said.

"Hi, are you Lisa? You are my only passenger today," he replied in stilted English.

Lisa wondered if she could run for it and make a quick getaway to her hotel in Nairobi. First, he was too young. Second, the plane was too small. Third, where exactly was she going?

As if he could read her mind, the pilot responded.

"Don't worry, Lisa. I have made this trip many times with only a few problems."

Lisa thought to herself, exactly what problems…? The pilot checked around the plane and spoke with airport staff to obtain flight clearance. He was wearing a pilot's uniform, impeccably clean and well-fitting, a bit too smart, she thought, for a trip to Juba. She wondered how she could extricate herself from this flight and the trip, but she knew it would be detrimental to her career to decide not to go, since her NGO had chartered the plane entirely for her, and there would be implications if she cancelled.

"That's fine. How long is the flight?" she responded, her voice faltering somewhat.

"It should take about an hour and fifty minutes. As we fly over, we should get a good view of Mount Kenya on the right side. Are you ready?" he said.

Lisa collected her bag and realized that the time for fleeing was over. She was destined to fly in this small plane with the child pilot.

The plane had six seats, and Lisa picked one at the back. She had read somewhere that the back seats would be the safest in the event of a plane crash. She settled in, closed her eyes, and clutched the sides of the seat. The plane took off smoothly. Lisa opened her eyes to blue skies and a magnificent view of Nairobi. The capital, in the 1980s, was still not overly built up, and there were few skyscrapers. Lisa had enjoyed her stay in Nairobi. She had thought that her first trip to Africa would be an exciting experience. However, she had been warned that Juba would be a striking contrast to Nairobi, and her expectations should be low.

She thought of her departure from the UK after her studies and leaving her family and boyfriend, Tim. She had met him at the Liverpool School of Hygiene, where she had studied for her master's. Although this was a relatively short trip of only five months, it still put a strain on a relatively new relationship. Tim was a PhD student at the school, and they had hit it off fairly quickly. However, Tim had been raised in a very traditional middle-class family. Lisa was a little too unconventional for him in her desire to work overseas and develop a career in international development. She was also sad to leave her family. In June, she had bought a house on the North Circular Road in London that she and her father had decorated from top to bottom before she left. She had almost become settled living in London.

"Why don't you come up front and sit beside me so I can show you Mount Kenya?" the pilot shouted out to her over the loud buzz of the engines.

Lisa shuffled up the plane hesitantly and sat beside the pilot. He had placed the plane on autopilot and was hunting around for something. Lisa was a little nervous that his attention was anywhere but on the aircraft's steering.

"Ah, here it is! My English notebook! I am trying to improve my English! Can you help me? In case you haven't guessed, I am Egyptian!" he screamed over the engine noise.

She hadn't guessed. She had thought he was Saudi Arabian. He proceeded to read sentences from his book for her to correct. She decided that if she were going to die, at least she would do it while helping someone. She wasn't sure, though, if English would be of much assistance to him in a crashed plane somewhere near Mount Kenya.

"My name is Reda, I was born and raised in Alexandria, north of Cairo. Do you know Egypt at all? It's a wonderful country. Although we are Muslim, Egyptians are very laid-back, and we take great pride in our culture. Alexandria is a fascinating city! It has far more history than Cairo and was founded by Alexander the Great in 330 BC! I love it. My father is a businessman, but my uncle runs the National Museum there, so I go there a lot."

"Sorry, I have never been there, but I would like to go," she responded. Lisa was intrigued by Egypt since she was fascinated by archaeology.

They proceeded with his English lesson for the next thirty minutes. After that, Lisa became a little tired.

"Would you mind if I went back and slept for a while? I didn't sleep much last night, and I need a little shuteye before we land!" She moved back to her seat before he could insist that she must continue.

After a while, she opened her eyes and saw land below. It looked like scorched earth, with a very brown, hilly, and barren landscape. To the left, she could see some buildings. Surely, this was not Juba! Somehow, though, she was pretty sure that it was…

The pilot landed on the short, untarmacked runway in Juba. He had to be skilled, as Lisa could not see the airport building. He turned the plane, and Lisa looked out to see if she could locate it.

As if the pilot was reading her mind, he said, "it's a small hut over there to your left. They don't get many visitors," he laughed.

Lisa thanked Reda. She wanted to get down on bended knees and pray to him, but she wasn't religious, and decorum ruled otherwise. She walked the twenty-odd steps over to the hut that served as the airport reception. She looked around her and could barely see any houses in the distance.

At the hut, a guard quickly checked her passport and beckoned her to a group milling around at the back. She recognized that he spoke Arabic to his colleagues, so she guessed he was most likely from Sudan rather than the south, where Dinka was the primary language. She saw a sign with her name and made her way over.

"Greetings. Our car is parked over there," the NGO driver said. His dark skin made her fairly sure he was from the South, not the North. She looked back to say goodbye to the pilot, but he was already gone.

The car park had only a few car spaces directly outside the airport hut. They walked over to an old Toyota Land Cruiser that had seen better days. The car coughed and spluttered its way out of the car park, thanks to the driver, who had mastered the complexity of this old jalopy.

The drive into Juba took about ten minutes. The town consisted of one- to two-story houses with mud cladding. They drove on a dirt road, which narrowed as they moved further away from the airport. It was bumpy and very dusty. Most of the way, Lisa's view was obscured by dust coming off the road, which created a red lens across her line of vision. Single-story houses were scattered on either side of the road, with a few larger buildings.

In the 1980s, Juba was a small city with buildings at most three stories high. Lisa had read as much as she could about the country before her arrival and was aware that oil companies had moved there in the late 1970s, with Chevron being the primary one. However, the companies did not do well in southern Sudan. Chevron and the government had proposed a package of development projects that included support for health improvements, drinking water, and education services. Neither the government nor Chevron lived up to these agreements due to arrangements that favored the North and not the South.

They arrived at a small one-story building originally painted white but now more like grey. The driver told her someone would visit her tomorrow morning to brief her as he carried her bags into the building. Lisa was relieved that she would have the evening to herself to settle and not have to commence her work immediately with a briefing. Her assignment in South Sudan was to run training for local government staff on controlling infectious diseases. She had recently completed her master's degree in public health, specializing in communicable disease control and epidemiology.

The first room had a worn sofa, a table, and, at the back, a small kitchen with a gas stove. There was a kettle beside the furnace and one saucepan. A small fridge contained essential foods such as eggs, butter, milk, and rice. The cupboard had cereal, bread, jam, and other items. The floor appeared to be concrete with a few worn, old mats. She saw a room off the lounge and entered the bedroom, which was worn but had clean bedding and a mosquito net over the bed. There was a radio in the bedroom, so at least she might have some communication with the outside world, she thought. The bathroom was attached to the bedroom, so she checked the water. It was running, but there was no hot water. Should she leave it running longer?

Lisa was tired, so she made a cup of tea and had some bread and butter with jam. She decided to sleep early, so first, she checked the locks on the doors and windows. She was a little concerned as she was on the ground floor, which was always more susceptible to break-ins. However, she was too tired to worry tonight, so she crashed onto the bed. She put on the fan in her room and was pleased to see that it worked.

She woke abruptly to the sound of loud music and checked her watch to find it was midnight. She peeked out the window to see which direction the music was coming from and could see a house further up the road where people appeared to be dancing. The music became louder, so Lisa made herself another cup of tea and tried to read a book. She knew she would not be getting back to sleep anytime soon. The music stopped around 4:00 AM.

Lisa got up rather wearily at 6:00 AM, washed, and dressed. She waited for the government official to visit her at the house. It was a Saturday, so she didn't expect much work to be conducted today. There was a knock on the door, and Lisa opened the door to a tall, distinguished-looking gentleman with light tribal markings on his cheeks.

"Greetings, Lisa. My name is Bortel, and I am the Community Development Director in the government of Juba. Anita, the Director for Africa-Action, is still in Mogadishu, Somalia, visiting her husband there as he has just been imprisoned," he stated.

Bortel must have been in his mid-thirties and at least 6 feet 5 inches tall.

He was dressed in a smart short-sleeved safari suit, and his face was quite handsome. Lisa thought he looked too young to hold a senior government position. However, she learned later that many senior government officials were young, since Khartoum was involved in their appointments and preferred younger people who were ambitious enough to follow the rules of the North.

"Let's go for a walk. I can explain a few facts about this region to you," he added.

"Is it safe to walk?" Lisa asked.

"Very. There have never been attacks on foreigners, and there has seldom been fighting in Juba unless at night," he replied.

They walked out into the street, down the dusty mud road, outside Lisa's residence.

Bortel started to describe the situation in the South. Lisa stopped worrying because she was accompanied by a very tall South Sudanese government official, who, due to his position, seemed to wield considerable power.

"You have come at a difficult time, as the civil war between the Southern Peoples Liberation Army (SPLA) and the government is intensifying. Although the first war only ended two years ago, we are amid a second war that started earlier this year. In 1983, President Nimeiri in Khartoum made several decisions that led to problems in the South, including the imposition of Sharia Law across the country and the abolition of the Southern Sudan Autonomous Region. In response, southern rebels, known as the SPLA, took up arms against the state. The problem is that most of the South is Christian or follows traditional faiths and will not accept Islamic rules. The region was converted by missionaries predominantly from Ethiopia," he explained.

"It must be difficult to live under the rules of the North, as from what I've read, they appear to have little empathy for the South," Lisa said.

"Indeed, you are correct. The northern people hold the South and its people in contempt. Even the more empathetic ones do not consider Southerners as equals. Most of us dread our visits to the North for work and other reasons, but as government staff, we are bound by their rules," he told her.

Lisa found Bortel very frank about the strained relationship with the North. She imagined he would be even more open. Still, she was working with an international NGO based in the UK, and perhaps he was nervous that information would be shared indirectly with the British government.

"Lisa, you are safe here since one of my staff members lives two doors down and has been told to keep an eye on your house. Don't worry about the discotheque at the end of the road. A Ugandan runs it, and although I would strongly recommend you keep from visiting it alone, there is usually little trouble from the people there," he said. As if she would be running down there every evening to dance her feet off, she thought and giggled to herself.

"Lisa, I would like to give you a tour of the town and show you where my government and the NGO offices are. There will be a car to collect you each day, so don't worry," he added.

Bortel proceeded to direct Lisa to his rather beaten-looking Land Rover. As a senior government official in Juba, he had a driver, so they sat together in the back of the car. Bortel talked a little about John Garang, the leader of the SPLA, but he was guarded in his comments due to the driver's presence. Lisa had heard about John Garang before her trip. He was an orphan educated in Tanzania and belonged to the Dinka ethnic group.[6] Bortel was also a Dinka. By the tone of his voice, Lisa could sense that Bortel was not a strong supporter of Garang. He explained that his people had experienced severe displacement as a result of SPLA operations.

"John Garang's ascendance to power from obscurity was soon after the 1983 Bor and Ayod mutinies and took many by surprise. Let's see how he progresses in his war against the North. The population of Juba is about 90,000, but with the civil war, more are coming to Juba to seek work and safety from recruitment to the SPLA," he said. She wondered about the tightrope that Bortel would have to walk here in the South. He was appointed to his position with the approval of the Sudanese government, so he had to be careful not to be heard supporting the SPLA. On the other hand, she was sure that many South Sudanese supported Garang.

6 The Dinka mostly live along the Nile, in the Bahr El Gazal, Upper Nile, and the Abyei Area of the Ngok Dinka in Southern Sudan and form forty percent of the overall population, being the predominant tribe of Southern Sudan.

Bortel pointed out key buildings to Lisa as they drove around the town. Most of the town's buildings were traditional mud-walled tukuls with grass-thatched roofs. She saw the university, which was small, but for Juba, it was most likely one of its most significant buildings. They drove past the Greek club, one of the better-kept buildings in the town.

"In the 1930s, when about forty Greeks were living in Juba, they set up a Greek-Orthodox church and a school. This building was a warehouse that stored wine, spirits, sugar, coal, rubber, and European imports, primarily from the UK. It is the same building that US President Theodore Roosevelt described in his memoirs, as he spent a night there," he replied.

"Can we go inside the Greek club to buy something to take out and eat? I am famished, she said.

"Why don't we just eat there?" Bortel replied.

When they entered the club, they saw many foreigners sitting inside, but there were also quite a few Africans eating. They ordered some bread called Kissra, a Southern Sudanese bean dish, Tzatziki, and Greek salad, which were all delicious. Lisa liked that no one looked at them as they ate, nor was anyone concerned about seeing an expatriate woman. She later learned through colleagues that it was one of the few discreet places in the city.

"I will introduce you to Oxfam staff tomorrow, as you will be running the training with their office. The training will be on the outskirts of the town, involving my government staff and women and men from the surrounding rural communities," Bortel said.

Lisa returned to her apartment and thought about her arrival in Juba. It was undoubtedly a novel adventure in Africa. She was still unsure whether she wished to continue her professional life in development, and this assignment was a good gauge for her to investigate this further. She was torn since she wanted more time with her family. She was also torn regarding Tim, her boyfriend. Tim had completed his first degree at Cambridge, which was expected in his family. In contrast, Lisa came from a very modest background, where she was the first in her family to attend university. She sat on the bed and read the book on Southern Sudan that she had brought with her.

This assignment contrasted with her prior development experience, since Lisa had never previously worked in a conflict zone, with most of her experience limited to working in refugee camps in Thailand. She was aware that there were predominantly two types of development workers: those who were more emergency-focused and moved from conflict zones to disaster recovery locations, often staying for only a short time, and those who were more interested in longer-term development programs. At this point, she had yet to decide where she wished to concentrate, as the former cadre, she considered, was far more exciting. However, her experiences had exposed her to the limitations of development projects, which often disregarded local knowledge. She was interested in working on projects that were country-led rather than donor-driven.

She cooked herself an omelet with tomatoes and onions, as it was all she had, and it was easy. Lisa then tried to call her mother in Ireland from the house, but was unable to, as the reception was too poor. Her mother was her confidante, and she had been looking forward to hearing her Dublin lilt. She tried to read while falling asleep to the sound of South African singer Brenda Fassie blaring out of the speakers at the Ugandan discotheque.

The next day, Bortel arrived early. Since it was a Sunday, he was wearing jeans and a T-shirt, which she found somewhat incongruous on him. She was dressed modestly in trousers and a long shirt. As they left town, Lisa saw the severe ravages of the region's drought. Bortel pointed to villages where Lisa could see tukuls in poor condition, with women carrying water pots on their heads as they collected water from the rivers. Only a few villages had piped water or a hand pump installed, and most women walked to the rivers, which were invariably polluted. Bortel stopped the car at Lisa's request so that she could talk to some of the women.

"Can you ask the women how long they travel to collect water daily?" Lisa asked Bortel to translate.

"They say they walk up to four hours daily to collect water. Often, the wells dry up in summer, so they have to travel even further. And, of course, it's the women and girls who travel for water and never the men," Bortel replied after translating the women's responses.

"Can you ask them about their children? Where do they take them when they're ill?" Lisa asked.

Bortel turned to the women again and spoke with them for about five minutes. Lisa noticed that the younger women were shyer, but the older ones welcomed the opportunity to talk with a government official.

"The women say if the child has diarrhea, they don't take them to the clinic as it's in Juba, and that's a one-hour walk. They will treat the child with local remedies. I asked if these worked, and they said only sometimes. If the child is coughing and experiencing breathing difficulties, they will take them to the clinic, but they will have to ask a neighbor to lend them a horse and cart, as they don't wish to delay the child's treatment by walking. A mobile clinic sometimes comes out for immunization services, so they will ask the health worker to examine the child. The problem is that the health workers are trained for vaccination services but not medically trained, so there is a limit to the support they can provide," Bortel explained to her.

Bortel continued talking to the women for twenty minutes, asking where their husbands were working. They were primarily working on the land, but some commuted into Juba, where they held unskilled labor jobs during the week and returned home only on weekends. Lisa thought that at least some households had a little income, even though it would only be a small percentage.

The training, conducted by Lisa on communicable diseases, would take place at one of the government's community development centers outside of Juba. More than two-thirds of the nation's population was either affected by blinding trachoma or at risk of infection. Another significant risk was Guinea-worm disease, which remains a serious threat, caused by drinking contaminated water that contains tiny, infected water fleas. Once inside the body, the worms would grow, pierce through the intestinal wall, and slowly migrate down to the legs or feet, eventually bursting out through painful sores. Lisa thought that a great deal could be done to prevent illness with limited funds and by providing relevant information to families. Guinea-worm was a disease of poverty, and in 1985, many African and Asian countries were still afflicted with the illness. Lisa knew that former U.S.

President Jimmy Carrie was interested in eradicating Guinea worm, and she had read about his efforts to develop a strategy to combat the disease.

Lisa walked around the village with Bortel. The children looked dirty, wearing little clothing made of rags and no shoes at all. Many had protruding bellies, indicating worm infestation, usually roundworm, which caused nutritional deficiencies. It was hard for Lisa to look at the children's condition, or at the deep poverty that clung to every corner of the village, without feeling a knot tighten in her chest. Tears gathered in her eyes. Now, with the civil war, these villages were less likely to receive assistance.

Bortel noticed her discomfort. "I know it's difficult to see this level of poverty. Most of the time, these families could have made more money by brewing Siko[7] or moonshine from dates and sugar. This is now prohibited, so they have lost a considerable amount of income. The economic situation in Juba is getting increasingly desperate, and many women continue to distil in their backyards illegally."

"It seems that little development assistance has reached these villages. It's as if there has been none in this region whatsoever," she commented.

"That's not far off the truth. Significant funding has been donated to Southern Sudan, but my department receives very little. Corruption, I'm afraid, is rampant. The Sudanese government allocates insufficient funds to the South and then places it in the hands of people who can't be trusted to spend it wisely," he replied.

"What about the children? If they don't go to school, what are they doing? Are they working in the fields?" Lisa asked.

"Well, that was the case until the Civil War. Now, the SPLA is recruiting children from most rural villages and training them as soldiers. Think about it: placing guns in the hands of eight-year-olds, sometimes even younger ones," Bortel replied.

Lisa was shocked. She had not encountered this before in her previous travels, but then she had not previously worked in a conflict country.

"The children are taken from their families and never allowed to return. They must be indoctrinated with the war's propaganda to make them shoot

7 Siko is a local term in South Sudan for a potent, often home-brewed alcoholic spirit.

the enemy, the Sudanese army. Even in my village, children are now starting to be taken. If you are in government, you can prevent it from happening within your family and relatives, but you can't protect others for fear of reprisals from the SPLA," he said.

"Surely the UN and the international community can prevent this?" she replied.

"The UN? Don't be fooled. They certainly can use their diplomacy to deliver food or medicines, but they can't interfere with the conflict, or their workers will be shot. There was an excellent Community Development Center at Wau. It took years to build the infrastructure and develop relationships with donors to support the staffing and courses run there. I hope Anita arranges for you to meet with the director," he said.

Lisa felt she should raise this with the UK government, but somehow, she knew that little action would likely be taken. Although she was still in the early stages of her career, she was aware that there were some battles where she had a chance to influence outcomes. Still, large political issues, such as the use of child soldiers, required a much higher level of engagement than what she could access.

At this point, she felt that she was in God-forsaken territory.

Chapter 2 · Adapting to the Environment

Lisa had been in Juba for a month. Anita, the NGO's director and line manager, arranged a dinner one night with a few people from the government and aid agencies who worked in Juba. The guest of honor was George, the Director of the Community Development Center at Wau, in the northwest of South Sudan. He was shortly to visit the UK to meet with government officials and present his work. George was about forty, although he appeared older. He was very thin and tall and, like Bortel, was a Dinka. Lisa sat with George before the dinner, interested in learning from him.

"So, George, how long will you be in the UK?" she asked.

"Well, I go once a year to talk at the London School of Economics and other venues, as they are very interested in what's happening in the South. The Center trains in community development and technical skills."

"Where do your trainees come from?" she asked him.

"Most are sponsored by the government and international NGOs. Our Center allows young people to learn a technical trade, and they help with our efforts to work with communities in the South," George responded.

Lisa asked, "but are you not worried about the increasing violence in the South and disturbances to the Center, due to the escalation of the conflict?"

"Yes, that is my greatest fear, since the SPLA are not fighting in the North. They are fighting the government here, which is affecting any development activities. It's not just the Center that worries me. I am worried about schools and health centers being damaged and destroying what is already a very fragile development framework in the South."

"I saw some of that on my field trips. There were abandoned school buildings, I presume, that were damaged by the conflict," Lisa said.

"Literacy rates and girls' enrolment at school are still incredibly low. There is so much to do. However, as you must be aware, politicians see winning as the only goal, and the damage along the way is ignored and forgotten," he replied.

"After what you have achieved, that must be soul-destroying. When did you start work on the Development Center? How did you get the funding?" she asked him.

"Most of the money is from British and European donors. They often invite me to visit their institutions to present our work. It's quite a shift for someone to come from here and talk to the West about development issues. However, this is the way it should be."

"You mean, less international expertise?" she asked him.

"Yes. We're often subject to international development workers coming over for one year or even a few weeks, determined to set their agenda and trying to push it on us at breakneck speed. They feel it justifies their salary," he replied.

The last sentence hit Lisa hard, as a consultant only visiting South Sudan for a few months. "That's a perspective I need to understand. You're right. One can come here with a fixed and almost superior attitude concerning results that need to be achieved without reviewing these with the government and communities."

"When I visit Europe, my role is not to lecture but to engage in dialogue on development issues. Of course, one of my greatest concerns is the duration of most development plans. Five years is nothing in the light of what needs to be done. Then, a new plan and new objectives are set without any real in-depth assessment of the work, with top-down evaluations conducted," George stated.

"Yes, five years is a very short time," she responded.

"I understand the need for donors to evaluate their funding, but I don't know why they can't use local companies or agencies to conduct these studies," George added.

Anita called them over for dinner, and Lisa reflected on her conversation with George.

Her work was now well underway with her training courses. She left her apartment early the following day and joined her driver for the trip to the training center outside town. She had now started training about thirty workers from the Department of Health and Community Development in disease prevention and control. She instructed staff on the factors regarding major infectious diseases prevalent in the South, and she enjoyed the training due to the participants' enthusiasm. The South Sudanese were motivated, interested, and keen to support their region. It was a level of motivation she had not experienced before. These people had so little, yet they wanted to do so much.

Anita frequently visited the training and was pleased with the progress. In her mid-fifties, Anita was an accomplished and experienced professional in international development. Her husband had been a government minister in Somalia but was now under arrest in a country with as many problems and conflicts as South Sudan. They often sat together in the evenings, drinking beer under the tree at Anita's house for shade, and talking about the UK, relationships, and working in conflict-ridden countries.

"Do you not feel very cut off here in Juba when your husband is in Mogadishu?" Lisa asked.

"I don't have much choice. I cannot remain in the city, or eventually, I will be arrested for conspiring with my husband. They will tolerate my short trips in and out, but I'm under observation whenever I visit," Anita replied.

"It must be tough for you. How did you meet your husband?" Lisa asked.

"I worked in Somalia in the 1970s. At that time, it was easier to work there. He worked for the government, and I was an NGO project officer," she responded.

Lisa asked, "didn't it worry you then that it would be difficult to continue the relationship?"

"We don't choose who we fall in love with. It hit me suddenly that I couldn't leave him, so we got married. I continued working there for a few years and then went back to work in London for a while, and he commuted back and forth," she responded.

"Would it have been difficult for him to move to London?" Lisa asked.

"Not really, as he could have based himself at a university. However, he didn't want to leave his country. As things deteriorated, he was placed under house arrest and imprisoned," she replied.

"What about children? Did you have any with him?" Lisa realized that her questions might now be too personal, but she was curious about how Anita could have had an everyday life despite her lifestyle.

"He has children from his first wife. We never had any, and I was in my mid-thirties when we got married. I fell in love with Somalia. It was such a beautiful country, but now it's being destroyed by warfare," she replied.

Lisa knew she would never have allowed herself to fall for someone who would have tied her down to one country. She wanted a career in development, which meant traveling extensively. She couldn't imagine living Anita's life, but she could see how devoted she was to her husband.

"I thought I had met someone special in Tim, my boyfriend, who was studying at Liverpool at the same time as me, but he called me a few days ago to say that he had met someone else at the school and he was now going out with her. He said the distance between us was too difficult for him to deal with," Lisa told Anita.

"Well then, he sounds rather superficial, and he would have waited for you if he were in love," Anita told her rather brutally. Lisa felt a little inadequate. Why had Tim not fallen in love with her? Lisa pondered if she had remained in the UK longer, could they have further developed their relationship, and would he have been more likely to stay faithful? However, she had to admit that Tim was traditional, and he would eventually want a far more conventional partner than Lisa. His phone call had hurt her, mainly her pride, but she would move past it. At least, she didn't need to worry now about leaving a relationship behind in the UK, if she decided to continue working overseas.

She changed the subject and asked, "do you prefer working in places such as Somalia and southern Sudan? Life must be tough, but I guess you really do see an impact from your work."

"The problem is that once you have worked in conflict zones, you tend to get offered positions in that category. Even though I frequently apply, I'm rarely considered for positions in more stable countries. I wanted a posting in Kenya since it would be easier to travel to Somalia, but I was turned down for a few senior manager positions," Anita replied.

"I guess it's easy to get labelled as a humanitarian specialist," Lisa responded.

"You don't need to worry about that yet," Anita replied.

On the contrary, Lisa thought she needed to think about that as soon as possible!

Chapter 3 · Precarious Living

Lisa began her course curriculum for the day in the tent that Oxfam had set up on the outskirts of Juba. She had now been in South Sudan for nearly three months, and she was used to the hot, dry weather as she taught her class under the light canopy with the sun streaming through the damaged canvas. Suddenly, she heard a loud bang, followed by rapid gunfire in the distance. Lisa ran out of the tent after asking her students to read quietly so that she could investigate what was happening. She hurriedly walked over to Nick, the director at Oxfam.

"What was that? Was there an explosion? I thought I heard gunfire?"

"I don't know, Lisa," he said rather nervously. "I think you need to drive back to your office now. Can you please close the training for the day? Perhaps you could politely ask the staff to undertake an exercise they can present tomorrow?"

"Good idea," she responded, but her mind was already heavily distracted. She returned to the tent, told the team that she had to leave, and gave them an exercise to complete. She hurriedly packed her papers and made her way to the car, where the driver had already started the engine. Lisa was not overly worried, but she knew she needed to return to the city as soon as possible. However, worrying about something she had so little control over was useless.

The driver took Nick and her to the road where the Oxfam office was, but the police had blocked the dirt path. The government soldier beckoned them to move forward, and Nick rolled down his window to talk to him.

"You can't go any further. A military plane has been shot down, we think, and it has crashed into the field outside the Oxfam office. Some of the offices have been hit by debris," the soldier told them. A few feet in front, they could see the debris of the small single-engine plane. The tail had broken off and was scattered outside the building on one side of the road. Near it were the burned remains of the cockpit. Presumably, the pilot had been killed, as Lisa doubted that he could have survived such a major crash. She hoped that his remains had been removed from the plane before it was allowed to burn away.

"Was anyone hurt?" Nick asked him.

"Not that we know of right now, but the pilot is dead. There was only one man in the plane," the soldier responded.

They could hear shooting in the distance, and the streets were nearly empty.

"The driver will leave you at Anita's house since it's safer than the office," Nick said as he quickly walked off to check the damage at his office.

Anita's house was right beside the office within the Afro Action compound, and she was in the house.

"Lisa, can you please go into my bedroom and close all the shutters on the windows? I need to contact the British Consulate to ask for their recommendation on what we should do next. Please also take at least four beers down to the bedroom, as we'll need them," Anita asked Lisa.

Lisa did as she was instructed. She still felt no fear and wasn't quite sure why she was so calm. She could see that Anita was very nervous, but for her, this was what she had expected when arriving in a crisis country. She had craved to learn what it was like to live in a country in conflict, and to her surprise, she found it all quite exciting, which also then led to a feeling of guilt as someone had died in that plane. She closed the metal shutters on the windows and sat on the floor beside the bed while she opened one of the beers. She was very thirsty, having spent most of the day in the field, and she quickly guzzled the beer down.

Anita came into the room after about thirty minutes, carrying snacks and water for both of them.

"John Garang and the SPLA have taken the airport, so there are no flights, and the military is firing at the airport. This isn't good," she stated.

"What do we do now? How long can he resist the military?" she asked Anita, who appeared more nervous.

"Nobody knows. But we may need to move out all non-essential personnel. Lisa, we may need to evacuate you in the next few days once the airport is secured," she responded.

"I understand, but if the SPLA has the airport, will any flights be allowed to leave?" Lisa didn't want to leave. This was too exciting, and she wondered if she was better suited to working under emergency conditions since it didn't appear to unnerve her.

"They can't hold it for long. The government will send reinforcements to take back control of the airport as soon as possible. Garang must know this, so he is just showing his hand to the government before he marches further into the South to control more territory and fight pro-government groups," she added.

They continued to hear the guns going off in the distance while they drank their beers. Anita placed two mattresses on the floor for them to sleep on, which they managed to do around 2:00 AM, after discussing everything under the sun, with the intensifying gunfire in the background. Lisa found it hard to sleep, as she had been experiencing an adrenaline rush throughout the drama.

They both awoke around 5:00 AM to complete silence.

"I think it's OK for us to sit outside to eat our breakfast as the gunfire has ceased for now," Anita said, and she went to prepare some porridge and coffee.

"The silence most likely means the SPLA has been forced to retreat. Let me call Bortel to see if he has any information." Anita entered her office to make the call while Lisa enjoyed the silence and the morning sun. She imagined that people living in crisis countries learned to enjoy whatever respite there was in the midst of chaos.

"Well, Bortel says that the SPLA took the airport yesterday and held it until early this morning when the government pushed them back into the hills. They live to fight another day!" she said.

"That's the first time that's happened, no?" Lisa asked.

"Yes, the SPLA has never got that far before. Our concern is how the SPLA destroys development in the South. We were about to launch a tukul thatching project a few months back, working in villages demonstrating improved thatching using UK techniques.[8] Now, it's too dangerous to run the training for fear of the SPLA moving around and recruiting in the towns," Anita stated.

---

8 A tukul is a traditional round hut with a conical roof that is found in eastern and northeastern Africa. Tukuls are made from mud, grass, and wooden poles.

"Do you see yourself staying much longer here, Anita?"

"I can't visit my husband in Mogadishu any longer. I am liaising with Amnesty to work on his release. But this job suits me as it's near," she replied.

"Don't you sometimes wish for a more conventional life?" Lisa asked.

"Well, the thing is, if you choose humanitarian aid, you do get burned out quickly. This is why many humanitarian workers typically stay overseas for five to ten years before returning to work in their own country. I will move home after this posting and see if I can work on my husband's release. It will be easier to get support for him there as well," Anita replied.

"But what will you do in the UK for a living?" Lisa asked.

"I'm interested in social work through career retraining. But I will also apply to Oxfam and other agencies," she responded.

Lisa could see that Anita's options back in the UK were limited. She reflected that if she continued working in international development, her options would also be limited if she decided to return.

Lisa left with the driver and returned to her apartment in Juba, where she packed her bags, as Anita had asked her to move in with her for security. She heard a knock on the door and answered to find Bortel standing outside.

"Hi, Lisa, I hope you have gotten over the incident yesterday. Things are safer now. John Garang has pushed his soldiers back to the villages, and I don't think he will infringe on Juba again soon," Bortel informed her.

"It was scary. Especially the plane crashing right in the town," Lisa replied.

"I know you are leaving in a few weeks, and I will be traveling to the UK for a workshop next week, so we could go to dinner this evening if that's convenient for you," he asked her.

Lisa wondered if this was advisable from a protocol perspective since he was her government counterpart. She had already sensed that he was attracted to her, and she had no idea if he was married. However, since she was leaving and somewhat trusted Bortel, she decided to go to dinner with him. First, she went into the bathroom to freshen up. Lisa was now in her late twenties, and although she could not be classified as beautiful, she was attractive to men. She was slim, and even under trying circumstances, such as in South Sudan, she made an effort to dress well. She applied some lipstick and combed her hair. She didn't wish to make too much effort in case Bortel misconstrued this as an interest in him.

They both left the apartment together, and Bortel directed her to his car, which he then drove to a restaurant in the center of town. The restaurant was in one of the better buildings, and other expatriates were present.

"What is next for you, Lisa, after you return to the UK? Are you going to work in Europe or remain in development?" he asked.

"I really don't know. I'm still torn. The idea of being overseas for two to three years at a time is daunting. On the other hand, I love this work so much that I can't see myself doing anything else that I would enjoy as much. Working in a country in crisis, though, is very challenging since anything can happen anytime!" she responded.

"Humanitarian workers are a special breed. They run on adrenaline and enjoy the stress of working eighteen-hour days, burning out, and resting for a few months back home. I understand your concerns. I have a stable position in Juba, but of course, this region is becoming more unstable due to the civil war," he replied.

"Where is your family, Bortel? Surely, you're married with children?" she asked him.

"No, Lisa. Even though I'm now thirty-seven, I can't afford to get married, although my family is pushing for it," he replied.

"Why is it expensive?" she asked.

"In this country, a dowry is required from the husband before you can marry. A man must pay in cattle to the father of the girl he's arranged to marry, and this can vary from fifteen to over a hundred head of cattle per girl. One head of cattle can cost up to $ 150. If the bride is educated, then the dowry is higher," he replied.

"Oh, my goodness. It's the opposite in India, where the female provides the dowry," she replied.

"It's also a good excuse to prevent my family from arranging a marriage I don't want. It's difficult since I have a master's degree from the UK, and finding an educated wife is a challenge. Young girls here, especially, are being denied an education because their parents want to marry them off for livestock," he responded. "I'm also not sure I want to have children when there is a risk of them being killed in this war. Maybe I should stay a bachelor!" he added.

"Do you see yourself staying in South Sudan or working overseas?" Lisa asked him.

"I don't know, really. Securing a position overseas can be challenging, but I'm eligible to apply to the UN due to my nationality. However, I feel a sense of duty to help as much as possible here. Few are as well-educated as I am, and there is much to do," he responded.

"Well, Lisa, would you stay in South Sudan and work in development?" he continued.

Lisa was silent. When she left Juba, she knew she would not return anytime soon. It was becoming more apparent to her that she wanted to work on longer-term development programs rather than relief assistance. She was also aware that although she was attracted to Bortel, she would never have a relationship with him. This would complicate her life and tie her to a place where she did not wish to remain.

"Do you want to visit that discotheque at the back of your house now? This is your last chance!" Bortel asked her.

"Why not? But for a very short visit only. I really don't wish to stay up late!" she replied, making her tone clear that this was her goodbye.

Bortel and Lisa visited the Ugandan discotheque, where Bortel seemed to know everyone, for about thirty minutes. They had a drink and a few dances to the music of Youssou N'Dour playing in the background. Bortel asked her for a slow dance, and since she was leaving, she agreed. He certainly was an attractive man. After another drink and talking about their different future career paths, Bortel drove her back to her apartment. She was concerned he might ask to come in, so she said little in the car. He accompanied her to the door when she got out of the vehicle. He kissed her politely on the cheek as he said goodbye. She felt a tinge of regret as Bortel walked away, which rapidly passed as she went inside and prepared herself a cup of tea.

Chapter 4 · Preparing for Departure

Lisa had finished the workshops with the Department of Health and Community Development staff. They were now working in nearby villages, setting up water filters to prevent Guinea worm infections and building demonstration latrines for villagers to replicate. They were training masons to construct latrine slabs and build a superstructure for the toilets.

Lisa was working with an engineer named Joseph, who was assigned to the Community Development department. Joseph was a highly motivated and hardworking Southern Sudanese Dinka. They identified indigenous materials that could be used to construct latrines in the villages, to help prevent water-related diseases.

"I don't think I have ever seen anyone work as hard as you. You are the first here in the morning and the last to leave at night. Why so much work, Joseph?" Lisa asked him.

"We are so far behind in development that it isn't easy to see if we will ever get out of this. Things have only worsened since the civil war was declared a few years ago. I don't see any end to this, so all I can do is keep working and try to help villagers," Joseph replied.

"I hope one day you are recognized for all the work that you're doing. You are one of the most impressive people I have met in development work," she replied.

"I trained as an engineer, but I can't get work so easily. NGOs only give me six-month contracts, and that's difficult for security. I want to work here, but I also need money for my family, and I worry about the war and how it will affect my children. Most of the engineers I trained with now work in Canada and the UK, where they studied for a further degree," he responded, shrugging off the compliment. Joseph struck Lisa as a very modest man. He wore a crucifix, so she knew he was not hiding his Christian faith, unlike most Dinka, who were polytheists.

"For me, it's normal to work hard, and I want to make a difference. I trained as an engineer in Khartoum for four years. I wouldn't say I liked it there, and the discrimination against me was harsh. But I was determined to finish my training and return home."

"Why was it hard?" Lisa asked.

"Because we were from the South! A few of us trained together, and we tolerated the bullying and the ridicule. We're so different from the Northerners. We share nothing, not religion, values, or outlook. We're like separate countries. We see ourselves as a separate nation. However, I am unsure that the SPLA cares how many of us die as we try to achieve that. They have their agenda. The government is now also targeting the Dinka since the SPLA recruits predominantly from that tribe. That's a grave concern as they will be indiscriminate in attacking villages," Joseph explained to her.

"But how will independence be achieved without John Garang and the SPLA?" she asked him.

"That's a good question. I don't know. But I'm waiting for a leader who doesn't believe that his agenda should be based on violence and who can negotiate with the North and Western leaders to obtain our independence. We need a Martin Luther King," he responded.

"Yes, and they silenced him," Lisa replied.

"Agreed. But come back here in thirty to forty years and see the devastation of the fighting and its toll on the country. And we will have to ask ourselves, was it worth it?"

Joseph sighed and walked back to inspect the technicians' work in cutting bamboo to make latrine slabs. Joseph then walked over to where wood was being cut for the latrine houses and took the saw to cut the wood himself. Lisa knew that even though Joseph was a qualified engineer, he would continue to work closely with communities. He was not political like Bortel. As things deteriorated within the country, it would be difficult for government staff to evade some form of corruption. However, having worked with Joseph for the past three months, she knew he would never allow that, and she feared for his future.

Lisa walked over to where Nick from Oxfam was standing, having just arrived to inspect the work, and greeted him.

"Well, Nick, I will be leaving next week. It was a pleasure working with you. Are you staying in Juba for long?" she asked him.

"How does one leave a region that never seems to improve? I have been working here for around seven years. When I was here before the war restarted, child mortality was decreasing. Now, it's back up to about two hundred per thousand live births. They don't know if that's accurate, since they can't conduct surveys in rural villages due to the conflict. Think about it. That's twenty percent of children dying before they reach five years old, mainly due to diarrhea, pneumonia, malaria, and tetanus, all diseases of poverty," he replied.

"I agree. You can train the government and improve some villages, but sustaining those gains takes time and effort," she stated.

"So, will you come back to southern Sudan to work?" Nick asked her.

She replied, "I'm not sure this type of assistance is where my skills lie. You're better suited for humanitarian work than I am. I am much more interested in longer-term development projects."

"Working in conflict countries is the most challenging and rewarding. The only problem is that we don't know how long the civil war will continue here. I'm worried about Garang's endeavor to build up his army at all costs. That means he will start to recruit children. That will be the worst as he works his way through the South. He needs a large army and will achieve this in any way he can," Nick told her.

"The border divisions created for this country certainly seem random with such vast cultural differences between the North and South," Lisa responded to him.

"The North has been an Islamic nation for more than four hundred years, and then it was under British control for sixty years until the mid-1950s. The British established the North and South under one government, ruled from Khartoum. The South has never forgiven the British for this. Of the eight hundred government positions vacated by the British in the 1950s, only four were given to Southerners. All we can hope is that Garang moves in the right direction to establish independence for the South. I agree with his motives, but I'm afraid I disagree with his methods," Nick explained to her.

"It must be frustrating that everything you do here can be wiped out in a minute if a village is bombed or schools are destroyed. It must be so demoralizing," she answered.

"You get used to it," Nick answered. "Before coming here, I worked in Congo. Many of the staff I worked with directly are no longer alive."

Lisa thought Nick was now quite numb to it all. She would be devastated if she were told after she left that Joseph had been killed. But perhaps a decade from now, she would be like Nick, she wondered.

Lisa said goodbye to Nick, Joseph, and the others. Then she directed the driver to the office to collect her bags. When she returned to Anita's residence, the place was empty, as Anita was traveling to the villages.

The driver took Lisa to the airport to check in her bags and prepare to depart the next day. In the distance, she saw a commotion, with aid workers and airport staff running towards the tarmac. She saw everyone grouped beside the runway. An expatriate ran up to Lisa.

"What blood group are you?" a pale man with red hair asked her.

"I'm not sure. I think it is B-positive since that's my father's blood group." Lisa looked at him, somewhat surprised and perturbed. Why would he want to know her blood group?

"No good," he responded.

He immediately ran off to ask someone else, and Lisa had no idea why he had asked for her blood type. She walked over to someone she recognized from the GOAL Ireland office, whom she had met a few weeks ago.

"Gerry, what's going on over there? Is there anything I can do to help?" she asked him.

"A missionary was driving back from Bor to Juba with his wife when SPLA soldiers stopped his jeep, and they demanded that he hand over the car and any money that he was carrying. There were about five soldiers, we think. They asked them to get out of the vehicle, but they refused to do so. The man then put his foot down on the accelerator and tried to drive away. They fired on the car, and his wife, who was sitting in the passenger seat, was shot in the stomach. He drove straight to the airport to get a flight to Nairobi for medical assistance. They have been on the tarmac for about two hours waiting for a flight. A doctor from Juba Hospital removed the bullet, but they didn't have enough O-negative blood for a transfusion," Gerry said. He was obviously upset by this event, and Lisa thought, most likely, about the implications for his travel in the country as well.

"So, what is happening over there now?" she asked him.

"They have set up a small tent with a blood drip. They are trying to get people with O-negative blood for the transfusion. However, it's a rare blood group, so it isn't easy to find," Gerry replied.

Lisa knew this was her mother's blood group, but she vaguely remembered being told that she and her sister had the same blood group as her father.

"I'm not optimistic that she will last before the flight. Their mission had told them a plane would arrive an hour ago, but it was delayed due to bad weather in Nairobi. They were driving to Juba to fly out for a month's holiday in the States. Just tragic," he added.

"Can she not wait at the hospital in Juba?" Lisa asked him.

"Have you seen the hospital? You wouldn't wish to be ill in Juba in your worst nightmare. All expatriate staff are instructed to evacuate immediately if they become sick or are injured. The level of hygiene is appalling, and it's teeming with people from the villages. If she goes there, she will be dead within a few hours," he replied.

"So, there is not much we can do to help her. I would be willing to hold her hand," Lisa stated.

"She is unconscious, and her husband is in a terrible state since he realized he should have given them the car when they demanded it. The rule is you give up your vehicle under such circumstances," Gerry replied.

Lisa left the airport and returned to have dinner with Anita at the house. She felt a terrible sense of grief for this family. The couple had been working in villages for a minimal salary, and this tragedy occurred while they were returning to the United States at the end of their assignment. Lisa realized how precarious working in conflict countries could be.

She was informed later that night by phone that the wife of the missionary had died on the runway before the plane arrived. Lisa felt great sadness. She came to understand that she needed to follow a path that offered some sense of stability—a place to work, a foundation to build on, and the ability to take calculated risks instead of living such an unpredictable life.

When she arrived at the airport the following day, it was calm, and there was no trace of yesterday's shocking incident except for the remains of the tent on the side of the tarmac. It was easy to walk through to the plane after clearing customs since her bags had already been loaded. Lisa stopped for a few moments and looked back at the town. She felt a mix of emotions, including guilt for leaving after only three months, relief that she could escape so soon, and sadness that she might never see any of these wonderful people again. She walked out a little further towards the runway and looked back again. In a flash, she thought she saw a woman walking towards the airport hut that looked vaguely like herself, but then she was gone.

She saw the Twin Otter plane in the distance and looked around. Lo and behold, the child pilot was there.

"Hi, Reda! I see you are flying me back to Nairobi?" She asked him.

"Yes, Lisa! It's good to see you again. You can tell me about your trip as we fly back!"

She got on board, this time without fear but with a great sense of relief that she was leaving a country that she was reasonably sure would not see much joy for decades.

Chapter 5 · Return to Juba, 2013

After her plane had landed on her return to South Sudan, she waited at least half an hour before the office sent a car to pick her up. She was on a one-week mission to visit rural development projects in the Equatorial region. Lisa looked around the airport. Thirty years later, this was now a paved runway rather than a clay mud one with an improved reception and customs building. She was told that the country's electrification rate had now reached seven percent.[9]

There was a mad rush of people milling around. They walked to the car park, which currently held about thirty cars. The town had remained the same. Few roads were paved, except for the one to the airport. The houses were as dilapidated as ever, and children played by the roadside, poor and ragged, with protruding bellies. They drove past the Greek club, and Lisa asked if the Greeks still owned and operated it. She was told that although a Greek man still owned it, the restaurant was called Paradise and was frequented by a mainly local clientele.

Lisa looked around the town as they drove to the office. She felt a pang of nostalgia for the innocent, trusting woman she had been when she worked here in the 1980s. Lisa was now the CEO of a British NGO based in London, working in more than fifty countries, primarily addressing social development projects, including micro-finance. When the opportunity arose for the start of a new initiative in South Sudan, she decided, along with project experts, to visit and review its feasibility herself.

As she traveled to Equatoria over the next week, she saw that nothing had improved within the country. South Sudan might have been independent, but little progress had occurred. Hundreds of millions of dollars had been invested, but most of it ended up in the pockets of politicians or was invested in infrastructure that was subsequently destroyed. The remarkable rural development center at Wau was damaged during the war, and its institutional memory was lost. Schools and health posts in the South were

9 In 2005, South Sudan declared independence.

destroyed during the civil war, and tens of thousands of children were recruited into the SPLA. The country was only beginning to recover from the devastation, which would likely take decades. The civil war had killed an estimated two million people and displaced more than four and a half million, most of them in the South, over more than twenty years.

George had been correct in their conversations in the 1980s when he had been concerned about attacks on schools and hospitals, as this had been widespread, including looting, vandalism, and destruction of facilities during military offensives. The army utilized any remaining facilities that were not destroyed, resulting in the halt of schooling in the South during the war. Thousands of children had been taken from their villages and forced to work for the SPLA. Those as young as eleven were recruited for this cruel war. No one knows the exact number of boys forced to fight, but it was in the thousands. Hundreds of children were killed or grievously wounded. Others died of starvation or disease. Many were subjected to severe beatings, and all lived in deplorable conditions. Rehabilitating these children and reintegrating them into their communities was an immense and daunting task. Lisa had met some of these children, now adults, through her NGO, and all of them were deeply affected and struggling to recover emotionally.

Lisa was thankful that she had not pursued a career in emergency support; instead, she had worked for several years in various countries in Africa and Asia on long-term development projects. She would have burned out after ten years or so, become far more cynical, and not enjoyed the sense of achievement that she had after thirty years of working in development. She had lived in many countries and was now settled back in the UK with her partner and child.

She had no idea what the future would bring to South Sudan. She recalled her conversations with Bortel, George, and Joseph during her visit in the 1980s and how much each had influenced her. She attempted to locate them during her stay but was unable to find any of them. She wondered if they were killed during the Civil War. The three men had influenced her to focus her expertise on longer-term development planning, working closely with national counterparts, understanding local and cultural needs, and not allowing her work to be too influenced by the Western world's political agenda.

She interviewed the staff of the NGO she had worked for in Juba and was amazed at their naivety and idealism. They had no idea that so little had changed since her assignment here in the 1980s, and she did not have the heart to discourage them. She was sad that she was only here for a week, but she was relieved to leave when the trip was over. She then felt an overwhelming sense of déjà vu as she recalled her departure from Juba in 1985. However, this time, she was leaving on a thirty-seater plane operated by Kenya Airways with a rather seasoned-looking pilot. And with a great sense of relief, she knew that she would never return to Juba.

Part Three

Lesotho (1986–88)

Marie Louise

Awakening

Chapter 1 · Arrival

Marie Louise walked down the hill from her hotel into town. It was chilly at eight o'clock in the morning, so she wore a sweater over her dress. She had on walking shoes and was enjoying taking in the new scenery. There were houses scattered on each side of the road, obviously owned by more affluent families in the city. She passed a few shacks beside these houses, where people sold cigarettes and beer, with children sleeping at the back. No one took any notice of her as she walked by. Marie Louise was quite fit, so she walked briskly down into the city, passing a small, quite smart coffee shop, where she entered and stopped to buy an Americano. The shop obviously catered to foreigners, and quite a few were seated at the front, sipping their coffee and enjoying croissants. Marie Louise picked up the coffee and then walked out. She passed a few beggars at the side of the road and gave them what coins she had in her purse. Marie Louise was still young enough at twenty-nine to believe that some of this money would benefit the recipient, rather than the pimp who sent the mother or child out onto the streets to beg. She saw that most local women wore mid-length skirts with cardigans or sweaters. However, many people were wearing blankets over their clothes. She learned later that the Basotho were renowned for their beautiful, colorful blankets that they wore during the colder months. They were often given as gifts during important ceremonies such as weddings and graduations and were considered a sign of respect and honor.

Marie Louise thought that Maseru seemed like such a small town rather than a capital city like Paris and London, where she had lived for nearly thirty years. She had checked into the hotel on the edge of the capital, the Lesotho Sun, owned by a South African billionaire renowned for gambling casinos throughout southern Africa. Marie Louise was already starting to regret this decision. She was assigned to support the Lesotho Highlands Development Authority (LHDA), working with the British Government, based in Leribe, which was even smaller than Maseru and 100 km north of the capital.[10] The Lesotho Highlands Water Project was, and still is, the largest bi-national infrastructure project between Lesotho and South Africa, diverting water from the mountains of Lesotho to South Africa. It provided water for South Africa and money and hydroelectricity for Lesotho. Marie Louise's role was to support the sociological aspects of the project and advise the engineers as they commenced construction of the dam. This was more of an infrastructure project than a development project, benefiting the people of South Africa. They would gain access to the water needed for the Orange Free State; meanwhile, Lesotho desperately needed the funds. The project aimed to create employment opportunities for the local population, potentially having a positive impact on the economy and the livelihoods of Lesotho's residents. Marie Louise had been attracted to the project because it offered an opportunity to assess a massive infrastructure project and its impact on the local population, which could boost her career development.

Marie Louise was of Anglo-French descent and was born in London. Her mother, however, was French-born and raised. She missed her family, whom she had left behind in Paris, and the friends she had made in London. Both cities were places where she had thoroughly enjoyed her life, and she was feeling disoriented. She thought that Maseru didn't quite feel like an African city should feel, as she had experienced in Nairobi or Accra. She had loved both cities and reveled in wandering through their streets and bazaars. Maseru had a strange feel to it. In most African cities she had visited, people stared at her as a foreigner. Here, however, she could sense a resentment towards her. No one appeared friendly or greeted her. Even the beggars in the street would put out their hands without a smile or greeting. She considered that apartheid next door in South Africa had affected the way she was treated, as there was likely a deep mistrust of white people.

She would have greatly preferred a posting in West Africa, where foreign visitors faced less resentment and, in her view, the culture was more vibrant. She came here because she considered it a good career move to work for the British government on this particular project. However, for black South Africans and Basotho, it wasn't easy to distinguish the British from

10 Leribe is now named Hlotse.

the Afrikaners. The British diaspora living in southern Africa was even more discriminatory. In 1986, South Africa was still marked by a deeply entrenched racial segregation and discrimination system. Apartheid had been the official policy of the South African government since 1948. It was designed to enforce strict racial segregation, institutionalize discrimination against non-white groups, and maintain white minority rule.[11] Finding any form of racism abhorrent, Marie Louise decided she would make the most of her time in Lesotho and then move on after completing her two-year contract.

Lesotho was a constitutional monarchy with a parliamentary system of government. King Moshoeshoe II was the monarch, and a prime minister led the nation. Moshoeshoe was named after the famous leader of the Basotho, who had stood firm against the British in the mid-nineteenth century. He was one of the most successful southern African leaders, fighting off the Boer and British forces and eventually creating a British protectorate rather than being colonized. Marie Louise thought that it must be difficult for South Africans to understand how this small country had withstood colonization and been ruled by African leaders. Although the Basotho remained predominantly poor, they were free to live and work wherever they chose, unlike black South Africans.

At the time of Marie Louise's assignment, Lesotho's economy was primarily based on agriculture, with subsistence farming as the predominant occupation. The country was mountainous, with a highland plateau covering most of its land. The elevation and rugged terrain made transportation challenging. The government faced several challenges in 1986, including political instability, poverty, and limited economic opportunities, and depended heavily on South Africa for trade and employment opportunities. Most men aged eighteen to forty worked in the mines. Before her arrival, Marie Louise had read that the terms of the Highlands Water Project had faced resistance from former prime minister Jonathan Leboa. In

11 When the project finance was agreed, South Africa, which would receive all the water from the project, was subject to international sanctions. To avoid the difficulties of international financiers openly aiding the then–apartheid regime, LHDA's financial advisers set up a London–based trust fund through which payments could be made. Although Lesotho was the nominal borrower for the project, South Africa was/is responsible for repaying the loans.

January 1986, just months before she arrived, he was found dead in one of his residences in Leribe—a death rumored to be connected to the project, as he had refused to accept the full terms demanded by the South African government.

She wondered if it would be a problem for the British Embassy that she was of Anglo-French descent, but it certainly had not been a problem in her application for the position. However, the British could be notoriously territorial, or at least the middle class were, which formed a large percentage of the diplomatic community. Working for the British expatriate community required frequent attendance at receptions and Embassy meetings, always adhering to standard protocol. She was sure a high percentage of them voted for the Conservative Party.

She continued walking through the town, which only consisted of a few main roads. Marie Louise was surprised by how cold it was. She was more than a little nervous to meet her counterparts. She had spent a month in Paris preparing for this assignment. She was to work with the World Bank project team, based in rather expensive offices in Maseru. The hotel's opulence stood in sharp contrast to the surrounding rural villages. The divide between the rich and the poor was highly apparent, which made Marie Louis somewhat uncomfortable, as this was her first long-term overseas assignment, and she wasn't used to such a divide.

Marie Louise walked a few roads to the Ministry of Local Development, where the social aspects of the highlands project were managed. She hadn't thought about security, but when she reached the office, she was alerted by the security guard at the gate that she shouldn't walk anywhere alone, even during daylight, for fear of robbery. That, again, was a new experience for her. At the Ministry, she was greeted by the national head of the project, who was managing the sociological aspects of the Highland Water project. He provided her with a comprehensive briefing on recent developments between the UK and Lesotho governments, as well as the project's status. After the briefing, she walked quickly back to her hotel, cognizant of the warning the guard had given her.

When Marie Louise woke up the following day, she took a hotel car over to the British Embassy. There was a security guard outside the Embassy, and she asked to visit the Second Secretary, her supervisor at the Embassy, for her assignment. The guard checked her bag and ushered her inside the compound, where she walked over to the offices. The Second Secretary was an older gentleman in his sixties, Nigel Barrymore, and was incredibly overweight. He could have been straight out of a Graham Greene novel. On his desk were various photos of himself with prime ministers and members of the British nobility. She was sure she even glimpsed a photograph of Nigel with the Duke of Edinburgh. His Saint Bernard dog was sitting in the corner of the room, nearly the same size as the Second Secretary, drooling at the mouth. The secretary, Bunty, looked over at Marie Louise, quickly at the dog, then back at the Second Secretary. She then stared back at Marie Louise, as if to indicate, 'Yes, this is precisely how you will be working with the British Embassy for the next couple of years.'

After introductions were made, Nigel asked Marie Louise to sit down on the couch at the table where tea was to be served.

Nigel stated, "Of course, you are aware, Marie Louise, the idea behind the Highlands Water Project began with the British High Commissioner to Lesotho, Sir Evelyn Baring, in the 1950s. He realized the potential within Lesotho's abundant water supply for future economic partnership with South Africa." Marie Louise was unaware of this and felt a little embarrassed, but she decided to research it later. Nigel invited her to lunch with him and his wife at a beautiful residence within the Embassy compound, which had a few acres of land. Marie Louise was about to sit on the sofa when the Saint Bernard took her seat. She moved over to one of the armchairs.

"Mr. Barrymore, how long have you lived in Lesotho?" Marie Louise asked him.

"About five years now. This is my last posting since I only have two years before retirement, so it's better to stay here to take lovely holidays in Durban and the Cape!" he replied.

"But with apartheid, isn't it challenging to travel around South Africa and work here in Lesotho with the government?" Marie Louise asked him.

"Not at all. The Afrikaners are incredibly hospitable, and South Africa is a fantastic country," he stated.

"But surely, it's difficult to tolerate how black Africans are treated across the border. They're not allowed into restaurants, public toilets are segregated, and there are many jobs they're not eligible to apply for, even if they're educated. I guess that's why Nelson Mandela was fighting for freedom," she added.

"Nelson Mandela was a terrorist. The African National Congress is a communist organization. They mined roads, bombed public places, and organized car bombings," Nigel responded, his voice becoming louder and sharper.

"He would argue he was fighting a war of repression against his people. We accept it for other wars—why not for apartheid?" Marie Louise responded to him very calmly, although she was also becoming incensed.

"We need to agree to disagree. You have an entirely different perspective, but then, of course, you're French," Nigel laughed. "I mean, you look so French, like Mireille Mathieu!" he laughed. Marie Louise was slim and petite with mid-length brown hair.

Somewhat angry and frustrated by this conversation, Marie Louise went into the kitchen to talk to his wife, who had said hardly a word throughout the meal, and thanked her for preparing a lovely lunch.

The next day, Marie Louise met the project team in Maseru at their World Bank office. Alan, an American, and Samuel, a British expatriate, ran the office. Neither looked too happy to see her.

"Hi, I'm Marie Louise. I presume you were expecting me." They looked at each other, turned away, and continued their business. Samuel gave her a gruff greeting and told her he had to finish a letter and would talk to her later.

"Hi, Marie Louise," Alan said. "We were not expecting you for another week."

"Hi Alan, I'm sure my technical adviser, based in Lilongwe, sent at least three emails to your office over the past two weeks regarding my start date." Marie Louise thought he had to be bluffing. Alan walked over to his desk and checked his computer for emails. After a minute or so, he looked up at her.

"Oh, I missed his message," Alan said quietly.

"Do you want to get coffee?" he asked. Marie Louise had already decided that she didn't like him, but she never refused coffee. They walked out of the building to a café around the corner. Alan was a rather sophisticated American, very tall and thin. The café was small, with a few expatriates and no locals, since the price of the coffee would be beyond their budget. Alan started to outline the project and the gains made over the past few years.

"So, what are your expectations working here?" Alan asked. He proceeded to answer the question himself. "Don't expect too much. The people are laid-back in the rural areas, and you won't get as much feedback as you expect from your surveys. We have collected information for the project for the past three years, and the data quality is questionable," he added.

Marie Louise was rather nonplussed that Alan admitted to the suspect quality of his work so nonchalantly. If the survey was well designed, there was no reason they shouldn't be able to collect good data.

"Alan, I have conducted social impact studies in Kenya and other countries. I am aware of the difficulties in collecting this type of information," she responded. She refused to feed into his belief that Lesotho was more challenging than other countries to collect such data.

"I didn't mean that," he quickly responded. "The Basotho people are laid back. They don't respond as quickly as you may require, and you may need to lower your expectations," he said.

"Alan, I really appreciate your concern," she said somewhat sarcastically. "This is not my first time undertaking this type of work, and I assure you, I know what needs to be done." She did not sugarcoat her response. She was not trying to impress Alan; he was now aware of this.

Marie Louise was already tired of their conversation. To her, Alan seemed somewhat condescending and overly confident. She wanted to return to the hotel and devise her strategy for starting her assignment in the north.

"Perhaps we could meet for dinner later, and I can explain how this country ticks," he quickly responded, seeing her tiredness.

"I think I really need to rest and digest all the reading material your office provided." Samuel had sent her a series of emails before she arrived, and more today.

The idea of an extra two hours of Alan in the evening was something that she knew she would not enjoy. He might have been quite attractive, but he was certainly not her type. She suspected that Alan was the type who blurred the lines between personal and professional relationships, and Marie Louise had strict rules in that regard.

She settled into the hotel and prepared herself for sleep. The next day, she would go to Leribe, the country's largest city in the north, where she was to live for two years.

Chapter 2 · Road to Leribe

The road from Maseru was well-tarred, mostly flat, and in relatively good condition. The Embassy had provided a driver and a Land Rover to take her on this first trip. After that, they would assign her a Land Rover to drive herself. As they traveled down the road, they passed groups of men carrying large bags, waiting for buses to arrive.

"Where are these men going?" Marie Louise asked the driver.

"To the mines in South Africa. They go back and forth all the time," the driver responded.

"Where in South Africa?" she added.

He explained, "the Tsepong gold mine in Orange Free State and Gauteng near Pretoria are the most popular for Basotho."

"How long do they stay before they return here?" she asked him.

"They work in the mines for as long as they can. The Basotho have been going to the South African mines for decades. We need this work, and South Africa needs our labor, so this won't stop anytime soon," the driver replied.

"Have you or any of your relatives worked in the mines?" Marie Louise asked him, hoping he wasn't becoming tired of her questions.

"My father did. Any money he sent home was used for food, health, and my education. That meant I could get a better job than he had had. But he died when he was fifty because of the poor conditions and the impact on his lungs," he told her.

Before she arrived, Marie Louise had read that, during the 1980s, many miners from Lesotho worked in the South African mining industry. The Basotho miners' migration to South Africa dated back to the late nineteenth century, when mining became a significant industry in the country. Economic factors drove labor migration from Lesotho to South Africa. Many Basotho men left their homes in search of employment opportunities in the South African mining industry, particularly in the gold and diamond mines. South Africa needed the workers, and this was the best means to earn a steady income despite the risks.

"Most miners work on contract labor arrangements. The money earned in South Africa is a big source of income for their families back home. But many fall ill since they work long hours without breaks, and they have few rights while living there," the driver explained.

"Before they can return home from the mines, they must be medically examined and obtain a clear X-ray before they can travel back," the driver said.

"How many fail the physical test?" Marie Louise asked him.

"About a third," he answered.

She knew what that meant. They would be forced to return to their villages, and most would not find work. Their health would further deteriorate, they would be unable to apply for expensive drugs, and they would eventually die young.

It took them about two hours to drive north to reach Leribe on a winding road in mountainous terrain. When they reached the town, they went to the house on the outskirts of the town that the British Embassy had allocated to Marie Louise for the next two years. Trees and hedges surrounded the house, making it invisible from the road. It was a single-story residence with a yellow-painted exterior. She checked the front door and found it was open, as she was expected to arrive around this time. She entered the hallway and went into the lounge. It could not have been sparser inside. There was little furniture except a wooden three-piece sofa set with worn cushions, a dining table, two chairs, and a few beds. There was a small garden at the back. The place was not very welcoming. It was a place to rest her head, but it wasn't a home. She was deflated by both her arrival in Leribe and by her prospective residence, as both were rather depressing.

She left the house and returned to her driver to head into town and meet some of the other British expatriates. There was a small club in the middle of Leribe, where she was to be briefed regarding her residence by a British engineer, as she had been informed in Maseru by the Embassy. He lived in the house beside hers within the same compound.

"Hi, Marie Louise. It's lovely to meet you!" John said. He left the table to walk over to her, as he was obviously expecting her arrival around this time. She could see he was in the middle of a working lunch with a few colleagues.

"Hi John, I have been over to the house. It's quite nice. I will need to get a few things. I guess I will need to bring some things up here from Maseru?" she asked him.

"My wife and I are quite comfortable where we live in the house beside yours," John replied, perhaps sensing her level of disappointment with the house. "We can access the Maseru Commissary to collect all our food from there. You will enjoy it here. There are quite a few expatriates, and we meet regularly for drink nights at my house or in town," he added. "I'm responsible for the British road construction project here, and this keeps me exceedingly busy, or so my wife says," he laughed.

He beckoned her to a nearby table and asked a waiter to bring a pot of tea for them.

"So, Marie Louise, what do you need to know to settle quickly?" he asked her.

"Well, I wonder if there are any security issues I need to worry about," Marie Louise asked him.

"My unit here, working on the roads, hires security guards to look after the construction warehouse and the British houses. It means there is always a guard watching your house," he told her. She felt reassured when he told her this.

"How long have you lived here now?" she asked him.

"About four years, but it seems shorter!" he said. "We leave in eighteen months!" he added.

"And do you enjoy it?" Marie Louise asked him.

"I love the work! To be honest, there isn't much else here. Leribe is a small town with no more than about thirty expatriates, and we don't really mingle with the locals," he told her.

Marie Louise wasn't surprised. John seemed like a nice man, but he wasn't here for the immersive experience. He was here to do a job and then leave for his comfortable life back in the UK.

"It would be best if you go over to the house and meet with my wife, who is in the unit beside yours right now, so she can help you settle in. She will be able to tell you where you can purchase most of the things you need," he added.

John got up after their tea was finished. "I am so sorry, but I have a working lunch right now. My wife is looking forward to meeting you," John excused himself and returned to his colleagues.

Marie Louise was beginning to feel even more unsettled, concerned that she might be unable to experience the culture of Lesotho and that her stay would be entirely an expatriate existence. She left the club, and her driver took her to John's house, next to where she lived. Marie Louise introduced herself to John's wife, Sarah, a slim, tall British woman, who chain-smoked throughout the thirty-minute meeting. She was obviously unhappy in Lesotho, which came across quickly in their conversation. However, she appeared very happy about the prospect of having another expatriate woman so close. Throughout her time there, Sarah provided immense support to Marie Louise.

After consulting with Sarah, Marie Louise went into her own house and sat at the dining table. She quickly made a list of things she would need to buy when she returned to Maseru. Marie Louise asked the driver to take her around the area so she could get some perspective of what the town was like. But after a few minutes of driving, the town abruptly ended. It was quite small. She drove over to inspect her office at the government agency responsible for the Highlands Water project. She was directed to a rondavel, a round building made of mud and brick with a straw roof, outside the main building where her office had just been established. At least it was ethnic, she thought rather sarcastically. There were a few cupboards and a desk already set up inside.

After a few days of furniture buying in town and settling into the house, Marie Louise went over to John and Sarah's house for dinner. She knocked on the door, and Sarah answered.

"Come in and sit down. Please make yourself comfortable. The French are always so stylish compared to us plain Brits," Sarah told her.

Sarah was dressed in jeans and a plain yellow T-shirt, along with sports shoes. She wore no makeup, and her hair was cut short, falling just above her shoulders. This was in contrast to Marie Louise, who wore a blue skirt suit with a white tie blouse and a light blue scarf around her neck. Sarah looked down at her shoes, and Marie Louise was a little embarrassed as she wore expensive French flat shoes that were not suited to the terrain of Leribe, where few roads were paved and the path to their houses was a mud track. Marie Louise had brought only a few pairs of shoes with her, including trekking boots, as well as some of her more expensive French shoes. She would have to buy some sports shoes like Sarah's.

"Thank you, Sarah, for being so welcoming."

"Yes, since John is always working! You're welcome to come here any time and join me for tea. I have two daughters your age, so you will help me miss them less. As you know, phone calls are costly, so we only talk once a week. I hope you're settling in well and enjoying this town. But it would be best if you were careful in Leribe. A Peace Corps volunteer was killed last year, stabbed multiple times in her bathroom. There was no apparent reason for the murder, and it was a suspected robbery," Sarah said.

Marie Louise was taken aback, as she had not been informed of this by either Alan or the British Embassy.

"As a result, the Peace Corps will not assign any more volunteers to Leribe. There are only two Canadian volunteers here," Sarah added.

"That's terrible! Did they catch the killer?" Marie Louise asked.

"Yes. They said it was a failed robbery. It's possible she was involved with a local who informed friends of her house and where valuables were stored. It was during the day, so perhaps they didn't suspect she would be home," Sarah said.

"Her family must have been devastated," Marie Louise commented.

"You should get a dog for protection. An Irish couple across the road is trying to find a home for their Rottweiler. The wife doesn't like him. He's a wonderful dog. A bit wild but very bright and quite a character," Sarah said.

That would be a first for her. She feared dogs. Fostering a cat was as far as her animal skills stretched to date.

"Well, no time like the present! Why don't we walk over there now and see if the dog is still available?" Sarah suggested.

"Well, I'm a bit scared now at the prospect of living alone, so let me see if the dog and I will get on," Marie Louise commented.

Sarah and Marie Louise walked over the road, about five minutes from her own house, to meet the Irish family who were seeking a new home for the dog. The dog was outside the house, sitting in the mud and looking thin and sad. Sarah went up and petted him, and Marie Louise went and knocked on the door. A man looked out and then quickly opened the door, greeting her.

"Grand to meet you, Marie Louise. Welcome to Leribe! You'll like it here," the man warmly said. She nodded politely.

"The dog has some history, I'm afraid. He's from a litter of Rhodesian ridgeback, mixed with Rottweiler. He may even have some German shepherd in him," he added.

"Is he safe? Does he bite? What's his name?" she asked with some hesitation.

"He only bites other animals, ha-ha!" Marie Louise didn't think that was very funny.

"He's called Matla. It's a Sesotho name given by the family that bred him. You will see that the doctor in Buthe Buthe has a similar dog from the same litter. Before my wife joined me, there was only Matla and me for two years, but then my wife brought over her German shepherd, and they didn't get along very well," the man said.

"How old is he?" Marie Louise asked.

"We think he's about three," he responded.

Marie Louise mentally added two years to that since she knew they wanted to get rid of the dog, and he certainly appeared older than three years.

"I warn you that he visits the house down the road frequently since another Irish colleague feeds him, but our friend there doesn't wish to adopt him," he said.

Marie Louise could not understand why you would feed a dog and not give it a home if you could. She walked up to the dog and crouched down beside Sarah to pet him. He looked at Marie Louise with his pitiful eyes, and she decided then and there that she would take him despite her fear. She didn't want him at this house for a minute longer. Besides, Sarah would surely help her if she had a problem.

"Shall I take him now? Do you have a leash I can borrow?" she asked.

She decided that even if she was afraid of this animal, it was best that he leave here, where he was not even allowed into the house and was not being fed sufficiently.

"Here, take this leash. It's old anyway." The man passed her a worn brown leather leash that had seen better days. She thanked him, inviting him to come over any time to visit the dog. However, he didn't appear very interested in doing so, so she put the leash on the dog, which he didn't seem to mind at all, and Matla gladly walked out the gate with her. They walked the animal the five minutes home, and he behaved well. They first went to Sarah's, who gave her a dish to use for the dog and some cooked meat from her fridge. She obviously loved the dog, and that made Marie Louise more secure about her choice. She wasn't going to second-guess herself after hearing about the Peace Corps volunteer's terrible demise. She would make it work with this dog.

After Matla was fed and given water, she let him into the house, and he followed her into the bedroom. For the only time during the many years that she had him, he climbed onto the bed and fell asleep immediately, not to wake up for about twelve hours.

Chapter 3 · Working in the North

Marie Louise sat in her makeshift office in Leribe, wondering why she had been placed in a rather large broom cupboard. They had told her no other room was available, and she did not argue. The positive aspect was that she had privacy. The downside was that there were no windows, and it was a muddy mess to walk over to the rondavel building when it rained. Since she had finished her work for the day and was waiting for one of the drivers to take her home, she was reading a book by Joseph Lelyveld, *Move Your Shadow*. Lelyveld, an American journalist, spent several years in South Africa as a correspondent for the *New York Times*. He covered major events in South Africa, including the apartheid era and the transition to democracy. He later served as the Editor of The *New York Times* from 1994 to 2001.

Move Your Shadow delved into the complexities of race, identity, and resistance while highlighting people's resilience in the face of their oppression. Lelyveld explored how apartheid affected every aspect of life in the country, from education and healthcare to employment and social interactions. Marie Louise found Lelyveld's detailed account of the plight of the average worker in both rural and urban settings intensely sad. She had a great sense of justice and found it difficult not to interfere when she observed someone mistreating others. In South Africa, this was happening every day through discrimination on a level that was beyond comprehension.

Marie Louise's dog followed her to the office every day. Sometimes, he had quite the dog pack following him to the building and beyond. He would leave her at the office and then come back around five o'clock when he knew she was leaving for home, or he would be waiting at home for her. She had no idea where he went during the day, but at least she had company in the evenings. Marie Louise planned her work for the next three months, focusing on the surveys she was there to conduct. The British embassy had provided her with a computer, which she set up at her house, fearing it might be stolen from her office. At least at home, there was security provided by John's project, and she had the dog whenever he listened to her. Marie Louise had been raised in cities. She was not scared as she considered herself quite careful regarding security. However, she knew she would have to be more cautious after the recent death of the Peace Corps volunteer and racial tensions within the town.

Marie Louise planned to survey the needs and aspirations of people living in project-affected areas, as a large infrastructure project could have a negative impact if their concerns were not addressed. This consultation process was critical for addressing potential social conflicts and ensuring the project benefited local communities. However, Marie Louise knew South Africa considered those aspects secondary to their water needs. They had little concern for how the project would affect local communities on this side of the border. Given that the project involved the construction of dams and infrastructure that could displace communities, sociological studies were needed to examine the impact of resettlement on affected populations. This would include assessing the adequacy of compensation, housing, and livelihood measures. The project posed threats to cultural heritage sites, for example, some of the ancient Bushmen rock paintings, many of which could be submerged or threatened by the construction of the dams. Marie Louise had to ensure that her work examined these impacts and explored ways to mitigate them. Her work also included studying the project's environmental impact on the highland's ecosystems.

After the questionnaires were designed and pretested, and enumerators were trained, Marie Louise commenced the surveys. She drove to the selected villagers in her Land Rover, accompanied by cars from the local development department. She had a team of four assistants from the Department of Local Development, which she had recruited after careful review. They set off for the first village along a winding track that was waterlogged in places, but the Land Rover was more than up to the task along the very rough, bumpy, wet road. When they arrived, they set up a meeting place with the villagers to conduct their questionnaire. The villagers, especially the Basotho women, always welcomed village meetings and the opportunity to share their views with the government and donor agencies, as they were pretty strong and vocal in their opinions. Few men were present, except the elderly and the young, since most men worked in the mines. This meant, however, that a steady source of income was being sent back to these villages through remittances.

Marie Louise walked up to the first randomly selected house where they would be conducting the surveys. It was a small rondavel, and the woman inside came out of the door to greet her. She glanced into the house, and she could see some furniture, a wooden cabinet, and a radio in the corner. It surprised Marie Louise that inside the houses would be all manner of furniture. Her staff told her that all the furniture was on hire purchase, usually from Ficksburg or Bloemfontein across the border. If people fell behind on the payments, the trucks would arrive promptly to haul away the goods. Marie Louise was surprised that no one offered tea or refreshments, which she had become used to in other countries she had visited. Even the poorest families would provide tea and something to eat, but not here. She asked one of her assistants why this was the case.

"Well, there is a level of indifference to foreigners who work in Lesotho, as the villagers are unsure if they will benefit. Most families either have someone working in the mines or know someone who does, and the treatment they receive is not good. They assume you're also racist," her assistant told her rather bluntly. Marie Louise wasn't sure how she could answer this, but she told her assistant that she wasn't racist at all. However, why should her assistant believe her when she hardly knew her?

Marie Louise and her assistants stayed an hour north of Leribe in Buthe Buthe, where they had lunch. She made good friends with the female assistants. It was more difficult with the men. They treated her respectfully but were distant. Buthe Buthe was smaller than Leribe, but was a district headquarters, and one of the power stations was to be located near the town. They walked over to the hospital and met the Mosotho doctor in charge.

"Greetings, we don't see too many expatriates at the hospital," he told her. The doctor must have been about thirty-five or so years old. He was tall and thin and looked quite exhausted. Later, she was told by her staff that he was one of the few native doctors in the country, and most were expatriates assigned to the hospitals.

"Hi, I was curious to visit your hospital to get some idea of the types of illnesses you see aside from the miners."

"Well, there are a lot of tuberculosis cases, even in addition to the miners. Malaria comes over from South Africa and other countries, and among children, diarrhea and acute respiratory diseases, including pneumonia, are prevalent," he answered her. "There is also a lot of malnutrition in under-five-year-olds. Most of the patients I have here right now are kids."

Marie Louise looked in the window at one of the wards and saw a group of mothers with children, cramped together, sitting on beds, feeding their children with spoons or bottles.

"I guess you give milk formula to the children?"

"Yes, formula if the mother can't breastfeed, but if they're over six months, then we give them porridge from maize meal and make sure the mothers continue to feed them, as they have too much to do and get distracted from the constant feeding a malnourished child needs.

Marie Louise was in awe of this doctor. He really cared. She walked out of the hospital, thanking him, and made a mental note to check in with him whenever she traveled north to verify any health data. As she walked out, she did a quick turnaround to see a clone of Matla walking out of the doctor's office, and she hesitated for a second, thinking he could not have come up this far. And then she remembered that the Irishman had told her the littermate of Matla lived in Buthe Buthe. They were eerily similar.

On one trip to the field, Marie Louise brought Matla with her to survey a village. That was a mistake. The pesky dog decided to go on a walkabout. He disappeared into the nearby hills, and the whole team spent the next hour calling for him. Matla's name meant 'virile strength' in Sesotho. Marie Louise wondered how his former owner had not checked that before naming him. This wasn't very comfortable for the staff as they shouted his name across the valley. She had thought about changing it, but she considered that he might be too old now for that. Eventually, he came out of the hills, strolled over, and hopped into the Land Rover as if nothing had happened.

One time, though, it was more serious. The team was driving up to Mokhotlong in the mountains, about a four- to five-hour drive from Leribe, and Marie Louise had taken Matla for the trip. When they reached a village to survey, Matla shot out of the Land Rover to wander around. When it was time to leave, the dog was nowhere to be found. Chris, a volunteer temporarily working with Marie Louise, insisted they depart for Mokhotlong as the sun was setting and it would be challenging to navigate the road, which included a river crossing. Marie Louise was heartbroken, and that evening she refused to eat with Chris, retreating to her room, where she forlornly stared at Matla's dog bowl. She could not return to town and tell everyone she had lost the dog, and by now, she was becoming very attached to him.

She told Chris they were going back to the village very early to search for Matla, and they would not be leaving for Leribe until he was found. So, Marie Louise got the car ready before breakfast to pick up Chris at the hotel's front entrance. Chris was frustrated and failed to understand the importance of the dog.

"I mean, it's just another dog, right?"

They set off for the two-hour journey back down the trail. However, when they got to the river crossing, due to the rains the night before, the water level had risen and was now at the same level as the base of the Land Rover. This was not going to stop Marie Louise. "Chris, you can wait on this side of the river while I cross over and look for Matla," she said. "Or I can collect you on my way back."

"No way, you won't come back for me, or you'll get lost. I'm coming!" he said.

"Well then, stop complaining. We're going to get that dog!" she told him.

Marie Louise was a skilled driver and navigated the water level safely to reach the other side; they then continued to the village. It was still early when they arrived, and they saw a few men in the distance walking out, most likely, to the fields to work. They stopped the car just outside of the village, and she opened the back of the Land Rover, poured a can of dog food into Matla's plate, and, without raising her voice, in case villagers became aware they had returned, she quietly called him. She didn't want to cause any issues by coming back to the village with no explanation, but she was pretty sure Matla had been locked away when they were leaving the day before. Otherwise, he would have come when she called him, as he always did. She wanted to retrieve him quickly before anyone was alerted to their presence. Matla was a large dog, and someone might have wanted him as a guard dog, as the average dog in Lesotho was a lot smaller.

After about ten minutes, she could see a movement in the hills above. Matla started crawling down from the hills where he had been hiding, and he came over to her and licked her hand. After a few attempts to jump up into the back of the Land Rover, she pulled him up, and he voraciously ate his breakfast in the back of the car. Marie Louise examined the dog and saw that its paw pads were cut up, where it might have been locked up and had scratched consistently to get out. Marie Louise quickly closed the back door of the Land Rover, ordered Chris to hop in, and they drove off before anyone had noticed. When they reached the river again, the water level was still high. Still, Marie Louise now considered herself an expert on river navigation, and she was running on the adrenaline of having found her dog against the odds, so she drove across quickly with no fear.

Chris was quiet by now. He would never understand Marie Louise since their perspectives were very different. For Marie Louise, Chris was a classic example of a somewhat idealistic young man who wished to work in Lesotho for a few years to help the local population. He was on a mission before he returned to the UK. Indeed, after his two years were over, Chris studied in Canada as a nuclear scientist, a far cry from the hills of Lesotho.

Once they were back on the main route from Mokhotlong, they drove straight through to Leribe, and she dropped Chris at his hotel. She rarely invited any staff to stay at her house, even though it was large enough to accommodate them. She needed the distance between work and her private life. She took Matla immediately to the vet to examine him, and he was given an ointment for his paws. She gave him an enormous meal and then gently tended to his paws. She was sure the dog was smiling…

A few months later, a local farmer knocked on Marie Louise's door with a shotgun.

"Have you seen a brownish-red dog with a bushy tail running in this direction?" the farmer asked her.

"No, I don't think so," Marie Louise lied rather nervously. "What did he do?"

"The dog killed a sheep on my farm. I want to kill that dog so there are no further episodes," he elaborated.

The farmer appeared to be hell-bent on finding him. He didn't scare Marie Louise for her own safety, but she was terrified for Matla.

"I think a friend owns that dog, and I'd be more than willing to help my friend by paying for your sheep," Marie Louise rather timidly suggested.

The farmer viewed her suspiciously, but he took the money anyway. Matla was hiding behind the house under the bushes, looking at her 'sheepishly' when she found him a few hours later.

After having him for more than six months, she had become very attached to the animal and would walk him when she came home after work or teach him tricks. The famous one Sarah had taught him was to identify the matchbox that contained the meat, so that he would get the treat. He loved that one, and Marie Louise didn't have the heart to tell Sarah that the dog could smell the meat a mile away. She would rarely leash him, as he hated it, and he walked by her side most of the time with no distractions. One evening, they went to dinner at the Irishman's house, the former owner of Matla. Matla was allowed to sit on the porch outside the front door but was not allowed inside. Marie Louise thought she would not remain long, as she wasn't comfortable leaving him outside at night. After the meal was over, she said her goodbyes, and Matla ran ahead of her to the car. Suddenly, she heard a scream. She ran out to see that her car door was slightly ajar, and Matla was up on his hind legs and had a man pinned to the side of the car.

"Matla, off! Now," she screamed as she didn't want him to hurt the man.

The man ran off down the alley as she ordered the dog to stay and not follow him. She wasn't going to report the attempted theft as she was aware how the police would approach it and most likely arrest someone who worked at one of the houses on the street just to solve the crime. Besides, she and the car were fine. But she knew now that Matla was truly a guard dog.

Chapter 4 · Crossing the Border into South Africa

Marie Louise had been living in Leribe for eight months and was far more settled, but she still didn't feel comfortable. She'd made a few friends in the town, but they were not really her type. Her friends in France and London were more avant-garde and politically and socially more aware. Most of the development workers in Leribe were there for the money. Their salaries were far higher than they would receive in their own country, so she restricted herself to short, polite conversations with them. Two of the easiest people to converse with were the Canadian volunteers, until the male volunteer suggested to her that, since there were few expatriates in the town, they should date each other. She just wasn't interested, so she avoided him after that. He was quite a nice-looking guy, but Marie Louise was not interested in having a steady relationship in Lesotho. At this stage, she was too eager to develop her career further, and she saw that as a distraction.

She had settled into her job and worked well with her team. However, she was somewhat uncomfortable with the amount of driving that the British Embassy expected of her. Road accidents were a way of life in Lesotho. One day, Marie Louise was distracted at an intersection and drove her Land Rover into the back of a Land Cruiser. Luckily, there was minor damage to the Land Cruiser as she had just hit the bumper, but the front of the Land Rover was severely dented. The accident was her fault, as she had not stopped in time; however, driving anywhere in the country was precarious. She decided to have the Land Rover repaired herself, as she was too embarrassed to report the issue to the British Embassy. She was the only female Technical Cooperation officer, so she could imagine what the comments would be at the Embassy.

She drove it over the border to have it repaired at a place recommended to her by her office. Marie Louise arrived at Barney's on the outskirts of Ficksburg, an Afrikaans town, a one-hour trip from Leribe, directly across the border from Maputsoe. Barney's garage was large, and there was only one white man on the premises.

"Hi, are you Barney?" Marie Louise asked him.

"That I am. Since you are British, looking at your license plate and the fact that this is a new Land Rover, you're from the Embassy assigned to Leribe?" Barney asked her.

"Yes, I arrived a few months ago. This morning, I crashed into the back of a Toyota Land Cruiser. It's all my fault since I'm still unfamiliar with the roads," she replied.

"At a quick look, I would estimate that's about 1500 Rand in damage. I'm pleased to repair it for you, and it shouldn't take more than twenty-four hours. Shall I send the bill to the British Embassy in Maseru?" he asked her.

"No, Barney. I'm responsible, so I should pay," Marie Louise told him.

"Well, that's good of you, but I doubt it would cause much of a dent in the British budget. You are welcome to bring your vehicles here for servicing and any repairs. I promise we will provide top service for your project. Please stop by sometime and meet my family. We often have a braai on the weekend, and you can meet other white folks nearby. I know there are a few expatriates in Leribe, and you may be very lonely there," Barney said to Marie Louise.

She was not surprised by his assumption that she would not make friends with the Basotho. Barney was a classic Afrikaner who believed that one socially associates only with one's own race. However, Marie Louise tried not to judge Barney. This was all he had ever known. As Joseph Lelyveld highlighted in his book, it would take a further twenty-five years to educate the white population about the importance of equality.

Marie Louise said goodbye to Barney and drove back, where she saw several South Africans trying to hitch a lift. She picked up a girl waiting by the side of the road who was returning to Maputsoe. It was about 5:30 PM, and the girl could not be more than sixteen years old.

"Hi. Were you waiting a long time for a ride?" Marie Louise asked the girl.

"About an hour," she replied.

"That's a long time. Are you here for shopping?" Marie Louise asked her.

"No, I work as a house cleaner on the outskirts of Ficksburg," the girl stated.

"So, how do you get there every day?"

"I wait in Maputsoe for anyone who's crossing the border. Most cars go through Ficksburg. It's easy to catch a ride at 7:00 AM or so," the girl responded.

"How long do you wait in the afternoon to return if you hitch a lift?" Marie Louise asked her.

"It varies, but it's usually about an hour. I was let go early today as my Madam is traveling to Bloemfontein. Usually, I leave at around eight o'clock in the evening," she replied.

"Isn't that dangerous to travel so late?" Marie Louise asked her.

"What choice do I have? My family needs the money," the girl replied.

Marie Louise was silent. She took the girl to her house on the outskirts of Maputsoe. It was a run-down shack, and an older woman came out of the house to greet her.

"That's my grandmother," the girl said.

"Where is your mother?" Marie Louise asked.

"She works in Johannesburg and rarely comes home. She works in a shop there," the girl responded.

"Well, if it's possible, please do stop by my office sometime for a chat," and she wrote her address down on a card for the girl.

She considered her own life of privilege as a teenager and the life of this girl. Life was a lottery ticket.

Chapter 5 · Tragedy

Marie Louise frequently visited Maseru to meet with government and World Bank staff at their offices. It was a small town for a capital city and was known for its raucous nightlife, but its day charm was sorely lacking. She had developed a somewhat problematic relationship with the office's head, Alan. Alan had worked for the World Bank for a decade, and although he was knowledgeable on development issues and the Highlands water scheme, Marie Louise and he clashed due to their different perspectives. Alan was far more concerned about getting the surveys conducted as quickly as possible. Marie Louise wanted to collect the data more slowly and ensure that sufficient qualitative data was also collected, as this would verify the quantitative analysis. Alan considered Marie Louise a nuisance, as he thought she acted too independently and rarely sought his opinion on any work matters. Marie Louise thought Alan was a typical expatriate, charming and diplomatic, but here for the money, not the cultural experience. He took advantage of being close to South Africa and often traveled across the border to shop or go out for an evening.

Very early one morning, Marie Louise reached the Leribe office to greet the staff before they were to drive to Buthe Buthe. They were to be joined by the United Nations volunteer engineer, Nestor, who was Filipino. Nestor had been in the country for about a year, working under Alan in Maseru. He had been due to arrive the previous night and stay in a hotel. When Nestor did not come after thirty minutes, Marie Louise set off for the village with her staff. When they arrived at Buthe Buthe, she stopped at the hospital to check in before heading to the town. The doctor called over to her.

"Hi, Marie Louise. I hope all is well. A message here says you need to call Leribe urgently."

Marie Louise called the office and reached the receptionist, who informed her that there had been an accident on the road from Leribe to Buthe Buthe involving Nestor's vehicle. It had overturned, injuring himself and two technicians whom he had picked up in Leribe, as they had also been late for Marie Louise's pick-up.

Marie Louise drove back as fast as she could, and she saw the Toyota truck overturned by the side of the road with blood marks around it. There were no signs of any staff, so she drove directly back to the hospital in Leribe. The hospital staff told her that their ambulance had driven Nestor directly across the border to Bloemfontein since he was seriously injured, and his UN Volunteer's office had recommended that he be moved there. The two technicians were waiting at the Leribe hospital. The first, Laurence, had a suspected head fracture and was bleeding from the ear, and the other, Sepipi, had only cuts and bruises. Marie Louise talked to both technicians to determine what had happened while walking Laurence over for an X-ray. She knew that Alan would need to know immediately, and she also knew he would unfairly blame her for the accident.

"He fell asleep at the wheel," Sepipi cried rather loudly. "I prodded him to wake up, and he lost control of the wheel, skidded, and the truck overturned."

"Where were you sitting?" Marie Louise asked. Wherever Sepipi went, there was always some problem.

"I was sitting beside him. I pushed him to wake up. I grabbed the wheel to make sure the vehicle stayed straight." This convinced Marie Louise that this was why the vehicle had overturned.

She discovered Nestor had driven from Maseru that morning instead of coming up the night before and staying in Leribe. When the accident happened, he had already been driving on a challenging and winding road for nearly three hours.

The next step was to call Maseru and inform the office. Alan's response was instantly accusatory. "Did you maintain the vehicle? When was it serviced?" Marie Louise put the phone down. She wasn't prepared to talk to him until he calmed down. Marie Louise always ensured that the northern project vehicles were regularly maintained, and the one Nestor drove had been serviced only a month ago.

She had to drive to Bloemfontein as soon as possible to check on Nestor. When Marie Louise reached the border, she showed her British passport and continued. It took two hours to get to the hospital from the border. She traveled with Arthur, the engineer from the Department of Local

Development. The problems began immediately upon their arrival at the reception. Arthur was a Mosotho and was not allowed to accompany her inside the hospital into the ward where Nestor was being treated, as this was prohibited. Marie Louise had no choice but to voice her displeasure to the hospital staff and leave Arthur outside while she visited Nestor. She reached his ward, where he was fully conscious and undergoing various medical tests.

"What do the doctors say, Nestor?" Mare Louise asked.

"I can't feel anything in my legs or arms. They first took me to the hospital for colored people only and would not take me to the whites' hospital until my UNV officer called them from Maseru and insisted they take me here," he said.

"They need to do X-rays as soon as possible. Let me find a doctor," she said as she walked to the reception desk.

The staff told her the doctor would not return for a few hours, but Nestor was due for X-rays and tests in the next thirty minutes. She thought to herself, at least he has a room to himself and is comfortable on pain medication.

"I can't get any information right now, but they are taking you for tests shortly. How is the pain?" Marie Louise asked him as she re-entered his room.

"Not as bad as it was. But I want to know why I can't move my arms and legs. It's stressing me out," Nestor cried.

Marie Louise stayed a few hours longer with Nestor until his tests were complete, and then met with his doctor, who told her his spinal cord was cut.

" His condition means he'll be living with quadriplegia long-term, and there is little more that can be done medically. You will need to prepare him for this," the doctor told her rather bluntly. They talked for a while longer before Marie Louise returned to Nestor.

She sat with him, but she couldn't bring herself to tell him the prognosis. She left Nestor sleeping at the hospital while she went back to Arthur, waiting outside.

"So, how is he?" Arthur asked.

"It's terrible. His spinal cord is completely severed, and he will be quadriplegic with no hope of recovery."

"Oh my god. The vehicle didn't even look that badly damaged!" Arthur said.

"The doctor said he was thrown out the window on impact, and that is where the ambulance found him, on the side of the road. He wasn't wearing his seat belt."

"And what about the others? Why weren't they seriously injured?" Arthur asked.

"Apparently, Sepipi was still in the vehicle and Laurence was thrown out, but not so far and hit his head on the side of the car."

"They should have all been inside the car and wearing seatbelts," Arthur complained.

"Agreed! And that's in the rules from the Maseru and Leribe offices. I don't know why they weren't."

Marie Louise and Arthur drove back to Leribe in silence, both depressed by what had happened. When Marie Louise got home, she rang Alan again to update him. He was now much calmer.

"Did you tell him?"

"No, not yet, I will tell him tomorrow," she replied.

"Wait, and I will go over tomorrow and tell him. He's my staff, so it's my responsibility."

"He fell asleep at the wheel, but if he had had his seat belt on, he would have been OK," she told him.

"Agreed. I'm sorry I accused you of not maintaining the car. Arthur told me all the cars had been serviced last week." Marie Louise thought he was polite now since he was at fault in his accusation.

"He will have to go back to Manila. His parents are arriving in a few days," Alan told her. Marie Louise thought that life can change in a second, and that's why it was so important to make the most of one's life, but to take care.

Chapter 6 · Friends and Company

After the accident, Marie Louise was somewhat shaken. Her staff were also affected, and everyone was more careful in driving safely. Nestor had been flown back to the Philippines and would never travel overseas again. Laurence had recovered from his skull fracture, and Sepipi still wasn't telling anyone what exactly had happened in the vehicle when Nestor had fallen asleep.

Marie Louise's life in Leribe consisted of working long hours at the office and visiting villages. She occasionally went out to dinner with a few expatriates. She made a close friend in the city, a stay-at-home wife, whom she would meet for long walks with their dogs. She was not entirely sure she was married. Her name was Carrie, and she lived with a rather grumpy Scottish vet, Donald, whom the British government had assigned to examine livestock in Leribe, but he also acted as the local vet. Carrie was the only person in town with whom Marie Louise had anything in common. She was intelligent, well-read, and attractive. Carrie was from the West Coast and had quite a colorful past. She had married young, giving birth to her son at the age of twenty. He lived with his father on the West Coast and visited her during his holidays. Marie Louise and Carrie often walked together in the forests on the outskirts of town, discussing their lives and experiences. In fact, they rarely talked about Lesotho. Carrie complained that she was unhappy and nearing the end of her relationship with Donald. Marie Louise had no idea why she was with him in the first place, as he was rather traditional. Carrie had a lover in the States, Paul, whom she met once a year in different locations, and who worked with the American primatologist Diane Fossey.

Carrie exclaimed, "I leave for Kenya in two weeks to meet Paul, who is flying from Kigali. I can't wait!"

"Would Paul consider a future with you?" Marie Louise asked Carrie.

"Hell, no. He has a steady girlfriend in California. We agreed that we would see each other once a year, which is enough," Carrie responded.

"But you want to leave Donald. What will you do?" Marie Louise asked her.

Carrie had no job to return to in the States. She had only ever had part-time jobs as a receptionist or veterinary assistant. She left school at sixteen with no qualifications.

"I will stay until the end of Donald's assignment, six months from now. He wants to return to the UK after this, as his children live there. I can't see myself living there, and he hasn't asked me," Carrie said.

"Where did you meet Donald?" Marie Louise asked her.

"In Kenya, he was working for the British, and I was visiting. We kept in touch, and he asked me to visit him here when he took the assignment. I guess I liked it at the time, so I stayed," she said.

Marie Louise thought Carrie was like the branches of the trees above them. She was swaying in the wind, moving in whatever direction the wind would take her. It was a life that she couldn't comprehend.

Another close friend of Marie Louise was one of the social assistants who supported the project. Mosela was married to a miner who worked most of the year near Johannesburg. However, she was in love with another man who worked for the Department of Community Development, and they had been having an affair while her husband was away. This was quite common in Lesotho.

"So why aren't you married, Marie Louise?" Mosela asked her.

"I don't think I have really loved anyone enough to relinquish my freedom," she answered. She thought to herself that when she considered the lives of Carrie and Mosela, she was rather pleased that her life was far less complicated. She wasn't relying on any man to satisfy her emotional or material needs.

"That's a strange reason not to marry. Surely, you wanted security and company," she asked.

"I can ensure my own security, and I have my friends for company," Marie Louise responded. She had had a serious boyfriend at university but had mainly been in short-term relationships since then. She didn't think she would settle down until her mid-thirties or so, and when she considered the lives of her friends in Lesotho, such as Carrie and Mosela, she thought this was rather wise. Both were living complex lives with partners they didn't care for, and unable to live with the people they truly loved. She had plenty of time to get it right and have a family.

"I married my husband when I was nineteen. I met him when I was a child, and we just really grew up together. It was accepted that we would marry," Mosela said.

"Well, that did not turn out too well..." Marie Louise said, and Mosela laughed. By now, they knew each other quite well and trusted that their conversations were confidential.

Mosela said, "the problem is that we only had a little time together before he had to leave for the mines where he has been working for the past ten years. I should have had a child, but I hardly see him. When he does come home, he's exhausted. After ten years working in the mines, he continually coughs, and I don't know how he even passes his chest X-rays."

"But you're in love with someone else," Marie Louise said rather judgmentally. It was difficult for her to understand why a person remained with someone they didn't love, but then she had sufficient income to ensure her independence.

"That doesn't mean I don't care for my husband. I just don't see a future with him any longer. I feel bad that the affair happened, but I can't stop it now," she said.

"Life is unfair, really. Working in the mines is not a life worth living. Yet the Basotho have no other viable options to earn a living," Marie Louise commented.

Since most men worked in either the mines or some menial job across the border, there was a high level of alcoholism in the country, and as a result, violence was a severe problem. Beer was sold at every garage. 'Don't drink and drive' meant that you didn't hold the can while driving, but it was perfectly fine to drink alcohol at the garage while you filled up with petrol. One night, when Marie Louise was driving back from Maseru alone, she was about to overtake a truck as she neared the town when the driver pulled out from his lane, nearly pushing her Land Rover off the road. She immediately pulled back and tried to regain control of her vehicle, under great effort to prevent it from veering off the road. Marie Louise stopped the car to collect herself before continuing her journey. She was severely shaken and sat in the dark for at least fifteen minutes to calm her nerves before she could even consider continuing her journey home. She could so easily have been killed or permanently injured like Nestor.

A few weeks later, one of the project's staff members, Sepipi, who had been involved in the accident with Nestor and had been fired mainly due to his laziness, came to her office. Marie Louise was working at her desk, and her dog was off wandering. Sepipi took a knife out of his pocket and threatened to kill her if she did not give him money. He was emotional and unsteady on his feet since he had been drinking. No one else was in her office at the time, and Marie Louise had only seconds to decide how to react. She stood up from her desk, and in her most authoritative voice, she said, "Sepipi, get out of my office. Now!"

"You are the reason why my contract was cut. Everyone blamed me for Nestor's accident. It wasn't my fault he fell asleep!" he screamed at her.

She stared straight at him and walked out from behind her desk and towards him. She had no fear.

"Sepipi, get out now!" she shouted.

Sepipi faltered, stepped back, and quickly ran out of the office. Marie Louise ran to her main office and reported his actions in case he returned, but he didn't. She never saw him again, and she was somewhat glad, as she did not want to see him taken by the police. She had always disliked Sepipi, but he was right; he wasn't responsible for Nestor's accident. However, he had lost his job due to incompetence and not because of the accident.

After these incidents, Marie Louise decided not to extend her contract past her two-year assignment as she couldn't predict what else might happen. She almost felt she was pushing her luck too hard if she stayed longer.

Chapter 6 · Jerome, the Architect

After fifteen months in the country, Marie Louise was getting on much better with Alan in Maseru. Whenever she came into town, they would have lunch and even laugh together during their meetings. She sensed that Alan was attracted to her, but luckily, he had a girlfriend in Lesotho, so she didn't need to worry. She wasn't really attracted to Alan, but she welcomed a better working relationship with him as it made her life far easier.

On one of her visits to Maseru, Alan introduced her to Jerome, a South African architect. Jerome was building schools in a few districts to serve as models for a more integrated and sustainable building approach. This was the first expatriate, Marie Louise thought, that she had met through her work who she considered interesting. When Alan introduced him, he shook her hand and stared straight into her eyes.

"Hi, Marie Louise. I would be pleased to show you some of the houses I have designed for the resettlement areas. Just say when is a good time."

Jerome had a strong South African accent and spoke confidently and assertively. He was about 6 feet tall and not particularly attractive, but he had striking features. Jerome was working with Alan on development projects near the Highlands Water Project, which would provide some benefits for the new resettlement areas supported by the South African government. He had studied in Cape Town, where he kept a house. Indeed, he was far more entertaining than Alan. They agreed to meet in Leribe, and Jerome would take her to the housing areas in villages where he was already making improvements.

On the walk through one of the villages, Jerome opened up to Marie Louise.

"I was assigned to Namibia for my military duty, which all South Africans at that time had to undertake," he told her.

"Was it hard? How old were you?"

"Yes, I only lasted nine months... I was twenty-one," he replied.

Marie Louise wondered to herself why he might have been discharged so early, but she thought it better not to ask. She thought he must be in his mid-thirties now, and she could see it still affected him.

After Marie Louise and Jerome visited the houses, they had lunch in a small restaurant in Leribe.

"What was it like growing up in Johannesburg and Pretoria?" she asked him.

Jerome paused before he responded. "It's difficult as a white. Even living in South Africa, things are changing so rapidly. I found it difficult growing up there during my teens. Even if you try not to discriminate, it's impossible as a white South African not to, especially with my affluent parents," he replied. "I had a girlfriend who lived with me in Maseru for several years. One day, she was cooking something on the stove. She left the kitchen for a few minutes, and there was an explosion in the oven. A bomb had been placed inside it. If she had remained in the kitchen, she would have been killed. We drifted apart after that, and she left to return to South Africa," he recounted somewhat quietly. As he described it, he still seemed devastated.

"How awful. Why would anyone stay under those circumstances?" Marie Louise exclaimed.

"I avoided close relationships after that event. I don't tell many people about it either," he added.

"Understandable. I guess it would also make it difficult to trust people. Why do you think there was a bomb placed in your kitchen?" she asked.

"They thought I was a spy," he quietly said. Marie Louise fell silent. "The African National Congress (ANC) was active within Maseru since many sheltered there to avoid the South African police. The ANC might have targeted me under the presumption I was an agent," he said.

She never again questioned him on this topic. She knew it might lead to a level of intimacy with Jerome that she was not ready to investigate.

Jerome was very devoted to his work and had conducted numerous social surveys while designing and building his schools. He had an inherent respect for the Basotho and the government. His father had inherited his fortune and never worked, and Jerome's parents raised him in Johannesburg. This was a sharp contrast to Jerome's work ethic. He loved his career as an architect and greatly appreciated the Basotho. His friends consisted of

Basotho and mainly British colleagues he had met in Maseru. He had a small apartment in Maseru, not quite the stately home where Alan resided, and he lived modestly.

Jerome became one of Marie Louise's closest friends. Whenever she needed to complain or was confused by her work, she called Jerome, and he often drove up to Leribe to offer his assistance. Marie Louise was sure she was attracted to Jerome. However, she was not ready to commit to a relationship, as she only had six months or so left on her contract. She had the type of loose friendship with Jerome that was very relaxed and supportive. Why would she ruin this by allowing it to drift into a physical relationship? The importance of what she learned about South Africa and apartheid from him was immeasurable. He would often touch her hand or brush against her, and most of the time, she thought this was accidental.

One day, Jerome and Marie Louise traveled to Berea, the district north of Maseru, to meet up with one of Jerome's friends, Stephen, who worked at the British Embassy. They brought a picnic and sat on the riverbank.

"I think that the situation in Lesotho will decline rapidly over the coming years due to the Highlands water project, and I don't see apartheid lasting much longer in South Africa with the unrest. I can see it dismantling in the coming years," Stephen declared.

Jerome agreed, "Lesotho will suffer significantly when apartheid ends in South Africa since there will be more pressure for recruitment within the country rather than continuing to employ miners from Lesotho and Botswana," he said.

AIDS was also beginning to make an impact in southern Africa. However, cases were still low enough as not to raise concern, and it was still considered a disease spread by homosexuals.

Marie Louise asked, "what about HIV infection in Lesotho? Indeed, that could become a problem in the mining population and impact this country?"

Stephen replied: "HIV infection will increase exponentially within southern Africa due to the migrant workers. Most miners are alone for months working in the mines and turn to sex workers for relief. I don't know why the health sector doesn't realize we're at the edge of a significant rise in cases. Once cases rise, they will never be able to control it since it would mean closing the mines. No one will do that, as it's big money."

"I agree. The sector's perspectives on this are mixed, but regardless, no one is working with the mines to spread health information regarding risks. That is the least they could be doing at this time. Southern Africa will be afflicted, including South Africa, Lesotho, Botswana, Zimbabwe, Zambia, etc.," Jerome said.

"Well, if that's the case, reaching the remainder of Africa won't take long. If prostitutes are spreading it through the mines, then what about migrant workers, truck drivers, etc.?" Marie Louise said.

It was still in the early days of the global HIV/AIDS crisis. The sad truth was that if a significant intervention had been made at that time to provide condoms to miners, it might have reduced the spread of the disease in Africa significantly.

Marie Louise and Jerome returned to Leribe, where he stayed the night at her house before heading off on his own the next day. Marie Louise prepared some tea in the kitchen, and as Jerome came up behind her, he cupped her hand in his. He looked directly at her, and she felt an intense wave of attraction between them. She moved away quickly.

"I have made up the spare room. I promise I won't let the dog go in there tonight!" she said as she tried to make light of what had just happened. She wasn't ready to take this any further.

They had breakfast together the next morning before Jerome set off for Mokhotlong. Marie Louise was glad to see there was no awkwardness.

Chapter 7 · Work Progress

"Nice grounds, Marie Louise. It would be best if you did something with the flowers here. Can you hire a gardener?" John asked. John, her technical supervisor, was based at the British Embassy in Maseru, and he visited every four months for a few days. He supported Marie Louise and frequently helped her in her arguments with Alan and the World Bank. This time, she invited John over to her house for lunch.

Gardening was not a forte of Marie Louise's. She thought weeds looked nice and should be allowed to flourish in peace. "Do you realize you have marijuana growing in your garden?" John said.

"No, John. I don't even know what that looks like." Marie Louise was rather shocked and made a note to pull it out as quickly as possible before any other project staff visiting noticed it. She didn't even smoke cigarettes, let alone weed, she thought.

John entered the lounge and took a seat. "So, what does the community data look like, Marie Louise?"

"I would say it's quite mixed. We surveyed the villages that will be expected to relocate due to the placement of the Katse dam first," she said.

"Farmers who will lose land to the project know they will have trouble re-establishing new livelihoods. There's little arable land in the mountains to replace what will be lost, and efforts to help them with new livelihoods will need to be heavily factored into the project," she added.

"We need to push the World Bank firmly on the issues of community participation in decision-making. We need to address people's perceptions of the project before we can tackle the social and physical needs of the communities. And right now, their perspective is that the project will ruin their livelihoods and local practices," she said.

John rolled up one of the marijuana leaves in his hand and crushed it, as he pondered the statement. "Well, we must follow the World Bank's guidelines. We conduct the studies and submit the results. If they wish to either ignore the results or do the minimum possible in terms of support to the affected communities, there's little we can do to push them." John was always pragmatic, but it wasn't what Marie Louise wished to hear. To her, the Highlands Water project was another example of South Africa railroading Lesotho and ignoring the needs of the Basotho.

"I am sure the World Bank guidelines, which are intended to ensure that projects are implemented without adverse effects on the environment and people, will not be adhered to. The project was approved based on a deeply flawed and inadequate environmental impact assessment. The World Bank has done little to ensure compliance. It's maintained the fiction that Lesotho was the borrower for the project despite South Africa being responsible for repaying the loans, as this has proved helpful in evading their responsibilities," she told John.

John never replied to Marie Louise. They continued to have lunch and then went for a walk before he drove back to Maseru.

After more than eighteen months of living in Lesotho and Leribe, Marie Louise was finally settled. However, she knew it was time to move on whenever she became too comfortable. She did not wish to become too content, and there were plenty of other places where she wanted to work. She felt that even if she developed more professionally here, she wasn't sure it would support personal growth. The pain of apartheid next door and the discrimination she faced as a white person were demoralizing. She preferred to go somewhere that would be a more welcoming cultural experience.

Marie Louise walked up the road to Carrie's house and knocked on the door. Donald, the vet, opened the door, muttering something in his strong Scottish accent, and then left Marie Louise to wait for Carrie.

"Hi, I won't be a minute. I'm just talking to my son in Los Angeles," Carrie called out at her.

"No worries. Perhaps I can try to convince Donald again to neuter Matla again. He will have to, since I intend to take him back to London with me!" Marie Louise said.

"Oh, he won't like that! He loves Matla, and he doesn't think it's a good idea to neuter animals as old as he is," Carrie told her.

"Tough luck. He must be neutered before he enters the UK," Marie Louise firmly said.

They walked over to the forest about ten minutes from Carrie's house.

"I've told the British Embassy that I won't be extending my contract and will leave in six months, completing two years. They were not happy, but they understood my perspective. There's not much more I can do here," Marie Louise said.

"Seriously, do you have to leave? You are the only real friend that I have here," Carrie replied.

"What about Donald?" Marie Louise laughed.

"It's not good. We hardly talk to each other now. Donald's family in Scotland wants him to spend more time with his children. Even though they are in their twenties, he thinks he should spend more time there. I'm not sure what I will do. He hasn't asked me to go with him. I wish I'd been born a man," Carrie sighed.

"Why would you say that?" Marie Louise asked. For her, she had never felt hindered by being a woman.

"I guess I never felt supported in doing what I wanted. I wanted to be a writer. However, I was a lousy student, and I was never encouraged to stay in school. I left school at sixteen and began working. I married at nineteen and then had my son a year later," Carrie said.

"Well, I guess I was always encouraged to get a degree. I had a supportive family. My mother was a teacher in Paris for decades, so she always had a strong work ethic. It helps if your parents are highly educated, but many children of less educated parents are determined to do well."

Carrie was quiet. They both understood then that they had less in common than they thought and most likely would not keep in touch when Marie Louise left the country, which made her a little sad. However, it was inevitable, since once she was no longer in Lesotho, they would have little in common.

Chapter 8 · Departure

A few months later, after wrapping up her assignment, Marie Louise drove to Bloemfontein to take a plane to Cape Town. She was quite excited about this, as it was her first visit to the country's south. She was to meet Jerome and tour the area around the Cape. She was quite excited, as she had not seen him for four months while she had been packing up and debriefing the Embassy and the project staff. She had felt no pain whatsoever in saying goodbye to Alan. She could see that he was sad to say goodbye to her and gave her a bear hug, which she was pretty glad to escape from.

She met Jerome, who was clearly pleased to see her, and lightly hugged her at the hotel. Jerome was now working at the University of Cape Town. He drove her to most of the famous spots within the Cape, including Table Mountain, which they walked up; Boulder's Beach, where he showed her some of the more expensive houses; and down to the Cape of Good Hope, which John II of Portugal named because its discovery was a good omen that India could be reached by sea from Europe, which to Marie Louise was fascinating. They talked as they walked along.

"So, was it difficult to leave?" he asked.

"No, surprisingly. I found it very easy. Although I enjoyed my time, I never really felt at home there," she told him.

"Maybe you have trouble putting down roots anywhere?" She wondered why he said that, as it was a rather strange statement, but then, perhaps it was true. She enjoyed traveling and didn't want to stay in any one place for too long at this time in her life.

"What about you?" Don't you have trouble settling?" she asked.

"No, not at all. I love Cape Town and will always keep a home here, but I love Lesotho, and I see myself going back and forth to work there for several years if I can find a new contract," he said.

Marie Louise was a little surprised as she thought Jerome would want to travel further than southern Africa. She was silent.

Marie Louise had a somewhat glossy image of Cape Town and did not realize that it had become one of the most segregated cities in South Africa until Jerome explained this. Racial discrimination was taken to the extreme as the apartheid regime forced different ethnic groups to live in separate places. This was supposed to prevent interracial contact under the pretext of 'separate development'. National laws governing the economy and society systematically favored white households over disadvantaged blacks. The result was that whites became increasingly better off than Indians/Asians, followed by coloreds, and then black Africans.[12]

Jerome drove Marie Louise to an urban slum named Khayelitsha, 25 km southeast of Cape Town. It was set up in the 1980s as a ghetto for black workers who migrated to Cape Town in search of jobs during the apartheid era. They left their expensive car and walked around the huts that served as houses. The paths were narrow and littered with rubbish. Children played in the dirt, and men argued as they smoked and sat around, playing cards.

"Residents here line up for hours at communal water pumps to fill buckets that have to serve all their needs for the day; thousands of homes aren't equipped with toilets, unemployment runs around seventy percent, and local police say they handle murders every weekend due to criminal gangs and other violence," Jerome told her.

"What a stark contrast to Lesotho," Marie Louise remarked. "Those communities may lack wealth, but they carry themselves with unmistakable dignity."

"The government established Khayelitsha as a township for black Africans. It was meant to consolidate all the black population in the Western Cape. The idea was to create four towns, each with 30,000 residents. The government then planned to move everyone to Transkei, the homeland created in the eastern part of the country. People living in existing townships near Cape Town fiercely resisted this. Fights broke out between the government and residents, leading to a surge in people moving here. I've been studying this regarding housing needs on behalf of the university," Jerome said. "Apartheid, for the South African government, has always been an economic necessity. Black Africans provide cheap labor, but they don't

12 Statistics South Africa, 2019.

want them living close to white families. So, more of them move out to the suburbs, and then they transport them by bus into the city for labor needs."

Marie Louise looked over her shoulder and noticed a gang was whispering on the corner of the road they were walking down. Jerome signaled to her to move quickly back to the car. Marie Louise cursed the fact that she had worn heels for this trip. They started walking swiftly, and she nervously looked back to see that the gang was beginning to follow them. They eventually started running back to the car, got in and locked it, and promptly drove back to Cape Town, hardly saying a word to each other.

The next day, Marie Louise said goodbye to Jerome at the hotel where she was staying. She would miss him, but they both knew they had no future. Jerome was firmly attached to South Africa and his work at the University of Cape Town. Marie Louise knew that it would never be her permanent residence. She was sad to say goodbye to him, but she was sure they would remain friends.

Chapter 9 · Cambridge, Massachusetts, 1998

Marie Louise joined Klaus in the back row of the auditorium. He put his hand to his lips, willing her to be as silent as possible as she shuffled into her seat beside him. She passed one of the cups of coffee to him, placing her own on the floor beside her feet. The auditorium was packed, and silence fell upon the room and its 25,000 occupants. President Nelson Mandela entered the room and made his way to the microphone. Marie Louise felt a shiver as she saw him walk onto the stage, as his presence was electrifying. He paused for a few seconds to drink his water and to view the packed audience at Harvard University. These were the sentences that hit Marie Louise the hardest[13].

> *The greatest single challenge facing our globalized world is to combat and eradicate its disparities. While in all parts of the world progress is being made in entrenching democratic forms of governance, we constantly need to remind ourselves that the freedoms that democracy brings will remain empty shells if they are not accompanied by real and tangible improvements in the material lives of the millions of ordinary citizens of those countries.*
>
> *Where men and women and children go burdened with hunger, suffering from preventable diseases, languishing in ignorance and illiteracy, or finding themselves bereft of decent shelter, talk of democracy and freedom that does not recognize these material aspects can ring hollow and erode confidence exactly in those values we seek to promote. Hence our universal obligation towards the building of a world in which there shall be greater equality amongst nations and amongst citizens of nations.*

---

13 Address by President Nelson Mandela on receiving an Honorary Doctorate from Harvard University : Eradicate the World's Disparities, 1998-09-18.

The disparity between the developed and developing world, between North and South, reflects itself also in the sphere of educational and intellectual resources. The precepts of the economic theorists who could so confidently prescribe to all now appear to have drawn much of their apparent intellectual validation from having been unchallenged by the day-to-day operations of a system that operated in the interests of the powerful.

Not only does this crisis call for fundamental rethinking and reconceptualization on the part of the theorists of the North, it more particularly and urgently emphasizes the need for thinkers and intellectuals of the developing world to sharpen their skills and analyses and for a genuine partnership between those of the North and the South to help shape a world order that answers to the shared and common needs of all peoples.

Marie Louise listened intently. You could have heard a pin drop in the room with the level of silence and respect for the President. She thought back to her years in Lesotho and how the plight of apartheid had affected her. Then, as his speech progressed, it struck her that Nelson Mandela didn't talk about racism; he didn't mention apartheid. Instead, he spoke about inequality, the gap between the rich and poor, and the need for education and learning. Marie Louise felt another shiver up her spine as she eventually realized that racism and apartheid were merely tools used by the rich and powerful to control people.

Part Four

Pakistan (1988–90)

Rebecca

Chameleon

Chapter 1 · Abrupt Arrival

It was a hot afternoon as Rebecca left the plane, and the heat struck her hard; it must have been at least 90 degrees Fahrenheit. The airport in Peshawar, North-West Frontier Province (NWFP) of Pakistan, was teeming with people. Rebecca had flown in on a direct flight from London to Karachi, a fifteen-hour journey, so she was exhausted. The airport was rather shabby and tired-looking but quite large. She noticed several guards around the airport, and she presumed this was normal for a country ruled by a military regime. Most of the women were either wearing saris or shalwar kameez, and their heads were covered with a chador or long scarf. A few were wearing black burkas with only a slit for their eyes. Rebecca had dressed conservatively for the journey, wearing trousers with a long dark blouse. The men watched her steadily, which somewhat unnerved her—she was alone and the only foreign woman at the airport. She slowly approached passport control, where they carefully examined her visa, which she had obtained just three days prior in London. The guard quickly stamped it and beckoned her to the baggage claim area. It was around three o'clock in the afternoon.

Rebecca picked up her two large suitcases, struggling to carry them, and went outside to the car park. The contents would have to last her until her shipment arrived in three months. She searched for a sign with her name for at least five minutes, to no avail. After thirty minutes, no one from the office had shown up, and she became increasingly nervous. Only local taxi drivers walked past, frequently offering her a lift. She went back to the airport hall, convincing the security guards that she needed to return to speak with the information desk inside. She walked over to the desk and asked the man there to order a chauffeur-driven car for her. She suddenly remembered that she had no local currency and tried to see if she had any dollars, but all she had were pounds sterling.

"We take credit cards," he replied.

"Oh, wonderful!" she replied, and then she suddenly remembered that it was late, and so there was no point in driving to the office. "Which is the best hotel to stay in Peshawar for tourists?"

"The best is the Pearl Continental Hotel, the only five-star hotel in town. The drive is about forty minutes," he replied. "They usually have rooms available, and calling them now may be difficult as their switchboard is often jammed with calls."

As she left the airport and walked over to the limousine, it was getting dark outside. She considered that she was most likely paying about five days' salary for the limousine and a few nights at the hotel, but she needed to feel safe on her arrival in Pakistan. She was praying that a room would still be available. Having worked in Asia previously, she understood it was far better to be safe than to worry about money.

The Pearl Continental was built in the 1970s, a well-maintained five-story building. The hotel was on the city's outskirts, making it a haven for foreigners. Rebecca entered the hotel after the limousine dropped her off at the front and walked to the reception desk. She asked the receptionist if there were any spare rooms and lied, saying she had forgotten to make a booking, and told him she had only remembered it as she drove toward the hotel. Luckily, his English was impeccable, and there were a few remaining rooms, so Rebecca paid with her credit card for three nights, in case the hotel became fully booked over the next few days. The man at the desk asked her if she wanted anything brought to her room. "No, thank you, I have everything I need for the evening," she managed to say in her most work-efficient voice.

The hotel's interior was quite beautiful. There were oriental carpets everywhere, old wooden furniture in the reception area, and Mughal-period paintings on the wall. Rebecca had already collected some small Mughal-era artwork on her visits to India. However, these were far more detailed and impressive. The North-West Frontier Province was famous for its wooden furniture. Rebecca later learned that most of the furniture in the hotel was from the Hayat Brothers furniture store. After the partition of the subcontinent, the business moved to Gujrat, Pakistan. The brothers went their separate ways, and in 1936, Abdul Aziz inherited his father's furniture business in Peshawar, which was now the most famous. Their furniture was made primarily of rosewood, which in the 1980s was not as rare as it would become later.

Walking to her room, she noticed groups of Pakistani men sitting in the reception. Her room was very elegant, with oriental carpets and a double bed. There was a TV that mainly had local programs and some foreign film channels. The bathroom was spotless, with a bath and shower and numerous toiletries provided. About thirty minutes later, there was a knock on her door. "Do you like a massage?" the young doorman said as she peeked out to see who was there.

"No, thank you. Not today, not ever!" Rebecca was slightly surprised by the offer but was too exhausted to think about it.

She locked the door tightly before falling asleep after her long flight.

Rebecca awoke at about 6:00 AM the following day and went to the ground floor for breakfast, as she had not eaten for more than fourteen hours since the last plane meal. From what she could make out, most of the tables were taken by Pakistani men talking business. There were no women in the room. She chose a Western breakfast of eggs and toast over a traditional Pakistani one of rice, meat, and vegetables, which was too much for her at this time of the morning. The breakfast room was overly air-conditioned, so it was challenging to gauge the temperature outside. As she sat there, she felt the men in the room were staring at her, so she made a lot of noise with her knife against the plate and slammed her coffee cup down on the saucer. Why not provide some entertainment for them?

When Rebecca returned to her room, she attempted to call her office to report her arrival. She tried the two telephone numbers she had been given by the NGO in London, but neither connected her to the office; instead, she was directed to a recorded message. She left her name and number at the location where she was staying. She decided to wait and see if anyone contacted her, or she would try again later. By this time, Rebecca was rather angry that not only had there not been a car to meet her at the airport, but the office had also not called her back at the hotel.

Rebecca tried to call again. Eventually, she managed to get through to someone.

"Hold, please. Putting you through to Nazar Ali, Chief of Office."

"Hello, Rebecca," this voice bellowed down the line. "We thought you were arriving this morning, not last night."

"I sent the details to your office a week ago and said my arrival would be last night," she said.

"Well, you should have waited at the airport instead of going to a hotel," Nazar said disapprovingly. Before she could explain that sleeping at an airport as an unescorted woman wasn't an option, Nazar cut her off.

"Wait at the hotel, and we will send a car. We have booked you at another hotel, which is less expensive," Nazar continued.

Rebecca took a deep breath.

"Nazar, thank you so much," Rebecca said. "But I think I will stay here for now, as my luggage is already unpacked. It would be a chore to pack everything up and move." Rebecca was sure she had found the safest and comfiest hotel in town, and she was not budging until she felt she was on safer ground. Even though she was conspicuous as a foreigner, she would be even more so in a less international hotel.

Nazar informed her that the car to take her to the office would arrive in forty minutes, so Rebecca got ready in her room. She decided to wear a dark red shalwar kameez that she had purchased in an Indian shop in London. She looked at herself in the mirror. Rebecca was slender, standing about 5 feet 5 inches tall, with brownish-red hair that fell to her shoulders. She knew she was attractive, but in Pakistan, she thought she might have to play this down somewhat so as not to draw attention. She tied her hair back tightly into a ponytail and decided not to wear lipstick, as she usually did. When she was ready, Rebecca walked downstairs. Since she had a little time, she walked around the hotel to examine her surroundings. It was a little chilly at this time of the morning in March. She walked through the back streets near the hotel, which reminded her of India, but there were fewer buildings compared to, for example, Calcutta. She could smell the garam masala and other spices of street food, as well as the floral scents of jasmine and roses. Most men wore a Pashto shalwar kameez or a kurta kameez, a more formal shirt over the trousers or kameez. All the women on the streets wore a burka; however, unlike at the airport, these were in bright colors, some blue, orange, and yellow. She did not see anyone wearing Western clothes. The way that the men stared at her made her very uncomfortable. She thought she was dressed conservatively, but obviously, to them, she was not. Rebecca wore a light cardigan over her shalwar kameez but didn't have a headscarf. It would be the first thing she would buy since she felt self-conscious without one. She wasn't accustomed to covering her head, but it was expected of women in public in Peshawar.

The town had a population of two million, but Rebecca had read that in 1988, due to the war in Afghanistan, a further two million refugees were living in camps both within and outside the city. Peshawar has a vibrant history as the third-largest city in Pakistan, with a history of Buddhism and Hinduism preceding the rise of Islam as the predominant religion. It was one of the oldest cities in South Asia. In 1849, the city was captured by the East India Company and later became part of the British Raj, under whose rule it remained until partition and Pakistan's subsequent independence in 1947.

Rebecca returned to the hotel and saw that the office car, with its NGO markings on the side, was waiting for her. The driver got out of the car and opened the door for her.

He greeted her with, "Good morning, Ms. Rebecca. I hope you had a pleasant stay at the hotel."

"Greetings. How far is it to the office?" Rebecca asked him.

"About thirty minutes from here. We will drive through the center of town," he replied.

Rebecca noticed many people walking through the streets, sitting at corners, and talking. They passed through the bazaar, which was filled with shops, with carpets laid out on the roads and cars driving over them.

"Why are the carpets strewn on the roads? Surely that will ruin them," Rebecca asked him.

"That's how you make a new carpet old. You leave it on the road for a few days…" the driver told her.

"Good to note," she responded. Rebecca made a mental note to check for petrol smells and tire marks before purchasing old Peshawar carpets.

"How far is it to the Khyber Pass from Peshawar?" she asked him.

"About one hour to the north-west," the driver replied.

Rebecca knew that from the 1960s until the late 1970s, Peshawar was a major stop on the famous Hippie Trail, which included the Khyber Pass entrance to Afghanistan. But, of course, tourists did not travel to Afghanistan any longer due to the war and the danger of landmines along the road. The car passed several beautiful old Mughal-style buildings with tiling and the clock tower that she had seen in articles. The clock tower was built by the British and had a colonial-style design. Most older buildings had overarching wooden windows with shutters. There were many small shops along the main road.

"When was the clock tower built?" she asked.

"It was built in 1900 to commemorate Queen Victoria's Diamond Jubilee. It was constructed by George Cunningham, the governor of the North-West Frontier Province at the time," the driver replied.

The city certainly had character. As they neared the office, Rebecca recognized the name of the street where there had been an attempt on the life of the Afghan leader, Ahmad Shah Massoud. Massoud was from the Panjshir Valley and was heavily involved in the resistance to the Russian occupation of Afghanistan. Rebecca had read of an attempt on his life on that very road only six months earlier. His forces were considered the most effective of all the various Afghan resistance movements. They were also considered the least corrupt group operating across the border. His men were professional soldiers, well-paid and trained, and, from 1983 on, they provided an effective strike force against the Afghan government outposts. Massoud was considered to have played a pivotal role in the fall of the Russians and their subsequent withdrawal from Afghanistan.

"Are there many Mujahideen in Peshawar?" Rebecca asked the driver.

"Most Afghan commanders visit Peshawar frequently to get funds or visit the province for firearms. They are not so interested in the refugee population since it consists mainly of women, children, and seniors, and they have little use for them in fighting," he replied.

They arrived at the office, which was a converted residential building with some surrounding land. The organization supported Afghan refugees and Pakistani communities by providing essential services, including water and sanitation, health, and nutrition support. Rebecca was to head up the health and nutrition component of the NGO for the next two years. She nervously entered the building, wondering what reception she would receive.

She knocked on Nazar's office door.

"Come in, Rebecca, and sit down," he bellowed. "I hope you are rested. We have a lot of work for you. Matthew mentioned you would be a hard worker, so I hope he is correct." Matthew was the head of the NGO's office, based in Islamabad, and the man responsible for recruiting Rebecca. After this comment, Rebecca was even more sure that Nazar would not become a friend during her assignment.

"Could you please summarize your experience to date for me, as I can't recall your CV so readily?" Nazar asked her.

Rebecca highlighted her experience and training for Nazar, noticing that he wasn't listening and was working on his desktop computer.

"Could you direct me to my office, Nazar, so I can start to brief myself and settle in?" Rebecca sharply asked him.

Nazar looked up, somewhat surprised. "OK, no worries. I understand that you wish to get settled. Later in the week, we can go for lunch."

Rebecca thanked him and was directed to her assistant, Matloob, by Nazar's secretary.

Matloob led her to a large office at the back of the building. There were two desks, and one was occupied by a Pakistani woman who introduced herself as Shahida, the officer in charge of gender and rural development. She wasn't very friendly either.

Rebecca decided to settle down at her desk and read the documents Nazar had sent by email.

"So, I hope you are settled at your hotel," Shahida said. She was about thirty-five, with long, loose hair, and wore a shalwar kameez. Since her head wasn't covered, Rebecca assumed this was only for the office, and that she covered her head when she went outside.

"Yes, it's lovely, thank you. Have you worked long for the NGO?"

"About three years or so," Shahida replied. I was born in Peshawar." She then glanced back at her computer as if to end the conversation.

Matloob walked over to Rebecca and handed her an agenda for the week's introductions to the government of the North-West Frontier region.

"Please tell me if you need to change anything."

"Will Nazar come with me, or will I be alone?" she asked him.

"Nazar wishes that you go by yourself." Matloob went back to his desk outside. Rebecca could see that her posting would not be easy. She wasn't sure why Nazar had decided he didn't like her, but she thought it was more likely that he would have this reaction to any expatriate joining what he considered to be his office.

Chapter 2 · Settling into Pakistan

Rebecca stayed at the hotel for another week before moving into a guest house in the town for a month. The food there was delicious, but she had little privacy. She was expected to search for her own home, and she had already started the process of contacting an agent.

After two weeks in Peshawar, she traveled to the NGO headquarters office in Islamabad to meet the team. The office was in the center of the capital, a modern city, by comparison, with a vastly superior urban layout.

Islamabad was developed as the capital city in the 1960s and was well-planned in terms of layout, compared to the old capital in Rawalpindi, located ten miles southwest. It was certainly a lot more modern than Peshawar. There must have been poorer areas, but that was less apparent than in other cities in the country. Islamabad had been constructed as the capital for several reasons. Pakistan needed money that was easily accessible from all parts of the country. Karachi, a business hub, was considered unsuitable, partly due to the influence of business interests on government affairs. Islamabad was also closer to the army headquarters in Rawalpindi and the disputed territory of Kashmir in the north.

She made her way over to Matthew O'Connor's office, the representative of the NGO.

Rebecca entered the room after being told to report there and looked at Matthew, who was standing at the window.

"Hello, Rebecca. I have heard some good things about you from your former supervisors. We waited a long time for you to join us!"

Rebecca had been working in Thailand and could not break her contract after applying for this position, so the NGO had waited a year for her to join the agency. Matthew was tall, about 6 feet, slim, and appeared to be in his early forties. He was also quite good-looking, well-dressed, and groomed. Rebecca was tired after traveling from Peshawar that morning and felt a bit self-conscious. She was dressed conservatively, in trousers with a long blouse. Her hair was tied back, and she wore no makeup.

Matthew talked for about fifteen minutes non-stop about Pakistan and Afghanistan, the politics, and the Russian occupation of Afghanistan. By the end, Rebecca wasn't sure if she should be working in Afghanistan rather than Pakistan. The man was incredibly knowledgeable about both countries. Rebecca noticed that he never entirely addressed her when speaking to her. It was as if he were lecturing. She felt oddly uneasy as she walked out of his office, as though he would play a part in her life that she had yet to discover.

After she finished the meeting at Matthew's office, she went to the man heading field operations, Zubair, an older gentleman of about fifty-five or so. He looked very stern, and as soon as Rebecca entered his office, she knew it was an ominous meeting.

"Hello, Rebecca, welcome to Pakistan. We hope you will be very comfortable here." Rebecca wondered if Zubair was welcoming her to prison or something similar by the tone of his voice.

"I have worked for this NGO for about twenty years now, and I have seen many country representatives come and go," Zubair said. Rebecca thought humorously that he was not greatly enamored of Matthew, which raised him in her estimation.

"'They all have different priorities and practices. At the end of the day, Pakistan always does its own thing, and whatever we decide makes little difference in the larger picture." Rebecca thought this was not reassuring regarding Zubair's belief in the organization's work.

He then went on to comment on her appearance. "Although your outfit is acceptable, it isn't suitable for Peshawar," Zubair said.

Rebecca was wearing a blouse that was thigh-length over her trousers. "Shalwar kameez would be more suitable. It would be best if you were careful with your practices in Peshawar, as people will be watching you. You cannot act as a Western woman, or your government counterparts will not accept you," he reinforced. She decided to accept his comment without arguing. Zubair reminded Rebecca of Nazar, her supervisor, but even sharper and more critical.

At this point, Rebecca was ready to end the conversation, but she thought she had to be tolerant since she would meet many 'Zubairs' over the next few years. Her ability to work with them would be a key factor in determining the level of her success. She met with some of the other staff. All were exceptionally friendly and kind, unlike the intense meeting with Matthew and the problematic discourse with Zubair.

Rebecca stayed in a guesthouse near the office. She liked walking around the streets of Islamabad as it was easier than in Peshawar. Fewer people stared at you as a Western woman, as it was more common to meet foreigners. It was far more cosmopolitan than Peshawar, with hotels, restaurants, and shopping areas, and it had the added advantage of being more relaxed. Rebecca was happy to stay a few days, arrange for her shipment to be delivered, and shop for 'more suitable' clothes.

Before leaving Islamabad, she spent the morning at the office, talking to some sector staff. In the corridor, she bumped into Matthew.

"Hi Rebecca, when are you leaving town?"

"This afternoon," she told him.

"Let's get a quick cup of coffee in the canteen." He guided her to the café and got two cups of coffee for them.

Matthew seemed conflicted, as if he was in a hurry but also appeared to want to talk to her.

"Be careful in Peshawar. There are many politicians and strange types. Please keep this to yourself and talk to Nazar or me if anything concerns you. I can't stay now, as I have a meeting at the Ministry of Health, but I will be in Peshawar soon and look forward to seeing you there."

Rebecca was a little unsettled by this conversation. She had not feared living in Peshawar, but now wondered if she should be more careful. If Matthew had wished to come across as mysterious, he had succeeded, and Rebecca was somewhat intrigued by him.

Chapter 3 · Culturally Acclimatizing

After a few months, Rebecca settled into her work. She avoided Nazar when she could, as he asked too many questions and seldom listened to her answers. She began working with her counterparts at the Ministry of Health and the Department of Local Development and decided to visit the field as soon as possible to explore the country further. She knew that sitting in the office would not help her understand the people she was here to assist. In the first few weeks, she made some friends in Peshawar: a British doctor called Suzy, who was rather absentminded and disorganized, but probably brilliant; and a Pakistani woman working for another NGO, Rubina, who helped her understand the culture more quickly than she would have otherwise.

With the help of an agent, she had found a suitable house in the University Town area, a planned residential community created by the University of Peshawar in the 1950s. The university was one of the oldest in Pakistan and was widely regarded in the 1980s as the best in the country. Until the mid-1950s, Peshawar was enclosed within a city wall and gates. Most expatriates lived in University Town as it was the safest area in the city. However, any Pakistani living there had to be affluent, as rents were very high. Rebecca found a house conveniently in the center of the town and only later learned that it was beside the home of the Afghan leader in exile, President Rabbani. Most of the time, this made little difference as she rarely heard anything from that side of the fence. However, she nearly had a heart attack one day when she received his phone bill by accident instead of her own, as it was for thousands of dollars. He obviously used the phone for international calls quite frequently. His assistant was extremely courteous when they exchanged bills; she received hers back, which was the monthly average of $ 150.

She hired a chowkidar, Hassan, to look after the property and guard the gate to the compound. He was a thickset Pashtun man in his sixties and of few words, although his English was good, as it was with most of the Pakistanis she worked with. She also hired a housekeeper to maintain the property and assist her with household chores, including cooking. She consistently felt guilty about her perceived extravagant lifestyle. It wasn't as if you could afford this level of support in Europe. However, the salaries were low, and the work was needed, she justified to herself.

One morning, she returned early to collect a file and found the housekeeper rushing out of one of the bedrooms, followed by a strange man.

Rebecca walked over to her chowkidar. "What's going on?" she asked.

"That housekeeper is no good. She brought a man over here," Hassan replied.

"Why didn't you stop her?" Rebecca asked.

"Well, I didn't feel it was my place," Hassan responded quietly.

"That is precisely what your role is! To ensure no strange people enter my premises!" Rebecca shouted back at him.

Rebecca was suspicious of Hassan's role in all of this. Something about Hassan was hard to trust, and she could not afford to entrust her property to someone she did not feel comfortable with. She reluctantly sacked Hassan and the housekeeper, giving them both a month's wages as she thought she had no choice. She felt most sorry for the housekeeper, but she would not discuss the event, as this would probably result in a police investigation, and she worried about retribution for the woman. She had met Hassan's son, Farouk, so she agreed when he suggested he would help her until she found someone. He was tall and thin and looked far more trustworthy than his father. She thought she would hire him for a month only until she found someone else recommended by a colleague.

"I am really sorry about my father's behavior. It was disgraceful. I cannot discuss it with him, but this was not the first time he has done this," Farouk said.

"I feel so sorry for the housekeeper, but I can't ask her to work here any longer," Rebecca replied. For Rebecca, the idea that her house had been used for prostitution was gravely offensive. She had no regrets about firing Hassan, and he was lucky that she did not report the matter to the police.

"I understand. I can clean and look after the property," Farouk said.

Farouk worked with Rebecca for the following two and a half years. He was an excellent support to her, and she knew she was wise not to judge him by his father. He never allowed his father to set foot on the property.

Rebecca found that the American club in the center of University Town was a haven for all the expatriates living there, and the food was good. It was launched as a guesthouse for visiting officials but soon became a refuge for "aid workers, missionaries, journalists, spies, and diplomats working the sidelines of the Afghan war[14]." Many journalists from the major international newspapers passed through the club. Most were very sympathetic to the Mujahideen, and there was rare criticism regarding any of their practices as opposed to the Russians. One of the most interesting people was Steve Masty, who ran the club. He was British but had spent a considerable amount of time in the United States, where he had served as a speechwriter for several Republican leaders. Steve was also very spiritual, and Rebecca often saw him engage in long conversations with groups on philosophical topics. Rebecca heard Masty saying, "the bartenders supervised and served the foreign lunatics with kindness, merriment, and unflappable aplomb." Prominent politicians, such as Charlie Wilson, a US Congressman, often seen sitting with his Johnnie Walker on the rocks, stayed at the club. Rebecca had to be told who he was, as she had no idea and had never heard of him or any other famous Americans who sometimes frequented the club. There were many famous journalists, but only their newspapers were known to Rebecca. Most of the social side of Rebecca's life was centered on meetings and dinners at the Club, when she wasn't entertaining at home or the home of one of her friends. She wondered where she would be categorized by club members under the banner of 'mercenary, missionary, or misfit'. Most likely the latter.

One day at the office, she saw an exquisite, tall, and well-dressed woman leave Nazar's office quite quickly, and she asked him who she was.

"Oh, that's Doctor Diane. She works for Matthew on the Afghanistan refugee program," he said.

Rebecca was surprised he did not suggest she talk to her, but she brushed

---

14 "Khyber (American) Club's bartender had frontrow seat to history in Pakistan" **Karin Brulliard**, published by *The Washington Post* on February 7, 2012

it aside. She had other things to worry about, and her priority was to work well with the government. She made her first field trip to visit health clinics and villages south of NWFP, in a district named Dera Ismail Khan or DI Khan. She ordered a vehicle and driver from the office and set off alone to meet government staff in the district offices and visit villages.

The district of Dera Ismail Khan (DIK) is on a fertile alluvial plain along the Indus River basin. The area is littered with ruins from ancient civilizations. DIK was on the path used by Alexander the Great, whose armies marched through Afghanistan, crossed the Indus, and briefly entered India before following the Indus to the Arabian Sea.

The drive to reach the district capital took about four hours. As they drove south, Rebecca noticed that the land was more fertile, and crops such as wheat, sugarcane, dates, rice, and mangoes grew. After consulting with Nazar, Rebecca decided that she would not cover her head in government offices but would do so in the villages. She met the health officer, a man in his thirties, who invited her to a meal with other government staff that evening. She wondered if it was wise, but she needed to work well with her counterparts, so she took her driver and went along. The meal was served outside, which was slightly chilly in the late evening. The food consisted of naan, goat's meat, lentils, spinach, and potatoes, heavily spiced with turmeric, Kashmiri mirchi, and garam masala. Rebecca asked what had been added to the meal and how it had been cooked, as it was so delicious. She was a vegetarian, but there was plenty of food for her, and no one questioned her for not eating any meat. It was an enjoyable evening. She never encountered disrespect or discourteous behavior during her field trips in the NWFP and was always treated with kindness and courtesy.

Most of the conversation that evening centered on health data within the area, but occasionally, it would veer into politics at the provincial and national levels. At that time, President Zia-ul-Haq was in power in Islamabad. In 1977, he had deposed President Bhutto and declared martial law. In 1979, following the Soviet invasion of Afghanistan, he adopted an anti-Russian stance and supported the Mujahideen. Zia-ul-Haq dominated Pakistan's politics for over a decade, and his proxy war against the Soviet Union was credited with stopping an expected invasion of Pakistan.

When they spoke of the president, it was in hushed tones, and they reverted to their local language, Pashto, much to Rebecca's disappointment. She knew the history of the president and his role in the coup to bring down Zulfikar Ali Bhutto, his subsequent trial and execution, which was condemned by many countries, but not perhaps her own under President Reagan. The Reagan administration had declared Zia-ul-Haq's regime as the 'front line' ally of the United States in the fight against the threat of Communism. The 'primary' policy or 'centerpiece' of Zia-ul-Haq's government was 'Islamization'. In 1977, before the coup, the drinking and selling of wine by Muslims, along with nightclubs and horse racing, were banned by Prime Minister Bhutto. Zia-ul-Haq went much further, establishing an Islamic state and Sharia law.

The next day, they visited neighboring villages on dirt tracks about an hour off the road. The villages were relatively poor, as was reflected by their houses and spartan furniture. However, she met wealthier families in some places, and they invited her to sit on cushions on their verandas and talk to the villagers. She was always given tea, biscuits, and sometimes lunch wherever she traveled.

There was a handpump in some of the villages. However, in most cases, there was none, and women walked on foot to collect water from uncovered wells, which were easily contaminated. She asked to examine some of the children's vaccination cards. The mothers were happy to share these with her, and after reading a few, she noticed a discrepancy. Many of the cards she examined were dated for the third dose of DPT (diphtheria, pertussis, and tetanus) at a future date. This meant that the immunization workers had not given most children in the village the third shot, but had recorded the child as already having received the full three shots. Rebecca, somewhat shocked, recounted this information to the health officer in DI Khan City and asked him why this was the case. He wasn't surprised. "Pressure is put on the immunization workers to produce results for the Ministry of Health in Islamabad. They are urged to raise immunization rates to eighty percent nationally, so the agents feel they must obtain these results as quickly as possible," he said.

"If they are not fully vaccinated, they can contract diphtheria, pertussis, or tetanus. They need all three shots," Rebecca said.

"I agree with you, but this pressure is from Islamabad. The agency doesn't feel I am responsible for the immunization program, and the responsibility lies directly with the Ministry in Islamabad. This is the only health project I supervise that is not decentralized," he replied. Rebecca understood that district staff were under pressure from their supervisors to produce results and felt sorry for them. She would share this information with Matthew as soon as she could so that he could advocate with ministry officials. However, she also knew the aid agencies pressured governments to achieve higher immunization rates. This was a good thing, but they needed to ensure the pressure wasn't being placed too heavily on poor field workers who needed their salaries at all costs. Rebecca was also concerned about the nutritional status of the children she saw, most likely exacerbated by childhood diarrhea and poor infant feeding practices. As she walked around the village, Rebecca saw many mothers breastfeeding their children. However, she knew the issue arose when the infant became older, as mothers would introduce other foods and water to the infant around four to six months. If bowls and spoons were not washed properly, the child would become ill due to poor hygiene. The safest method was to introduce hygienic practices for weaning while continuing to breastfeed for two years. Rebecca always carried oral rehydration packets to give to mothers when their child had diarrhea so they could rehydrate and replace essential salts. She would have a lot to talk about back in Peshawar.

While returning to Peshawar, Rebecca accompanied the technician to a village near the Punjab border. Exploring the area, she came across ancient ruins, which the technician identified as remnants from the era of Alexander the Great. Among the scattered stones, a gleaming blue fragment caught her eye. The technician explained that Alexander and the Macedonians used this type of blue mosaic to reinforce and embellish their structures. Fascinated, Rebecca took the stone home, keeping it for decades. Each time she gazed at it, she was transported back to her field visits, where every trip to the southern region of the North-West Frontier Province felt like stepping through a time machine.

Chapter 5 · Entering the Spider's Web

After returning to Peshawar the following week, Rebecca expected Matthew's visit. This was the first time he had come to Peshawar during her assignment, and she wasn't sure if they would get along well. She was also nervous since he was the Director of the NGO, and she had found him to be somewhat magnetic in Islamabad. She walked around University Town and went to the house of a friend, a woman from the UN, Monserrat, an expert on Afghan refugees. Montserrat gave Rebecca the latest information on the refugees and their movements. Most Afghan refugees in Pakistan were Pashtuns, housed in refugee camps established by UNHCR throughout Pakistan's two westernmost provinces, the North-West Frontier Province and Baluchistan. Over the years, the camps evolved into villages that appeared like any other Pakistani village. Many refugees carved out reasonable and stable lives, at least compared to what they could expect in Afghanistan. Most found at least subsistence work in the local economy or rented land to cultivate. Many families maintained a foothold in both countries by living in Pakistan while hiring tenant farmers to work their land in Afghanistan. During the 1980s and early 1990s, religious schools known as madrasas gained popularity among Afghan refugee populations. Ultra-conservative groups, primarily based in Saudi Arabia, Pakistan, and Afghanistan, funded the schools. Later, it was discovered that the madrasas were the breeding grounds for the Taliban movement.

Matthew strolled into the office the following day, wearing a smart western suit; no kurta shalwar for him, Rebecca thought.

"Rebecca, why don't we leave the office and go to University Town for a coffee at the American Club?" he called across the room.

Rebecca wasn't sure that was a good idea, considering it was more than a twenty-minute drive.

"Can we not just stay here and work in the conference room?" Rebecca asked. She wasn't sure she wanted to be in a more relaxed environment with Matthew. First, she needed to demonstrate to him her professional skills.

She was here for the work and to further develop her career.

"I think we need a place where we can talk freely," he told her in a subdued voice.

There wasn't much she could argue with in this request. It was true that there was always someone hovering around the office, listening, and since he was the Representative, this was even more likely with his presence in the office. She agreed, and they drove to the club. When they arrived, Matthew was in his element, approaching most people, including journalists. Rebecca was not familiar with most of them. Matthew stopped at one table and talked to an American journalist for about ten minutes. Rebecca decided to order the coffee herself, as she thought it might take a long time for Matthew to tear himself away.

"Sorry about that, Rebecca. I needed to deal with some business." Matthew then talked for about fifteen minutes about the agency's support for Afghanistan and the refugees. During his monologue, there was little chance for Rebecca to ask questions, which did not surprise her as it was similar to how he had addressed her when she first met him in Islamabad. Matthew told her the Afghan response was run from Islamabad with a skeleton staff in Kabul. The agency supported the Mujahideen groups through development assistance, including supplies and equipment, as well as technical support to the refugee camps for health and nutrition. Some support was provided for early child development and education materials. Rebecca was a little tired of Matthew's monologue on Afghanistan and the work across the border.

"Matthew, I thought the major thrust of my work here was to support rural communities within the Northwest Frontier and neighboring Afghan communities. Surely, sufficient other partners are working in the refugee camps in and around Peshawar?" She understood most development funds were directed to the Afghan refugees, mainly those three million living closest to the city. However, she would not spend the next two years supporting those areas, as she was sure she was needed elsewhere.

"While I was traveling, I examined the villages in the south closely, and there are significant health and nutritional issues in children that we are duty-bound to address." Now, she was giving him a lecture and enjoying herself.

Matthew sat back in his seat, listening, and stared at Rebecca intently. He was about forty-five or so years old; regretfully, he was also tall, dark, and handsome… He was quiet as if considering something, and then he spoke.

"I understand, Rebecca. If you wish to prioritize Pakistan villages at this time, I will support you. I know you will ensure that services are equally provided to neighboring refugee communities." This comment caught Rebecca off guard, as she had expected resistance from Matthew.

"Oh, I thought you would oppose me on that," she told him.

"Why would I do that if I know that you're perfectly capable of seeing where the major problems are? It serves the refugee population well if neighboring Pakistani villages aren't resentful of the aid provided, and if there are needs, they should be addressed. But we need to ensure we balance our funding, so the donors know we're supporting both Afghan and Pakistani populations," Matthew said.

Matthew then told her he was from California. "I lost my father when he was very young and was raised by my mother with my brother, near Los Angeles." He had the air of a Californian, a little brash, very confident, and somewhat flamboyant. Rebecca was rather surprised he opened up to her about his past.

"What about you? Tell me a little about your background?" Matthew asked her. "Why did you agree to come to Pakistan?"

She replied, "I thought it was an interesting assignment, and since I had experience working in Asia, I thought it wouldn't be too difficult to adapt."

"And now, what do you think?" he asked her.

"It's more complicated than I thought it would be. The mindset of Pakistani men, especially in Peshawar, is somewhat limited. It's easier in the field to relate to both men and women," she answered.

"How so?" he further asked. Rebecca felt like this was an inquisition.

She responded, "my field visits in DI Khan were far easier. Most government officials don't judge me as a woman but for my professional skills. The men are very respectful."

"But that's because you're American, and they don't expect the same standards as for their own women," he replied.

"Yes, I realize that. I visited a village where I was debating with the local Mullah, and no local women were allowed into the room. Then, I was allowed to sit with the women afterward. Different standards!" she stated.

"And what are your plans after Pakistan?" he asked her.

"I don't know yet. Maybe settle down back home. Get married and have children," she said.

"Really?" Matthew said.

"Maybe not! I don't know. It isn't easy working overseas all the time. This is now my third assignment overseas in rapid succession. I love the work, but it's draining, setting up a new life in a new country, making new friends, and then moving on when the work is completed," she replied.

"I've lived overseas since my early twenties, and I can't imagine not working in development. I don't think I can live back in the United States," he said.

"It's easier for a man since your wife will most likely follow you and live with you overseas. Most men don't follow women to their assignments unless they both get jobs in the same country," she stated.

"I was married. She didn't like India. I loved it, so we divorced," Matthew said.

"OK. So, there are exceptions," Rebecca responded. Somehow, she was sure Matthew was the exception to all rules. She refrained from commenting on his divorce in case the conversation became more personal. By now, she knew Matthew was a little interested in her. She just wasn't sure if it was attraction or general curiosity.

The following month, Rebecca was invited to a major NGO meeting that Matthew facilitated at Murree Hills on the outskirts of Islamabad. The meeting was to plan the development of the next five-year Pakistan program. Most staff in Islamabad were only working on the Pakistan program, and only some supported the Afghan refugees, unless Matthew asked them to provide support through the Peshawar office. This was an opportunity for Rebecca to get to know other staff and see if she should imagine a future with the NGO. At this point, she wasn't sure. She was also unsure whether to shift to the UN since Montserrat, her neighbor, appeared quite content with them. Rebecca also realized that she was a little excited to see Matthew again and maybe a little attracted to him.

They stayed at a resort for tourists, and the view was incredible, with the snowcapped mountains of Kashmir in the distance. Murree was Pakistan's most developed and popular hill station. There were about thirty participants from the office, and Zubair opened the workshop but didn't say much. All Rebecca heard from that speech was to avoid being too innovative, be cautious, and not work too hard. Then, Matthew breezed into the room with his coffee. He sat on a chair and swung his legs onto the table. He then proceeded to contradict everything that Zubair had said. He talked for about forty minutes about the program, his changes since his arrival, and what he expected from the staff. He was far more animated than she had seen from her prior meetings with him. His talk was interesting, but again, there was little opportunity to ask him questions or engage in a proper dialogue. Rebecca glanced around the room, and most people were looking at Matthew with awe and respect. She wasn't quite as impressed as they all seemed to be by his words.

In the evening, a workshop session with Matthew and some of his staff members turned into a social gathering, continuing until the early morning hours. Rebecca attended only for the relevant work information and rarely stayed for the drinking afterward. Since everyone who remained late was an expatriate, the wine bottles could be opened later. One night, Rebecca was curious and decided to stay for a drink. There were mainly women sitting around: Sarita from India, Tasneem from Bangladesh, and others. It was plain that the women hung on Matthew's every word. He had already worked in Pakistan for over three years when Rebecca arrived. When Matthew made any statement, none of the others ever contradicted him. They talked about influencing people. Matthew then spoke about manipulation and its importance in the workplace. Five people were left in the room at this point, and the drinks were flowing. Rebecca thought it was a strange topic to discuss.

"Sometimes you need to use manipulation to influence others to undertake certain tasks. You can manipulate emotions positively to boost morale," Matthew said.

"You shouldn't," Rebecca responded. "Manipulating people is certainly dishonest. If you can't explain upfront to motivate them to undertake a task, then you shouldn't ask them to do it," she said adamantly.

Matthew almost turned red in the face.

"Bullshit," he said. "Everyone manipulates other people. Look at marriages. Would people stay married if they weren't manipulating their partner somehow?" Rebecca could see by the force of his response that Matthew had had one too many whiskies. Looking at the remaining few in the room, she could see they weren't surprised by his response.

"It's unacceptable to fool someone into undertaking a task they would not do otherwise," she stressed. The others in the room were dead silent as Rebecca became more uncomfortable with the conversation. She could hear her heart racing as she shifted around in her seat.

"You will never persuade me that manipulation is a positive tool. It's fine to influence people when you're sharing information, but manipulation is a different thing altogether. You are using coercion and deception to get people to change their behavior. And it's subjective, as it's based on your individual needs. Enough of this. I'm leaving!"

Rebecca went off to her room, fuming with anger. She could not understand how everyone was comfortable with Matthew's approach, but then she realized this was how Matthew worked. He would get to know someone, identify their weaknesses and strengths, and exploit both. Rebecca avoided being alone with Matthew and stopped attending the night sessions. She had made friends with Aina, a Finnish woman working in health for Pakistan, and she stuck closely to her until the end of the workshop. Matthew noticed that Rebecca had avoided him for the rest of the time in Muree Hills. As they said goodbye, Matthew invited her to dinner at his place on her next trip to Islamabad. Rebecca hoped he would forget that invitation. Now she was worried that he could also be attracted to her, and what the implications of that would be on their subsequent encounter.

When she returned to Peshawar, Rebecca became more involved in sector meetings with Pakistani and Afghan representatives, focusing on health services within the refugee camps and in Afghanistan. It always irked her that the Pakistani male counterparts would shake her hand, but the Afghan counterparts refused. Rebecca hoped to see Ahmad Shah Massoud, the Mujahideen leader, at these meetings, as she had yet to meet him. However, she met Gulbuddin Hekmatyar and a few others. Hekmatyar was an Afghan politician and a suspected drug trafficker. The sessions were always too long and rambling, with more demands being made and both sides, Afghan and Pakistani, complaining they were the wronged party. Rebecca hated these meetings as no one listened, and the emphasis was on making demands and securing commitments. She left the meeting, wrote the minutes, and shared these with Matthew and Nazar.

Rebecca did not enjoy working at her office, as her relations with Nazar and Shahida were strained, and it was obvious that few people liked her, being the only expatriate. Even her secretary never listened to her and worked primarily for Shahida. Shahida was very close to Nazar, dangerously so for a Pakistani woman since Nazar was married. Nazar's wife and children lived in Karachi, his permanent home, where he would retire to. Rebecca was often invited to field trips with Nazar, and Shahida would join them at the last minute. Rebecca wondered if she was a cover for a clandestine relationship between the two. She didn't care as both were superfluous to her mission in Pakistan. She could be polite to them without becoming close to either. However, the power dynamic struck her as being somewhat unfair to Shahida. Did she choose to have a relationship, or was she coerced into it? As a Pakistani woman, it would be impossible for her to marry if people knew that she might be involved with Nazar, and gossip was dangerous.

Rebecca traveled at least once a month within the province, and she frequently went back to DI Khan in the south. During one of her trips to the south, Nazar requested that she visit a village where the chief had requested a water supply system. She was taken directly to his house, which was almost like a fortress. It was a large compound with walls approximately 30 feet in height surrounding the house and compound, featuring barbed wire on top and guards in towers with guns positioned around the perimeter. By now, Rebecca was aware of the abundance of Kalashnikov guns and had seen many since most guards in University Town carried them. Most of the Mujahideen in meetings also carried guns. But witnessing this fortress and the ammunition strewn around the compound was quite intimidating. The village chief invited them to have lunch with him and his wife. Rebecca was unsure where his family was, but she had caught a glimpse of a woman covered in a burka when she entered.

On their way back to Peshawar after the visit, Rebecca asked the driver why the place was fortified and why there were so many guards and guns in the compound.

"The village chief was an officer under President Bhutto. During the riots, which were organized by those who believed that Mr. Bhutto's Pakistan People's Party rigged the March 7 elections in 1977, the village chief fired on a bus full of protestors that was leaving Peshawar to join the riots against the president," he told her.

"About ten people were killed. More than a hundred protesters were killed in total during the bloody crisis. Bhutto gave the order to crack down heavily," he said.

"How awful. But they were only demonstrating. Why would he try to stop them?" she asked.

"Emotions were high at the time. People said that the election of President Bhutto was rigged," the driver told her.

"But why, all these years later, are the families still seeking revenge?" she asked.

"This is the way in Pakistan. It's called vendetta. These disputes can persist for decades, even hundreds of years, between families. For Pashtuns of the North-West frontier, it's part of Pashtunwali, our code of honor. All the affected relatives are still intent on a vendetta against him and his family, even if this occurs several decades later," he told Rebecca.

She said, "That is scary for his wife and children. She can never feel safe and must worry whenever her children leave the compound."

"If they don't kill the old man, they will kill his son or his grandson. It's inevitable," the driver told her. They drove the remainder of the journey in silence.

Rebecca thought to herself that nothing was simple in Pakistan. Politics were complex at all levels, and she felt more unsafe than she ever had in the country.

Chapter 6 · Dinner in Islamabad

Rebecca attended a refugee meeting hosted by her NGO in Islamabad. During the meeting, Matthew seemed distant, so she was happy to keep her distance and engage with government counterparts attending the conference. At the end of the two days, Matthew strolled over to her.

"Where are you staying, Rebecca?"

She replied, "I'm with Aina for a few days, but I intend to return to Peshawar on Friday." She was trying to avoid being invited to the dinner he had mentioned.

"Wonderful. You're invited to dinner tonight with Aina. I have already asked her, and she confirmed. Seven thirty will be fine, and don't bring anything. I have more than enough of everything."

Foiled, she thought. She knew she could not be angry with Aina.

They arrived at seven thirty in the evening at Matthew's house on the outskirts of town near the Margalla Hills. The view was magnificent, with lush greenery and rolling hills set against an orange-red sunset. Matthew's house was large, featuring Pakistani, Afghan, and Turkish rugs, as well as a few carpets from Kashmir. Rebecca was becoming somewhat of an expert on rugs, having acquired her own in Peshawar, so she was excited to examine them and guess which country and region they were from.

She was pleasantly surprised that his house was beautiful, with many artifacts, including intricate Indian tapestries and wooden Hindu carvings. Before moving to Pakistan, Matthew had lived in India for over fifteen years. She wondered if the government had found his resumé problematic to approve due to this connection. The elegant woman from Peshawar that Rebecca had seen at Nazar's office, Dr Diane Beaumont, arrived a few minutes later. She was dressed in a very elegant Western suit, which made Aina and Rebecca appear like a couple of country bumpkins in their cheap shalwar kameez outfits. Rebecca had not changed from her outfit for the workshop, and the creases had now set in. Diane was tall and slim, with well-groomed hair and a touch of makeup. Rebecca never wore makeup in

Pakistan and now seldom ever wears Western clothes.

"Hello, Rebecca!" Diane almost screamed. "Nazar and Matthew have told me so much about you!" She glided over to Rebecca and shook her hand. Rebecca was surprised to see that she was wearing heels, which, again, was something she had never done in Pakistan, as it might have drawn attention to her.

While Matthew walked into the kitchen, Diane breezed over to the drinks cabinet and made herself a whisky on the rocks. Her thick American drawl identified her background as being from the Midwest, specifically Kansas. Matthew returned, sat on the sofa, and beckoned Rebecca to sit beside him. Rebecca looked across at Aina and wanted to join her on the opposite side of the room, but thought it might be considered rude, so she reluctantly sat beside Matthew on the couch. A few minutes later, Ben, the operations manager, joined them.

As Diane spoke with Aina, exchanging health information, Rebecca engaged in small talk with Matthew and Ben. Matthew kept popping off to check on the food in the kitchen, though a Pakistani house assistant was watching over it as it cooked. Rebecca and Ben listened to Diane, talking animatedly on the other side of the room.

"Seriously, I despair of supporting camps with immunization and health services, as supplies and vaccines are always late from Pakistan, and I am always waiting for the Afghan staff," Diane exclaimed.

Diane worked with NGOs inside Afghanistan on cross-border immunization, maternal health, and infant nutrition services. She also discussed her recent trips to Jalalabad and Kandahar across the border, which were undoubtedly precarious due to the presence of landmines scattered throughout the area, including under the roads.

"Rebecca, we must have dinner in Peshawar since we both live in University Town," Diane said.

Rebecca found there was something rather scary about Diane. She didn't wish to get close to this person as a friend. While Matthew was still in the kitchen, Diane moved across the room and sat beside Rebecca.

"I don't know if Matthew told you, but I'm married to a French journalist who is considerably older than me and works for Le Monde. He is presently in Mindanao, the Philippines, studying and traveling with the Moro National Liberation Front, an armed insurgent group fighting for independence," she told her.

If Rebecca felt dull and inadequate before this introduction to Diane, she certainly felt more so now. She wondered why Matthew had also invited Diane to the dinner, as they would hardly become great buddies.

"He travels a lot," Diane said. "He comes here about every four months for a week or so." Rebecca wondered what kind of marriage that was.

Rebecca noticed that Diane stared at Matthew a lot, and her eyes followed him around the room, but she was not surprised. Matthew was the sort of man who expected attention from men and women.

Matthew returned, ushered his staff to bring the plates into the room, and put them on a side table.

As they ate, Matthew pushed himself into a space between Diane and Rebecca and continued talking to her. "So, Rebecca, have you considered what you intend to do after Pakistan?"

"I'll continue in development. Perhaps I might consider shifting to the United Nations," she said. "I'd also like to have more work experience in Africa."

"Interesting. I have plenty of friends in the UN, so I am sure I could help you there," he told her. Of course he did, she thought.

"So, where is home in Maryland?" Matthew asked.

"My parents live in a small town called Monkton, about a forty-minute drive outside Baltimore," she said. "I'm close to my parents and sister, and keep in touch through phone calls. They have a modest house with about four acres of land. My dad is a mechanic who worked for Ford for years."

"I know Monkton," Matthew said. I spent time in Virginia and Maryland a few decades ago, so I am familiar with the area. It's famous for its horses! I love Baltimore. It has lots of character!"

Rebecca could sense that he was interested in something about her. She just wasn't sure what it was. After Diane had finished her meal, she began discussing her work with Matthew and what she needed from him. Rebecca could see he was attentive to her professionally, but not in a personal way.

Diane had her hand on Matthew's knee and leaned in, almost whispering to him. There was a level of intimacy between them, yet he still appeared somewhat distant. Rebecca tried to catch Aina's eye to indicate their departure. She was ready to leave and wanted to keep her distance from Matthew. She wasn't sure why, but she knew it would not be suitable for her to fall under his spell.

"You're leaving so soon?" Matthew appeared concerned. Rebecca wondered if he was genuinely sorry that she was leaving, and she thought he might be.

Yes, I will be leaving for Peshawar early tomorrow morning, so I need to get some sleep," she answered. Aina looked at her suspiciously, knowing she wasn't leaving until the afternoon, and wondered why Rebecca was lying.

As they got into the car, Aina commented, "What an interesting lady Diane was!" Rebecca was silent. She was too busy thinking about Matthew.

Chapter 7 · Precarious Politics in Peshawar

It was August in Peshawar, so the weather was hot and humid, with occasional showers. Rebecca was sitting on the porch outside her house. There was no electricity, and she was drenched. She felt somewhat sorry for herself, as the temperature was 100 degrees Fahrenheit, and there was nowhere to escape the oppressive heat. She was also slightly shaken by the latest developments in the country.

Muhammad Zia-ul-Haq, the president of Pakistan, had just been killed in an aircraft crash in Bahawalpur, about 300 miles south of Islamabad. The American Ambassador, Arnold Raphel, and twenty-eight others died with him upon impact. This was a shock as speculation was that explosives were hidden in a crate of mangoes loaded on the plane. The Pentagon said the robust four-engine aircraft was unlikely to have crashed due to mechanical failure. There was much speculation regarding the cause, and many military leaders living in Peshawar were sure it was sabotage. Rebecca had made friends with some of Pakistan's retired military officers, who were also members of the Rotary Club, supporting immunization and polio eradication efforts. They were convinced that India was involved due to Zia-ul-Haq's support in building the country's nuclear capacity. Rebecca was warned that it might lead to instability in Peshawar since President Zia-ul-Haq had strongly supported the Mujahideen.

The Russians started withdrawing from Afghanistan, leading to more bustling and competition between Afghan groups and NGOs. Following the Soviets' departure, the Mujahideen made considerable advances. They were even able to take and control several cities, but they failed to unseat the Russian-appointed President Najibullah.

One of the leaders who frequently attended high-level meetings in Peshawar was Hekmatyar. The US had been supporting his group, Hezb-e Islami, since the Russian invasion in 1979, and he received more support than any other Afghan leader, including Massoud. He was also heavily supported by the Pakistani government. As the war ended, Hekmatyar used the funds and weapons the CIA and Pakistan intelligence (ISI) provided to establish his organization as one of the leading heroin producers in the region. It doesn't take much imagination to realize how many Afghan and Pakistani organizations based in Peshawar became secretly involved in moving that heroin across the border. In 1979, Hekmatyar took a young Saudi Arabian citizen under his wing who had just graduated, intent on liberating Afghanistan from the 'infidels'. His name was Osama Bin Laden. Rebecca watched Hekmatyar's people move around Peshawar or at meetings. The drivers always knew who they were.

Since they had met in Islamabad, Rebecca occasionally met with Diane for lunch at her request. She often talked about her work in health with the Mujahideen leaders, including Hekmatyar.

"Some of the meetings I attend are borderline dangerous," Diane said. "Despite being a qualified doctor, they do not respect me as a woman. These Afghan leaders expect me to cover my head and only talk to answer their questions," she said. "I am never treated respectfully, and all they ever do is make demands for medical supplies, primarily for their troops and not for their people!" Rebecca was not keen on meeting with Diane, as she found her somewhat intimidating, but she agreed to the lunch meeting out of a sense of duty.

Diane opened Rebecca's eyes further, that this love the Americans had for the Mujahideen in fighting the Russians was very one-sided, and they chose not to recognize the violent and ruthless side of the groups.

"Would you like copies of my reports and summaries?" Diane asked. Rebecca was grateful to have this level of information, as it helped her be more efficient at the Afghan meetings. However, what surprised Rebecca somewhat was the level of detail within the reports. They were far more elaborate than required for health sector information, including the geographic locations of Mujahideen groups across the border, the names of senior officers, and the number of members of each group. Rebecca wondered if Matthew had asked her for this level of detail and why he would have required it. She knew that some of the NGOs that worked cross-border were almost neurotic about providing detailed information in case it was detrimental for the Afghan groups.

In September, the NGO organized a workshop in Peshawar for all principal staff to design the new country program. Rebecca did not wish to stay during the workshop evenings since she wanted to avoid socializing with the Islamabad staff. The workshop at Murree Hills had made her somewhat wary of mingling with some of the female staff, as they frequently asked questions about her personal life. However, after the first day, Rebecca relented and stayed for dinner and drinks with the group in the evening. She briefly spoke with Matthew to update him while he was in a group with a few others. He seemed a little distracted, and she realized he avoided looking her in the eye and gave curt answers. Rebecca dismissed it and made her way home.

The next day, the session started early, and when Matthew entered the room, he looked over at Rebecca a few times. Rebecca sat at one of the circular tables with five or six other staff members. There were about six tables in the room with about thirty staff members. Matthew started his session by discussing the new country program and its goals. Then Rebecca felt strange. She had no idea what was happening, but it was as if there was a direct connection between her and Matthew, and no one else was in the room. Rebecca looked around to see if anyone else noticed, but it seemed no one else had. Matthew glanced over once more and then continued his session. And then he lost his concentration, stumbled over his words, looked over again at Rebecca, and tried to continue. Rebecca was perplexed about why she was feeling such a strong connection. She had not realized until now that she was falling for Matthew. How could that be the case when she knew he was everything she didn't want in a partner? Matthew stopped, looked at Ben, and said he needed to stop for coffee as he was exhausted that morning. Rebecca ran out of the room at full speed to the bathroom. She did not want to talk to anyone, let alone Matthew. When she re-entered the room ten minutes later, she realized Aina had noticed hers and Matthew's reactions to each other, and she was looking at her strangely but supportively. She got up from their table and fetched a glass of water for Rebecca.

Rebecca managed to avoid Matthew for the remainder of the meeting, but their eyes occasionally caught each other. The rumor at the Islamabad office was that Matthew would leave for a promotion sometime next year. Did she want to get involved with someone who would only remain for around six more months when she had a two-year assignment to complete? Rebecca managed to avoid attending any small group meetings with Matthew. She did not want to lose concentration. She decided the best course of action was to pretend that this had never happened.

One day, before the workshop ended, they heard an explosion outside the hotel, and everyone immediately rushed to the window. A bomb had exploded outside the main gate of the hotel. Rebecca looked around the room for Matthew and saw him walking away from the window with a worried expression on his face. Luckily, the explosion was minor, and no one was hurt. The staff were told that Afghan rebel groups had planted the bomb, but no one knew which group was responsible. Decades later, in 2009, the Pearl Continental was damaged considerably when a truck was driven through the back of the building by rebel groups, supposedly to stop US interference in Pakistan.

Chapter 8 · Matthew's Visit to Peshawar

It was late October when Nazar called Rebecca to his office.

"Rebecca, Matthew is coming in this afternoon, and we want you to join us for a meal in town with Shahida."

Rebecca didn't think she could avoid this, and so she agreed. At about two o'clock in the afternoon, Rebecca walked into the room outside Nazar's office and bumped into Matthew. He stared at her and smiled.

"I hope you are joining us for dinner tonight," he said.

"Yes, Matthew. Do I have any choice?" she said somewhat nervously. They stood in the room together, staring at each other, and Matthew smiled. This was the first time after the workshop that they both acknowledged that there was something between them.

"No," he replied.

Matthew was staying at the Greens Hotel, the second largest in town. In the 1970s, it was known as a traveler's hotel and was popular with tourists. Rebecca travelled there with Nazar and Shahida in the office car to collect Matthew for dinner. They ate at an Indian restaurant near the hotel, renowned for its good food. Most of the conversation centered on Nazar's difficulties managing the Pakistani government's expectations. Matthew glanced at Rebecca furtively and then dived back into his discussion with Nazar. Rebecca was relatively silent during the dinner.

As they all walked Matthew back to his hotel, Nazar asked when he was planning to leave Pakistan.

"Most likely December," Matthew replied.

This was a surprise for Rebecca, as she had heard that Matthew was going, but she thought it would be sometime next year and was a little disconcerted.

"Why are you leaving?" Rebecca asked him.

"HQ is transferring me to Africa to head up another office, possibly in Ethiopia," Matthew replied.

"Do you want to leave?" Rebecca asked.

"I don't have much choice," Matthew said. "Too many forces are working against me remaining here."

He did not elaborate. As they reached the hotel, Nazar turned to Matthew and said, "I am escorting Shahida home. Goodbye to both of you." Rebecca's eyes darted to see if another vehicle had been left for her, but she saw none. She decided to accompany Matthew into the hotel. Matthew took her hand as they entered the hotel.

Matthew directed her into the bar through a closed door and to a couch. He then went over to the bartender and called to her.

"I am ordering you a gin and tonic, no? That's what I've seen you with."

Rebecca nodded her head and looked around her. The bar was dark, with rosewood furniture and red upholstered couches. There were a few expatriates sitting at the bar who nodded to Matthew. Rebecca thought she might have seen them at the American club. Matthew returned with her gin and tonic, a whisky for himself, and peanuts.

Rebecca stared him straight in the eyes.

"Why are you interested in me?" She was surprised at her own words, as this was quite forward for her, but by now, it was evident that he was.

"You don't compromise. Your values aren't for sale. I don't think you have ever tried to influence others to change."

"And I thought you said at Murree Hill that it was OK to manipulate others to change their views."

Matthew said, "Views are fine to change, but values aren't. You don't compromise your values."

"Surely there are many people you meet like that."

"No, actually, there aren't. Most people will do what you ask if the price is right."

"Do you compromise yours?" Rebecca asked him.

"Not my core values. Sometimes, for those, I have to influence others."

"So, what's next, Matthew?"

"For me, or for us?" he said to her with a smile.

"For us."

"Why don't we just see how this goes, a day at a time?" he said, finishing his drink and guiding her to the elevator with his hand.

Chapter 9 · Intoxication

Matthew left the next day for Islamabad, but they talked every few days by phone. They were now involved, and Rebecca knew she was completely infatuated with him as she found it difficult to focus on anything else, including her work. Sometimes, she felt like she was walking a few feet off the ground. It was a completely new sensation for her, unlike any other experience she had had in a relationship. Occasionally, however, she would panic somewhat when she considered that Matthew was leaving in December.

Although preoccupied with Matthew, Rebecca prepared for an important field trip to Swat and Chitral, north of NWFP, visiting health clinics and observing maternal health projects. Chitral was among the world's highest regions, located in the Hindu Kush. To get up there, one either drove or flew, and sometimes flights were not advised due to the weather. Despite having excellent pilots, many planes crashed into the Chitral mountains, so Rebecca preferred to travel by road. She loved Chitral and her visits there, as it was ethnically and culturally different from Peshawar. It was one of the country's most beautiful areas, situated at the confluence of the Karakoram Mountain range and the K2 Summit. Perhaps she loved it there since it did not adhere to strict Islamic rules. The valley was a major center of early Buddhism until the seventeenth century, when it became predominantly Muslim. Only the driver and she traveled the eight-hour road to Chitral, stopping in Swat for lunch. They continued on the road for another four hours to Chitral. When they arrived, Rebecca was quite exhausted. They checked into a shabby but clean guesthouse.

She was unable to make any calls from Chitral due to poor reception, so she was unable to contact Matthew. Chitral was situated at an elevation of 5,000 feet and is intensely beautiful, with its snow-capped mountains and dense forests. The Kalasha women of the region typically wore long, black robes, often embroidered with cowrie shells and featuring a red lining, which distinguished them from the general population. In contrast to the surrounding Pakistani culture, the Kalasha did not generally separate men and women or frown upon contact between the sexes. For Rebecca, the major problem was that girls frequently married young, as young as ten years old, and little education was reaching the population to prevent this practice. She spoke to the government staff about halting this and improving women's hygiene practices. In Chitral, menstruating girls and women were sent to live in a 'bashaleni', a village hut, during their periods until they regained their 'purity'. They were also required to give birth in the bashaleni, which was unhygienic and dangerous if any complications arose. The challenges in the north differed from those in the south of the province, but were just as challenging. At least her mind was distracted from thinking about her budding new relationship.

The following week after her return from Chitral, Rebecca drove to Islamabad to see Matthew and to rest after a hectic month of travel and intense work on the Afghan and Pakistan programs. Matthew had made a few visits to Peshawar since they had started seeing each other. It was always low-key, and he would stay at the Greens Hotel. Nazar was always aware of Matthew's movements for security reasons and informed Rebecca so she could meet him at the hotel. Matthew was in his office when she arrived. He hugged her and returned to his desk, beckoning her to sit down.

"I was worried when you didn't call," he said. "Did you bring any security with you when you visited Chitral?"

"No, she replied, why would I?" She didn't understand the question, as she had traveled everywhere in NWFP with just the driver.

"Rebecca, you need to be more careful. I won't be here in another few months or so to give you any protection," he responded.

"They have already selected my replacement. He's a good British candidate and very qualified. Far more qualified than I was, and he will only be undertaking one job, to be an effective Country Director," he said.

Rebecca assumed he meant the replacement would focus only on the Pakistan program rather than Afghanistan. They talked briefly and then left the office to have lunch together. Most of their conversation was around Rebecca's trip to the north, in which Matthew appeared interested. Still, she could already see he was considering other matters as she talked, as he kept looking over at the door as if they would be interrupted. She stayed the night at his house and left the next day to return to Peshawar. She drove back herself along the Grand Trunk Highway, which was a two-and-a-half-hour journey. She had no one in the car with her, as the visit was very low-key since it was unwise for her to stay at Matthew's house alone in Pakistan. Aina was not even aware that she had stayed overnight in Islamabad.

Two weeks later, she drove up to Islamabad with Nazar, Shahida, and others to Matthew's house for his party. He had not answered her calls for the past two weeks, so there had been no interaction between them. First, she went to the office and looked for him, but he was absent. She bumped into Sarita outside his office. Sarita was the Communications Chief, and she had worked with Matthew in New Delhi.

"Hi, Rebecca. Do you want a coffee?" Rebecca knew that Sarita had worked with Matthew in New Delhi, India, and she had noticed at the Murree Hills workshop that she was one of the women infatuated with him.

"Hi, Sarita. Have you seen Matthew? I've been looking for him," she replied.

Sarita sat down slowly and passed a coffee to Rebecca.

"Have you not heard, Rebecca? The Pakistani government requested that Matthew leave the country within five days. He must pack up his house and will most likely be escorted to the airport," she whispered.

"No…?" Rebecca replied, somewhat confused, since she had not heard this information from Matthew or Nazar.

"I have been asked to leave as well, and so have Ben, Yuriko, and Astrid, the head of the Lahore office. We've been asked to pack up our houses and leave within a month. Matthew was given less time," she continued.

"I'm confused…. why is this happening?" Rebecca asked her. She wanted to swear, but not in the Islamabad office in case anyone heard her.

"Matthew said that they think all of us have been spying for the Indian government, including him and me, due to our work in India before coming to Pakistan. I'm unsure why the others were asked to leave, but we all must leave within the next month," Sarita explained.

"Do you have a letter from the government asking for your departure?" Rebecca wasn't sure she believed Sarita.

"Matthew has a copy of the letter, which is confidential. The government informed Matthew of this, so the NGO is handling all our transfers, covering all costs and reassignments. I imagine the letter would damage the NGO if it's released widely since, as you know, some of our staff might leak it to the press," she elaborated.

Rebecca got up from the table and abruptly left Sarita to digest this news. She searched for Aina, whom she could rely upon for the truth. Aina confirmed what Sarita had said.

"It's all very confusing and damaging for the agency," she said.

"But why so sudden?" Rebecca asked her.

"No one knows," Aina told her. "They said in the office it's because the government suspects that Matthew has been passing information to India about the AJK (Azad Jammu and Kashmir) regions, which has to be rubbish. You know that Pakistan can be paranoid about India."

"This is terrible," Rebecca said, mainly thinking about herself and the impact this would have on her.

"Shall we go together to Matthew's leaving party tonight?" Aina asked.

"Yes," she said hesitantly. "Can I stay with you tonight?"

"Yes, of course," Aina replied.

When they arrived, Matthew was sitting with Ben and a few other men, knocking down whiskies. He looked over and caught her eye. She could see his expression, which combined guilt, concern, and fear. For a group that had just become 'persona non grata', they certainly didn't appear to be suffering. The group was cracking jokes, ribbing each other, and generally having an enjoyable time. Rebecca could see that Matthew was avoiding her, and she wasn't sure what to do about it as she didn't wish to attract any attention to their relationship. Aina suggested they leave and have a quiet evening at her home. Aina did not drink, and the party became more raucous as time passed.

Rebecca got up to leave with Aina and exited the house. Matthew came out after her.

"You can't leave yet!" he said.

"Oh, yes, I can," she said. "There is no point in staying. You leave in a few days and didn't even tell me you were going!" she yelled at him.

Matthew came over and put his arms around her, and she didn't resist. Rebecca tried to stop herself, but tears began to well up in her eyes. He kissed her and didn't seem to mind if the other staff saw him. Aina stepped outside to wait in her car. "There is nothing I can do," he said. "I must go. The agency expects me to leave as soon as possible."

"And what about me?" Rebecca cried.

"You knew I was leaving at some point. The government just demanded it much sooner. We could meet in the States before my next assignment?" Matthew said somewhat hesitantly.

"So, we dash around countries for clandestine meetings?" she asked. He was quiet. They kissed again and held each other silently for a long time. She abruptly pulled herself away and ran to Aina's car. She didn't look back as they drove away.

Chapter 10 · Shifts in the Country

Rebecca was depressed after she returned to Pakistan from a few days' leave in Dubai, where she had taken a short break for Christmas. She would have gone to the United States and tried to meet Matthew before his reassignment, but Pan Am Flight 103 came down in Lockerbie, Scotland, in late December, which led to flight cancellations and her changing her plans. Her father, somewhat traumatized by what happened, preferred she return at the end of her assignment when it was safer.

She had talked to her father a few times over Christmas. She did not mention the details of her relationship with Matthew but spoke about the five staff members of the NGO that the Pakistan government had asked to leave the country. Her father was very focused on Rebecca's career and never mentioned marriage or children to her, as if these were not essential goals for her. She called her father on New Year's Day and then explained what had happened in December to the staff members who had been asked to leave the country. Her father paused before he replied.

"Who was the American?" he asked. "The rest were a smoke screen for his exit. There may have been a death threat against him." Her father was razor-sharp and intelligent. She hung up the phone and stepped away into her garden. She was stunned that this had never occurred to her. Then she wondered about the timing. The Russians were withdrawing from Afghanistan, so why would they see any CIA agents as a threat? Perhaps some of the Afghan groups had turned against the Americans and knew that Matthew was passing information back to Washington. Rebecca thought the most likely group may have been Hekmatyar's.

By late 1988, the Soviet withdrawal from Afghanistan was underway, and the US was beginning to scale back its involvement. Some Mujahideen factions, particularly hardline Islamist groups like Hekmatyar's Hezb-e Islami, began to view the US with suspicion.

Many radical fighters believed that the Americans had used them as a tool against the Soviets and would now abandon Afghanistan without helping establish an Islamic government. During the 1980s, thousands of Arab fighters, including members of what would later become Al-Qaeda, had joined the Afghan jihad. These foreign fighters were often more extreme in their ideology and saw the US as another imperialist power like the Soviets.

Rebecca talked to a few people in Peshawar and learned that some radical Islamist groups there saw Western NGOs and aid workers as spies or agents and that there had been quite a few death threats.

Rebecca settled back into her life and work in Peshawar, trying to think as little as possible about Matthew, as it was too painful. She had not returned Matthew's call in February, and he had not tried to call again. She knew he had been assigned to Nigeria as the new head of office and would start there in April. Rebecca decided to cut all communication with Matthew as it was too painful for her to remain in Pakistan and conduct her work when there was little chance of their meeting anytime soon. Rebecca had received a brief letter from him in April, a few months after his attempted call, stating that a position in Nigeria would become vacant shortly and that she should apply, as she was more than qualified. The letter said little else with no terms of affection. Matthew had not used formal channels to send the letter, as obviously, the Human Resources Department could follow up on this and consider it preferential recruitment. She wasn't sure it was a good idea to apply, as it would be challenging to have a relationship under such circumstances, given that they would be in the same office and he would be her supervisor.

Diane left the country in June of that year. After Matthew had left, she never tried to contact Rebecca again and slipped out of the country without anyone noticing her departure. A few months later, a new Afghan office staff member, Dr Akiko, contacted Rebecca and asked if she knew that Diane had been running a bank account at BCCI (Bank of Credit and Commerce International). The bank had contacted Dr. Akiko, assuming she was Diane's successor at the NGO. BCCI asked Akiko if she wished to withdraw the remaining funds from the account, as these were substantial. BCCI was well known for shielding payments to Afghan Mujahideen groups. Rebecca was not surprised, as there had always been something off about Diane.

Rebecca tried to enjoy herself in Peshawar, and she went out with Suzy and John, her New Zealand friend. John asked to rent a room in her house for a while. She knew that John was keen to become involved with her, but she viewed him only as a friend. One night, John took her to dinner, and as she said goodnight to him outside her bedroom, he asked to sleep with her. She decided to allow him, but when they were lying together, Rebecca only permitted him to hug her and not to kiss her or anything further. They slept together all night, fully clothed. The chemistry between John and her changed after that, as he felt rejected and decided to move out of the house a few weeks later. Suzy chastised her as she loved John and thought he was a good match for Rebecca. She knew she wasn't over Matthew, and listening to the lyrics of the singer Tracy Chapman in the evening only made her feel more morose.

"Why, oh why, couldn't you give it a go with John?" Suzy said to her, talking over the song Fast Car by Tracy Chapman.

"I like him, but I'm not attracted to him. Maybe I could be, but Matthew is too recent for me, and I'm not over him!" Rebecca told her.

Suzy added, "John really likes you, and I think he asked to move in here because of that. He likes eccentric women, and let's face it, Rebecca, you're different."

"He needs a more conventional partner. I can't give him what he needs," Rebecca exclaimed over the music.

"You'll regret this, Rebecca. Matthew will never be what you need, and now he's halfway around the world!"

Rebecca ended the conversation by going into the garden to sit by herself.

In September, Jack Hanley, the head of health for the NGO in New York, decided to visit Pakistan and the NWFP, and Rebecca was asked to accompany him on his field visits. Jack was easy company, a laid-back gentleman from the Caribbean who was highly knowledgeable and entertaining. Before he left for Islamabad, they had lunch in town.

"Rebecca, I came to Islamabad for a reason. Our staff there told me how effective you were, and we would like to recruit you to New York as a senior adviser," he said.

"Why me?" Rebecca said. "There must be other good staff to recruit who have been at the agency longer than I have," she said.

"Because you have built up a reputation in a difficult country in a short period," he responded. "Working in New York is not easy. And I think you have the kind of strength to handle it. It's bureaucratic, stifling, disconnected from the field, but if you are persistent, you can move policy and programs a long way," he said. Jack was hardly making it sound attractive, Rebecca thought.

She asked, "can I think about it for a while?"

Jack was not the type to be patient. "Don't ponder for too long, Rebecca. Many people would be very grateful for this position," he responded.

Rebecca was enjoying her life more in Peshawar. She had a good group of friends and interesting work, but she knew she would be ready for a new challenge by the end of the year. She was questioning what had occurred between herself and Matthew, whether it was real, and whether the person she had fallen for was a different character altogether.

Rebecca applied for the position in New York since she knew it would be an interesting challenge. She thought it would take at least six months for the application to go through the necessary channels and for the recruitment to be complete. However, after three months, Rebecca had heard nothing from Jack Hanley regarding the New York position, and she began to wonder if he had changed his mind and was no longer interested in recruiting her. In a moment of weakness, missing Matthew, Rebecca applied for the post in Nigeria. She didn't message him to confirm this as she considered it unprofessional. She determined that fate should take a hand in this and decide whether she should be assigned next to either New York or Lagos. Two months later, Jack rang her in Pakistan.

"Rebecca, why did you apply for the position in Nigeria? Are you no longer interested in coming to New York?" he said in a somewhat frustrated tone. "Now the representative in Nigeria is asking human resources to fast-track your recruitment ahead of the New York position, and he may succeed," he said.

"I am so sorry, Jack. I had not heard from you in over three months, and I was worried I would be left with no position," she weakly argued.

"Well, which post do you want, Rebecca?" he asked.

"Jack, I want to come to New York. I think it would be better for me," she replied.

"Well, you had better contact Human Resources, and I will do my best to push forward on your recruitment. I don't like that Matthew is playing games right now. I know you worked with him, but it's not acceptable for him to try to push his recruitment through the appointments committee first," he complained. Rebecca came off the call feeling both excited and disappointed by Matthew's behavior. She was tempted to let the process take its course, which would likely mean she would end up in Nigeria. However, career-wise, New York was an excellent opportunity, and the post was a grade higher than the one in Nigeria.

Rebecca wrote to Human Resources the following day, requesting that they temporarily hold her application for the Nigeria position. She needed at least two weeks to decide whether to pursue this position. She did not mention her application for the New York position.

In December, she was offered the position in New York and accepted immediately. There was no further message from Matthew. Jack had succeeded in ensuring his recruitment was put forward to the appointments committee before that of Nigeria, and she was set to transfer to the United States.

Chapter 11 · Leaving Peshawar

In a few months, Rebecca would be leaving Pakistan for New York. She was now sharing her office with Zaidi, a tall and thin Pakistani who had been transferred four months ago from the Islamabad office. Rebecca never talked at length with Zaidi. She considered him dangerous and was very wary of sharing information regarding her work or her Afghan counterparts. She knew he was knowledgeable and heavily engaged with the NGO staff in Islamabad.

By now, she was aware that some of the Islamabad and Peshawar country office staff were working with other NGOs within Peshawar, transporting heroin produced across the border, mainly from Hekmatyar's factories, into Pakistan and down to Karachi for shipment. She had no proof of this, but her NGO partners had told her, and the implications were that senior staff were receiving payments for these consignments. Unsurprisingly, drugs were crossing the border since many Mujahideen groups had been producing heroin from the opium grown in Afghanistan to pay for arms. However, it was surprising that staff within her agency were engaged in this, which Rebecca knew was dangerous knowledge.

Zaidi asked Rebecca to join Nazar, Shahida, and him for a meal for Nazar's retirement, and she agreed. He walked over to her desk and offered her some Dalmut, a local snack that he had left for her, which she was happy to partake of, as she loved Asian snacks. She left the packet on her table as she left the room. They all traveled to the restaurant together and had an Afghan meal. That was a little difficult for Rebecca, as she was a vegetarian, and most Afghan meals primarily contained meat. As the meal ended, Rebecca started to feel lightheaded and went to the bathroom. She saw that Zaidi was observing her as she left the table. She looked at her eyes, and Rebecca noticed that her pupils were dilated. She nervously returned to the table and asked Nazar if she could leave the restaurant early to check something at the office. Rebecca could feel herself shivering in the car with fear as the driver took her back to the office. When Rebecca entered her office, she picked up the packet of Dalmut and asked the driver to take her home. She rang Rubina, her Pakistani friend, and asked her to come over.

"Rubina, I don't feel well. My head hurts, my arm is aching, I feel lightheaded, and I think I might have been given something. Could you taste this Dalmut and tell me what you think?"

Rubina took a little of the Dalmut packet and lightly licked it. "This is weird," she said. "It tastes like quinine?" I am calling Dr Akiko at the Afghan office to come over and examine you," she responded.

Dr Akiko arrived within an hour and took Rebecca's temperature and blood pressure.

"Your blood pressure is high, Rebecca, at 150/80. Have you been carrying heavy goods or over-exerting yourself?" she said.

"I must have done," she said. Rebecca's blood pressure was usually 95/60; she suffered from low blood pressure, but she didn't want to discuss her suspicions with Etsuko since it might get back to the office and lead to a confrontation with Zaidi, which she didn't want. She didn't have much time before she was due to leave Pakistan, and she wanted to depart the country safely and unharmed.

"You need to rest for a few days and don't go to work," the doctor said. "You don't need to go to the office anyway. You are leaving soon for the US, so you can do some of your work at home and in a relaxed manner."

Rebecca was stunned. She had been poisoned in her own office, and why? Had they meant to harm her or to warn her not to discuss what she knew about the drugs smuggled across the border when she arrived at headquarters? A week later, Rebecca was informed that a staff member in Islamabad was stabbed to death thirteen times outside his house. The rumor was that it was related to drug operations, as he was no longer useful and knew too much.

Before she left the country, Rebecca took a trip to Mohenjo-daro in the south of the country with a friend from the NGO's new Afghan office. They took a third-class compartment on the train and sat next to some chickens, as there were no other seats. It took them a twenty-hour train ride with little chance of sleep. When they arrived, they found a restroom and took turns sleeping, keeping guard for each other in case they were robbed. It was a fitting trip for her last journey in Pakistan. They did not look too far out of place and wore local clothing that became very dusty and creased after the train journey. Mohenjo-Daro was one of the largest cities in the ancient Indus Valley civilization, developed around 3000 BC. The immensity of history and culture contained in the ruins was overwhelming. During the trip, Rebecca had time to reflect on how dangerous it was for her to stay in Pakistan any longer and how deeply shaken she had been by the poisoning incident. While Pakistan was rich in history, culture, and religion, its other face—marked by corruption and political turmoil—was starkly real and unsettling.

When she returned to Peshawar, she said her goodbyes quickly and left. She was sure she would keep only a few friends from Peshawar or Islamabad.

Chapter 12 · Matthew's Memorial, 2002

Rebecca walked into the church in New York. She was dressed elegantly in a high-quality black suit. She had lost a significant amount of weight since her days in Pakistan. Her hair was lighter with highlights, and she wore her engagement ring and gold earrings. Rebecca prided herself on always dressing elegantly and fashionably at work and for social gatherings. She slipped into one of the pews and sat quietly while others streamed in slowly. Rebecca kept her distance from anyone she recognized in the church, as she no longer worked for the agency.

The memorial was for Matthew O'Connor, who had died of cancer in Cambodia, where he had been assigned after his time in New York. It was a one-hour service featuring speeches by the CEO of the NGO, one of the deputy CEOs, and several staff members who had worked with Matthew. When the Deputy walked back to his pew, he stared directly over at Rebecca, and she saw that he knew there had been a relationship between her and Matthew. She knew the deputy well, having worked with him in New York.

Rebecca had seen Matthew a few times when she worked in New York. In 1992, he had become ill with cancer. She had traveled down to Arkansas, where he had been receiving treatment, and had stayed with him for three days with his girlfriend at the time. She had pleaded with Matthew to return with her to New York so that she could look after him in her apartment in midtown. But she could see that he would not rely on her for support. After his treatment, Matthew moved into an apartment in New York while he convalesced. She visited him to check on his recovery, but they remained only friends. They were distant, and Rebecca never discussed her suspicions regarding his role in Pakistan. Over the past ten years, they had bumped into each other a few times, with Rebecca feeling increasingly disconnected from him with each encounter, until she eventually became indifferent whenever their paths crossed.

Rebecca felt a tear slip down her cheek. She tried to remain collected and aloof. The deputy looked at her once more with empathy. He had regarded Matthew in high esteem.

When the service was over, she discreetly left the church, talking to no one, and passed by the photo of Matthew, taken in his forties at a workshop, with Bach's Brandenburg Concerto Number 2, Andante, playing in the background. This time, she could feel herself breaking into tears, and she ran outside quickly before she collapsed.

Part Five

Egypt (1994–98)

Anna

Mortality

Chapter 1 · Life and Death in Egypt

"Everybody duck!" Manou screamed. A rapid succession of gunfire sounded out. Anna dived down behind the taxi driver's seat. She tried to scramble further down, but there was no more space between her and the front seat. She started praying. Next to her, she heard people praying in English, Persian, and Arabic. Everyone in the taxi was whispering.

A thud of a bullet entered the body of someone in their car. Anna did not see it, but she thought she recognized the sound. It was the type of human sound, a suffocated cry that she had only heard in films, and then, the next second, a second shot, with the same gasp of breath. Then, silence. She had an unshakable sense that whoever had been struck was no longer alive. She just hoped it wasn't the driver or Nicholas, the Italian social development officer, who were both seated in the front seats, with little space for the driver to duck down behind the steering wheel.

"Reverse, reverse, reverse," she murmured, almost as a mantra. She kept repeating it, but how could the driver reverse if he was shot? Was he shot? She kept repeating the words. Six people were in the car, an old Peugeot 504 station wagon with three rows of seats.

A few seconds later, the driver reversed the vehicle and sped back on the road they had just traveled. He initially zigzagged as he tried to avoid the next round of shots. Still in reverse, the car shook and trembled until he swung it around in a two-point turn and pressed on the gas at full speed back on the Luxor Road. Manou, the Country Director of the UN Cooperation Agency in Cairo, was the first to get up. He had crouched down next to Anna. He looked over at Dalia with panic in his eyes, and then at Anna, crouched on the other side.

"Anna's been shot," Manou screamed.

At that point, Anna got up from behind the seat. "No, I'm fine," she surprised herself with how calm her voice sounded. For some unknown reason, she swung around to look behind her. Labib, who had sat directly behind her, was leaning against the window with lifeless eyes. There was a small, red stain on his chest. Anna let a gasp of breath escape from her mouth.

"Nicholas, can you crawl back over our seat and check Labib?" she shouted. She knew that Nicholas was trained in first aid. He climbed over the middle seat to examine Labib. He looked at Anna with a pained expression.

"He's dead, Anna. There is nothing I can do. He must have taken a shot to the heart."

Anna slumped back in her seat, feeling shocked and frightened. It could have been her sitting in Labib's seat. This was all too surreal even to imagine.

"Please check Dalia, then, Nicholas." Anna could tell that Dalia was in shock, and her head was bleeding, but she was fully coherent.

Nicholas examined her head.

"I think she is okay. There is no sign of a bullet," he said.

Anna looked at the car's ceiling, and there were two bullet holes. Dalia was crying quietly; she wasn't sure if she was injured, but she was reassured when she was informed that there were no bullet marks. After a few minutes, they saw a bus traveling towards the terrorists. Manou told the driver to stop and warned the bus to turn around and return to Luxor. Anna told their driver to go straight to the hospital. They stopped at the checkpoint to alert the police and for them to send officers to recover the bodies of their police escort.

Everyone in the car was running on adrenaline and was very shaken when they reached the hospital. As they got out of the car, Anna could feel her legs shaking. She looked around at Nicholas.

"Nicholas, can you help the staff take Labib out of the car?" Somehow, she wanted one of their staff members to accompany him inside as if he were still alive.

Nicholas moved around to the other side of the car to assist the hospital staff in removing Labib from the back. She could see that he was also unsteady on his feet.

The hospital staff took Labib inside on a stretcher and determined he was dead. Later, they informed Manou and Anna that Labib had taken two bullets to the heart. Dalia had been hit by shrapnel from the top of the vehicle as the bullets entered the car, and they treated her wound.

While Anna and Manou were waiting in the office of the head administrator for the hospital, recounting their attack, the police entered the office and asked to interrogate Dalia and Nicholas. By now, Dalia's head had been treated for the cut, and she had been given a sedative. The police would not interrogate Manou and Anna due to their senior positions within a UN agency.

"I will accompany Dalia for the interview," Manou said. "Please, Anna, can you accompany Nicholas?"

Anna thought that was a good idea since the police in Egypt were notorious for conducting heavy interrogations and bullying people into confessions to solve cases quickly. Manou and Anna were also worried about the driver, so they requested that his interview be delayed until Nicholas could accompany him. This process took about two hours, and then they were all escorted back to the administrator's office, where the Chief of Police for Luxor joined them.

The inspector asked, "so, what exactly did you see?" For the second time, Manou and Anna recounted the whole incident.

"What about the police who escorted us? Did you recover their bodies?" Anna asked.

"We don't know if they are dead. We don't think they are," he responded.

Anna was sure this was a lie. They had seen the terrorists open fire on the police car with their Kalashnikovs. There was no way they could have survived that.

"Why were you going to the health clinic?" The inspector asked.

"We were opening a clinic there supported by our agency," Manou responded. "You know the agency we work for!"

Their interrogation by the inspector went on for another hour, and he finally admitted that the four officers of their police escort had all been killed. Anna thought that by now there was no way they could avoid admitting it, and in all likelihood, the press had hounded them for a statement.

By late afternoon, they were allowed to return to the hotel to pack their luggage. As they left the hospital grounds, they saw the police car that had escorted them parked in the front, where it had been towed back from the Qena Road. Anna noted in an almost emotionally detached way that it was riddled with bullets.

All of them were very quiet on the ride back and barely acknowledged the others' presence. Anna felt emotionally drained, and she still felt nervous. She thought she would continue to feel like that until they were out of Luxor. The office had booked tickets back to Cairo late that evening.

Anna thought back to the events of that early morning. She had woken at about 6:00 AM that day in the Luxor hotel. It was light outside, and she could hear the imam in the distance calling for prayer. She had now been in Egypt in her new assignment for two weeks. She had flown down with her supervisor, Manou, the Country Director. Planes in Egypt were efficient and timely, and the flights were full of tourists en route to the ancient city, home to the Tomb of Tutankhamun, the Temple of Hatshepsut, and other prominent ruins.

She had walked outside the hotel that morning to see what kind of day it was. It was hot, around 90 degrees Fahrenheit, and dusty. They would be taking a taxi with a local driver they often hired to open a health clinic that the organization had funded in the district of Qena, about an hour south of Luxor. Yesterday, they had taken Anna to visit the tomb of Tutankhamun on the outskirts of Luxor. As they left the tomb, a girl of about eight ran up to Anna and pushed a blue stone into her hand. The stone was shaped like a scarab and was given to people to protect against evil spirits.

At the breakfast table on the morning of the attack, Manou, who was Iranian, briefly described the town they would visit that day. Qena was a large market town on the River Nile, which was also one of the poorest governorates. Nicholas, the social development officer, and Dalia, a young rural development officer, were to accompany them. Nicholas was of Swiss-Italian descent, over six feet tall, handsome, and intelligent. He had lived in Egypt for at least two years before Anna's arrival. They were then joined by Labib, the photographer, to take pictures of the event. This was her first time meeting Labib, and he was somewhat subdued at the breakfast table, not appearing pleased to have joined them on this trip. Later, Anna was told that Labib had never wanted to join the trip but had been convinced by his supervisor, Nadja.

"Well, Anna, we must make your first visit memorable," Manou said.

"I don't need it to be memorable. Qena is one of the poorest governorates in the country, so we certainly need to be working there," she responded. "I just would like to see some of our work."

"We have done a lot of work regarding health and education. You will be impressed," Manou added.

Anna was rarely impressed after working in development for fifteen years. She hoped to be proven wrong. Manou was a very confident man who had worked for the agency for about twenty years, and nearly all his positions had been as Country Director. He was in his fifties but remained very enthusiastic about everything and was full of boundless energy.

They left the hotel to pick up the car. The idea of taking a local taxi and driver was to lower the risk of being recognized as an expatriate while traveling in the region. A year ago, a bus was attacked on the same road, so it was safer to use an unmarked car to travel in the field. Dalia had used this taxi driver many times over the past few years and trusted him.

Anna was a seasoned international development worker, so she was used to traveling in risky areas and had little fear on this day. However, she remembered that it had taken her at least ten seconds to decide where she would sit in the Peugeot station wagon with its three rows of seats. It wasn't like her to worry about such matters, but as the new deputy director, she thought she should be more concerned with protocol issues. Manou sat in the second row, and Dalia got in beside him. Labib sat in the back row, and Nicholas sat in the front seat beside the driver. Anna was a bit disconcerted that she was being forced to decide to sit in the back row with Labib, the photographer. After what appeared to her to be quite a considerable time deciding, she thought Dalia would have to squeeze up so she could sit in the second row with Manou. She didn't know Labib well enough to sit beside him. Anna got into the car's second row, and they drove away. Her seat was quite comfortable, so she sat back and perused some papers regarding the project site they were visiting.

About fifteen minutes outside Luxor, on Qena Road, the taxi stopped to share the passenger's details with the police checkpoint. Dalia got out of the car to share their details with them. There were two guards at the checkpoint. Dalia returned to the car.

"They wish to send a police car with us to accompany us to Qena," she said.

"OK," Manou replied. "But tell them to drive ahead and not behind us," he said.

Dalia returned to the car on Manou's side, and Manou shuffled beside Anna. Anna continued to read her papers as they moved off slowly. The police car, accompanied by four guards, drove ahead of their vehicle, but Anna noticed they were only traveling at about 15 to 20 miles per hour, which seemed excessively slow for an armed escort. A checkpoint was ahead, where the police stopped. The guards at the checkpoint wore turbans and walked up to the police carrying what Anna recognized as Kalashnikovs. They talked for about two minutes, and the police got back in their vehicle and drove on with their station wagon following closely.

"We are too close to the police car. Can you please drop back?" Anna shouted to the driver. Manou looked at Anna, not understanding why she had asked for this.

"If we hit a pothole or anything, we are at risk of slamming into their car," Anna said to him.

The driver agreed and pulled back a little. Anna felt a little strange. Ahead, they could see the police car slowing down for what appeared to be another checkpoint.

This time, three to four men left the side of the road, carrying Kalashnikovs, and started firing on the police car in rapid gunfire. The driver stopped abruptly, about 30 feet behind the police car. Anna could see up ahead that the police were not firing back from within the vehicle. She guessed that it was too quick for them to respond. Or was it just that it was unexpected for them? Why had they slowed down? She had frozen at that point before Manou shouted and aroused her from her state of shock, and she ducked down behind the front seat.

She couldn't believe that she hadn't been shot.

When they returned to the Luxor Hotel from the hospital, Manou, Nicholas, and Anna sat in the reception for a while and stared blankly while Dalia went to her room to rest. Anna wanted to order a strong drink to calm her nerves, but she would wait until she reached her room. She was in a Muslim country, and drinking publicly was not condoned for women. Anna walked slowly to her room, wondering if the shooting had happened, as it felt so unreal. After entering her room, she opened the minibar and reached for the small bottle of whisky. She poured it into one of the glasses on the dresser and retrieved some ice from the fridge. Anna sat on her bed for a few minutes and drank it down quickly. She didn't want to think for too long about what happened, but she was desperate to leave the hotel and Luxor as soon as possible. She packed her bags and went downstairs.

Tickets had been booked by the office for all of them to leave on a 7:00 PM flight to Cairo, but Manou decided they would only go if Labib's body could accompany them on the same plane. They made their way to the airport by taxi, and after they cleared check-in, they sat in the airport reception and waited for the police inspector to inform them that Labib's remains were cleared to board the plane. About thirty minutes before departure, they were told the body was being taken directly onto the plane. They quickly collected their things and prepared to board. Before they went, they instructed their driver to come to Cairo as soon as possible and report to their office. Both Manou and Anna were worried about him and did not trust the police in Luxor to try to interrogate him further or to pin part of the blame for the attack on him. They owed him their lives, and they needed to protect him.

On the plane, Anna sat beside Nicholas, who was also in shock but proceeded to relate anecdotes of his escapades in Egypt throughout the flight.

"Well, Anna, welcome to Egypt! Not the best way to welcome you, eh? I think Manou thinks you are courageous! Did I tell you about his brother? I invited the Swiss Ambassador to dinner, and his brother was playing footsies with her under the table. The problem is that I think the Ambassador was enjoying it," Nicholas said in his strong Italian accent.

"She is very nice and often comes to my place in downtown Cairo. Next time I have dinner, I'd better invite her husband to supervise her," he laughed.

Did Nicholas think that she was in the mood for this? On the other hand, this saved her from having to discuss the attack with him. He didn't seem to want to talk about it either.

Anna looked down and was stunned to realize that her blouse was stained with Labib's blood. She was surprised that she hadn't noticed this at the hospital or hotel. She was too paralyzed to walk to the bathroom and remove it. As she reached into her pocket, she felt Labib's tie, which they had taken off when Nicholas had examined him. Anna sat back, closed her eyes, and pretended to sleep in case Nicholas started up once again on his stories. She felt a tear slide down the side of her face.

They arrived in Cairo just over one hour later. They were escorted off the plane by airport staff before the other passengers and taken to the side where Labib's coffin would be removed. Nadja was there to greet them. She was the chief of communications for the agency, and it was apparent that she had been crying. She hugged everyone and then walked over to the airport staff to wait for the coffin to be unloaded. Nadja was in her late forties, a seasoned communications and media professional, and she had already managed the press that had been incessantly contacting the office for details of the attack. Anna had had no opportunity to meet Nadja before departing for Luxor and Qena, but she was impressed with her skills in managing their arrival at the airport and her handling of the press.

Nadja told everyone they would drive directly to Labib's house to meet with his family, as she had already been there earlier to tell his wife of her husband's death. After the body was loaded onto the vehicle and everyone had their luggage, they drove the forty minutes to Labib's house in Heliopolis, a suburb of Cairo. Labib's wife opened the door, and Manou, Anna, and Nicholas entered and sat down. Labib's wife had been crying but was remarkably calm and gracious in greeting them. His two children entered the room. Anna noticed that both were most probably under ten years of age. They had been informed of their father's death, but it was apparent that they had not grasped the gravity of this news. Anna could not help but stare at the children and feel an overwhelming sense of their loss. Due to a senseless attack only hours ago, they would suffer for the rest of their lives. She tried to conceal her tears, but they were now running down her face. If she had decided to sit in the back row of the car, then it would have been she who was killed. Now these poor children would grow up without their father. She couldn't say anything to his wife and was silent throughout the conversation led by Manou and Nadja. They left the house an hour later, very subdued and exhausted.

Anna was driven to the hotel in Zamalek, where she checked in and went straight to her room. She went to the porch and walked outside for a moment into the courtyard. Again, she considered why she had taken such an unusually long time deciding where to sit in that car. The implications of this decision hit her hard. She then went back inside and locked the door. She collapsed on the bed but could hardly rest before receiving a call.

"Hi, Anna. Are you OK?" It was Ted, the acting head of Human Resources in New York. "What happened?"

Oh no, Anna thought, I can't go through this again. By now, she wondered if the attack had even happened and whether it was all her imagination. Except Ted, on the other end of the phone, was asking her about it.

"Everyone is worried about you," Ted said. "You are lucky that all of you are alive. It could have easily gone the other way." Anna was already aware of this. She didn't need to be reminded, but it was bad enough that five people had died, including the police officers.

"We are arranging for a consultant to contact you all shortly for post-traumatic stress counselling," Ted stated. "We need to send someone quickly to Egypt. Do you want me to contact your parents?"

"No, Ted," she stressed. She wasn't even sure she would tell her parents until a few weeks later, since they would be so nervous. She rarely told them whenever she was in danger since they would worry terribly. A year ago, she had been in Herat, Afghanistan, on a mission, and she had told them she was in India.

"Well, you need some rest now," he said. "Please tell us if you need any time off, and I will talk to Manou."

She put down the phone and ordered room service: soup, fish, and a chocolate dessert, which was delivered within ten minutes.

Anna tried to sleep for a while, but she no longer felt sleepy, so she got up and made herself a cup of tea with the kettle in her room. She turned on the TV. The Euro News channel was on. A few minutes later, a headline lit up across the screen.

"Five UN staff members were attacked in a car near Luxor. Five people were killed, including a UN staff member and four police escorts."

The map portrayed the location of the incident. Anna stared at the screen... this was too surreal. She hoped this wasn't being reported in the UK newspapers at the same time. She was too tired to call her parents, but she would ring them early the next day. She turned off the TV and fell asleep almost immediately.

Anna got up at 5:00 AM the next day and remembered what she had just survived the day before. She wasn't hungry, so she prepared a black coffee in her room. She wore a mauve suit, a white blouse, and a scarf around her neck. She wanted to dress in dark colors in respect of Labib's death, but she didn't have a black suit. She selected a pair of black shoes with small heels and left for the hotel reception, as her pickup vehicle was scheduled to arrive around 7:00 AM. It was a twenty-minute drive to the office, and upon her arrival, she found only the drivers and a few administrative staff members. They appeared somewhat surprised to see her. Did they assume she would be resting with smelling salts at the hotel?

Anna walked briskly to her office, sat down, and read her mail. There was a letter from her close friend Sheila waiting for her. Sheila had worked with Anna in Watford, outside of London, for a few years before Anna decided to work overseas, and she had remained a close friend. She opened the letter quickly and read it. Sheila's cancer had recurred and had metastasized to the brain. She had been given only one year to live. Anna dropped the letter on her desk.

For the next few months, as Anna was adjusting to living in Egypt, she would continually relive the terrorist attack in her mind. It troubled her deeply that if they had taken one different step, they all would have lost their lives in the car. She realized that she was becoming somewhat obsessed with replaying the scenario in her mind. The agency arranged a few sessions with a PTSD specialist, but that didn't really help. Anna decided the best method was to put it out of her mind and continue as normal. She thought it strange that the agency didn't suggest that she transfer to another country, but in many ways, she didn't want to leave. She wanted to tackle what she had experienced and move past it. She was also feeling some depression concerning the fate of her friend in the UK, who was dying. Life seemed so unfair at times, and yet, here she was, alive, due to good karma that day.

Anna eventually settled into her life in Cairo. She had found a wonderful apartment in Zamalek with views of the Nile. The building must have been about 250 years old, with an old-fashioned elevator that moved up to her fourth-floor apartment very slowly and with a creaking sound. Anna managed to find a taxi driver to take her to work each day and pick her up in the evenings, which worked well as she knew that driving in Cairo was like taking your life in your hands. Due to the incident, Anna constantly changed the time she left the house, just in case... However, since the attack, her nerves had been affected. She was on edge whenever she heard a noise or anything out of the ordinary. Her experience had obviously frayed her nerves.

Anna had been fascinated by Egypt since she visited the British Museum as a twelve-year-old. She was intrigued by the Rosetta Stone, the key that unlocked ancient Egyptian hieroglyphs, which remains one of the museum's most famous objects. One summer, her mother had taken her to the New Museum in Berlin, where she had seen the bust of Nefertiti. The sculpture was about 19 inches high, and its form and colors Anna had considered wonderful. Nefertiti was the wife of King Akhenaten and one of the most fascinating women of ancient Egypt. Akhenaten was known as 'the heretic king'. He married Nefertiti when she was thirteen years old during the first three years of his reign. The bust was exquisite, and it motivated Anna to draw the sculpture. She was not interested in art; she rarely drew or painted and had decided not to pursue it as a study, instead opting for the sciences. However, she was compelled to draw this image. Since then, she had never forgotten the intrigues and complexities of ancient Egypt.

Since arriving in Cairo, Anna had frequently visited the Egyptian

Museum, which housed thousands of artefacts. The museum was always fascinating, as it contained so many pieces in excellent condition that it was possible to stand in one spot and rotate to see incredible artifacts in all directions. This was quite a contrast to the British Museum, with its well-organized layout, fewer artifacts, and detailed descriptions for each. She preferred this rambling and packed display with scant descriptions of items. In the museum was an unfinished bust of Nefertiti, an incredible likeness to the one she saw on display in London. At stressful times, Anna would retreat to the museum to ponder and reflect. For her, it was more effective than any of the post-traumatic stress sessions organized by the office.

Anna also loved walking the streets of Cairo and milling through the bazaars. In the 1990s, moving around as a woman was still relatively easy, and one was not expected to wear a chador that covered one's head and face. She often went to the museums or the bazaars by herself and stopped for coffee after shopping. Anna fell in love with Egyptian jewelry, particularly items that copied the designs of the Pharaonic period. A shop in Zamalek was owned by Azza Fahmy, who mixed Egyptian and medieval designs to create unique pieces. When Anna wore these pieces, she admired how they reflected the artistry and symbolism of ancient Egyptian culture, contemplating the thousands of years of history they embodied.

It took a lot of work to escape Cairo, as it was such a sprawling city. However, despite what she had gone through, it never diminished her awe for the country's history and archaeology. She frequently visited the pyramids at Giza or the step pyramid of Djoser, where tourists flocked in large numbers. She was often accosted by young children seeking money or selling unwanted goods, but she tried not to give them money since many were forced on the streets to beg by either their parents or an agent. The worst was when children begged on the streets, coming up to cars, seeking money. Many of the children were disabled, as they were more likely to receive funds. She knew that if she gave money, she was perpetuating the cycle of them being forced onto the streets to beg. Cairo was a dichotomy of expensive plush hotels against streets filled with poor people begging or selling small goods. It was rapidly prospering, but inequality was worsening.

Chapter 2 · Anna's Special Mentor

After a month in Cairo, Manou introduced Anna to Aida, a regal lady of around seventy-five years of age. Aida was not tall, about five feet. Still, she appeared very formidable. Anna was unsure whether Aida would accept her in her position as deputy director, given that she was only in her mid-thirties. Anna needn't have worried. Aida was a champion of women, determined to give any woman in a senior position her support and confidence. Colleagues at the office informed her that Aida was close to Mrs. Mubarak, who relied upon her for advice regarding development projects.

Aida invited Anna to join her for a field visit to an urban slum development project in Cairo, which the First Lady also supported, focused on providing small loans to low-income families. The First Lady, whose husband gave her a wide rein in domestic policy, championed causes such as women's empowerment and preventing harmful practices such as female circumcision. Anna was aware of her husband's critics but liked the First Lady. She behaved fairly and supported women from modest backgrounds in professional positions.

"So, Anna, what do you think of our project?" Aida said.

"It's a good project," Anna replied. "But there are so many people living in slums in Cairo. Is there any plan to expand it?"

"Funds are always the issue, Anna. You are correct that the number of people benefiting from the project is insufficient. We need to expand to additional areas," Aida responded.

"Well, you don't have to do everything yourself. Other projects and the government can use this model for expansion elsewhere. Your NGO can be engaged in training and sharing skills that you have learned and applied successfully," Anna added.

Aida invited Anna to her apartment for a drink with Manou the following week. She had a small apartment over the Nile in Zamalek. It was very comfortable but not ostentatious.

"Well, Anna, how do you enjoy working with Manou?" Aida asked her.

Anna tensed up slightly as she found it difficult working with Manou. She liked him as a person, but he was an unconventional manager, and if he wanted to pursue an idea, he didn't care how it was done.

"It's interesting and Manou is very dedicated." Anna furtively looked at him as she gave her answer. Aida laughed at her answer.

"Well, Anna, I couldn't have put it better if I'd tried." Aida laughed as Manou looked at her with a questioning look that indicated he wanted to ask her what she meant, but decided against it.

"Well, if you two ladies don't mind, I think I will go back to the office for a few more hours' work," he said.

It was already 6:30 PM, and that was part of Anna's concerns with Manou. He would work all hours at the office, but most of that time was spent in conversation with staff rather than in productive work.

After Manou had left, Aida sat back down with her drink and looked over at Anna.

"Some things are within your control, while others aren't. Learn to make peace with the latter so they don't hold you back in your career." With that, Aida changed the subject and talked about her early career at the UN, which Anna was very interested in hearing about.

"I worked in the UN for over thirty years in senior positions, including Regional Director in Nairobi and Geneva. The most significant lesson I learned was to always retain a sense of humor, even under the most difficult of circumstances. I never felt pressured to behave in a way that was expected of a man. I was always proud to be a senior professional woman in the UN. And never worry about the opinion of others, only those that you hold in high esteem," Aida told her.

After that first visit, Aida took Anna under her wing and mentored her professionally. Anna made a monthly ritual of visiting Aida for Manhattans, as Aida indeed mixed the best she had ever tasted. Even in New York, they were never as good as Aida's.

One day, she went over to Aida's early in the day.

"Hello, Anna. This is early for you. Is there anything wrong?" Aida asked her.

"I need your advice, Aida. Manou has complained that I am too harsh on the staff and need to be more compromising. But it's challenging because so much is unregulated in the office. Projects are passed if Manou likes them, and an assessment is seldom made to ensure they are cost-effective or sustainable. Most of the staff go directly to him if they want project approvals, and he always agrees. I admire his skills most of the time, as he is an excellent diplomat, and the government listens carefully to him. I am sorry to burden you, but I need an objective opinion," Anna said.

"Anna, most of the staff you supervise are women, no?" Aida responded.

"Yes, they are, and most of them are older than I am. I respect them, but they are very persistent," Anna said.

"Welcome to Egypt, Anna! Never underestimate the women. They are some of the strongest women you will ever meet. Every time you question one of their projects, I am sure they go directly to Manou's office complaining about how difficult you are," Aida stated.

"Well, yes. Sometimes, I have passed back a proposal for correction, and it is returned to me under my closed door for approval, late in the evening, with little changes made," Anna said.

"Manou is the Director. His job is to schmooze the government and keep everyone happy. He wants a happy office. That's his nature. On the other hand, you want an efficient, honest program that delivers results," Aida explained.

"So, how do I balance this?"

"First, you need to get those ladies on your side. They need to recognize your value. It would help if you could discuss your views with them further to balance your needs with theirs, while ensuring the agency's needs are also met. I imagine Manou has had his way for quite a few decades, but you mustn't be labelled at this point in your career as difficult," Aida responded. Anna thought back to Aida's message to her on her first visit, to focus on the things that she could change.

"I think I am already there... but I see your point," Anna said. "I have suggested that we undertake joint field visits to get to know each other better."

"If the staff sees your value, they won't mind the criticism if it adds value to the work. Most of those ladies are dedicated to their mission," Aida said. "I agree with that. Few people in the office don't work diligently," Anna added.

"Do you want to be a UN bureaucrat, or do you want to be someone who's known for achieving results? Don't be perceived as someone only concerned with dotting the i's and crossing the t's and adhering to rules. From what I have seen of you, you have your own considerable skills. Come out from behind Manou's demands and inspire the staff with your knowledge and direction. You will be a director yourself one day, so start leading now," Aida said. Anna pondered this. Manou was considerably older and her supervisor, so she had acquiesced to his program direction to a considerable extent. Perhaps it was time to consider the role she wished to play in Egypt carefully.

"There is one woman in your office, though you should be more careful with her," Aida told her. Now Anna was curious as she suspected who this was, but she needed Aida to confirm.

"Your operations officer, Marwa. She is older than the others and more complex." Anna wondered what she meant by complex, but this was undoubtedly the woman whom she had considered the most difficult.

"You don't need to do anything, just be aware of what she does," Aida said, no more about Marwa, and closed that part of the conversation as they discussed lighter topics over their Manhattans.

Chapter 3 · The Artist

Nicholas became Anna's closest friend in the office. He helped her understand Manou's perspective on work issues and assisted her in navigating some of the more challenging relationships with the local staff. Everyone loved him for his sense of humor, joie de vivre, and exuberant personality. Nicholas was a fun companion, and going to dinner with him was always a wonderful new adventure. They would go to some place downtown that Anna had never been to, offering excellent cuisine and the most awful Egyptian wine, which he had made them order, as it was far cheaper than purchasing French or Italian options.

Nicholas had a small apartment on the second floor of a distinguished but deteriorating building in the heart of the old city. After a few months of living in Egypt, Nicholas invited Anna to dinner at his place. When she arrived at the building, she discovered that there was no elevator, so she walked up the rather old and worn staircase to his apartment. As Nicholas let her in, she noticed that the hall walls were painted a rather garish red, which was surprising since he usually had such exquisite taste. As she walked into his lounge, she saw a mural painted on the wall.

"Who painted this, Nicholas?"

"I did. This is my real love and hobby," he replied. "Right now, I am painting a mural at the house of the UN Secretary-General, Boutros Boutros-Ghali, but his wife keeps wanting me to add items, Anna. It's driving me crazy!" Nicholas could be pretty dramatic at times, Anna thought.

The painting on the wall primarily depicted forests, flowers, and buildings. Nicholas had spent most of his youth in Italy, as his mother had died when he was very young. He had been raised in a very eclectic and artistic upbringing surrounded by artists and actors, unlike his brothers, who had remained on the farm near Geneva and went straight into agriculture.

"Why do you work in development then?" she asked.

"It pays the bills," he responded. "It's difficult to become known as an artist. I had an exhibition in New York. Lots of people came, and I didn't sell a thing."

His work was quite detailed and beautiful. Moreover, Nicholas was also talented as a social scientist, and he helped Anna gain a better understanding of Manou and Middle Eastern culture. In another life, Nicholas might have belonged to the Middle East, for he related to its people more intuitively than Anna and embraced the rhythm of life with a fluency she struggled to attain.

They took Arabic classes together, but during the sessions, Nicholas drew cartoons that made Anna laugh, and she seldom learned anything. Anna would have fallen hard and fast for Nicholas, but she suspected from rumors within the office that he was either gay or bisexual, and the complexity of becoming involved with him would not have brought her much joy. Nicholas mentioned a woman who was a close friend based in New York, but he never talked much about her, and Anna did not prod him. She, however, did confide in him regarding her past loves, and he was most opinionated in his responses on her poor choices. Once, after a few glasses of wine, Anna tried to kiss Nicholas, and he gently pushed her away, telling her how much he liked her, but he didn't want a physical relationship. Wonderfully, it never affected their relationship, and they remained close.

Nicholas gave Anna the most exquisite presents for her birthdays and Christmas. He gave her a tapestry from former Zaire, which was hundreds of years old, and she had no idea how he had obtained it. He often gave her Egyptian jewelry from Azza Fahmy's shop and other locally obtained items. His generosity was boundless. It was Nicholas who helped her develop a great love of Egypt despite the challenging start to her assignment. Some of the most entertaining times with Nicholas were at Manou's home, where he often invited them for dinner. Most of the office staff loved Nicholas as he was never angry; he always told interesting stories and never allowed anyone to be distressed in his presence. He was far more popular than Anna, but she never felt threatened by him, and he made it clear to everyone that he supported her professionally.

Sometimes, though, Nicholas drove her crazy. She invited two friends from the Italian embassy to her apartment for dinner. Nicholas was to join them and cook the meal. The idea was that he would arrive an hour earlier to prepare everything since he was an excellent cook. At about eight o'clock in the evening, there was no sign of Nicholas. The doorbell rang, and the guests were at the door, with Nicholas behind them. Anna let the two Italians into the apartment and angrily closed the door on Nicholas. She left him outside for five minutes before she eventually let him inside.

"You said you would be here at seven! Now the guests are here and no meal!" Anna told him as she ushered him into the kitchen.

"Malesh, Anna! They don't care as long as they have a glass of wine in their hand. Did you give them any, Anna, or have you left them sitting in the lounge in misery?" he asked her.

"I will plonk a bottle in front of them, but now I need to help you produce a meal in ten minutes!"

Anna left the room with a bottle of St Emilion to bring to her guests and then regretted that she hadn't bought a bottle of Barolo, considering that Nicholas was cooking Italian pasta with sauce. She left her guests with the bottle and went back to the kitchen. When she entered, she found that nearly every pot and pan in the kitchen was being used as he prepared the meal. Nicholas was almost prima donna-like as he shouted directions to Anna for ingredients, utensils, and plates. She wasn't sure if she should whack him with the frying pan or pass it to him.

Anna told Nicholas she was taking annual leave the next week to visit her friend Sheila in the UK, who was dying of cancer.

"Anna, always remember. It's a privilege to be with someone who is dying," he told her. She remembered that during her last visit with Sheila in Oxfordshire. Anna was amazed that she never complained about why she should get cancer at thirty-seven. Her only regret was that she would not see her five-year-old son, Owen, grow up. Anna knew that she would never see Sheila again after she left, and it struck her that since her assignment to Egypt, this was the first time that death was confronting her so abruptly.

One day, Nicholas and Anna took a boat ride on the Nile with a friend of his from Florence.

"Anna, you know I lost my mother when I was ten. My father raised my two brothers and me. Being raised in an all-male household wasn't very nice.

My father was very tough. He was a farmer. He died a few years ago. He left the farm to my oldest brother, but he did share some of the proceeds with my other brother and me. I never wanted to work on the farm, so that was no loss," he said.

"That's tough, Nicholas. You strike me as the least likely person to be raised on a farm! My father was also raised on a farm and ran away from it as soon as possible," Anna told him.

"When I was in my twenties, I wanted to end my life, so I went to a forest a distance from my home and walked for hours and then fell asleep under a tree. When I awoke, I looked over and saw my mother's shadow under a tree with a bright white light around her. It remained there for about ten minutes before it disappeared," he recounted.

"You are very spiritual, Nicholas, so I am not surprised you experienced that," Anna told him.

"I always felt abandoned by her. But of course, it wasn't her fault," he said.

At some point, Anna hoped Nicholas would leave development and pursue his passion for art, as he was immensely talented. Years later, she learned that a writer based in New York had used Nicholas's work to illustrate a series of children's books. She assumed she was the woman Nicholas had mentioned.

Two years after Anna had arrived in Egypt, Nicholas caught a severe infection from a mosquito bite. Anna wanted to go over to see him, but she was about to start a training course.

"Nicholas, you need to see a doctor. Let me come over this afternoon, and I will see if you need anything."

"Don't worry, Anna. Try to concentrate on the training." Anna talked to his friend, Sami, who said Nicholas would be fine. It was just a minor infection.

The training absorbed most of her time until eight o'clock that evening. She rang Nicholas soon after, but a man she didn't recognize answered the phone.

"How is he? Shall I come around?" she asked. "No point," he replied. "He is sleeping, and I doubt he will wake up this evening."

At four o'clock in the morning, Anna was suddenly awakened by the sun's warmth streaming into her apartment and nearly scorching the bedsheets. This was the first time it had been so intense, enough to wake her up. She felt very peaceful, though, and so she dozed off again until she rose at seven o'clock.

Anna went over to the Nile Hilton Hotel, where the meeting was being held.

"Have you heard, Anna?" she asked as she entered the hotel, one of the staff rushing over to her in the reception, her face raw from crying. Anna was still a little tired after her early morning wake-up and needed at least two more cups of coffee to be wide awake. However, she woke up quickly when she saw how upset she was, and how red her eyes were.

"Nicholas was taken to the hospital in the early morning hours and died around 3:00 AM of septicemia. They say it was dengue fever that led to the septicemia."

Anna was utterly stunned and didn't respond. She walked back to lean against the wall and stared straight ahead of her at the hotel fountain. When she had talked to him early the previous day, he was coherent. He had not seemed like he was near death. She asked to be driven to the hospital. When she arrived, she asked if she could see his body. She felt very numb and hardly said a word to the other staff member who accompanied her. She couldn't believe he had passed and wanted to be sure.

Nicholas was very pale as his dead body lay on a white sheet in the hospital's morgue. Anna was stunned at the sight of him, as he seemed alien to her, unlike her close friend and confidant. He should not have died. He was still young. All life had passed from his body, which was now cold to the touch, reminding her of Labib's death in Luxor. Again, Anna was struck by the fact that Egypt had forced her to confront death as she had never had to before.

At the funeral, Anna ensured sunflowers, one of Nicholas's favorite flowers, were placed on his coffin. The church was packed with staff and friends. It was unreal to believe that he had passed, and she felt his presence with her for a long time.

Chapter 4 · An Angry Irishman

After Nicholas's death, Anna became almost mechanical in her work within the office. And there were many problems. Although Manou was honest, his management style was weak. A significant issue was that he could not control the manipulative Operations Manager. Marwa was an Egyptian who had headed up operations in the Cairo office for over a decade. However, her management style involved gathering sufficient information on staff members to control them, using a personalized file in which she compiled all the information she could use against each of them. Anna had never met or worked with anyone quite like Marwa, who was in her fifties and was married to a senior police officer. It was rumored that Anna's predecessor, Dorothy, had left Egypt after receiving an indirect death threat from Marwa.

"Four policemen died because of your visit to Luxor and Qena. They left wives and children," Marwa said to Anna. Anna thought that there were no words of sympathy for Labib's wife and children, nor was there any sympathy for Anna and the others, who still suffered PTSD from their involvement in this incident. It was a strange and cruel statement to make after the attack. She had complained to Manou, but he was almost scared of Marwa and told her to ignore it.

In late 1997, Eamonn, an Irish auditor, arrived to conduct the country audit. Anna had never seen him in New York and assumed he must be new to the department. Eamonn and Anna were sitting in her office in Cairo around her meeting table.

"Hi Anna, I have heard a lot about you from staff in New York. They all seem to think that you are good," Eamonn said.

"That statement sounds like you don't believe it," Anna responded. Eamonn changed the subject. "I have gone through the files in detail, and it appears some of your national officers have engaged in some real messes and compromised their positions." He slowly related this to her as if he were pronouncing a death sentence upon them.

"You have only been in the country for one week, so it is virtually impossible that you could have reviewed all the files and discovered such damning evidence of wrongdoing," she very sharply responded to him.

"After my review, I am convinced that most senior Egyptian women working for the agency should be sacked as they are all 'furthering their crusades' rather than the goals of the organization," he firmly stated.

Anna looked at Eamonn, shocked at his words. What about the men? Abrahim, the Health Officer, worked at the TV studios as a morning host each week, but no mention was made of his extracurricular activities. Anna knew that all the information had come directly from Marwa. She collected her thoughts to avoid overreacting.

"Eamonn, this is concerning. However, it would be best if you documented these cases so I can talk to the staff member concerned. I will stand by my staff until you provide direct evidence of inappropriate transactions."

"One of your officers, Hanaa, is heavily engaged with a national NGO outside the office. She is on their board of directors, and her mother is the agency's CEO. You have been providing funding to the organization," Eamonn lectured.

"That funding was provided before my assignment started. I am sure you know how reputable the organization is, and the CEO is a member of the Committee on the Elimination of Discrimination against Women (CEDAW)," Anna related to him.

"The issue is that Hanaa is on its board of directors, and that is against the rules, if payments are being made," he emphasized.

Anna knew this was prohibited, and approval had to be sought for any membership on a board of directors before engagement. This was another example of Manou's rather sloppy management style, as he approved the NGO's payments, but that wasn't most likely the fault of her officer, Hanaa.

"Eamonn, Hanaa raised the issue with me, so she obtained the necessary approval from Manou and New York last week on the understanding that she would resign from the board of directors of that NGO immediately," Anna told him.

Hanaa oversaw women and gender projects within the country agency.

She was at least ten years older than Anna, as were many women in the office. She was formidable, incredibly talented, and one of the hardest workers Anna had ever encountered. Most of the time, they performed well together; however, initially, it was a rocky start. Over time, Anna adapted her style to become more consultative and supportive. Aida had enlightened her in developing a far better management style than she had when she arrived in the country.

One of the issues that Hanaa championed was the elimination of female genital mutilation (FGM). Those who practiced FGM in Egypt believed it to be a 'good tradition' in that it controlled both female sexuality and enhanced fertility. Instead, it negatively affected women's reproductive and psychological health. Estimates indicated that seventy to eighty percent of Egyptian women had been circumcised. The high figures were mainly due to the class divisions in Egyptian society.

Furthermore, some prominent Islamists asserted that FGM was an Islamic practice. When Anna learned of the statistics, she had difficulty believing the number of women who were circumcised, and she often wondered how many women in the office might have been affected. It was such a traumatic experience to undergo at the age of ten or eleven, to be physically held down by other women while the cutting was carried out, usually by a traditional midwife. The whole idea that this was used to control a woman's sexuality was vilely abhorrent to Anna.

The second case that Eamonn was investigating was more complex. One of the most impressive programs was the community schools project. This was managed through the education department, supported by the private sector and local communities, which provided the premises for the schools to operate. Heba was a dedicated and brilliant officer who oversaw the project. Anna had had plenty of clashes with Heba on her arrival, and the faults were on both sides. However, if there were a few impressive projects she had visited, this was one of them. Establishing such a project, where village schools were created to reach the poorest children within communities, especially girls, was a significant challenge in Egypt, and Heba had successfully made it happen. Anna had visited at least ten community schools in Qena, Asyut, and Sohag, Upper Egypt, and the outreach in these impoverished areas was impressive. What was also very impressive was that the Ministry of Education, at the central and sub-national levels, owned and managed the project.

"Well, Anna, the community school project is rife with problems," he said. Anna was by now rather bored of Eamonn's complaints and started fidgeting with papers on her desk. "There was a problem with selecting the private sector company," he said.

Anna then became more alert. "What is the issue in the selection?" she asked.

"Well, only two companies were considered, and the one selected was only one person with a history of working with Heba as a consultant rather than a company," he said.

After the rather tedious meeting with Eamonn, Anna decided to conduct her research on this matter rather than go to Heba, as she knew she could be hot-headed and might speak directly to the auditor before Anna had a chance to review and clear this matter. Anna was sure of one thing in her time in Egypt: the women were far more impressive than the men. Heba worked all hours, rarely rested, and had put her heart into establishing the project over the past eight years. However, as with all the Egyptian women Anna supervised, woe betide you if you stood in their way. She learned that careful negotiation was always the best way forward. She collected numerous references outside the agency for the consultant concerned and obtained a letter of recommendation from the government after conferring with Heba.

Eamonn had come to Egypt with a mission to "clean up the office". However, it had taken its toll. Anna was exhausted from working fifteen-hour days at the office for two months straight and felt little appreciation for this effort.

"Well, Anna, it was either you or me who was going to lose on this one," he said, at the small leaving party arranged by Manou.

"What do you mean?" Anna asked him.

"I was informed that this office was in a mess by New York, but I think you'd cleaned up most of it by the time I arrived." He looked over at Manou on the other side of the room. "He's a lovely guy. I'm glad you were able to do that." Eamonn made no further comments and went over to Manou to say goodbye.

Anna was surprised by Eamonn's comments as she didn't expect any praise from him. She noticed, though, that Eamonn left without bidding farewell to Marwa.

Chapter 5 · Shifts and Changes

Anna had now been living in Egypt for two and a half years. Manou retired at the end of 1997, and Anna was both relieved and sorrowful. She had learned a lot from him regarding working with ministers and senior-level government officials. Manou would sit, joke, and gossip with ministers for an hour, and then deliver the punch line to lobby strongly on behalf of poor communities, as poverty was a severe problem in the South. As much as his lack of discipline wore her down, she knew of his tremendous force and power in achieving formidable results regarding the agency's work in Egypt. Anna knew that sometimes she had been a thorn in Manou's side, but he also appreciated the discipline she had brought to the program.

Theresa, the new Director, arrived in the country a month after Manou departed. However, since the UN Coordinator had been asked to leave simultaneously, Theresa was requested to take on this role immediately upon her arrival. She invited Anna to take over daily management of their agency as Officer-in-Charge (OIC). Theresa and Manou had arranged with support from HQ for the Operations Manager, Marwa, to be transferred to a regional office in Nairobi. Anna could not quite grasp how they would move such a difficult officer to a key office. This was a classic example of shifting the problem. It reminded her of the statement made by one of her former bosses: "If you perform poorly, Anna, you will be promoted very rapidly." Most UN bureaucrats opted to shift the problem rather than dismiss the officer concerned due to the ramifications of a possible legal case.

After a few meetings with Theresa, Anna was sure their working relationship would be tense. This was her first assignment as country director. Anna thought it was most unwise of her to accept the role of UN Coordinator, as she would not have time to adapt to the country and grasp the office's issues, given that the UN role would consume most of her time and attention. Anna was indeed correct regarding Theresa having no time for the Egypt country office. However, she needn't have worried about the office as complete responsibility was placed upon herself. With Marwa having left, Anna took on the role of country OIC and was now responsible for operations management. Anna had few friends in Cairo with whom she could relax after work. Aside from Aida, it was unwise to have social relations with people at the office, and since the death of Nicholas, there were few in whom she could confide. Abrahim, the Health Officer, was a good friend, but she knew better than to get too close to a national officer, where the lines between professional and personal could quickly blur.

Anna traveled to the Aswan district in the south with the Maternal Health Officer and Abrahim for a one-week trip visiting projects. Most major cities in Egypt were beside the Nile, and towns were spread out on both sides of the river. In the 1970s, two dams were constructed at Aswan to control seasonal flooding and provide water for agriculture. The dam was one of Gamal Abdel Nasser's most outstanding achievements. Egypt built the Aswan High Dam to enhance its agricultural production and power supply.

It was scorching hot at 105 degrees Fahrenheit. They registered at the rather run-down guest house with poor air conditioning, but Anna didn't mind staying at run-down hotels or guest houses if she was on the road. She ended up editing papers until 3:00 AM. Then she heard the sound of shots in the distance. Anna scrambled off the bed onto the ground and waited, her heart beating violently. There were no further sounds, but Anna slept on the floor all night. The next day, she asked what the sounds had been. "Only a wedding," Abrahim said, observing Anna's nervousness. Anna realized she still had PTSD, even after three years, but she didn't want Abrahim to see how much the shots had disturbed her.

They visited the rural development projects and some of the health posts. Maternal health was a real challenge since there were insufficient trained midwives for deliveries. The local midwives were unqualified for complicated deliveries, and they were also responsible for female genital mutilation. Anna knew that they had credibility in the villages and were trusted by the elders, which was a serious problem. Getting to villages when there were complications in delivering was also a challenge. Obtaining transportation to villages could be difficult, and invariably, by the time the woman was transferred to the health facility, it was too late for the clinic or hospital to save her or the infant.

At the end of the week, Abrahim and Anna decided to take a half-day trip to Abu Simbel. They went by boat from Aswan to the temple on the western side of Lake Nasser. The temple was built during the time of Rameses II (c. 1279–1213 BC), who undertook an extensive building program throughout Egypt and Nubia.[15] This magnificent monument risked destruction as the reservoir lake resulting from the Aswan Dam was set to flood it. Egypt asked UNESCO for help to safeguard its Nubian heritage. UNESCO took up the challenge and activated a spectacular rescue operation. They convened top experts—hydrologists, engineers, archaeologists, architects—who devised a radical plan: the temple would be dismantled, moved to higher ground, and reassembled. The result was spectacular, as the ancient temple was successfully melded with new engineering technology to ensure its survival despite the dam. It was one of the most amazing archaeological sites that Anna had ever seen, and she was enthralled to learn that Patricia Kennedy had sought support from UNESCO to preserve the monument after visiting the site with the president.

As Abrahim and Anna walked together, Abrahim said, "Anna, you have been here for a long while and are highly regarded in the country. I often wondered why you stayed here after the attack."

"Well, I often wonder that myself. Headquarters didn't give me any other option. I could have asked, but I was concerned it would be perceived as a sign of weakness," she answered. "I love Egypt. I am glad I had this opportunity. But of course, if I had known what would happen that day, I would never have come! I didn't think this country was high risk, as I have been in far more difficult places like DR Congo and never experienced such a threat. There had never been such a threat to UN staff before our incident. Who knows how many more there will be now? Our vehicle was targeted that day as they knew a UN convoy was traveling to Qena, and the militants were angry with Mubarak and his government. Of course, now

15 Nubia was one of the oldest civilizations in the world. Its history is often intertwined with Egypt to the north. They were sedentary agriculturalists, traded with the Egyptians and exported gold.

we know that it was an attack by Al-Qaeda, initiated most likely by al-Zawahiri, who was living in northern Sudan at the time with the leader of the group, Osama Bin Laden," she related, avoiding answering Abrahim's question as to why she had stayed.

"Yes, well, Al-Qaeda recruits young Egyptians from Upper Egypt—from Qena, Aswan, and Sohag—since those areas are underdeveloped. Of course, the government has fallen short in providing development assistance, so the terrorists support the families and recruit their young boys in exchange," Abrahim explained. "The staff respected that you stayed. They all consider you quite formidable."

Anna knew why she had stayed. In her life, she had never given up on any task or job, and for her to do so would have been a sign of weakness. She could have asked for a transfer, and no doubt they would have given it to her, but she wanted to demonstrate her strength to the organization. Anna didn't know how to admit when she was beaten down, and this country had certainly done that to her.

Chapter 6 · A Visit from Headquarters

It was March 1998, and Anna had been in Egypt for three years. HQ decided to send their security adviser to Cairo for one week. The Country Director, Theresa, requested his visit to understand security issues better. At about six o'clock in the evening, Mark Scott knocked on the door of Anna's office and entered without waiting for a response.

"Hi Anna, sorry to disturb you at this time, but Theresa said you were still working here, and we won't be disturbed this way," he said.

"Well, it's a bit late, and I was going to leave in a few minutes."

"This won't take long. I wanted to ask you a few questions regarding the attack you encountered a few years ago in Luxor," Mark asked.

Anna knew that Mark had only worked for the organization for one year. Before this, he had worked for the Pentagon.

"Can you recount precisely what happened that day in as much detail as possible?" he asked Anna.

Anna thought to herself, oh no, here we go again. She had compartmentalized the incident very carefully in a locked chamber within her mind, and now, she was being asked to take it out again! She told Mark everything she could remember in more detail than she had even provided at the hospital after the attack. She was rather irritated that three years later, she was being asked to recount this attack once again.

"I could so easily not be here today if I had decided to sit at the back of the car," Anna told Mark.

"Why do you think your car was targeted?" he asked her.

"Well, I suspect it was because we were UN staff, and this incident occurred immediately after the International Conference on Population and Development, during which the president clamped down heavily on security throughout the country," she answered.

"But how was only Labib killed? Why weren't more people shot in the car? There must have been a sharpshooter aiming at your vehicle, firing through the roof to kill him. The shots could not have come from the people firing at the police vehicle, since the bullet holes were in the roof of the car. If a marksman were targeting your vehicle, then they may have been aiming to kill only one person. The shooter was most likely positioned in a tree by the road. He wasn't firing to kill the driver, or the windscreen would have been shot out," Mark elaborated. Anna became more alert as she listened to Mark, and she wondered how he knew so many details.

"But then why kill the police in the escort car?" she asked Mark.

"Collateral damage..." he answered her.

Anna wasn't sure what Mark was implying. Was he alluding to the fact that she had been the target? Why would she be targeted? And if Mark was as knowledgeable as he most likely was, he was already aware that Anna was no CIA agent...

"Do you think I was the target or Manou?" she asked him.

Mark paused before he responded quietly. "I think that you were the target, Anna. You had only been in the country for two weeks. Maybe they had been passed information concerning you," he told her.

"Well, Mark. With your background, I am sure you are aware that my ability as a spy would be sorely lacking," she laughed as she responded.

"You were brave to stay," Mark told her as he ended their conversation and bid her farewell. That night in her apartment, Anna thought carefully about what Mark had said. It had taken her three years to get to a safer place after the attack, but now she was unnerved by this conversation and felt herself threatened again.

Chapter 7 · Walking on Quicksand

When Anna returned home that day, she had a glass of wine. She knew that she was drinking more in Egypt than she should. She would often have half a bottle of wine in the evening by herself. This, for Anna, was a problem, as she had contracted hepatitis early in her career, and her liver was not as strong as it should have been. Even two glasses of wine were too much. She sat in her lounge and looked at the boats passing on the Nile. This at least calmed her. She contemplated all the work she needed to address at the office in the coming week.

After taking the taxi to her office one day, it struck her how dusty the road was, with the sounds of heavy traffic on the main road, horns blasting, taxis running in and out of traffic, and the imam calling to prayer. She had become used to all these sounds, but today, for some reason, they stood out to her.

Anna entered the building and walked up the stairs. Before she ascended, she greeted the security staff and the admin officer on the ground floor. The security officer greeted her and swiftly looked in her bag. Anna became increasingly tense as she climbed the stairs, unsure why. Badra, Anna's secretary, greeted her as she entered her office at the end of the corridor.

"Good morning, Anna. You look a little pale. Are you alright?" Badra called out to her.

"I'm fine—I just got back late from the field trip yesterday," she answered.

"Theresa wishes to see you in her office as soon as possible. Shall I make you a cup of coffee?" Badra asked her.

"Badra, you are a star! I will go over there when the coffee is ready! What would I do without you?" Anna smiled at Badra and hugged her.

Anna walked down the corridor to Theresa's office, greeted her secretary, and entered the Director's room.

"Sit down, Anna. How are you? You look a little tired," Theresa commented.

Anna tried not to display her exasperation at another comment on her appearance.

"I am fine, Theresa. I was a little tired after the field trip. You do remember that I was in the field for one week," Anna stated sarcastically.

Theresa had been relieved of her duties as Resident Coordinator the previous week. She had applied for the post, but it had been awarded to a man who had worked within the UN system for decades.

Theresa displayed an expression of pained concern, somewhat transparently false.

"Anna, I have received some news from the UN Security Coordinator that there is a death threat against you. I don't have any details, and he promised to investigate the matter and inform me," she told Anna.

Anna froze and stared at Theresa. "Where does this information come from? This is right out of the blue. Why would I be a target of a death threat? I have been here now for three years after the terrorist attack. If they wished to target me, would they not have done so before now?" she tensely responded.

"As I said, Anna, I don't have the details. The security staff were concerned, so they brought the matter to my attention. Considering this, you should start making plans to leave Egypt. It will take at least six months to find another position, so starting now is probably a good idea," Theresa told her.

Anna shuffled in her seat, looking increasingly uncomfortable, her eyes fixed suspiciously on Theresa.

"I think I should apply for a new position. This also allows you the opportunity to settle into your role as Director. You've been responsible for overseeing all UN activities in Egypt, so time was limited to focus on our office. But now you can allocate a hundred percent of your time to here," she responded, again with sarcasm in her voice. She wasn't sure she believed Theresa, and she was also thinking back to her conversation with Mark.

"Have you thought about taking time off? What about applying for another master's degree or taking a year at home in the UK? The Kennedy School at Harvard offers a one-year degree course. Why don't you apply?" Theresa asked Anna.

Anna wasn't sure she wanted to step out of the agency at this point in her career. Anna also knew that Harvard applications were highly competitive, and her chance of acceptance was probably only ten percent unless her agency sponsored her. She thought that Theresa wanted her out of this office as soon as possible. Was she threatened by her?

"Do you think the agency would sponsor me? That would make it far easier," Anna responded.

"I doubt that, Anna. Priority is given to more senior staff seeking further qualifications," she answered.

She answered Theresa in a louder voice: "Theresa, I understand your concerns. I will initiate the process of seeking a new position. However, let me be clear. I have been overburdened with work since you arrived. I have had to carry two jobs, operations and programs. Now, I understand you want your office back. Bearing this in mind, I will gradually pass over all operational matters to you, continue with programs, and start preparing for my exit."

Theresa shifted around in her chair.

"Please don't take this personally, Anna. You have had a heavy workload in Egypt, mainly due to my predecessor's shortfalls. It would be best if you were prepared to leave for your own good," Theresa responded.

Anna looked at Theresa, and her expression made it clear that she did not believe the last sentence. She wondered if Theresa was threatening her. Anna rose from her chair.

"Theresa, thank you for this recommendation. I will take the necessary action," Anna replied.

Anna marched back to her office, closed the door, and burst into tears. She felt that all her hard work in Egypt had not been appreciated or recognized.

Over the next month, Anna decided to apply to Harvard. However, she was not optimistic about her chances. She was unsure whether she had applied for senior positions, and if she had, whether she would even be considered, given that her reference from Theresa might not be so strong. She took the examination required for postgraduate studies at the US Information Center in Cairo after taking home practice tests from a manual she found in a bookstore. At the exam, she was surrounded by young Egyptians in their twenties applying for graduate school. She took the test with three sections: analytics, quantitative, and verbal reasoning. Anna was surprised when her marks were displayed at the end of the test on the screen, showing scores over 600 for all three categories. She was aware that to be admitted to Harvard, all scores needed to be above 600.

Anna spent Christmas at home in the UK and frequently became angry for no reason, losing her temper with her parents and siblings. She decided to take a week's holiday in the US and visited the Kennedy School at Harvard. Anna knew then that this was her answer. She needed time away from her organization and time to think about her future. Perhaps she would not remain in development, but she knew she desperately needed this time out or her career would derail.

Two weeks later, Anna flew back to Cairo. One afternoon back at the office, Abrahim walked straight into her office without asking Badra. He appeared somewhat nervous and tense.

"I am sorry, Anna, but your moods are affecting me. You are always tense and angry. I can't seem to do anything right. I am doing my best in polio elimination efforts in Egypt, but you don't seem to think that I am. I have complained to the Director and to the WHO," Abrahim told her.

Anna looked surprised and felt like she had been kicked in the stomach. She did not expect this conversation and had thought Abrahim was coming to brief her on program developments. She had considered Abrahim a good friend.

"Abrahim, I have just returned from the UK and the States! I always have questions about programs; you know this about me. I don't think our recent conversations have changed from our regular ones. Why would you complain to the Director and to the WHO?" she asked him.

"Anna, you've been very tense, and it always comes across. You're irritable, question our actions, and lose your temper," Abrahim responded.

"I have never lost my temper with you. I understand that you may perceive me as tense—my workload has been heavy, and I am tired. I apologize if I have brought this into my work." However, Abrahim was not listening to Anna and was nervously shifting around in his seat.

"It's not good enough, Anna. I can't take it any longer. I can't work with you any longer."

Anna was silent and shocked. She wondered if Theresa had incited Abrahim to criticize her in such a manner. Anna was beginning to feel that everyone in the office was turning against her.

"Abrahim, if you feel that way, I understand. However, I ask that you discuss these matters with me rather than with external agencies, such as the WHO. This is internal. I know you are speaking to our director, but we must be careful in discussing such issues with partners," she replied.

"There! This is another example of you trying to control everything. Nick from the WHO is a friend of mine. I am entitled to talk to him and say anything that I wish!" Abrahim got up, pushed his chair away, and stormed out of the room.

Anna sat staring at her desk, not quite sure what had just happened. After ten minutes, she packed her briefcase, walked out of her office, and descended the stairs. She got into her taxi, which was waiting outside. Her taxi driver, Sami, greeted her as always, having now worked with her for three years.

"Are we going home, Ma'am?" he asked her.

"Yes, Sami. Please drive as fast as possible," Anna told him.

Anna was tense and needed to get home and calm herself with a drink as soon as possible.

"Please go faster, Sami. Going left would have been far more direct," she instructed him.

Anna leaned forward in her seat and sighed deeply in the back of the taxi. She started frowning at Sami's slow progress through heavily built-up traffic.

"Sami, this is terrible. This route is not the best, as traffic is so slow. There is no excuse," she shouted.

"Enough! I am trying my best!" Sami responded.

But Anna could not stop displaying her frustration with Sami. She made more exasperated sounds as she expressed her frustration.

"At last! Now, we are making some progress!" Anna replied.

"I am sorry, Ma'am," Sami stated morosely.

Eventually, Sami pulled up to the apartment. He looked sad and disappointed.

"Ma'am, do you want me to come tomorrow morning?" Sami asked her.

"No, thank you, Sami. I will make my own way to the office this week," Anna told him.

This was the first time Anna had not asked Sami to pick her up. But she couldn't shake herself out of her dismal and angry mood. Anna went to the elevator and pressed the button for the fourth floor. After pouring herself a glass of wine, she closed the door, sat on the couch, and stared at the wall for at least thirty minutes without emotion, feeling numb. Sami stopped coming to pick her up in the mornings and evenings, and she never saw him again before she left Egypt, despite her attempts to contact him through the office. He told her assistant that he preferred to work elsewhere as he could earn more.

A few months later, Anna was sitting in her office. She was on a call to Headquarters in New York. They had placed her on hold for thirty minutes, and now she was about to talk to Timothy, the Deputy Director of Human Resources.

"Hi Anna, how are you doing?" the Deputy Director asked her. "It must be pretty stressful there."

Anna had no idea why he would make such a statement out of the blue. Even before she asked her question, she was aware of the tension in his voice. Anna was already irritated. No small talk, she decided, and just went straight to the question.

"You know I applied to the Kennedy School. I don't know if I will be accepted, but will the agency allow me to take a year off, and will they pay my fees?" she asked him.

"I understand your situation, Anna. However, we think you should take a three-month stress management training course instead and then take a less challenging position at Headquarters. Your Director, Theresa, is concerned regarding your ability to cope with stress. She feels you must handle yourself better within the office and work more collegially with your direct supervisees," he responded very matter-of-factly.

She paused for a moment before she responded.

"So, the thing is, Tim, the harder you work, the more stressed you become.

The more stressed you are, the more likely you are to become a problem to the organization. I would have been better advised to leave straight after the terrorist attack to return to New York at that time. I probably could have returned at my professional level rather than take a demotion.... if you knew I was stressed, why didn't you move me from here three years ago?" she asked him.

"I hear you, Anna. I understand. Look, I've only recently come into Headquarters myself. If you get accepted at Harvard, talk to me then. Otherwise, please seriously consider this option," Tim responded.

Anna left the office at midday as she saw no point in staying when her conversation with Tim had stressed her, and she decided to work from her apartment. On the way home, Anna stopped her cab at the bazaar of Khan el-Khalili[16] and walked through the narrow streets filled with stalls selling food, jewelry, baskets, antiques, and souvenirs. The bazaar dated back to the fourteenth century, with its old architecture, stone-gated entrances, and cobbled pavements. She found El Fashawy, an old coffee shop in the heart of the bazaar and entered. She remembered the times she had come here with Nicholas. She tried to think about what would come next for her. People stared at her, a woman alone. She sat, drank her coffee, and had a pastry. She tried to think about how to get through this difficult time.

A week later, Anna entered her apartment after meeting with Theresa at the office, who was pressing for her to leave in July. Her cat did not come to greet her as usual. Anna went into the kitchen and saw that she had left the window open. Anna leaned out of the window. She went back into the room and called the cat's name repeatedly. Her voice became louder and more frantic as she called his name. She looked out the window again. She was sure the cat had jumped out the window, as she never left it open. She collapsed on the floor and cried. In her mind, she had lost everything: her job, her apartment, her remaining friends in Egypt, and now her cat... She couldn't stop crying.

The doorbell rang. It was her landlady, Nadia.

16 Khan el-Khalili is a famous bazaar in the historic center of Cairo, Egypt. Established as a center of trade in the Mamluk era and named for one of its several historic caravanserais, the bazaar district has since become one of Cairo's main attractions for tourists and Egyptians alike.

"Anna, your cat is on the stairs on the 2nd floor. I would have carried him to you, but he bites violently," Nadia informed her.

"Nadia, oh, thank you so much. Please wait here, and we can have coffee. I will go and get him," Anna responded.

Anna ran down the stairs and saw the cat trying to decide whether to continue down or retreat up. She grabbed him quickly and returned to the apartment.

"Nadia, thank you so much. I was sure he had jumped out the window. I feel so attached to him since I raised him here as a kitten," she cried.

"Anna, why are you crying? You look so upset. Is this only about the cat?" Nadia asked her.

Anna started crying again.

"Nadia, I am afraid I will have to leave Cairo in July as my office wishes to transfer me back to New York. I am so sorry, as I have loved living in this apartment, and you have been a wonderful landlady," Anna said.

"It can't just be that alone making you so unhappy." Nadia came and placed a hand on Anna's shoulder.

"All my efforts until now in my career have been in vain. I didn't do this work solely for my career. I love working in development. But I haven't enjoyed these past few years. I feel so burnt out and unappreciated," Anna told her.

"Anna, listen to me. Egypt is a wonderful country, but it is not where you should wish to remain. Things are becoming far more difficult here with the growth of the Muslim Brotherhood. Soon, it will be difficult for women to go out without wearing a head covering. Fundamentalism is creeping in gradually," Nadia informed her.

"I know you're right, Nadia. I know my time in Egypt is coming to an end, but I wish it could have been a happy exit instead of feeling like my time here has been wasted. I know that I've contributed a lot here, but my career in development is over," Anna cried.

"Wait before you make those kinds of decisions. Give yourself time after you leave Egypt. Rest and enjoy your friends in the UK and the US. Life is short, Anna, and you're still young. Please try to enjoy your life more. It would be best if you found a good partner and married," Nadia replied.

"That is the last thing on my mind, but thanks for cheering me up," Anna laughed.

Nadia passed the mail to Anna. There was a letter from Harvard. She opened it quickly, tearing the envelope violently. She scanned it and looked up at Nadia.

"Nadia, I have been accepted to the master's in public administration course at the Kennedy School at Harvard," she shouted.

She read extracts of the letter to Nadia:

> *Faced with many more talented and highly qualified candidates than it has room to admit, the Admissions Committee has taken great care to choose individuals who present extraordinary academic, extracurricular, and personal strengths. In making each admission decision, the Committee keeps in mind that the excellence of Harvard depends most of all on the talent and promise of the people assembled here, particularly our students. In voting to offer you admission, the Committee has demonstrated its firm conviction that you will make significant contributions during your year and beyond.*

Anna and Nadia hugged and cried again, but this time with tears of joy. They could hear the cat meowing insistently for food. After Nadia left, Anna read the letter at least three more times. She couldn't believe she had been accepted, as her confidence was at an all-time low. She read again that Harvard thought she had "extraordinary talents and strengths". For the first time in ages, Anna was starting to feel appreciated and felt perhaps she was on the path back to regaining her confidence and strength.

Chapter 8 · Packing to Leave

After a month of fighting with Theresa and Human Resources, everyone agreed that Anna should attend the master's course at Harvard. However, the agency would not pay for the course but would offer three months' leave with pay. Anna had three months of leave available that she could add, so she decided to make it work financially.

Anna looked at the men packing up the furniture at the apartment. It had already been five hours, and only half of her furniture and goods had been packed. She had performed this task too many times. It was always emotional and so final.

Upon arrival, Anna was always excited to receive her shipment and feel more at home in her new country. It always helped her to become more settled. However, packing up was such a solemn task. She was glad to leave Egypt, but the process was painful. The packing was a manifestation of the end of her life here in Egypt.

Nadia approached the apartment to see how far along Anna was in her packing.

"I will miss you, Anna. I am giving you a small table and a painting. Both are quite old, and I am sure you will treasure them," Nadia told her.

"Nadia, that is so generous of you. I will make sure they are both packed immediately. At this stage, I always feel like I'm being packed into boxes, as if I'm being divided into hundreds of small pieces… I created a life here in Egypt, and although this was undoubtedly my most challenging assignment, it was also the most fascinating country in which to live," Anna said.

"You're sad now, and yes, you will miss Egypt, but it's time to leave, Anna. You look exhausted, have lost weight, and you never have time for anything except your work," Nadia told her.

"Nadia, you're right. I must learn to balance my work and personal life! Studying will be good for me as it will allow me to slow down and think about my priorities," she responded.

"I hope you will come back to Egypt to visit. There are many places you have yet to see!" Nadia wistfully said.

Anna thought to herself that she was pretty sure she had visited most places in Egypt. Nadia returned downstairs.

Anna packed the cat into a special crate for collection and transportation to the United States. She looked around again at all her belongings, which would be put into storage for a year while she studied. She realized she had no idea where the boxes would arrive next and where the next chapter of her life would start after completing her master's degree. This ritual of packing and unpacking was no longer a physical exercise she undertook. It was an emotional rollercoaster that symbolized a new life in a foreign environment, a different culture, and the adoption of new customs and habits, as she molded her character to adapt, almost creating a new persona for each new country. Who would put themselves through that process again and again?

Anna arrived at the office after saying goodbye to Aida. She was very sad because she was sure she would probably never see her again. She walked into Badra's office and embraced her.

"Anna, I will miss you," Badra said. "I have worked for many bosses in Egypt. You are one of the few people I have seen make a real difference in this country through your work. You really care."

Hanaa and Najwa embraced Anna, expressing their emotion upon her leaving.

"Anna, I will miss you. You must be one of the best bosses I have ever had. You always supported us regardless of the pain you got from those above. You really care about the country," Hanaa told her.

Theresa entered the room, and everyone fell silent. She gave a short speech thanking Anna for her efforts and wishing her well on her journey. Anna looked for Abrahim, but he was not there to say goodbye. She briefly thanked everyone, carried her presents to the taxi, and left the office, thanking the administrative staff profusely for their support. Anna did not look back, and a smile crept onto her lips.

Chapter 9 · New York, 2007

Anna emerged from a meeting with the Deputy Executive Director in New York. As Program Deputy Director, she had been asked to lead the development of a new medium-term development plan. Her secretary, Candice, entered the room.

"Anna, Abrahim in Cairo called for you while you met with the Deputy Executive Director," Candice told her.

Anna looked puzzled and wondered why Abrahim had called her. She had not heard from him since she left Egypt, so she called him back immediately.

"Abrahim, how are you? It's been a long time! Nearly ten years!" she exclaimed.

"Anna, Aida has passed away in Cairo. I know you would want to be informed. You talked about returning to Cairo for her funeral," Abrahim said.

Anna felt very sad. She was silent for a while before answering Abraham.

"Thanks, Abrahim. I'll consider whether I can return for her funeral, but it's unlikely. However, I will write a short speech that can be read at her funeral."

Abrahim and Anna made some polite small talk. Candice came to the door to remind her that she was due in a meeting in five minutes.

"Goodbye, Abrahim. Do keep in touch," Anna politely told him.

Anna put down the phone and recalled her time in Egypt, the immense stress she had felt living there. She wanted to attend Aida's funeral, but she knew she would not. She sat and pondered for a few minutes how hard her time had been in Egypt. She walked over to the wall where Nicholas's painting was hung, touched it, and then left her office for a meeting with the Executive Director.

Part Six

United States (2000–2005)

Geeta

Ambition

Chapter 1 · Making Career Decisions

Geeta stood in the elevator of the agency's high-tower building on 45th Street in mid-town Manhattan. Her chest clenched more with every floor she passed on the way up. She readjusted her name tag, "Senior Officer for health management." It had come loose in the eighteen months she had been on the job.

Being called to the Executive Director's office this morning without having coffee seemed jarring. On the 13th floor, Geeta stepped out. Deborah's office door was open, and Geeta gently knocked and stepped through.

Deborah bent her head over a pile of papers. She only looked up briefly and gestured for Geeta to sit. She sat down, catching a whiff of coffee from the staff kitchen. She waited. A few seconds later, Deborah looked up, put her pen aside, and stood up.

"Good morning, Geeta," she said politely. "How are you?"

Before Geeta could answer, Deborah went on.

"I want to express my gratitude for the work you are doing in health. Your support for the development of the new AIDS Section was stellar. Your list of achievements is impressive, including your work on polio eradication and support for the Global Alliance for Vaccines and Immunization, as well as your reports on the World Summit goals. However," Deborah raised her voice just as Anna opened her mouth to thank her for the compliment, "I have something else to discuss with you. I want you to take over the Water Section. Are you interested?"

Geeta struggled to take it in. The Water Section? She certainly was very interested, and it had been her dream to work again in her primary area of expertise. She took a deep breath to buy herself some time. Why had Deborah asked her this out of the blue?

Geeta sat up straight and said, with a voice slightly thinner than she'd hoped, "Deborah, I would be very interested."

Deborah abruptly continued, hardly waiting for Geeta's response. "The Water Section is in a lot of trouble. You are aware of the arsenic contamination issue in Bangladesh. We are getting into deeper waters there, pardon the pun," she said. "The government blames us for the contamination issues since we have installed the most pumps. And the water drilling rigs in India are also under investigation. And now, Copenhagen has been implicated in favoring the procurement of water drilling rigs through a particular company. This is a mess that is now a major prosecution case against one of our staff."

Geeta could feel the tension rising within Deborah with each issue she raised. Clearly, Deborah wasn't finished.

"I know you're highly capable of handling crises, Geeta. You have an engineering degree, and you have the experience."

A challenge, then, Geeta thought.

Geeta had been aiming to get a posting in New York after completing her master's degree in international development at Columbia University eighteen months ago. They had requested that she take a posting as a deputy in China, but she was loath to go again so quickly to a new assignment overseas, as she had been working in challenging countries for fifteen years. When they asked her if she wished to assist in managing the Health Section, she jumped with joy. She had always been drawn to the health sector, and it would allow her to explore her future career path.

Deborah continued, "So I'm going to ask you to take over the Water Section."

"When would you wish me to start, as there is a lot of work in Health to tidy up first? And what would you like me to focus on in Water?" Geeta asked.

"You're going to shut the whole Section down."

"Excuse me?"

"You will take it over and gradually close it down quietly, so others won't suspect immediately. We have enough on our hands with Health, Education, and Child Protection. I hope it won't be noticed if we let other agencies take over the work." Deborah had spoken the last few words quietly but with a sharp edge.

Before her health assignment, Geeta had been a water specialist for fifteen years. Water was the most critical issue in development: shutting it down would destroy decades of work. Geeta sat up straight and leaned forward.

"Deborah, can I think about it? I really enjoy my current work in Health."

"You have twenty-four hours."

With a racing pulse, Geeta left the 13th floor and walked back to her office, her legs not quite as steady as she wanted them to be.

She glanced into David's office as the Chief of the Health Section was talking to staff members about mother-to-child transmission of HIV, gesturing wildly with his hands. Geeta loved working with David. He was brilliant and knowledgeable, and she loved the intellectual stimulation.

Why would Deborah wish to close the section that was crucial to supporting developing countries and one of the most critical priorities of the UN system?

It didn't make sense. Geeta thought back to the time when she was studying for her master's degree a few years ago. One evening, she turned on the TV and watched Deborah, who was being interviewed on the BBC. They had pushed Deborah regarding the arsenic contamination issue in Bangladesh and asked her if her agency was responsible for the water contamination from the handpumps. Deborah made an error that most highly experienced leaders, like herself, don't make. Deborah had apologized for the problem. The problem was the groundwater, not the hand pumps installed by the agency.

Geeta stopped by David's office after his meeting. He held out a chair for her and smiled. Then he got up and made her coffee at his Nespresso machine.

"You don't look so good, Geeta. How did your meeting with Deborah go?" he asked her.

Geeta stared at her shoes because she knew what she would say before the words formed in her mouth.

"Deborah has asked if I want to head up the Water Section as Director. And I think I'm going to accept," she responded.

He shook his head and rubbed his chin. "We need you in Health. Water is not as important as what you and I are achieving here," he said quietly, knowing that Geeta had already made up her mind and he would not be able to deter her.

David started pacing around the tiny office while Anna drank her coffee. Sip by sip, she tuned out his objections, kindly countering each one with suggested solutions, and a plan formed in her head. She would take the job. And she would do precisely the opposite of what Deborah wanted. She would save the Water Section within the agency.

Chapter 2 · Experiencing 9/11 in Manhattan

Geeta walked out of her apartment on 25th Street and 3rd Avenue, wearing a fashionable raincoat and scarf with running shoes for walking briskly. Like most New Yorkers, she kept her high heels at the office to change into on arrival. She walked down 3rd Avenue. At 8:45 AM, she looked at her watch. She didn't notice anything else. She entered her office ten minutes later and closed the door as she started to check her email. There was a knock, and her colleague, Kamal, entered her office.

"Have you heard?" Kamal asked her.

"No, what is it?" she responded.

"A plane has crashed into one of the World Trade Center towers. It must have been out of control. Maybe the pilot had a heart attack?" he exclaimed.

"How? What plane? When did it hit it? Which Tower did it hit?" she asked him nervously.

"They say at about a quarter to nine. All communications are down. I will try to find out more. The plane struck Tower One near the top," Kamal told her. He left the room to find out more information.

As Chief of Water and Sanitation, Geeta was due to fly to Washington, D.C., that day to visit the World Bank, but she had an early meeting with the Regional Director for East Africa, so she could not leave early. Geeta was about to exit her office for the airport, but she had an ominous feeling and decided to stay put.

A few minutes later, Kamal returned to her office and poked his head in.

"They say the plane was large. They think it was a passenger jet. How could they be that far off course?" he said.

Kamal looked at his phone as it beeped.

"There is another crash into the second tower. How can this be happening?"

"What? How? There is no way that both towers can be hit accidentally. Let me go and see Faheem and see what he knows," Geeta told him, and left her office immediately.

Geeta walked over to Faheem, the Director of Programs. His office was at the end of the corridor, overlooking the East River. She stepped straight in, which was unusual. Three people were already in his office, looking out the window at smoke billowing at the end of Manhattan over the East River.

Everyone in the room appeared nervous and panicked. Geeta tried to appear calm, but she was becoming more anxious by the second.

"Faheem, do we need to evacuate? If planes are going into buildings, the UN is a target."

Geeta could see Faheem had not even considered this yet, as he was in a state of shock.

"Geeta, let me go upstairs to the 13th floor and see what we need to do," he replied.

Faheem was an elderly gentleman, approximately sixty years old, from South Sudan. He was a very gentle soul who feared any dealings with the Executive Director. Geeta could see Faheem steeling himself before he met with Deborah.

Faheem made his way to the elevator to the 13th floor. Geeta decided not to use the elevator and walked down two flights of stairs to meet the Regional Director for East Africa.

"Hi, Geeta. I think our meeting is cancelled, don't you? Let's talk briefly and set up another appointment for next week," the Regional Director told her.

"Yes, I think my flight to Washington, D.C., may no longer be a good idea!" she said with sarcasm.

"I don't think so, Geeta," he said, as he looked down at his phone. "A third plane has just gone into the Pentagon," he said with shock registering in his voice.

"This is unbelievable. Oh my God. How many more planes will crash into buildings?" Geeta responded.

Geeta ran back upstairs into Kamal's office. She felt the tension rising within herself. She knew that if buildings were being targeted, the UN was a prime one to take down.

"We must send our staff home immediately if this building and the central UN tower are targeted. I don't care when the office announces it; we must leave this building now," Geeta told Kamal.

"I agree, Geeta. I will quietly tell everyone to exit, go home, and remain there until we hear otherwise," he responded.

Geeta passed anxious staff blocking the corridors and told them the Director's announcement should come soon. She returned to Faheem's office. As she was walking in, they both heard a loud boom and rushed over to the window. The smoke emanating from the side of Manhattan Island had increased considerably and was now entirely black. Faheem went to pull up the news on his computer.

"World Trade Tower Two has just collapsed...." Faheem quietly said.

Faheem and Geeta looked at each other in shock. This could not be happening. Geeta recalled the joy in seeing those twin towers as a beacon in the distance on every trip into Manhattan, coming in from the airport by cab, as if they were welcoming you back home.

"The top floor is now announcing an evacuation order for the building. Security will announce it on the speaker system in a few minutes. We are all to return home except those living near the Towers and the Financial District. We are working on a list of the staff living in those areas so that others can help them," he told her.

They opened the window wider and could see more black smoke billowing out. But this time, they could also smell the ashes. Geeta went back to her office. Only Kamal within her section remained there. They listened as the message was broadcast over the speaker.

"This is a message from the Director. Due to the events unfolding at the World Trade Center, everyone should return home immediately. Please consult with your supervisor if you live outside of the city, as transport may be affected. Thank you for your urgent attention."

Kamal and Geeta looked at each other in silence as the announcement was made.

"Kamal, can you go home? Is the trolley bus working to Roosevelt Island?" Geeta asked him.

"Yes, but all trains out to the suburbs have been stopped. And the bridges into Manhattan have been closed," he responded.

"Go home, Kamal. I will call you," she told him.

Geeta called Deirdre, who lived in Copenhagen but was in Manhattan for a few weeks for training.

"Deirdre, can you come to my office now? You can't get back to Tarrytown as the trains are down, and no cab can get off Manhattan right now. Come back with me to my place and stay there!" she told her.

"I need to make some calls to Copenhagen. Can I make them from your place?"

"Of course you can. I need to call my parents and Lance in Niger as well, but you use the phone first." Geeta had been seeing someone in Niger for the past year, but she didn't consider it to be a very serious relationship.

Deirdre met Geeta at her office, tense and worried. They left the building together. As they left Second Avenue, they sensed everyone's tension as they rushed down the streets. Geeta and Deirdre looked up at the sky and saw four or five fighter jets flying low and fast. Both were in emergency mode, walking quickly and taking in everything that was happening around them. As they turned to step up Third Avenue, they gasped when they saw droves of people walking toward them covered in white dust, as if they were in a trance. Deirdre tried to talk to one of them, asking if they had arrived from the World Trade Center, but there was no response, as if they hadn't heard the question or just didn't want to stop to talk while moving away from the trauma.

They must have passed hundreds of people, covered in dust, walking along in a zombie-like fashion with no expression on their faces, not even fear or horror. Very few people were carrying anything. The roads were empty of vehicles except for fire brigades speeding down Third Avenue, with sirens on at full blast and police cars following them. They reached Geeta's apartment. The doorman was missing, and they walked up the stairs to her apartment.

No sooner were they through the door than Deirdre turned on the TV for the latest news. Geeta made some tea and heard a loud bang on the news report.

Deirdre rushed over to tell her. "Tower One has just gone down..."

"This is not possible. How can both Towers come down so quickly after being hit by planes?" Geeta exclaimed.

Geeta hugged Deirdre. Deirdre's former boyfriend worked in Tower One at Cantor Fitzgerald. He always arrived early at his office. Geeta thought back to one of the times she had met him a few years ago at Grand Central Station.

Geeta, Deirdre, and Todd had sat at the bar at one of the restaurants at the station, having margaritas and chips. This was the first time Geeta had met Todd; indeed, she was not impressed, considering him somewhat arrogant.

"Hi, Geeta. Deirdre talks a lot about you. She said you've lived in dangerous countries. I imagine that must have been terrible. Thank God we live in a safe country."

Geeta was quiet.

"I work for Morgan Stanley, but as of next week, I have a new job as VP for a relatively new company. It's a promotion with more money," Todd told Geeta.

Todd handed his card to Geeta, which was embossed with Cantor Fitzgerald.

Todd talked most of the next hour about himself and his tedious job, failing to mention his wife and children, which Deirdre had told her about... She disapproved of their affair, but it wasn't her business, and she was very fond of Deirdre.

"It's a new company and an excellent career move for me. Tell me, Geeta: Do you have a boyfriend? You're not getting any younger..." Todd asked her. She escaped after an hour while Todd was in the bathroom.

Deirdre and Geeta, after being glued to the TV all day trying to fathom what had happened, decided to go out to eat—there was little in the kitchen. As they walked down Third Avenue, it was eerily quiet. Manhattan felt like a different place without the usual sound of traffic. There were no cars on the street except the occasional police car. Most shop doors had people sitting outside with a lit candle, and fighter jets were still flying overhead. All the restaurants were full—everyone seemed to have had the same idea: to eat out and see how others were reacting to the morning's events.

They walked to one of Geeta's usual haunts on Third Avenue and quickly ordered red wine to calm their nerves. Everyone was speaking in hushed voices. There was little joy or laughter in the room. Although it was September, Geeta noticed the fire had been lit, and a group of people sat silently around it in armchairs, lost in thought. Even the servers moved slowly, making as little noise as possible as they served.

"Have you heard from Todd?" Geeta asked Deirdre.

"Still waiting. I keep texting him, but I get no response. I have a bad feeling about him, Geeta. Cantor Fitzgerald offices are near the top of the World Trade Tower One, where the stairs were cut off, unless he didn't go to work that day or was late," she said despondently.

"He may just be busy and helping others in the aftermath. As you said, Cantor Fitzgerald must have been heavily hit, as it would appear all of the stairs were blocked in the initial plane crash, and they were on the 101st floor upwards," she replied.

"I don't think this city will ever be the same again. How do you get over this?" Deirdre said.

"The government said that terrorists were responsible for the attack, Osama Bin Laden and Al-Qaeda," Geeta said. She had encountered the impact of Bin Laden during her visits to Egypt, where it was said he was responsible for the Luxor Massacre on 17 November 1997.[17] Indeed, the last place she had expected that she would live through a terrorist attack was in the United States.

Geeta and Deirdre walked home along the quiet streets, and as they did so, they watched people put up pictures of missing ones who had not come home that evening. They decided to walk around the neighborhood to gauge people's reactions. They wandered down to First Avenue and found a group of people outside the bookstore. They were putting up a notice board and a stand.

"Do you mind if we ask what you are doing?" Deirdre asked.

We're putting up pictures of our daughter," a woman responded. She must have been in her fifties, looking tired, and her eyes were red from crying. "She lives with me in that apartment block," she said, pointing

17 https://en.wikipedia.org/wiki/Luxor_massacre.

behind her. "She started working at One World Trade Center a week ago. She's only twenty-four." She started tearing up and walked away to a man standing nearby, who also appeared to have been crying, and hugged her. Geeta looked at the pictures attached to the board and the writing from her mother underneath, pleading for information on her whereabouts.

On this day, no one was yet talking about lost lives as families were still hoping their loved ones were still alive and were on their way home to them. It was so tragic. When Geeta revisited First Avenue a week later, the information board had been transformed into a memorial to the young girl, created by her family and friends, with many bouquets placed underneath.

After 9/11, Manhattan gradually returned to some level of normalcy. The financial district around the fallen towers was cordoned off for months. When Geeta visited Tribeca, she saw the barriers with soldiers checking the IDs of those entering as if it were a military zone. However, even once all the visible signs of 9/11 disappeared, Geeta was sure it would take years, maybe even decades, for New Yorkers to get over the intense shock of what had happened that day.

Chapter 3 · Meeting Lance and Saying Goodbye

As she was late, Geeta ran down the street and met Lance on 3rd Avenue. He was sitting on the wall outside one of the shopping centers, reading a book. They hugged and then walked a few blocks to the nearest restaurant. Lance was Dutch, about forty, stocky, and very attractive.

Geeta had been seeing Lance on and off for two years, as he was based in Niger in a senior position for the same agency. She thought the relationship was finished when they last saw each other in March. She was unsure if she wanted to see him, but he asked to meet with her while he was in New York.

"Geeta, you look great. New York suits you!" Lance told her.

Thanks, Lance; I'm enjoying my work at the Water Section. It's fun but challenging! What's been happening with you?" she asked him.

"I am transferring to Ethiopia in a few months. I am quite happy to make the shift. We did not part on good terms last time we met, so I wanted to see you before I left," he told her.

"Are you still seeing Julie?" Geeta asked him.

Geeta had discovered that Lance had been seeing someone else as well as her. He had left a note on his table in Niamey from a woman, and Geeta casually asked him who the note was from. He had told her he had been seeing another woman for the past year. Yet, in some ways, she could understand why it had happened. He was isolated in Niger, and she was in New York. He needed someone he could see more frequently. However, she was still angry that he had not told her, and she had ended their relationship on her last visit.

"Yes, but it's not serious," he replied.

"Well, apparently, it wasn't serious with me either," she answered sarcastically.

"I'm sorry that I didn't tell you earlier and that you had to find that note," Lance told her.

"Long-distance relationships are tricky, and she was nearer. I get it, even if it upset me," she answered.

"We could try again?" Lance asked her.

"How, Lance? You're going to Addis, and I am still based in the States. How can we make it work? And what about Julie?" Geeta replied.

"Well, we can't make it work if we both work for the same agency. You could leave and join me in Ethiopia," he suggested, ignoring her question about Julie.

"I cannot just give my job up like that. It means a lot to me. And there is no guarantee it would work with us," she replied rather heatedly.

"You could find work with another agency in Ethiopia," he responded.

Geeta thought that she had worked far longer with the UN than Lance, and her position was senior to his, yet he expected her to give up her career, home, and friends to follow him.

"This job is really important to me. I'm not what you need. You need a less ambitious person than me. I can't see myself following you to Ethiopia. I want to achieve results in my work. I want my work to make a difference," she explained to him.

They undoubtedly had a strong attraction, but she had never loved him and didn't think there was any future. Although Lance was good to talk to and they had fun together, he was far too conventional for her and would always expect her career to be secondary to his. Geeta was unsure why one person fell in love sometimes after a week, yet it just didn't happen with others. However, she also strongly believed in karma, which drove her to remain in her present job and see it through. She thought to herself that she was more in love with her work than she was with Lance. Lance walked her back to her apartment, and she invited him up for a cup of tea. Still, she didn't sit beside him on the couch, but instead sat opposite, as she didn't wish to resume a physical relationship with him. She wasn't sure she trusted herself to be too near him, as he was exceedingly good-looking. She didn't want to give him any mixed messages.

"I've always loved your apartment, Geeta. You have such great taste in furniture; your paintings and carpets are marvelous as well." Lance sat back on the sofa and slowly sipped his tea.

Geeta worried he was getting a little too comfortable on the sofa. "What are your plans for the rest of your visit here?"

"Well, I leave for Niger in two days, and then start packing. You could always visit me in Ethiopia and think about my offer."

"Lance, I did like you, and maybe we could have had a future if you worked for another agency." She was well aware that she had used the past tense with him. "But we both work for the same agency, which means it will compromise me if I follow you. Let's agree to remain friends, and I will write to you," she continued. "Do you want to go out and get a quick drink before you return to your hotel?" Geeta moved towards the door and put on her coat, giving Lance a clear message. He followed her out the door.

Chapter 4 · Bangladesh and the Arsenic Problem

On a freezing January morning in 2003, Geeta left her apartment at 6:00 a.m. for her week-long trip to Bangladesh. It was a very long flight with a transit in Singapore. She tried to sleep on the plane, but she was suffering from a heavy cold. The flight attendant was worried that she might infect other passengers, so she upgraded her to first class for the entire journey. However, despite being comfortable, it was still difficult for her to sleep.

Geeta was tired as she left the plane at Dhaka airport after the final flight from Singapore. As she left the plane, she breathed in the air slowly. She was hit by the fact that she had returned to South Asia once more and felt at home. The atmosphere was filled with the pungent scents of diesel fumes, sewage, curried meat, dust, ashes, and coriander. Geeta walked out to the baggage claim area. She waited for the National Institutes of Health (NIH) team from Washington to greet her and accompany her to the city, as she was expected to meet a doctor and an epidemiologist for the conference they would attend.

A man confidently walked over to her. She assumed it must be the epidemiologist, as she knew the woman was a medical doctor.

"I assume you must be Geeta, as you appear to be waiting for someone," the man said.

"How did you know I was waiting for you?" she asked inquisitively.

"Well, there aren't many expat ladies waiting in the baggage area for anyone," he answered.

"I didn't see you on my plane?" Geeta asked him.

"We didn't see you either, as we had expected to meet you in Singapore before we boarded," he informed her. Geeta then remembered she had been sitting in first class, and she was likely seated by the time they boarded in business class.

Geeta was a little taken aback and didn't respond immediately. She had no idea why she suddenly became somewhat shy, as she was usually highly confident in any work context. Robert was about 6 feet tall and dark, with a solid American accent. He appeared to be of Asian or Hawaiian descent.

"Hi, you are Robert, then. Where is your colleague?" she asked him.

Robert pointed to Barbara in the distance, searching for her luggage. Robert and Geeta kept looking at each other, obviously feeling something between them without knowing what it was. Barbara walked over to them and greeted them. Then, all three left the airport lobby and searched for the UN agency car, which they found quickly. After a forty-minute drive, they arrived at their guesthouse. Geeta was conscious that she felt a connection to Robert during the drive through the city.

They were shown to their rooms, each with a rather unusual layout. There was a long corridor to the bathroom beside the bedroom. Half an hour later, while Geeta unpacked her suitcase, Barbara rushed into her room.

"Geeta, about 1000 dollars is missing from my purse. I left my wallet on the bed as the gentleman took me down to see the bathroom, and when I came back, I checked my wallet, and the money was missing," she exclaimed.

"Barbara, are you sure? The penalties are severe when we accuse anyone in this country of doing something like this," Geeta said.

Barbara was sure she was correct. Geeta rushed to check the bag she had left on her bed, and she found 400 dollars missing, half of the cash she had brought.

"It seems that we were both robbed while they showed us the bathroom at the side—clever! I need to contact my office as we cannot stay here after this."

Geeta went down to reception with Robert accompanying her and burst into a lively argument with the man at reception, who denied everything and said that both women were lying. Geeta thought it was best for the office to engage with the staff to retrieve the funds if this man became overly aggressive. She contacted her office and requested a vehicle immediately to take them to a new guest house. Geeta was already jetlagged, but losing 400 dollars on arrival had undoubtedly woken her up rather quickly. It also did not bode well for working with the NIH team since Robert and Barbara were not impressed with the administration of the office. Although Geeta had made many trips to Bangladesh, she usually stayed in a hotel and was unaware of why this had changed. Most likely due to rising prices in Bangladesh, it was cheaper to book regular guesthouses. Robert had not left anything on his bed, so he was not robbed, but he appeared concerned for them both.

"Geeta, you're right in insisting that we move. I don't think it's safe to stay here or anywhere near, as a police investigation is needed for the thefts, and we may become targets for revenge. I'm really sorry that you've both lost so much money. That's tough," Robert stated.

They took the agency's car to the second guest house, about twenty minutes from the first one. The second place was more of a hotel, cleaner and better organized than the first. The office ensured that the police were sent to investigate the theft. Both women were pretty sure they would never see their money again. Geeta thought it was tough for anyone in Bangladesh, especially those in the hospitality industry, not to be tempted to steal, given their low salaries. Here came the wealthy Westerners, leaving their money lying around.

The three of them went down for dinner that evening in the hotel restaurant.

"I am sure we will not see that money again. I hope your agency acts against the guest house and ensures the thieves are arrested," Barbara stated.

"Well, being arrested for such crimes in Bangladesh is not a pleasant experience. They can be thrown in jail for years without a trial, and invariably, they can arrest the wrong people just to satisfy the needs of a UN agency. So, is that really what you want?" Geeta asked her.

"A thousand dollars is a lot of money to have stolen," Barbara continued.

"A thousand dollars is one year's salary for an unskilled worker at that guest house. The problem is, even if we request action against the staff, they will likely find a scapegoat to take the fall and hand the person over to the police. I am sure that the hotel receptionist gave the instructions to steal those funds," Geeta responded.

Barbara was in a quiet mood for the rest of the evening and left the table early, leaving Robert and Geeta alone. The tension between Geeta and Barbara did not seem to affect Robert, who remained at the table for an hour or so after she had left.

"So, how did you end up at this agency? Do you enjoy it?" Robert asked her.

"I worked overseas for about fifteen years before my appointment to New York. I love working there, but I now live in Connecticut. It was too much after 9/11," she answered him.

"That's a long time working abroad. I imagine you enjoyed it. I love New York, to visit for short trips only!" Robert laughed.

Robert leaned back in his chair and ordered a beer. He looked over at Geeta, expecting her to order something as he clearly wished to continue their conversation. She ordered a glass of wine.

"I have lived in Virginia for the past twenty-odd years working with the NIH. I can't say I like D.C. much. I ended up there after qualifying as an epidemiologist. I am Hawaiian by birth and grew up on the main island," he told her.

Geeta felt very comfortable talking to Robert. He was soft-spoken, listened well, and was calm.

"I have a son. He's twenty-five now and lives on the main island in Hawaii. I got married when I was nineteen, and before I finished my studies, my first wife was pregnant. And I am afraid I had another failed marriage after that one as well, but no more children," Robert told her quietly.

"Gosh, do you ever see your son with your busy schedule?" she asked him.

"Not much, as he's close to his mother and not me. I was too young to have children." Geeta could not imagine becoming a mother at nineteen. It was difficult enough to contemplate it now at forty-three. They got up to go to their rooms and lingered a little while saying goodnight.

Geeta was a little unsure of what she was feeling. Although she had only known Robert for a day, she felt elated while she was with him.

The next day, all three decided to walk to the bazaar before the conference started in the evening. They walked to Shankaari Bazar beside the Buriganga River. The bazaar also had the largest concentration of Hindu temples in Dhaka. The temples were small but well-decorated with ornamental motifs on the entrance and walls. Bicycle rickshaws, mainly driven by children and young people, raced down the small, cobbled streets, tooting their horns continuously. Geeta and Barbara bought some spices and silk. They walked from there up to the botanical gardens at Balda and sat for a while to talk about the conference. Robert walked behind Barbara and fell back to walk beside Geeta. He looked over at her for a second and then looked away as they walked in silence.

The conference was addressing the problem of arsenic contamination in groundwater in Bangladesh. Robert and Barbara would present at the meeting on the epidemiology of transmission and the clinical results on the human body. According to the World Health Organization, in 2000, Bangladesh was quoted as having suffered the most significant mass poisoning of a population in history due to groundwater contamination with arsenic, where it was estimated that more than forty of the sixty-four districts in Bangladesh had concentrations of arsenic in groundwater above the cut-off level recommended by the WHO.

In the evening, Barbara retired early to prepare her presentation. Robert and Geeta decided to walk a little, and they ate at a small restaurant around the corner from the hotel, ordering a mix of dishes that took advantage of Geeta's expertise.

"Have you spent much time in India since you started working overseas?" Robert asked her.

"Not as much as I would like. My family lives in New Delhi, but we are originally from West Bengal—not so far from here! My mother gets very upset with me, but I call her a few times a week."

"Do you think you will return to India at some stage to live?" he asked her.

"No. I don't think I would fit in very well, as I'm in my forties, unmarried, and have no children. But there are far more career women in India today than ever. It's much easier for me, though, living in the US; I can merge into the background and live my own life," she explained to him. Geeta found it easy to talk frankly to Robert as she didn't think he was judgmental and felt compelled to be open with him.

"I guess that is a similar situation to mine. There are expectations from my family in Hawaii. But I may go back at some point, most likely when I retire, since I could continue to work part-time," he stated.

"Do you enjoy your work at NIH?" she asked him.

"Yes, a lot. It challenges me, and I guess I am somewhat of a workaholic," he said.

"Really? You seem a little laid back to me," Geeta told him.

"It's a veneer. Being Hawaiian, people expect you to emulate the island life. If I had wanted that life, I would have remained there," he told her.

"Whereas, with me, everyone expects me to be hot-headed, and I am!"

"It's difficult in the UN system as a professional woman. They give you the position to fulfil their quotas, but rarely support you to succeed. Or so I am told! I have a few friends in the system," Robert told her.

"Spot on!" she exclaimed.

"Do you intend to remain in the UN system until you retire?" he asked her.

"I'm not sure. Sometimes, you stay because it's financially secure. But my intuition is I will call it a day at some point and work either with NGOs or as a consultant. I don't want my career to only be about my work with the UN," she responded.

"And what about your partner?" She'd wondered when he would raise the issue of romantic relationships.

"I just broke up with my Dutch boyfriend. It was difficult as he was living in Niger. He was preparing to move to Ethiopia and asked if I would accompany him. But then he wanted my career to be secondary to his," she explained.

"And when do you think you will put your career as equal to a partner?" he asked.

"I don't know..." Geeta responded.

They returned to the hotel and went to their rooms to prepare for the next day's conference. Robert looked intensely at Geeta as he walked past her to his room further down the corridor.

After the conference and spending two days together in Dhaka, they visited a nearby village where arsenic contamination levels were high. The government had marked the handpumps with red paint where the arsenic contamination rate was too high, but Geeta saw that people were still using these pumps for water since they were conveniently near their houses. Barbara examined some people who were showing symptoms of long-term exposure to high levels of arsenic, which were usually observed in the skin. They included pigmentation changes, skin lesions, and hard patches on the palms and soles of the feet. Geeta knew that if they continued to be exposed to arsenic, it would eventually lead to cancer. Undetectable in its early stages, arsenic poisoning takes between eight and fourteen years to impact health, depending on the amount of arsenic ingested, nutritional status, and immune response of the individual. The most affected people in Bangladesh were poor women and children.

Geeta questioned one woman while the driver translated into Bengali. The woman looked about fifty but was thirty-five, according to the driver. In poor rural households, it was the adult female who was generally the most malnourished and most vulnerable to disease.

"When her husband discovered symptoms of arsenicosis, he refused to allow her to stay under the same roof. He wants to send her back to her parents for treatment," the driver said.

"In most cases, husbands leave their wives if they develop arsenicosis. As a result, these women are forced to leave the village and become destitute," the driver continued.

"What about the men who are affected?" Geeta asked.

The driver again translated for the woman, and she laughed and answered: "The men are looked after by their wives. They don't leave!"

When Geeta and Barbara heard these stories from the women in the village, they were dumbstruck, and they had no idea how to stop these actions. They left the village rather sober and returned to their hotel to pack for their trip home the next day.

Robert, Barbara, and Geeta were flying via London, where they planned to take different flight connections back to the United States. While checking in at the counter, Robert asked for a seat next to Geeta. Geeta was a little surprised but rather pleased at his request. They boarded the plane and made themselves comfortable, with Geeta taking the window seat. She was a little nervous for the flight, as she wondered if they would have enough to talk about. She needn't have worried.

"You haven't explained how you ended up in development?" Robert asked her.

"I was fourteen or so when I decided to work overseas. I had no idea what

I wanted to do professionally, but I knew I needed to travel. I applied to go abroad quite early in my career, at twenty-three, and it was so difficult for my family to accept. But I was excited. I never quite fit in within India and always felt like an outsider," she told him.

"It was difficult for my parents to accept since they never wished to travel far outside India and could not understand why I'd want to live in poorer countries and witness high levels of poverty. My mother's family had been relatively poor," she continued.

"My parents died when I was young. My mother died when I was fifteen, and my father died when I was nineteen. My sister helped raise me as she was ten years older," Robert told her in a subdued voice.

"Oh, that's awful," Geeta said. "I can't imagine losing my parents at that age."

Robert looked over at her and didn't respond. He ordered a whisky, and Geeta asked for a wine. As they settled into their seats, Geeta flicked through the in-flight movies, her fingers hesitating just slightly, aware of him beside her, and unsure why his silence unsettled her so much.

"Did you never want to get married, Geeta?" Robert asked her.

"No. I was never in one place long enough," she laughed. "It's a good excuse! But it's pretty unheard of that an Indian woman gets to my age and is unmarried!" she replied. "It's much easier for men living this type of expatriate life, where your wife will invariably travel with you. Few men will follow the woman as she pursues her career!"

Robert was silent.

"I have always been very independent. I never leaned on anyone much except perhaps my father, who always guided me well. I never wanted a very conventional life. I would have liked a child, but I am not ruling that out yet!" she said.

"Although I have a son, I felt I was absent too much as he grew up. My career was so important to me, and I was accepted to study at Johns Hopkins in Baltimore. I wouldn't mind being a father again as I would give it more time", he told her.

Robert continued to talk about growing up in Hawaii and his family there. Geeta had never been to Hawaii and was keen to visit it someday. Eventually, Robert suggested they watch a film and then try to nap. Geeta glanced over at him, sensing a quiet, peaceful connection between them—one where silence felt natural, not awkward.

After a while, Robert turned to her, "You must come to Virginia, and I'll show you around."

"When?" Geeta responded. Robert smiled.

They both slept for a while before they landed at Gatwick. The three of them had to take a transfer bus to Heathrow, so they boarded the bus and sat at the back with Robert beside Geeta, and Barbara opposite. Robert moved so that his leg was touching Geeta's, and he left it there throughout the one-hour bus journey as the three of them talked.

When they arrived at Heathrow, they all made their way through security, but Robert and Barbara's departure was too abrupt for Geeta. Barbara rushed Robert, telling him they needed to run to their gate. Robert looked over at Geeta with a pained expression, said goodbye, and left. She walked away, already missing him.

Chapter 5 · Visit to Washington, D.C., and Virginia

Two months later, Geeta flew into Reagan National Airport in D.C., got a cab, and booked into her hotel. She had experienced a hectic few months in New York working on a major conference with the office of the Secretary-General. However, she was excited to see Robert again after their trip to Bangladesh. She waited outside the hotel to meet him, and he arrived in a green sports car.

"Funny, Robert. I did not see you as a sports car kind of guy." He laughed, and they hugged.

She was a little daunted by the car and wondered if Robert had a playboy-type edge. Indeed, it wasn't the type of car she would expect an NIH epidemiologist to drive.

Robert took Geeta to see his modest and nicely decorated house on the outskirts of Arlington. He gave her a tour of the home, which resembled a bachelor's kingdom, but it felt abandoned, as if Robert didn't stay there very often.

Geeta was somewhat shy at his place and preferred they leave and eat. He took her to an Indian restaurant in Arlington. After dinner, Robert asked Geeta if she would go home with him, and she knew this was what she wanted to do. They talked late into the night about their dreams and aspirations.

After staying the night at his house, Robert took Geeta on a tour of Arlington Cemetery. This had always been a special place for her, as it is where John F. Kennedy and his brother are buried. They saw the gravesite and the eternal flame there. JFK's stillborn son, Patrick, was also buried there. The Kennedys had always fascinated her and contributed to her interest in the United States. Robert touched Geeta's shoulder frequently when they stopped to read gravestones, as if to assure her that she was important to him. Robert was fascinated by the gravesite of Thurgood Marshall, one of the most significant Supreme Court Justices and the first African-American to join the Court.

"He was a good man with his overruling of 'separate but equal' and education rights for African-Americans. Have you suffered any discrimination in the US as a Hawaiian?" she asked him.

"It's more subtle for my ethnicity, but it's still there. You must prove yourself twice as hard as anyone else," he told her. Geeta was thoroughly familiar with this experience as an Indian woman forging her career in the UN.

"It was hard as my family didn't have much money, so my studies were delayed until after my marriage. It probably didn't help the relationship that I was always studying. My son feels some level of discrimination when they come over to the mainland, but not in Hawaii itself. It would have been easier to remain in Hawaii, but studying at Johns Hopkins in Baltimore was the best opportunity for my career," he said.

"How do you think this discrimination affected you?" she asked him.

"I always tend to underestimate my skills, which I rarely see in my colleagues within NIH. They are so overly confident," he said.

"Women tend to underestimate their own skills because of the discrimination they face. I remember when I was promoted early in my career, there was one man in my division who believed that this was solely due to my gender, and he never really gave me credit for the work I accomplished. He also undermined me with other staff. One day, I took him aside and asked him to join me for lunch. Then, I told him he had fifteen minutes to share all his concerns about my work and what he thought I should do to address my weaknesses. He spent fifteen minutes telling me how professional he believed I was, how much he admired me, and how difficult it was for him since I had been promoted to a senior position at a young age. After that, our work together improved considerably," Geeta explained.

"I think overconfidence is overrated anyway. It's always good to underestimate yourself before any significant task, as I can then rise to the occasion," he said.

Robert and Geeta continued to walk around the gardens of Arlington Cemetery, exclaiming as they saw a grave they recognized, such as Lee Marvin's, and Geeta shed a tear when they witnessed a mother and children crying over a fallen soldier's grave. Geeta was surprised to see tears at the corner of Robert's eyes and how this had also affected him. He looked at her for a few seconds and then turned away. They left and took a trip to D.C. to visit the Smithsonian before they returned to Arlington. They found a small restaurant nearby to have lunch.

"You must come and stay at my house in Connecticut. We can then go to New York and visit the Metropolitan Museum and the Guggenheim!" she told him.

Robert paused and appeared pained. He looked at his phone, put it away, and turned to Geeta.

"Geeta, there is something I need to tell you. I've not been honest with you. I have been dating someone for two years, and we recently became engaged. She also works at NIH and is a doctor," Robert explained.

Robert wiped a tear away as he said the words. Geeta was dumbstruck, glanced at Robert, and then looked away. She was surprised that he had not told her before now, and she felt anger and pain rising in her. She had sensed that he was holding back some essential information.

"If you are engaged, I guess it's very serious," she said quietly. Robert didn't respond and looked away.

Geeta was surprised by what she didn't say. She didn't ask him to continue whatever this relationship was at this point. She didn't ask him to break the engagement, and she didn't ask about his fiancée. She didn't want to know who she was.

"Robert, I need to return to my hotel and pack before I leave tomorrow," Geeta said rather icily.

Robert looked at her, but Geeta looked away. She wanted to discuss whether this was serious, but she knew if she didn't leave, she'd burst into tears. Robert finished his tea, gulping it down, and then rose from the table. They were both silent on the drive back.

Geeta said goodbye to Robert outside her hotel. She hugged him lightly, but her anger prevented her from giving him a warm embrace, and she certainly had no words to say to him. She left and didn't look back as she entered the reception.

Chapter 6 · Planned Rendezvous, New York

Three months later, Geeta organized a one-day meeting on global arsenic contamination in New York. Barbara and Robert, among other experts, were attending the event. The aim was to develop an operational research strategy for arsenic contamination in Bangladesh and other affected countries. Geeta was both excited and apprehensive about seeing Robert again. She knew that she was falling in love with him, and unless he left his fiancée, she didn't want this to get any more complicated. Robert called Geeta on her cell phone before the meeting, while she was at home.

"Hi, Robert. How are you? I presume you are coming tomorrow. It will be good to see you and Barbara. I hope she's still not going on about her stolen money in Bangladesh," she laughs.

"Yes, Geeta. I will be there. Can I stay at your place?" Robert asked her.

Geeta felt a great sense of elation but also fear. She had not contacted Robert since they had been together in Virginia, partly because she was angry that he had not told her earlier about the engagement and because she had a principle of never becoming involved with anyone who was either engaged or married. She assumed that Robert wanted to talk to her and decide whether they should pursue a relationship. However, she needed to clarify that he couldn't just continue an affair with her while he was still engaged. She paused a moment and then replied.

"Yes, Robert. How long will you stay?"

"A few days," he replied. "I would like to talk, and perhaps we could visit the Metropolitan Museum. I need to clear my head a little, and I'd like to see you."

Robert talked a little longer about his work, the conference, and expectations, and then hung up. Geeta was surprised that neither of them mentioned his fiancée. She was too scared to ask. Geeta wasn't attracted to many men and was so committed to her work that she had little time to meet anyone or develop any meaningful relationships. And yet, in the back of her head was the sheet she had written out when she left Cambridge,

Massachusetts. You were asked to write about where you saw yourself ten years from now. She had clearly outlined her rise within her organization to a senior level. She had listed her move to the suburbs of New York or Connecticut; however, she had also indicated that she would be in a committed relationship, living with her partner and with perhaps a child. She had written about transitioning to consultancies to balance her work and personal life.

She started making plans in her mind. She would remain at the agency for another year but then transition to consultancies. Perhaps she would move to Virginia. She knew that she was serious about Robert. Maybe a little voice in her head also told her that she was getting ahead of herself...

The day of the workshop arrived, and Geeta prepared her house for Robert's visit. She ordered food so that she could cook for them both. She wore her navy dress, jacket, and blue flowered scarf and applied her Yves St. Laurent perfume. She put on some lipstick and mascara. She instructed the cat to behave at its best and not leave a mess, and then she left to take the train to Grand Central. The rain was heavy that day, with thunderstorms. When she got to the office, Glenda, her assistant, informed her that all preparations were in place for the meeting, which was to be formally opened by one of the Deputy Executive Directors. She saw a text from Robert, so she escaped to her office to read it.

"The plane has still not taken off from Reagan National Airport due to bad weather. Delays could last several hours."

Geeta replied, "text me when your plane takes off."

Geeta returned to ensure all papers were placed in the meeting folders while somewhat worried that Robert would arrive late for his intervention. She emailed the other key speakers to confirm they were prepared. The conference was scheduled to start at 10:00 AM, so it would have to begin without the NIH guests.

The meeting commenced with the keynote addresses and a short speech from Geeta. The guest speaker from Columbia University provided an overview of global arsenic contamination in water. The speeches spilled over time, so she was able to eliminate the NIH interventions. Geeta became absorbed in the proceedings and failed to notice Robert's texts. She only read them at midday.

"All flights are cancelled until late afternoon. Is it still worth coming, as the meeting will end by five?" Robert texted her.

Geeta read this and didn't respond. She felt a great sense of deflation and sadness. She somehow believed that if Robert had been destined to come to New York and they had been able to talk to see if they wished to pursue a relationship, his flight would have arrived. Although she was a fighter, she chose her battles carefully and realized that she rarely fought hard for her personal life and relationships. She cried herself quietly to sleep that evening and tried to let go of the dream she had slowly been creating. Her intuition told her that any future with Robert was over.

Three months later, Geeta was settling back into her house after a productive trip to Ethiopia, where she had met with the Dutch government for a field visit to negotiate a thirty-million-dollar grant for their agency's Water, Sanitation, and Hygiene (WASH) services in six countries in East Africa. As a result of the visit, the first country, Ethiopia, would commence within three months. Geeta rested on her couch and reviewed what she needed to do that weekend. Her cell phone rang, and Geeta picked it up, which she rarely did, as she tended to let calls go to voicemail.

"Hi, Geeta. How are you?"

"Hi, Robert," she said in a subdued voice.

"I tried to call you several times over the past few weeks but couldn't get through," Robert told her.

"Sorry, Robert. It's good to hear your voice. I was in Ethiopia for the past ten days. It was a great trip except for the flights in single-engine planes around the highlands. At one point, we had to land on a muddy runway uphill with a tree in the middle of it. We had to abort our landing and make a second attempt. Unnerving!" Geeta told him. She realized she was rambling on and that Robert wished to speak.

"Geeta, I wanted to update you on my news. Angela, my girlfriend, and I have decided to get married within a year or so. I think it's the right thing for us both. I wanted to tell you first. We both want a child; she is now forty and has little time left. I know this might be difficult to hear, but I needed to talk to you," Robert told her.

Geeta did not ask about Angela and her details. She didn't want to know.

"Robert, I am unsure why you're telling me all this," Geeta pointedly told him.

"At any other time, we could have had a chance. But my career is in Virginia, and yours is in New York. How could we work it out?" Robert was reaching out to Geeta, but she didn't know how to open the door for him.

"I get it, Robert. Your life and your relationships are there, and moving would be difficult. And I don't see how I could give up this job when there is still so much to do. You've been with your partner for a long time, while we've only known each other for a few months and have met only a couple of times. Please stay in touch," she asked him, but she knew that he wouldn't. Geeta ended the call and cried a little. She walked over to the table, sat down, and opened her work emails.

Chapter 7 · Women's Leadership Training

A year later, Geeta was enjoying her role as head of the Water Section and was beginning to see the results of her toils. More money was coming in from donors, and countries were developing new programs. However, sometimes Geeta wondered if she needed to focus more on her own well-being and happiness. Her work absorbed most of her time and attention.

In early 2003, Geeta attended a leadership training program on the Canary Islands for women leaders, alongside women from various UN agencies. Agneta, the Swedish woman running the training, was a seasoned professional who had trained hundreds of women in leadership skills and had written numerous books. Midway through the training, Agneta took Geeta aside and talked to her.

"Geeta, I know you've done well in your career and are highly respected, but there is one aspect that worries me," Agneta said to her.

"I didn't receive much support except from a few individuals I met along the way!" Geeta answered, ignoring the second part of her comment.

Agneta continued, "Geeta, you'll be frustrated and may not go as far in your chosen career path unless you balance your personal life better with your career."

"Are you talking about a partner?" Geeta asked her.

"It's finding someone who supports you and makes you happy. You deserve that and your professional success," Agneta replied.

"It nearly happened a year ago. I thought I had met the person who would make me happy and with whom I could live. I haven't met many that fulfilled that requirement!" Geeta wistfully told her.

"What went wrong?" Agneta asked.

"He was engaged before he met me, and married her," Geeta continued.

"Maybe there's someone else more suited?" Agneta asked her.

"It's challenging. I want to slow down and prioritize my private life. I envisaged this when I was studying a few years back, but I fear it, too," Geeta told her.

"Why fear?" Agneta asked.

"Because you expose yourself to getting hurt in a way that career and work never do. You can control your job, but managing a relationship is super difficult."

"This is an issue for highly successful women. They feel they must control all aspects of their life, and you cannot. Fate happens; weather happens; tragedies happen. You can never control everything. You have to learn to move with the wind sometimes."

"I will try to address that part. I know I need to be happier than I am right now," Geeta answered.

"You can go further professionally if you have more support. Why should women always have to choose one or the other? Why not allow yourself to try?" Agneta asked her.

Geeta considered Agneta's words. She knew she could have tried harder with Robert, but feared rejection. However, he had failed her, too, by concealing his engagement. She understood that control was an issue for her. She had successfully managed to control so much in her life. However, controlling her personal life proved to be much more complicated. She didn't consider herself to have much fear regarding most of the challenges in her life. But she had a great fear of intimacy, not in terms of physical closeness but in terms of opening herself to another person and sharing her life. She wasn't sure how she would change that.

Chapter 8 · Tsunami Response in Asia, 2005

Kamal burst into Geeta's room with excitement.

"Have you heard the news? President Clinton is coming to our office next week to announce a joint UN initiative for water," he told her.

"No, Kamal, but no doubt the Director will inform me shortly," she commented.

It was a cold March morning in 2005. She had been working for the past few months in response to the tsunami in Asia. Her staff were in Sri Lanka, Thailand, and Indonesia, expanding the agency's response. She worked from home and in her office for sixteen hours a day, mobilizing staff and funding to support the agency's work.

She thought back to that day in December when she was celebrating Christmas at her house in Connecticut with her sister and friends, and suddenly, a news flash came across the screen of a tsunami hitting Asia. She watched the screen as the tidal waves started demolishing houses, sweeping people, cattle, and cars along with their total devastation. She was on the phone all day on December 26, communicating with offices in Indonesia, India, Sri Lanka, Thailand, and the Maldives. The following week, she stayed at the office each night until late, working with Human Resources to identify people to fly out for support. She called Kamal and Mark to her office the day after it happened.

"We need to mobilize quickly to get support to all these countries. This is a surge response like we have never managed before. I need you to work with HR today to identify the best people for short and long-term assignments and check languages or previous experience in these countries."

"I think Kamal and I need to go out, too," Mark said.

"What's your suggestion?" Geeta asked him.

"I suggest Kamal heads to Sri Lanka, and I head to Banda Aceh, and we will coordinate responses from there. We can be assigned for six weeks to get things up and running and then make sure someone suitable replaces us."

"Okay, but this is not easy, Mark. You're going in straight after chaos, and no organization is yet in place," Geeta commented.

So, within days, two of Geeta's senior staff headed out. Geeta stayed behind to organize the response and mobilize people. She worked closely with the Supply Department for everything that needed to be sent over at warp speed. It was very intense.

One morning at her desk, she got a call from Mark in Indonesia.

"Geeta, I need help. I've lost my laptop, passport, wallet, everything..."

"What happened, Mark?" she asked him, somewhat surprised as Mark was always so organized.

"Well, I got permission from the government to go into Bandah Aceh, and really, Geeta, it was awful. Bodies everywhere, debris, cars, and trucks overturned. Most people, I was told, were swept away by fierce waves that carried everything with them. There has been no time to clear anything, and children are walking around with no one accompanying them, wearing no shoes, and asking for food. I didn't know what to do. All I had was a bar of chocolate with me... I gave it to one girl. And I had to wade through water up to my knees to inspect pipes and see what could be done to restore the water supply."

"It sounds so bad. Is the government sending any support? Tents and food? I hope your shots are up to date?"

"Not yet. Yes, I got extra shots before I left. It's taking a heck of a time to get organized."

"So, what happened?"

"I had taken a cab, and when I got out at the hotel, I left my bag with everything in the back of the cab. I have to go to the Embassy tomorrow to report the lost passport. I've called them already," Mark told her, his voice trembling a little as he spoke.

"Don't worry. How much was in your wallet?" Geeta said, trying to calm Mark down.

"About two hundred dollars, but my credit cards were also in there."

"Well, look, we will contact the hotel and pay your bill, and I will work with you on your passport. If you send an email with details, I can make calls from here to cancel your cards."

After Geeta had calmed Mark down and hung up, she thought about the stress of what he had seen out there. Nearly 160,000 people had died that day in the province of Banda Aceh, and it would take ages to clear bodies, bury the dead, and deal with the aftermath. It's one thing to see one dead body; it's another to see bodies wherever you look and see dead children. It must have been unbearable. Geeta worked with Mark to get him home over the next week and ensured a replacement was sent out immediately.

Geeta was not surprised that the Executive Director had yet to inform her of President Clinton's visit to the office. Their relationship had deteriorated over the past year as the section's profile within the agency rose, and more funding became available. Deborah was uncomfortable discussing water and sanitation, although Geeta knew that she no longer wished to shut down the sector, most likely since its profile was now significantly larger. Geeta called up to the office of the Executive Director and spoke to her assistant.

"Hi, Geeta. Deborah is not available right now. I understand your concerns regarding President Clinton's visit. Please prepare talking points and send them to my office for the Executive Director," the assistant told her.

Geeta decided to prepare a comprehensive speech for Deborah. She understood why the Director was upset. President Clinton, her mentor, was coming to the UNC office to speak, not on health or education—those were areas of expertise of Deborah's—but on water, which she had never professed to know anything about and had never tried to gain any expertise. He was to launch a water improvement initiative with the agency, as part of the tsunami response.

"Geeta, why would she not inform you of such an important meeting for our section?" Kamal asked her.

"You know why, Kamal. She didn't support us. On the other hand, she didn't stand in our way, so give her some credit," Geeta told him.

"Geeta, you could lose your position on this one. She'll want to stand beside President Clinton, and now she sees you as a thorn in her side. It's good for the section, but it's not good for you," he told her.

"I know that, Kamal. But I could never take on a job and decide not to give it everything I've got, and that wasn't what she wanted," Geeta replied.

"Watch your back, Geeta. She will try to remove you," Kamal warned her.

"It doesn't matter if she does now. I think we are headed in the right direction. I can go back to the field or whatever. I have options. But I couldn't live with myself if I hadn't given the section my all," Geeta replied.

Geeta thought about the next few months and the tightrope she had to walk to complete her role as Section Chief and then transition to a new posting. She was also aware that Deborah's term ended in December 2005. She was upset that she would not be attending the event with the former President, but there wasn't much she could do about it.

After Kamal attended on behalf of the section, Geeta met him in the corridor outside her office.

"There weren't many people, really," Kamal told her, trying to make Geeta feel a little better. "I think the Director wanted to keep it small for the former President. He talked about the agency's work in the sector and its leadership. And he talked about the good work he heard about in Banda Aceh and Sri Lanka," Kamal told her. "He said that the Foundation was looking forward to working closely with us in all the affected countries and leveraging more funds. It was great he came, Geeta, and that's due to your leadership."

"Thanks, Kamal. I'm so grateful that you were there. How was Deborah's speech?"

"She didn't use much of what you wrote. I think she had someone else provide the points. Not very strong."

Geeta returned to her office, closed the door, and cried quietly at her desk.

Two months later, Geeta arrived in Oxford after flying in from Sudan. She had spent the last month in Darfur developing the water and sanitation response for the refugee camps. She left Sudan through Chad, taking a fourteen-hour road journey to Ndjamena before flying out. She flew to Paris, then London, and caught a train to Oxford. Geeta met her consultant, Julian, at the hotel on the outskirts of Banbury. They were due to meet at Oxfam the next day.

"Hi, Julian. Do we have an outline of the terms of reference for the

WASH Cluster for emergencies? I know you sent me a rough draft a few days ago," she asked him.

"Geeta, I need to review this with you now. It will be tough for Oxfam to accept that the UNC will coordinate WASH for all major emergencies. Until now, this has informally been their role," Julian told her.

"I know, Julian. However, we are an impartial UN agency and can rise to the challenge."

The following day, Geeta walked around Banbury, realizing that working for Oxfam could have been her destiny. Despite her lack of diplomacy, she ended up with the United Nations. However, over the past years, she had become far more skilled in negotiations. She walked back to the Oxfam office in time for her meeting.

Geeta met with the Oxfam technical staff, accompanied by Julian. After a long debate, they agreed to support her UN agency in taking the lead. Now, she could share this information with the UN Emergency Coordinator in New York, who would expect Oxfam to be on board.

Geeta knew that taking charge of the Emergency Cluster would significantly put the agency's WASH agenda back on the map. She laughed as she realized this was far from "closing down the section". Managing the emergency response on behalf of the UN would be an engine that would take on a life of its own. She had seen that clearly during the tsunami response and her trip to Darfur. This work was of great importance, and no UN agency was as strong as UNC in rising to the occasion and providing leadership during these complex emergencies.

Chapter 9 · Reflections in Connecticut

Geeta locked up the house in Rowayton and drove to Westport to meet her good friend Stephanie for dinner. They met at a restaurant beside the river, their favorite haunt.

"I leave for India in a few days to see my parents, so I'm glad I got to see you before I depart," Geeta told her.

"Hi, Geeta. I was at Deborah's leaving party yesterday. It was sad after ten years. She did so many good deeds for the agency," Stephanie said.

"I agree, but WASH perhaps wasn't one of her greatest interests," Geeta said sarcastically. "However, most of the time, she left me alone to do my own thing. My time in the sector is also coming to an end. I reckon I'll need to look for a new job in another few months. It's now been five and a half years, and that's the longest I have ever been in any position," Geeta replied.

"I know. Deborah loves education. I bet her next assignment is related to that. It would be best for you to consider another UN agency or look at charities," she told Geeta. "Or you could see what the new Director is like and develop your relationship with her," she responded.

"I don't know what sort of challenge is best next for me. I feel I completed my dream job. Maybe it's time to focus on my personal life. I would have been frustrated if I had given up this job for Robert. Perhaps he'd have been frustrated if he had followed me to New York?"

They sipped their mimosas, enjoyed their lunch, and laughed at the latest news in the agency and beyond...

Geeta returned home and then went for a walk by the sea. She considered what she had given up by undertaking this work. She had always put her personal life on hold. She knew she would try to turn this around over the coming years. However, she would not sacrifice her career. Somehow, there must be a way she could balance both. Perhaps Robert and she could have tried to make it work long-distance. But Geeta knew she had not made enough effort to convince Robert that it could work with her. And then she realized why... she had never been able to give herself entirely to a partner. There was always something holding her back. She had never considered a conventional life for herself and didn't want to deprive Robert of a more conventional relationship and perhaps another child. She had never really seen herself having children, and she still had so much more to prove to herself.

She was excited for what came next and knew she would rise to that challenge. Geeta was now forty-seven and felt at the peak of her mental and physical development. She was in the throes of perimenopause, but it would not defeat her. She considered herself embarking on the next chapter of her life as more resilient and robust to take on significant challenges.

Part Seven

The Philippines (2008–2011)

Patricia

Disillusionment

Chapter 1 · Ithaca, Upstate New York, July 2006

Patricia's drive to Ithaca was exhausting. She arrived in the evening, having been on the road for six hours on a warm July afternoon, but her mood lifted instantly when she saw Eric was waiting outside his house, leaning on the gate. They had not seen each other for ten years, but she felt a flutter in her stomach. Eric looked like he hadn't slept for a year, haggard and tense. He was about six feet tall and carried more than a few extra pounds now with the paunch of a middle-aged man. He smiled at her, and she saw the younger, blond hunk of a man for a split second. The one she'd fallen for instantly. He was still dressed in jeans and a T-shirt as if he had never left his twenties. She had only brought a small bag with her, which she handed to him somewhat reluctantly when he reached out, as she was more than capable of carrying it herself. They walked down the many stone steps to his small house beside Lake Cayuga. He told her he was renting it from the owner of the adjoining larger house.

Patricia was now in her early fifties. She felt blessed that her hair was still brown with blond highlights and not a trace of grey. She was dressed smartly for her senior-level position at the United Nations, and she had driven straight from her office at the main UN building in midtown Manhattan.

In his kitchen, he made her a cup of coffee, no sugar, with milk, and then made his own. He had not forgotten.

"It's good to see you after so long. I didn't think you would come," Eric said and took a sip.

"Well, you sounded terrible when we talked." Patricia glanced around the kitchen. "So, how is Linda?" The sink was clean, but underneath, Patricia could see the bin was full of take-out meal containers. She had contacted Eric a few weeks ago after she received an email from him stating that his marriage was on the rocks.

"She is okay, but she's taking it badly."

Patricia nodded. "So, are you legally separated?" she asked.

"Yes, I have the papers. They were signed and notarized a few days ago. It wasn't good in the end. We hardly even talked to each other. I'd come home and go straight outside to sit with a beer."

"Are you sure you couldn't make it work? When I met her, she seemed to be deeply in love with you." Patricia had visited Eric when he was engaged to Linda. She had liked her, but she could see that it was an unbalanced relationship. Linda didn't work, and when the three of them had gone out for the day, Eric had paid for everything. Patricia was too independent ever to be entirely reliant on a partner.

Eric hesitated. "Maybe it would have been easier if we'd had children."

Patricia remembered that when they were together, in their twenties, the trouble with Eric was that he was infatuated with romantic love. However, once he was in a committed relationship, the work always became a burden for him. There had been other serious relationships in her life since then, including a brief marriage that had only lasted a year, as both of them were often traveling.

Still in the kitchen, Eric mixed two frozen margaritas, crushing the ice, and Patricia thought to herself that they were immediately relaxed and at ease with each other, just as they had been in the past.

"Let's walk down to the dock with our drinks and sit outside," Eric told her.

They walked out onto the dock and sat down in chairs positioned at the end, overlooking the water.

When Eric married Linda, she was too old to have any more children. She had three from her previous marriages.

"Linda had suggested that we should adopt," Eric told her. "But I resisted it. I knew I would never leave if we had a child."

Patricia told him about her latest role at the UN Secretariat, where she supported protection initiatives, her recent trip to Senegal for a major meeting, and her visits to Denmark and Norway for conferences.

Eric listened with eyes wide open, a hint of envy on his face.

"I could never travel as much as you have," he said slowly. "I still enjoy my work here as an environmental engineer. I have my old friends, a good support network even without Linda."

This was Eric's third failed marriage. The first was when he was in his twenties, and his wife had left him. Eric had married about eighteen months after he and Patricia had split up. The second one, to a farm owner, ended after five years. With Linda, it was different; she had adored him.

"I'm surprised you didn't go overseas to work, Eric. I mean, we met in Asia, and you loved working abroad."

"Well, I wanted to, but then I got married, and when that didn't work, I studied for my master's and was offered a job after that. It just didn't happen."

Patricia didn't understand that statement since she had made everything in her life "just happen". But she remembered that aspect of Eric when they had been together, as even in his twenties, he was full of self-doubt.

She was pleased to be here talking to Eric, and she was very relaxed sitting out on the deck after her margarita, but she wasn't anticipating anything more than friendship. She still had many things she wished to do career-wise. She thought that she was over Eric, but as she was sitting there beside him, she felt the draw to him again. She didn't want to step into the trap of falling in love with him again. She had been very much in love with him when they were young.

They talked all night down on the dock. They watched the sunrise over Lake Cayuga and spent about an hour walking around the lake.

"You seem to have a good life. Why didn't you settle down and remarry after Dan?" he asked.

"I didn't have time. I decided to focus on my work, and really, of all the people I dated, I didn't want to marry any of them. Let's face it, my marriage to Dan failed as I was always traveling," she told him.

They laughed.

"I wonder if you and I should have gotten married?"

Patricia turned away and looked out over the water. Although she had been devastated after they split, she had moved on and picked up the pieces.

As the temperature continued to drop, Patricia and Eric walked back up the path to his house. She started to feel that clingy, toffee-like feeling of being drawn back into a maze that would be difficult to extract herself from…

Chapter 2 · Arrival in Manila

It was a hot, dry day in Manila in July 2008, and Patricia was waiting in the studio apartment, pacing back and forth in the room. That morning, she had arrived in Manila from New York to take up her new position as the head of the UN Development Assistance (UNDA) agency and was jet-lagged and nervous. Her agency had rented this small studio for her on her arrival, so it would be easier for her to settle into the country. Eric and she had not seen each other since February, when they had met in Thailand for a holiday. They had been involved for nearly two years after that weekend in Ithaca and had managed a long-distance relationship between Ithaca and New York with some difficulty. Eric had decided he wanted to work overseas and accepted an assignment in the Philippines, leaving in October 2007. Patricia was surprised as they had been getting very close by July, and then he suddenly pulled away and broke up with her by email. Who breaks up by email?

"I'm sorry, Patricia, but I think you should know that I don't see us being together in the long run. I love you, and I always will, but we want different things." She was shocked as she read the message on the train on her way home. So, she broke communications with him until he rang her on her birthday in October and told her he was on his way to the Philippines.

"I'm sorry, Patricia. The message was cruel and harsh. Look, can we try to meet while I'm in Asia? What are your travel plans?"

Patricia was terse in her response to him.

"I have a conference in Bali in November, so if you want to see me, you will have to come over there."

"I think I can do that. I can try to get ten days, and we can travel around the island."

They had an idyllic time there, traveling by road to temples, beaches, and hill resorts. As always, they got on well and talked late into the night. There was a strong physical chemistry between Patricia and Eric that had always been present since their twenties, and it had remained strong. However, there was also a peace between them that meant they could sit together for hours in silence, each reading their books or working and feeling perfectly content.

Patricia had enjoyed their time together, but it was somewhat jarring at the airport as Eric walked off for his flight back to Manila with barely a hug and a glance back.

There was a knock at the door of the apartment. Eric sauntered into the room, and they hugged for ten seconds. Eric leaned back and looked at her, his hands still on her shoulders.

"When did you arrive? Swanky apartment! You must be tired! Are you up for eating out? There is a place around the corner that serves excellent Filipino food. You will love their Lechon Baka with roast beef!" Eric exclaimed, all in one breath.

"Eric! Have you forgotten that I'm a vegetarian?" she said exasperatedly.

"I am sure they can make something for you. I have been out in the field all day, working on an environmental clean-up job for one of the oil companies. It's been tiring these past few months. When did I last see you?" Eric said.

"Last February in Bangkok," Patricia said as she sighed at the memory. When Patricia met Eric there, it had been a tough week since she had last seen him at Christmas. Patricia had arrived from attending a high-level panel on protection issues in Tokyo and had made a detour to meet with Eric, who was on assignment in Bangkok for a month.

She had arrived at his hotel in Bangkok, which she immediately disliked, as it was somewhat rundown and seedy-looking. Eric was saving money, she thought to herself, as he was undoubtedly on a decent salary. They had visited some temples and the floating market and enjoyed the days of sightseeing. Still, the evenings were rough as Eric was determined to argue about anything and was very distant. He felt it would only be possible for the relationship to survive if they weren't physically together in the same location. They had agreed to split up, again, and Patricia was quite torn as she flew back to New York. There was little communication between them until May, when Patricia had told Eric that she had been offered a position in Manila and had accepted, as it was a good career move. In fact, what had happened was that the Head of Personnel had offered her a few posts to consider, and one of them was in Manila. She decided to apply and was accepted.

They left the apartment block and walked a couple of roads over to the Filipino restaurant, which was small, with shabby décor but very clean.

"Well, the next two years should be exciting with you in your position and mine with my company. I didn't think you would be able to take a posting here. How did you get it?" Eric asked her.

"The Head of Personnel contacted me since someone was interviewed for the Head of Office position, but the Executive Director was uncomfortable with his appointment." Patricia thought to herself that that part was genuine. "I didn't expect the Head of Office position to open up. It was serendipity," she replied.

Eric shrugged and looked over to his side. A man of about seventy was sitting at a table with a very young-looking Filipina. Patricia frowned.

"It's not acceptable that men of his age should be with a Filipina so young. I wonder how he met her," Patricia commented.

"Don't knock it. He needs someone to look after him in his old age. I am sure he spends enough money on her," Eric responded.

Patricia was a little shocked by Eric's response. While working in Asia in their twenties, Eric had been one of the few who never considered a relationship with a local at that time, deeming it inappropriate. His perspective was undoubtedly different now that he was in his fifties.

"I worry about myself when I get old. Who will look after me when I am eighty, in the throes of dementia…" Eric commented.

"Well, you will be on your tenth wife by then, so I am sure she'll look after you!" Patricia laughed.

"Funny! But it's a fact that the most expensive thing in the US is elderly care. Most people can't afford it and end up in a state institution," Eric forlornly commented.

"Eric, don't be so depressing. I am sure you will be fine," Patricia replied.

This was the side of Eric that Patricia found hard to tolerate: his pessimism about his future! He was bitter about his former wives and the financial cost of the three marriages. Yet it was easy to see why the marriages had failed. Eric craved a traditional relationship with a wife at home by the cozy fire, and yet he was attracted to intelligent career women.

"You know that sex trafficking here is an enormous problem. Many young girls take up with older expatriates to gain money or to obtain a foreign passport," Patricia told Eric.

"Well, you can't blame the women wanting to escape a life of poverty," Eric replied.

"And what about children or any girls or boys under eighteen? That's a severe problem here. Surely, you don't condone that?" Patricia asked him as they got up from the table. Patricia was starting to wonder if Manila was bringing out the worst in Eric.

"No, I agree. Children are off limits."

At least they agreed on something.

"How old do you think that girl is with that old man?" Patricia asked, preparing for an argument with Eric.

"Over eighteen..." he responded.

"I reckon she is seventeen, tops. Shall I ask her?" Patricia asked.

"I don't want a scene. Let's leave!" Eric walked to the counter to pay the bill. Patricia got up and gave a filthy stare to the senior man at the table with the young girl. She would have said something if Eric had not been with her. She wondered if following Eric to the Philippines had been a good idea. Although she had not compromised her career in doing so, she would have progressed faster if she had remained in the United States.

Patricia had taken a gamble in following Eric to the Philippines. However, it struck her then that since she was at the pinnacle of her career, it was safer now to commit to a relationship and give more attention to her personal life. She felt that before, she had never been afforded that luxury.

Chapter 3 · First Day at the Office

Patricia was picked up at her apartment by the office driver, who drove her to the agency building. UNDA was housed in a multi-story modern building in one of the most affluent areas of Manila, Makati. She was rather surprised by the ostentatious building, considering their programs focused on addressing poverty in the poorest regions. She took the lift to the 20th floor and walked over to her office.

It was the size of her first studio apartment in New York. There was a table for meetings, chairs for staff discussions, and a large desk for her. Perfect. Her assistant, Atty, greeted her before she entered and said her coffee was already set up in a flask in the office.

"We have briefing sessions set up for you throughout this week. We have also arranged field visits for next week to projects for child protection, health, and education. Next month, they want you to visit Mindanao, the poorest province in the south. They would also like you to see the north of Baguio and then Sagada, which is in the far north, two months from now," Atty told her.

Atty was very soft-spoken and polite. Before her arrival, Patricia had been told that it was important never to lose one's temper in the Philippines, and she knew she was lucky to have an assistant such as Atty, who would advise her on the correct behavior in any situation.

Patricia was keen to visit the south of Mindanao as it was conflict-affected and received the least attention from development agencies. She was unsure about Sagada, a mountain province that was also a tourist attraction. The photos reminded her of Nepal due to its rice terraces. There was undoubtedly some poverty there, but far less than in the south or Masbate in the country's center. Patricia went to her desk, put on some music, and basked in the sun streaming through the glass window wall.

Nigel, her deputy, entered the room. "Hi Patricia, I hope your flight was smooth. I didn't want to disturb you yesterday as I thought you needed to get over your jet lag."

"Thanks, Nigel. Let's get lunch today and talk about the programs," she said to him.

Nigel had prepared an excellent briefing package for Patricia on the country and its programs. Patricia was struck by the progress in the Philippines, which had risen from a least developed country to a lower-middle-income country over the past fifty years. However, the development challenges had shifted dramatically over the past ten years, with the rise of disasters due to heavy typhoons hitting the coastal regions. The country also needed help with the least developed regions, such as Mindanao, where development indicators were much lower.

During lunch, Nigel talked about the country.

"You know, Patricia, this country was devastated by the Japanese occupation during the Second World War. They occupied the country for three years, controlling around fifty percent of the land. The people were treated brutally by the Japanese, and Manila suffered the most. It's now mostly a new city since so many buildings were razed to the ground. About one million people were killed."

"I didn't know it was that bad," Patricia responded.

"The suffering they went through during the war meant that they would never tolerate such oppression again, and the people expressed this in the uprising against President Marcos in the revolution of 1986, after the assassination of Ninoy Aquino[18]. The Filipinos are very kind people, but if you push them too far, they won't tolerate it." Patricia glanced quickly at Nigel to sense if he was trying to convey any message to her and then dismissed the thought.

"I read about Aquino, Marcos, and the revolution. Quite incredible." Patricia knew from her Filipino friends that they contained a quiet resilience whilst retaining a calm and graceful countenance.

Nigel continued, "we have an event this afternoon on child protection. That's our most extensive program due to the problems of child labor, sexual exploitation, trafficking, and, in the south, armed conflict. We're meeting

18 Benigno "Ninoy" Aquino Jr., a former Philippine senator, was assassinated on August 21, 1983, on the apron of Manila International Airport

with the government this afternoon to review the program and consider where additional support is needed. Would you like to join us?"

Nigel was British and had worked for the agency for over thirty years. He was set in his ways, but the staff respected him, and he was a solid rock within the office. Patricia had already decided, however, after reading the reports before she arrived and speaking with former staff who had worked in the country, that she needed to encourage the government to adopt more innovation.

"I would love to attend that," Patricia responded. She was aware that eighty percent of Filipino children experienced some form of violence either at home, in school, or online.

Back at the office, Atty reminded Patricia that she needed to present her credentials to the Ministry of Foreign Affairs.

On the way out, Patricia looked again at the plush multi-story building, got into the BMW provided by the office, and wondered if this was how the agency should be perceived within the country.

In the evening, Patricia returned to her apartment and prepared dinner for Eric and herself. At about 8:00 PM, Eric arrived and threw himself on the couch. His feet dangled over the end of the sofa as he shuffled to make himself more comfortable, forcing Patricia to sit on the bed facing him. After their meal, she poured each of them a whisky from the mini fridge in the room.

"Difficult day for me. How was your first day? I am sure your deputy wasn't exceptionally pleased to see you. You said he has been running the office as Officer-in-Charge for four months? How many staff are there?" Eric asked her.

"There are about a hundred and twenty staff or so. The budget may need to be larger, given the scope of work, so we will need to conduct additional fundraising. I met most of the Section Heads today. They are a lovely group of people. How is your work?" Patricia asked him, quickly changing the subject since she was aware that Eric was still somewhat surprised that she was heading up the office in the Philippines, and she wasn't sure he was entirely comfortable with it. Patricia had reached a senior level within the UN, and her salary was significantly higher than Eric's, so she was cautious in playing down her role somewhat, as Eric had become even more conservative with the passing years.

"It's okay, but some executives are dissatisfied with our work, so much needs to be done. It doesn't help that I leave for Everest Base Camp in four weeks and will be gone for nearly two months," he told her.

Patricia thought to herself that this was another example of Eric planning his world without her. He was spending two months in the Himalayas with his old school friend, and he had never suggested that she might wish to join them, even for a week at the end of his holiday.

"My father sends you his best wishes. I think he misses you more than me," Eric commented.

Patricia loved Eric's father. He was a prominent, blustery university professor with a large heart and generous soul. She often wondered why Eric was not more like him. His father consistently worried about Eric, having already been divorced three times, and was convinced that Patricia was Eric's best choice for the future. The more his father pushed, the more Eric was riled. Their relationship was complex, with Eric struggling to accept his father's advice. It didn't help that Eric's first wife was one of his father's students. They had been married for eighteen months when she left him for another man. Eric had been devastated and had returned home, where it had taken him a few years to recover. Even now, Eric saw himself marrying again, unlike Patricia, who saw it as a bind that would tie her down and hinder her independence. However, she was more open now to the idea of a life partner than ever before. She knew she would miss him while he was away in Nepal, but it would give her a chance to throw herself into her work with no distractions. It would also allow her time to find a suitable house and set herself up fully in Manila, and then she realized that she would be doing all of that with no participation from Eric.

Chapter 4 · Tagaytay

It was mid-January 2009, and Patricia met Eric at Mandaluyong Shopping Center. This was the first time they had seen each other after a month apart over Christmas and New Year's. Both had spent Christmas in the UK and the US with their respective parents and extended family. Patricia had been in Manila for five months, and the work was going well. However, the relationship with Eric was not.

Eric had come back from Nepal in late October and was not impressed with the house that Patricia had rented, as he considered it too large. She had rented it because the garden was large enough for her four dogs, which she had brought over from the US. Her dogs were deeply important to her as they were all rescues that she had saved over the past five years. She really didn't care what the house looked like as long as there was about an acre of land for them to run on. As it happened, the house was suitable for her to hold receptions, as this was necessary for her role as Head of Office.

Patricia and Eric both agreed that, for appearances, in a Catholic-dominated country, it was better for him to keep his apartment and not move in since they were not married. However, that was not the real reason. Eric didn't want to move in as he felt that this was Patricia's place, and he didn't wish to be perceived as the spouse of the head of UNDA. Since his return from Nepal, until Christmas, they had enjoyed many weekend trips to the hills and the sea, all of which were enjoyable. However, she also sensed that he was distancing himself again from her before they departed for their Christmas vacation.

After they did some light shopping, Patricia had their driver pick them up to drive them to Tagaytay in the hills. Tagaytay was a famous holiday mountain town south of Manila, known for its mild climate. It sat on a ridge above Taal Volcano Island, an active volcano surrounded by Taal Lake. After an hour's drive, they found a restaurant and ate.

Patricia cut right to the heart of the conversation that they needed to have.

"Eric, I'm not sure this is going to work. We need to spend more time together and discuss the future. How long do you intend to stay in the Philippines?"

"I will stay for a few more years," he said.

"But what comes next?" she asked him.

Patricia had never really broached this subject with Eric before. She had followed him here. Hadn't that been the problem in the past? They had never been in the same place at the same time for any extended period.

Eric looked over sympathetically at Patricia. "I agree, Patricia. Let's see where we are at the end of the year, and then, if we feel ready, we can take the next step," he said to her. "I'm not sure how long I'll stay here as my contracts are year to year."

Patricia felt a mixed response to Eric's statement, as it was the most committed he had sounded since they reconnected in 2006, but it didn't help pin down any future direction for them. He immediately seemed less tense, and they ordered some food.

"How is your brother?" she asked him.

"He's good. He wants to visit next year. However, since his third divorce, he has been dating this other woman. She's not the brightest button, but he seems happy with her. She works in a shoe shop in New Jersey, near where he lives," he told her.

Patricia tried to fathom how the two brothers now had six marriages between them. Their mother was a warm, welcoming person. The father had married his childhood sweetheart and, most likely, had never strayed.

Eric then changed the subject and started to talk politics and his devastation that John McCain had lost the election to Barack Obama. Patricia wasn't surprised that Eric had shifted to a safer discussion. He hated talking about their relationship and his feelings. In terms of political views, a significant gap existed between Patricia and Eric. Eric was a Republican who had never voted Democrat except once for Clinton against Bob Dole in 1996. Some of his views were beyond Patricia's comprehension. Eric believed that once a woman had children, she needed to put her career on hold, fearing she would not be able to provide enough care for them. He was also uncomfortable with a partner being more successful than he was.

He had accompanied her to a few events where she gave speeches, but he would often walk off, and she would spend ages afterwards trying to locate him with her driver. He never really asked about her work or what she was trying to achieve. This was a thorn in Patricia's side, as she was a senior official in the UN, and her position as Head of Office in the Philippines was a crucial one.

On the other hand, he sometimes took pride in her achievements. It was a little schizophrenic. Eric's favorite John Lennon composition was *Jealous Guy*, while Patricia loved *Imagine*. Maybe that was a good indication of the chasm between them.

They went for a one-hour walk, laughing most of the time, and then drove home, changed, and went to the swimming pool at the back of the house. Eric brought out two glasses and a bottle of wine while Patricia stepped into the pool.

"Here you are," Eric said, handing a glass to Patricia as he sat on the steps in the water. Patricia loved having the pool even though she was a poor swimmer and never went up to the deep end.

"So, do you think this year will be easier for you workwise?" she asked him.

"I don't know. There's a new guy from the States, who's decided that he doesn't like me very much, and spends his time trying to impress the directors in Dallas."

"Well, this I know: you're not very good at kowtowing to senior staff," Patricia responded.

"You know, maybe we should get married," Eric said. Patricia was surprised that he should raise this now, after their conversation earlier. She looked over at him and decided that maybe, after his second glass of wine, she shouldn't take him too seriously. She changed the subject to the state of the garden, kissed him, and sat down beside him on the steps. She realized she wasn't comfortable discussing making any commitment to Eric at this point. They continued to talk about Eric's work.

Chapter 5 · Setting up a Sub-Office in Mindanao

Patricia and the office team went to McDonald's for breakfast in Cotabato, Mindanao. Now it was a haven amid chaos, although a bomb had exploded outside the restaurant the previous year and had blown out the side windows. The restaurant was now repaired, and the team sat down for breakfast, although Patricia did look around her constantly to see if there were any suspicious-looking people. The idea of eating pancakes saturated with syrup was a comfort to Patricia and the team in a war zone, and they were certainly enjoying themselves as they tucked in. They were visiting Cotabato to establish a new Mindanao office that would assist with emergency programs in the poorest region. They had seen four potential buildings and settled on the safest, which had a 14-foot compound perimeter wall and the office set well back from the street. She had two senior staff members traveling with her, Leonard and Anders.

"Well, we have the office selection settled, but we must meet with the Moro Islamic Liberation Front (MILF) tomorrow.

"As of 2008, as many as fifteen percent of the MILF's forces were under eighteen years old. The problem is that the rebel group is committed to eliminating child soldiers, but there are differences in their definitions. Boys older than thirteen are usually considered adults in Islamic law. If born into families involved in the fight for independence, they are duty-bound to help their families," Leonard informed her.

"Who are we meeting? Is it safe?" she asked him.

"Yes, we meet with them frequently. They don't threaten us and provide complete protection for our meetings, including armed guards," Leonard told her.

"That's good. What do we hope to achieve tomorrow?" she asked, as she didn't wish to ask too much about the need for the armed guards, as that might scare her more than she wanted to be at this point.

"Well, the MILF has agreed to start releasing child soldiers back to their communities. However, in exchange, they are asking for development projects within the villages where the children come from, including primary education, health services, and learning aids and wheelchairs for children with disabilities," he said.

"It seems like a fair ask. Can we draft a proposal and approach the Canadians or the Australians for support? Since these villages are poverty-stricken, we should also focus on income-generating activities that engage women. We could ask the Department of Social Affairs to support the conditional cash transfer program in these villages," she suggested.

The conditional cash transfer program in the Philippines was one of Patricia's favorite programs, run by the Department of Social Welfare and Development with its amazing Secretary, Dinky. Dinky was 5 feet tall, extremely charismatic, and incredibly energetic. Patricia loved meetings with her, since they always bounced ideas off each other and had mutual respect. The cash transfer program was targeted at the poorest communities and provided funds directly to mothers, based on the number of children they had. The conditionality included that children were fully immunized, enrolled in early childhood development and primary schools, and that mothers and children received regular check-ups and participated in family planning and nutrition sessions held by the project.

"Australia has already indicated its interest, so it's possible," Leonard told her.

Leonard and Patricia continued their conversation and walked back to their hotel, which was down the road, with the drivers following in their cars for protection.

Patricia noticed that the windows in her room were at the top of the wall, safer in case of any nearby explosions. She felt quite secure as she slept for the night, and anyway, she was too tired to worry more than she wanted to at this time. The hotel was frequented by many expatriates, and security guards were stationed at the gates. The next day, she met her staff at the hotel's breakfast bar, and they drove off to meet the Liberation Front. Before the meeting, they stopped to talk to local government officials.

"Patricia, you will need to cover your head for the meetings with the Liberation Front. It's not necessary for the local government meetings," Leonard said.

Patricia had not been accustomed to covering her head for a while, since she had worked in the Middle East. However, they were in Maguindanao, in Mindanao, which was predominantly Muslim, so she considered it necessary. She borrowed a scarf from a colleague to use when they traveled further on to the MILF meeting that afternoon.

She looked over at the side of the street where they had stopped at a checkpoint. A man was watching them; he retrieved his phone and talked to someone. She thought nothing more of it at that point.

After the meetings, they stopped at McDonald's again for lunch.

"There was a blast at the checkpoint we passed on our way to our meeting. It happened about five minutes after we passed the checkpoint," Leonard told her, as he put down his phone. "The government just informed me."

Patricia thought back to the man who was observing them. He was obviously making sure that they were clear before the blast was set off.

"Who do you think set the blast?" she asked him.

"It could be dissidents within the MILF making their displeasure known to the government. The government is very fearful of any donors being killed in Mindanao. However, I don't think we were the direct target," he told her.

"Was anyone hurt?" she asked.

"The guard on the post was injured, but it was not a large blast, so passers-by were not injured," he replied.

"This place is still unsafe, and we were warned that this would be the case. HQ was wary of us setting up an office here," Patricia told her staff. "This is going to be very challenging, but if ever a sub-office was needed, this is where it should be. Anders, we need to develop an excellent case for HQ to establish this office, including a comprehensive security plan to protect staff residing down here and those like us who will visit periodically."

"We will get that case prepared over the next ten days or so," Anders responded. Patricia was used to winning her battles with HQ, and she wasn't going to lose on this one.

Chapter 6 · Vacationing in Palawan

The next few months were busy with preparing the necessary papers for setting up the office in Mindanao and discussing the project with staff in New York. By the time Easter came, Patricia was exhausted and planned to take a short vacation of a week or so with Eric visiting Palawan, an eco-tourist island, to spend time together and rest from their stressful jobs. Palawan was one of the best places to visit in the Philippines, renowned for its stunning white sand beaches, picturesque islands, crystal-clear blue waters, diverse marine life, and towering limestone cliffs. They flew into the capital, Puerto Princesa. Patricia had booked a hotel, the Taj, which was supposed to be a short taxi ride away. Eric pulled over a motorized rickshaw driver rather than a cab to save money and take them to the hotel.

"Are you sure that it's a Taj hotel? As in an Indian Taj hotel?" Eric asked her.

"Yes, I went online and booked it. Mind you, it seemed cheaper than a Taj hotel should be..." she commented.

After about twenty minutes in the rickshaw, they arrived at a dilapidated building.

"Well, I can say this one only gets one star..." he laughed in a "I told you so" manner.

Patricia walked to the reception, but no one was there. She eventually found a woman in one of the rooms.

"Hi, is this the Taj Hotel?" she asked.

"Yes, Miss, do you have a booking?" the woman asked her.

"I think we do, but before we finalize, we would like to see the room where we're staying," Patricia said.

Patricia was led to a dilapidated room with dirty bedding and no bathroom, except a communal one down the corridor. She thanked the lady and rushed out the door quickly to return to where Eric was standing.

"We'd better search for a cleaner hotel in town. This definitely is not part of the Taj chain..." she told him.

"Next time, you may need to verify online a little better. How many people did you say worked in your office?" Eric chided her.

"I don't use the office to make private bookings. I booked this myself online. Sorry for the inconvenience," she told him rather pointedly. She had thought it was a bit strange that she had never heard of this Taj in the Philippines, but she was so busy with work, she didn't have time to check thoroughly before their departure. Eric always made her feel somewhat impractical and slightly incompetent when it came to managing simple tasks. They found a hotel in the center of town that was not full and had a clean room. Patricia paid the bill, and Eric carried the bags upstairs. She never argued about bills, since she earned about twice as much as Eric did, but it would have been nice if he had offered this time.

"I need to call Ithaca. Peter said my ex-wife rang him as she didn't know what to do with her tax return. I'll be back in fifteen minutes," he told her. Peter was Mark's childhood friend and the closest person to him aside from his family. The two had grown up and attended school together in Ithaca and had even shared girlfriends in the past.

Patricia looked around the room. Since they were only staying one night, she only unpacked lightly. They would take a bus to the coast and then take a boat up to the top of Palawan, stopping at a few ports as they made their way up the coast to El Nido. Eric came back to the room.

"Linda is having problems completing her taxes. She is asking to delay the divorce for at least a year so we can file together," he said.

Patricia did not comment and went to the bathroom to comb her hair. She was unsure how she felt about this, but she thought it gave her a degree of safety. After his half-hearted proposal at the pool at her house, she was sure that she didn't want to make any decision about a long-term future with Eric until at least the end of the year, when they would know whether they could perhaps live together successfully. She had never pushed Eric for the divorce since he was legally separated. He ensured that he had filed the papers before starting the relationship with her, as he knew she would never consider being involved otherwise.

"Peter is well. He said he is still not over our trek to Everest Base Camp. It's funny, really, as I thought he was far fitter than me. He sends you his best wishes," Eric told her.

Patricia knew that Eric was lying. Peter had no time for Patricia and considered her a nuisance in his relationship with Eric. Eric was also heavily bonded to Peter. Then Peter married, settled down, and had two children, while Eric had three marriages and no children.

"How is Peter's wife?" Patricia asked.

"They're still not talking to each other. I think it's been six months now. They won't divorce because they would have to leave the house and sell the land, and neither will do that," he said.

"Shall we go for a walk?" Patricia suggested, not really interested in Peter's life and problems.

"Sure, let's get something to eat," he said.

They arrived at a restaurant near the hotel and sat down to eat. Eric ordered a bottle of wine. Patricia looked over disapprovingly, as she didn't want to drink too much before a four-hour bus ride tomorrow morning, followed by a boat trip. She was also concerned about Eric's excessive drinking.

"So, you have been here for eight months. Do you think you will stay in the Philippines for a while?" he asked her.

Patricia was slightly surprised as Eric talked as if they were on separate missions. However, she knew that Eric was torn between staying in the Philippines for a few years and returning to Ithaca to be near his parents, who were growing older.

"I have to commit to at least three years now. It's unfair to leave before that; otherwise, they have to find a replacement, and we are in the middle of designing a new country program," she replied.

Patricia knew, as she said this, that it sounded like she was making independent decisions without Eric, but she had no choice. She had requested this posting and had to complete the assignment before leaving. Patricia knew she had a loyalty to the agency that she had to fulfil.

"Well, I guess let's see if I stay. I am offered only one-year contracts, and I don't know if these will be renewed before October of each year," he told her.

"Understood." She was quiet. She wasn't sure she wanted to pursue this conversation.

"Let's plan tomorrow's route and see where we should stop on our way up the coast," she said.

The next day, they traveled to Sabang by bus and stayed at a beautiful hotel on the coast that Eric had found online the previous night. They ate by the sea and retired to a cabin on the beach. The following day, they took another boat to San Vincente, where they found a lodge. They had a wonderful day walking, eating, and discussing development issues. Patricia and Eric never tired of discussing topics and confiding in each other regarding their work and current affairs. Patricia could never fully reconcile the two dominant aspects of their relationship. On the one hand, they could talk for hours, engaging in deep, intellectually stimulating conversations. On the other hand, they—or more accurately, Eric—would get into arguments over trivial matters, or he would express views that were entirely at odds with her own.

The following day, they set out for the port. Patricia sensed from early morning that Eric was pulling away. She wondered if this was due to how close they had become the previous day. She dismissed that thought as they got on the next catamaran to El Nido. They were joined on the boat by four Dutch tourists, and they talked together for at least thirty minutes about the Philippines and their work. Patricia noticed one of the women sat beside Eric and spoke to him. Eric decided to sit at the end of the boat for a while to watch the waves as the rain started pouring down and the water became very choppy. The Dutch woman walked down to the end of the boat and joined him. They continued talking for the rest of the journey, while Patricia grew increasingly unsettled.

The boat docked at El Nido, where everyone jumped off and waded a few feet through the water before reaching the beach. The Dutch people asked where Eric and Patricia were staying. Patricia curtly told them they were waiting for another boat to take them to Miniloc resort, one of the islands in the distance.

"What's wrong, Patricia? Did you need to be so rude to them?" Eric asked her.

"I was not rude. That's my brusque manner. I work for the UN, so I keep my distance," Patricia responded.

"Something has riled you up," Eric persisted.

"You're well aware of what this was," Patricia said.

"Have you been upset since I talked to that woman on the boat? Don't you think that's a bit childish?" Eric said to her.

"What was she talking so avidly about? She can't be more than in her mid-twenties, no?" Patricia responded sharply.

"She's on holiday with her brother. She'll stay in the Philippines for a few months and then travel to Cambodia and Vietnam," he replied.

Patricia looked at the coast of El Nido, where they had arrived. There were a series of small hotels and kiosks on the shore, and some fishermen milled around preparing their boats for an evening haul of fish. Children dressed in rags were kicking a football, and a few tourists were at the top end. The resort where they were staying was costly, yet it appeared that the surrounding villages were not benefiting from any of this investment.

Patricia saw the resort boat approaching. She stopped talking and waited for it to collect them. There were no other passengers on board, but they were silent for the half-hour trip.

When they arrived, they were taken to a cabin over the sea. Patricia decided she was unhappy with the place and told reception she would prefer a room for them in the main lodge with a sea view. The cabin was too intimate, and she needed to put distance between Eric and herself.

They unpacked their bags in silence, and Patricia lay down on the bed to check her emails.

"Let's go and eat!" Eric said. Patricia ignored him and continued reading her emails.

After Eric left the room, Patricia tried to fully understand why she was so unhappy. She couldn't put her finger on the problem. It couldn't just be that she was upset because Eric had talked to a woman on the boat. Then it hit her. He always made her feel insecure, as if it was the only way he could keep hold of her. He enjoyed consistently pushing her off-kilter.

Eric was sitting by the beach bar when she went down, with two margaritas in front of him. He was talking to the barman about the resort. Patricia recognized the barman's Australian accent and wondered why he was working here. Eric passed one of the drinks to her.

"Let's look for a table by the sea. You're not still mad at me, are you? The barman is very interesting. He's traveling the whole of the country, and he pays for it by working wherever he can. I would love to join him!" Eric told her. Typical, Patricia thought. Eric would love to be young again with a rucksack on his back, traveling through Asia.

The resort was expansive in front of the sea, with cabins on one side and the multi-story hotel on the other. There was a flurry of boats docking and leaving, with people taking evening trips to the surrounding islands for arranged meals, night diving, and stargazing. Patricia walked over to the pier and signed Eric and herself up for a few trips over the next few days. She knew that Eric would be happy just to sit at the bar and talk to the Australian for the four days they were here, maybe with some snorkeling. The contrast between the resort and the poor towns and villages Patricia usually visited on her field trips struck her hard. She felt guilty about visiting such a lavish resort when the region was still impoverished, and even the resort staff were likely on meagre wages, despite the hotel's revenue. Patricia increasingly struggled with guilt over the contrast between her own life and that of the communities she worked to support in developing countries. Early in her career, the divide hadn't felt so stark. But as she climbed the professional ladder, earning more, living more comfortably, and surrounded by support staff, the gap between development workers and the local populations they were meant to assist felt wider and more unsettling than ever.

"I am not mad any longer. Look, we've paid quite a bit for this holiday. I would prefer we avoid any problematic conversations and enjoy ourselves," she told him.

"That's fine by me. We agreed anyway that we would see how we would fare over this year and decide at the end whether we would break up or not," Eric quietly said.

Patricia ignored his comment as it would just start another argument. They had gone far past the "how we would fare" benchmark. It hit Patricia hard that she would never be the type of woman Eric could remain with for longer than a few years. She was too successful professionally and would never wait for him at home with hot chocolate and his slippers ready. As he had aged, Eric had become far more conservative. There had been some hope for them in their twenties as they were on the same wavelength. The distance between them now was becoming palpable.

Patricia sat with Eric and had a meal. They ate silently, with Eric distracted, watching the tourists around them. She decided they would have an excellent time for the coming three days.

Chapter 7 · Child Exploitation, Manila

Patricia was sitting in her office when Atty entered to inform her that the Chief of Child Protection, Nadia, wanted to speak with her.

"Patricia, we have a problem. Remember all the police officers we trained in child protection and the prevention of child harassment? Well, one of the officers found an expatriate in a locked car with a child two nights ago, and they arrested him. He is now in custody," Nadia told her.

"Well done! It would appear the project was successful if the police arrested the criminal. How is the child, and where were they taken?" Patricia asked.

"The child, male, is with the Department of Social Affairs and is getting the support he needs. However, there is a problem. The expatriate is a UN staff member from another agency, and his office has already contacted me to request the police drop the charges," Nadia told her.

Patricia was appalled.

"Well, what do we do? It will not look good with how we have trained the police to suddenly declare it's OK and release him," Nadia continued.

"What is his name?" Patricia asked.

Nadia gave her the name of the perpetrator, and Patricia was shocked. She knew the staff member because he had been a health consultant in New York for at least a year. His work was excellent.

"We don't request the police to release him. He must remain in jail, and the Philippine government needs to determine whether he will be prosecuted. This is a local matter, and it's not our job to interfere," she replied.

"I agree. I will relay that message back to the police and to the Department of Social Affairs," Nadia told her.

Patricia pondered how this man could have descended to such a level and was alarmed that he might have been doing this for a long time in the Philippines. He held a senior position and was highly regarded by his colleagues.

"The Secretary for Social Affairs is on the phone for you, Patricia," Atty told her.

"Hi, Patricia. I guess you have heard about Martin Hedges by now. We are receiving numerous calls from his agency and the Australian government, as he is an Australian citizen. We are ignoring both. However, we're worried since he is suicidal. We will place him under watch for now, but do you agree that we must request the Ministry of Justice to develop the case against him?" the Secretary asked her.

"Absolutely, Dinky. We must proceed with this; otherwise, we will have no credibility. And it's a grave crime that he committed. It's like stating it's not important since the child was impoverished and the perpetrator comes from a connected and privileged background. We need to support this case as an agency," Patricia responded.

"Apparently, there are more children he exploited. He had a local pimp. We are getting pressure to release him so he can go home to Australia, but that sets a bad precedent," Dinky added.

Patricia agreed with the Secretary. She had no sympathy for Martin as the power dynamic was so skewed. He had given the boy eight dollars, and since the pimp managed the boy, he would not even see the money. This exploitation of children had to be stopped. Patricia saw in her messages that there was a call from Martin's supervisor. She didn't ring him back.

Chapter 8 · Harassment in the Office

Patricia entered her office and found three women sitting around a table. Their voices were heated, and one woman quickly exited the room.

"What's going on?" Patricia asked.

"We talked about this last week. Enya is taking a case against Anders," Grace told her.

Anders was the office's Operations Chief. He was very competent, but his weakness was women. Enya had accused Anders of harassment, so she was now working in another section.

"Does Enya wish to file an official case against Anders?" Patricia asked her.

"She is not sure. She wishes to move to another section, but also wants a promotion. She feels she deserves this. She has requested I represent her as her ombudsperson, and I have agreed," Grace told her.

Patricia knew that this was going to be a complex case. This wasn't a straightforward harassment case, where the staff member made a complaint that could be corroborated by other staff. The staff member had worked with the Chief of Operations for two years and never raised an issue. Now, she wished to move, which was acceptable, but demanding a promotion was not, as it could be construed as the price for her silence. She asked Anders to come to her office. He had been on leave, so there had been no chance to talk to him before now.

"Hello, Anders. I hope all is well. You are aware of the case that Enya has brought against you. I am signing the note for the record today since all details must be shared with New York for their recommendation. She wishes to leave your section and move to another, which would require approval from HQ. However, she is also requesting a promotion. Let me ask you bluntly. Is there any truth to the accusations that she is raising? HR will question you on this, anyway." Patricia asked him.

"No, Patricia. I never harassed her, but I did sometimes lose my temper with her because her work could be shoddy and late in submission," Anders responded.

There was another complication. There had been a prior harassment case against Anders when he was working in Kenya. His ex-wife had been pushing for the case to be taken against him. However, it was resolved in his favor, and the organization took no action.

Patricia had to be careful, as the assumption would be that Anders was guilty due to his record; however, she needed to address this case independently and not be swayed by his previous case. The first stage involved in-house arbitration, accompanied by careful documentation for HQ. If that failed, the issue would be referred to New York for resolution.

She told him, "I have requested another UN agency to help with the arbitration as an independent entity unfamiliar with the staff members concerned, but again, this will need to be approved by HQ."

"Is that wise?" Anders asked her, and Patricia could see that he was trying to control the outcome by influencing her. Well, that won't work, she thought.

"Anders, the only other alternative is that we call New York immediately to address the issue. The first question will be why we did not address it through our own channels. This case must be dealt with fairly!" she told him rather stiffly.

Anders shrugged his shoulders and left the room.

After Anders left her office, Patricia called in Enya and Grace.

"Enya, I want you to know that we are doing our best to examine this case to the fullest extent possible. We are requesting that another agency undertake the arbitration process, but I must ask you a question before proceeding. Would you prefer I take the case to New York and ask them to investigate immediately?" Patricia explained.

"No, I am ready to go through the arbitration process, but I can no longer work with Mr. Anders," Enya responded.

"I agree. As an interim measure, we will transfer you to Child Protection while we review other vacancies you can apply for over the next month," Patricia told her.

Patricia returned to her office after accompanying Enya to the Child Protection Unit to introduce her to the staff there. She then called the

Resident Coordinator to explain what she was about to do and the process she had recommended.

"What do you think happened?" the Resident Coordinator asked her.

"I don't know, since Enya has yet to provide the actual details of the harassment, and her ombudsperson is correct in not divulging that information if she indeed wishes to present a formal complaint to Headquarters," Patricia explained.

"Do you think that they had an affair?" The Coordinator asked her.

"I can't speculate on that. I don't know. All I do know is that a serious complaint was made by one of my staff," Patricia told her.

"It's your decision, but it makes sense to me. It would be best if you were seen to be impartial," the Resident Coordinator told her.

Patricia, exhausted, was driven home to her house in Makati, where her dogs greeted her. Eric was sitting at the table, working inside.

"How was your day? Mine was terrible," he told her.

Patricia explained the entire case to Eric, as he was not familiar with any of her staff, so she considered it safe to confide in him.

"Sounds like he did it," Eric said.

She could argue that Eric was a little chauvinist, but she was sure of one thing: he would never be accused of harassment in the workplace. He was far too professional and careful regarding such matters, and he had told her that he never had relationships with work colleagues.

"I can't make that assumption. My gut reaction is to support the woman, and considering Ander's record, that might be the right approach. However, there is no proof, and this new case needs to be reviewed independently of his history," she told him.

"Oh, throw the book at him!" he laughed.

Patricia thought, so much for a rational, independent opinion. Eric didn't appear to care if Patricia got her hands burned on this case. Patricia was well aware that if she made one wrong step, her chances of further promotion were in jeopardy. She went to the kitchen and poured herself a glass of wine from the bottle that Eric had already opened. Eric suggested that they go for a meal in Greenbelt.

Eric and Patricia found a Mexican restaurant, and Eric ordered margaritas.

"So, when are you flying to the UK?" Eric asked her.

"I will fly out in a week. What about you? When are you flying to New York? I am sure your parents will be thrilled to see you," she told him.

"Yes, but Dad wants to leave Ithaca for good now and live in Florida. Mom would prefer they spend winters only in Florida, but she agrees with him for an easy life! He keeps harping at me to come home and settle down. He feels too old to make the flight here," he told her.

"Well, he does have some heart issues. He's right to be a bit worried," Patricia responded.

"Well, today the office told me that they might not extend my contract past December. So, I'll consider going home, or Shell Company has discussed hiring me directly. Another option is to move to my company's office in Australia," Eric told her.

"And what about us? If you leave here, I don't think I can leave this position before 2011 due to the seniority of the post and a new country program under development," Patricia replied, somewhat concerned.

Eric ordered more margaritas, sighed, and sat back in his chair. Patricia had had such a hard day dealing with the harassment case that she quickly drank the second margarita.

"Well, we'll play it by ear. I'm not sure about any plans right now, so I can't make any commitments," Eric said quietly.

Patricia was confused because Eric had nearly proposed to her by the pool a few months ago, but she brushed it off because he had too much to drink.

"So, I am supposed to coast along and wait for you to make your plans independently. Eric, I came here since you were working here! I wouldn't have come this far away from my parents at their age," Patricia told him.

"This food is good! Let's order more margaritas…" Eric started on his third margarita and then ranted about his problems at work.

"Let's go home and talk for a while. I feel a bit tired," Patricia told him.

Eric ignored her comment. "I can't believe the directors are listening to Keith over me. He has far less experience than I do and is making all his moves to impress those above him. He doesn't care about any of his fellow workers. And he treats the Filipinos as his subordinates, even though Ferdinand, a national, is in charge of the office." Eric ranted on, becoming louder.

Patricia shuffled in her seat as if to distance herself from him.

"I think we should walk home," Patricia told him.

Eric looked at Patricia angrily and turned to say something to the person at the next table, commenting on their food. Patricia asked for the bill.

"I'm not ready to leave yet. Let's go down the road and try their margaritas, too," Eric told her.

Patricia paid the bill, got up from the table, and left Eric alone. She walked home to the house, got herself a coffee, and sat down with the dogs. About thirty minutes later, Eric stormed into the house.

"What was that? Why did you leave me like that? It was highly embarrassing! I looked around, and you were gone," he shouted.

"Eric, you were not listening to me all evening. I've had a long and tiring day, and I wanted a quiet evening. I agreed to go out but not to drink all night and have a hangover tomorrow," she told him.

Eric came up close to her.

"That was too much! It was disrespectful," Eric said to her.

He pushed Patricia hard on the shoulder. She fell back onto the couch, stunned. She was silent, but Eric had not stopped ranting. He started to move closer. At that moment, Mattie, Patricia's German shepherd, walked over and placed himself in front of Patricia. Eric looked at her and then stormed out of the house, slamming the door behind him.

Chapter 9 · The Shooting

It was October 2009, and Christmas decorations were already being displayed around Makati and Manila. As Patricia was being driven over to give a speech at a conference in the early morning, she thought back over the past three months. She and Eric had spent their summer holiday with their respective parents, and when he returned, Eric came over and apologized for his behavior at her house in July. She decided to give him another chance. She loved him even though her intuition told her that they would not last beyond the end of the year. In October, they took a two-week trip to Cambodia. One week was spent at a regional representatives' meeting in Angkor Wat, and the second was spent traveling in the country. It had been a good trip and helpful in repairing their relationship, but tension between them remained. Patricia was having trouble getting past the incident in July at her house. Eric had pushed her, and no man had ever laid a finger on her, ever before.

After Patricia had given the speech and was walking over to the car, a call came from Anders, the Operations Chief. He sounded somewhat tense, but she considered this was due to the ongoing harassment case against him. The case had been referred to Headquarters since it had not been resolved by arbitration.

"We have had a major incident. I am afraid it's bad. Alberto, our driver, was visiting Mindanao to visit a girlfriend, and he was shot in the stomach by her brother. She's Muslim. He has been taken to the hospital in Cotabato. Of course, he was on vacation time, but he had no authorization to visit Mindanao, and he needed that for insurance purposes in a conflict zone," Anders told her.

"Awful! Have we talked to the hospital?" she asked him, rather shocked.

"Yes, and they are not giving him good chances of survival. Thirty percent odds he will survive the shooting," Anders told her.

"We need to evacuate him to Manila as soon as possible. I need to talk to the hospital," Patricia insisted.

"We can't evacuate him as he is not covered through insurance. We have already talked to the hospital," Anders replied.

"When were you first informed of this incident?" Patricia asked him.

"About three hours ago. We are handling it, Patricia," he told her.

"Why didn't you tell me about it then? From now on, I will be responsible for approving all actions. Please pass me the phone number for the hospital directly," she asked him.

Patricia called the hospital and was put on hold. Eventually, the doctor managing Alberto's case came to the phone.

"I am afraid Alberto has been severely injured. The bullet exited from his back after entering the front of his lower torso, but seven organs were struck. We are operating on him right now, and he has been in surgery for the past two hours," the doctor told her.

"Do you have security guards at the hospital?" Patricia asked him.

"We have security downstairs," he told her.

"We will send over extra security to put a guard on the door if the perpetrator returns. What do you need?" she asked him.

"We need more blood. We are short right now, and the Red Cross has no more here to provide," the doctor replied.

"We will send blood and one of our doctors to Cotabato by Medevac as soon as possible. The same plane will bring Alberto back to Manila," she said.

Straight after, Patricia got a call from Brenda, the Communications Chief.

"We need to get a press release out, as everyone is reporting that a UN staff member has been killed in Cotabato. We need to make it clear that he is still alive," Brenda told her.

"I'm sorry, Brenda. Why would we do that? We're not releasing a press release at this time."

"But this looks so bad," Brenda told her. "And the UN will expect us to comment quickly."

"No statement will go out today or tomorrow. The brother of the girlfriend tried to kill Alberto, and no arrest has yet been made. We can't take the risk that they may think he's still alive, so no word should get out until Alberto is safely on the helicopter back to Manila," Patricia insisted.

Patricia ended the conversation with Brenda and then called Medevac services for a plane to be dispatched immediately to Cotabato carrying two office staff to support Alberto on the journey back. She called Anders to see if he had secured payment for the helicopter from the insurance company, but this had not yet been approved. Patricia called Alberto's wife and updated her without providing the information concerning the girlfriend or why he was shot.

Patricia returned to her house, and Eric was not there. She went into her lounge and called the doctor in Cotabato.

"Alberto is still in surgery for another three to five hours. There was internal bleeding that required urgent attention. Your staff has just arrived with the additional blood, so thank you!" he told her.

"Will he survive the surgery?' Patricia asked him.

"I don't know. He appears strong, but the bullet very severely injured him," the doctor told her.

Patricia thanked the doctor and walked over to the drinks cabinet, where she poured herself a whisky to steady her nerves. She received a text from Eric saying he had heard about her staff member and was sorry. He would be out that evening with friends. Given this crisis, Patricia wondered why he would not come home on this day. She knew this didn't bode well for them.

Patricia made two more phone calls during the night to Cotabato staff for updates and was pleased to hear that Alberto had survived the second operation and was now sleeping. She asked the staff there to ensure the door to Alberto's room was under guard.

At 6:00 AM, Patricia received a call from Cotabato, informing her that Alberto was on the plane with a hospital doctor and her staff, and he was en route directly to Makati Hospital. She felt that now she could get some sleep and go to the office later that morning.

Chapter 10 · The End of the Relationship

It was early January 2010, and Patricia had just returned from the UK, where she had spent Christmas with her parents and sister. Eric and Patricia had parted under bad circumstances in November. After Alberto's shooting, they had argued by phone about his absence for those few days when she had needed his support. They did not see each other before they departed for their leave.

However, in December, she received a call from Eric while she was in London, who told her that he missed her and wanted to see her as soon as she returned. Patricia was mildly optimistic that they could move past the difficulties this time. However, it was a challenge for her to put out of her mind the incident where Eric had physically pushed her. She was not over it yet. They had both decided to give the relationship until the end of the previous year before deciding what would come next. Yet here they were, in a new year, without any resolution or direction. Perhaps when Eric came over later, they could talk this through and start anew with a deeper understanding. Patricia was still in love with him despite his shortcomings.

After her first day back at the office, she came into her house and was greeted by her four blustering dogs before she checked the kitchen to decide what she would eat. She heard Eric enter. She went out and hugged him.

"I missed you. How is everything? How are your parents?" he asked her.

"All is good. Mum could be better, but they are as well as can be expected. How are your parents?" Patricia asked him.

"They are very good and send you their love. They both miss you," Eric told her.

Patricia realized she had never invited Eric to meet her parents.

They sat out in the garden on the bench and drank wine.

"My office was impressed by how your agency managed the typhoon last November and wants to contribute to your organization. Shall I pick up the check, and we can pocket it?" Eric said.

Patricia looked at him aghast. Did he really think she could condone him taking money from her organization?

"I'm joking! It's difficult being back at the office, and I was tempted to stay in Ithaca since there is no guarantee of work here past this July," he told her. Patricia thought it was a poor joke.

"I get it. You need to follow what's best for your career. But I need to stay at least until the end of 2010. I could be released after that," she replied.

They went to the kitchen, where Patricia's housekeeper had left out ingredients for her to make an omelet and had left rice in the slow cooker. Eric turned on the gas stove and prepared the frying pan with olive oil, salt, and herbs. He added some tomatoes, spring onions, and spinach that had been cut and prepared for them. Patricia grated some cheese while Eric proceeded to make each of them an omelet. Patricia sprinkled the cheese on top and got the plates ready. They decided to sit and eat in the TV room where they would watch a film together.

"You know, something strange happened to me at the office today," Patricia recollected. "The head of our fundraising had asked me to purchase something for her in the UK. As I pulled this item out, a letter from an old friend from Egypt slipped out of my bag." Eric looked across at her curiously.

She had no idea how the letter had gotten into her purse, since he had written it to her a long time ago, but she knew the contents of the letter, having kept it long after her friend's death.

Patricia continued, "The letter includes the sentence, 'although my eyes may stray from time to time, I remain loyal to the one I love,'' she told him. "This letter was written to me more than fifteen years ago. I don't quite know how it ended up in my bag today."

Patricia turned to Eric and asked him, "have you slept with someone else recently?"

Eric looked across at her and then looked away. "Yes, it didn't mean anything. I met her in a bar in Ithaca over Christmas, and since you and I broke up last November, it happened. It was only one night," he smiled very faintly as he responded. What surprised Patricia was that he didn't even seem to be embarrassed about it.

"We did not break up! We argued. That's different!" she told him.

Patricia got up from the couch. She walked slowly over to the dining room. She turned back to look at Eric.

"Please leave the house and don't come back. You can collect your things later, or I'll send them to your office," she calmly told him in a quiet voice.

Patricia walked into her bedroom and closed the door. She heard Eric drop his set of door keys on the table.

As he left, he shouted out to her, "we always break up for the same reason!"

Patricia realized that this had been coming for a while since she had given Eric an ultimatum last January. The strange thing was that he hadn't even tried to hide or be embarrassed by what he had done. She knew now it would never work out between them. The younger Eric was much more supportive, but over the years, he had evolved into someone who had little in common with her and even resented her success. This time, it was over. Patricia felt a heavy grief, and she cried to herself for most of the night, trying to work out what Eric was alluding to. Was it trust?

The next six months were challenging for her. Although Eric was still working in Manila, she didn't see him again. She asked to see him in April to address their breakup, but at the last minute, she decided not to go and instead took a trip to Cebu for a short holiday. She managed to mask her grief from the office staff, but she was suffering. She immersed herself more in her work, which at least she continued to enjoy. Later that year, Eric left the Philippines to take an assignment in Australia with the same company. Patricia didn't try to see him before he left. She mourned the relationship for most of the year, but it didn't affect her work. She had decided that she would try never to see Eric again unless they accidentally met somewhere. Gradually, she overcame the heartache and understood it would never have worked as they were such different people.

Chapter 11 · The Dismantling of Patricia's Career

Patricia waited in her office, knowing this would be one of her most difficult days. Atty announced that Sarina, the Regional Director, had arrived at the building and was on her way to her office.

"Good morning, Patricia. It was a pleasant flight, and the hotel last night was excellent. Please thank Atty for all her support regarding the arrangements. Now, I suggest we go for lunch immediately. OK?" Sarina ordered her, so she knew there was not much choice in the matter.

They went to Greenbelt for lunch, about fifteen minutes from the office. The restaurant was one of the nicest in the shopping mall, offering a variety of salads, as the Regional Director was a vegetarian. Patricia looked across at her nervously as she was aware that Sarina didn't like her. She steeled herself to be prepared to respond forcefully. Their relationship had been fraught with issues since the Executive Director visited the Philippines a few months back, and Sarina had not been invited to join her. She had never forgiven either the Executive Director or Patricia, even though there was little that Patricia could have done about this, since it was all arranged through the New York office. The problem with many senior staff in the agency was their egos.

Sarina did not wait long before she launched into attack mode.

"Well, Patricia. It appears you have a serious problem with the Child Protection Officer, as she refuses to work with you and Ahmed, your deputy," she stated. Ahmed had replaced Nigel about a year ago and was Nadia's supervisor.

"I rang you, and I explained the situation! She is angry as she has to terminate her husband's contract, which is being paid directly by our agency to one of the NGOs we support. I don't need to stress that the rules clearly state that we need HR approval before any spouse can be employed through our funding. Because this was not done, I asked her to give the NGO three months' notice on his behalf. If we go through the proper channels, perhaps this could be changed later. Right now, it is a serious audit query if we don't do something fast," Patricia explained to her.

"Forget the issue of her husband. You have a problem with getting on with your staff," Sarina replied.

"I have to interrupt you there. The problem is only with Nadia. Where are the other issues?" Patricia rather impatiently asked her.

"There are some. For example, you and your former deputy had problems working together," Sarina continued.

Patricia knew then that Sarina had flown in for a reason unrelated to solving the problem with her Child Protection Officer. It was intended to label Patricia as a problem, which would ultimately destroy her career within the agency. She was silent as Sarina continued. She could feel the color draining from her face, and she clutched at the side of the table. She had no idea how she would manage this attack.

"It's time for you to leave the Philippines. A spell back at Headquarters would be good for you. You do not appear to manage pressure well," Sarina continued.

"Are we avoiding the issue that a staff member broke the rules, and that doesn't matter? I handled it as diplomatically as possible, but I cannot change the outcome, so we must terminate her husband's contract with the NGO now," Patricia continued to try to explain to her. Still, she could see she was not listening, as Sarina checked her phone for messages.

"As I said, Patricia, that is not the issue," Sarina replied.

It struck Patricia that Sarina had already consulted with HQ on this issue, and they had agreed that Sarina would clear it. Even though there was no record of approval for the husband's employment, this allowed Sarina to proceed as she wished, to remove Patricia from the Philippines.

Patricia knew it would do her no good to continue arguing with Sarina about her case. The Regional Director had decided, and Patricia was aware that she had not consulted anyone else in the office except Nadia. Patricia had no problems with any of her other officers. However, she knew that people would want to please the Regional Director, so she could slant a question in a particular manner to obtain the response that would back her claim that Patricia was a problem. She knew the agency would not take her side on this issue, so she needed to end this meeting as quickly as possible, collect her thoughts, and decide on her next steps.

Chapter 12 · Leaving Manila

It was November 2011, and Patricia looked over the nearly empty apartment as she watched the packers finish wrapping up the last furniture and items. Her housekeeper was finding more items in the cupboards and packing them.

She had been both happy and extremely sad here. She had entertained numerous guests over many happy evenings. She had enjoyed her life in Manila. Now, after three and a half years, she was due to end her time here and move back to the UK for a short while to support her father as his health declined. She had applied for six months' leave without pay, which had been granted. She was still determining what would come after that. Her drivers, Reuel and Alberto, came to the house to bid her farewell.

"I will miss our drives and Starbucks stops, Patricia. We had good times. Where are the dogs?" Reuel asked her.

"They were shipped back to the States yesterday to kennels and then to my house in Connecticut," Patricia replied.

"Ma'am, you deserve all the kindness and best wishes for your next assignment," Alberto said.

Alberto had recovered well from the shooting and was living a good life, exercising regularly and supporting his family. Patricia felt proud of the office's effort to save his life. The previous evening, the office had hosted a party featuring Lady Gaga songs and performances, as she was one of her favorite singers. It had been a wonderful evening, full of fun, leaving Patricia sad to leave. Her Communications Officer, Brenda, had choreographed the whole musical presentation, including costumes and performances.

"We will miss you, Patricia," Brenda told her. "You always supported us women, and we appreciated that."

"Thanks, Brenda! And I will miss you all terribly!" she told her.

"What comes next?" Leonard, the Child Protection Officer, asked her.

"Well, I need six months at home in the UK with my father as he is declining rapidly," she told him.

"Will you miss the Philippines?" he asked her.

"Yes, I will miss having summer every day, even at Christmas. I will miss my trips to the field and landing on some island, where a feast of seafood, fruit, and assorted sweets always awaits my arrival. I will miss my times with the Ministers, such as Dinky, who was the warmest and kindest Minister I have ever met. But, Leonard, what I think I will miss the most is what we all worked together to achieve. We have made a significant impact on Mindanao, particularly in child protection and health. You really all are a wonderful team," she told him and the others, and then she walked away quickly to hide the tears streaming down her cheeks.

She had no regrets about coming to the Philippines. She felt that significant achievements had been made. As she walked out of the office for the last time, she knew intuitively she would never return as a UN staff member.

She had made good friends in Manila and knew she would never see many of them again. This was the nature of her work, and she had accepted that when she signed up for international development work thirty years ago. However, it was always painful to leave your friends, your home, and your environment, and to leave behind the persona you had created in each new culture, tailored to the country's needs.

She watched the boxes being loaded onto the lorry. When all the boxes were packed, she banged the door shut after her as she got into the car, and then they drove to the airport.

Epilogue

Brighton (2024)

The Women

Echoes of Seven Lives

Patricia was about to enter the hall at the Institute of Development Studies in Brighton. As usual, the weather in England was cloudy and overcast. She missed the clear blue skies at her home in Worcester, Massachusetts. She entered the building and made her way into the conference hall. Sir Robert Briggs, an eminent expert in international development, was giving a speech. Patricia had always considered him rather pompous and theoretical.

Sir Robert was talking about participatory governance. He mentioned programs in Pakistan and Mozambique that focused on aspects of citizen-led accountability, including linking local concerns to policymaking, and bridging grassroots movements with structural reform. Additionally, there was a mention of donor-led empowerment. Patricia wondered why donors needed to be further empowered. Were they not already holding all the purse strings? After forty-five years of working in development, she wondered how far the donors had really come. She sure knew that in every country where she had worked, local experts were up to the task of leading their own development efforts, and there was undoubtedly a resentment towards yet one more donor or development agency arriving with pre-packaged solutions, assuming authority, and sidelining the very people who best understood the challenges and the context.

She stayed until the end of the talk, suppressing her yawns and resentment. She was meeting her friends that evening for dinner at a local restaurant. Most of them had not seen each other for nearly forty-five years when they took a one-month course at IDS at the beginning of their international careers. Patricia thought back to that time and how naive they had all been.

She entered the lobby of the Grand Hotel, where she was staying, which had a history with terrorism, as it was the site of the 1984 blast during the Conservative Party conference when Margaret Thatcher was staying there. It was a beautiful old hotel with immense character. Patricia was rarely in the UK these days since her parents had passed away, and her other family members were all living in the US. An hour later, Patricia left the hotel and walked down the road to the restaurant. She entered and asked for the table she had booked. As she walked in, she saw that Nancy had already arrived and was seated at a large table by the window.

"Hi Nancy! My gosh, good to see you!" Patricia was surprised to recognize her immediately. "You look the same as when we met in '79." Except Patricia noted that Nancy was much slimmer. She pulled out a chair and sat opposite her. Nancy was already drinking a glass of wine, so Patricia ordered one as well.

"Good to see you too! I arrived here this afternoon, so I am still quite jetlagged. I mean, it's quite the journey from Thailand!" Nancy responded.

"I'm a bit jetlagged myself, but that's just flying here from Boston! Less than your journey!" Patricia ordered some hors d'oeuvres when the waitress walked by their table.

"Remind me, what are you doing there in Thailand?" Patricia asked.

"I have my home in Bangkok, where I work as a consultant. After my second divorce, it made sense to stay where my son was working, as he is based there. I undertake consultancies for both the UN and NGOs, so I am kept busy most of the time," Nancy said.

"I had no idea you married again after you divorced Martin. You got married after Nepal, right? You were so in love with him? What went wrong?" Patricia asked.

"That's a long story! Are you sure you really want to hear it?" Nancy asked her.

"Sure! I have my own complex stories! Don't we all?" Patricia responded.

"Well, after we had Isaac, it wasn't easy. I married Martin about two years after we worked together in Nepal. He made it clear that it would only work if I followed him to the States and studied for my master's degree there. After that, I followed him on his overseas assignments and never had time to develop my career," Nancy explained with her voice becoming quieter as she went on.

"It was unfair of him to expect that," Patricia exclaimed.

"I wanted to study, but my attention was on Isaac. And Martin never really carried his weight at home, so the burden was on me. He now lives in Australia with his fourth wife. I am happily twice divorced, have a steady job, and my son is nearby! I guess Nepal was my longest and happiest development experience. Being a consultant is very intense, and since donor agencies usually pay my fees, their needs often don't align with the country's needs. What about yourself?" Nancy asked.

"I married once but never had children. It lasted a few years, and we're still friends. No regrets. I now live in the States. I've mainly worked for NGOs and on their Boards for the past eight years and love it. But I only work for agencies engaged in humanitarian assistance. I've soured on international NGOs working in development, as there are so many excellent local non-profit organizations. There's still a need for international support for full-scale emergencies," Patricia said.

"But you had a really great career. I tracked your path. I often regret not remaining with the UN in some way," Nancy replied.

Geeta, Lisa, and Marie Louise entered the restaurant. Patricia stood up to greet them, and they all hugged each other before taking their seats. Patricia thought they all looked similar to when they first met, except Geeta. She had aged considerably.

"Now we are just waiting for Rebecca. She'll be late, I am sure, due to her meeting in London," Patricia said. The women had a WhatsApp group where they updated each other on developments, marriages, divorces, and new jobs.

"Well, ladies, as you drink your wine, an expensive Bordeaux for our French friend here, what have you all been doing for the past few decades?" Patricia asked them.

"Well, since my life is the least interesting, I'll go first," Lisa said. "You all know that, after South Sudan, I decided to work in emergencies. I went back to live in London first and then went to DR Congo for six months, but it completely burned me out. There were things I saw that I never want to remember. I went back to London and retrained in behavioral sciences and worked for the private sector for twenty-odd years."

Patricia wondered how Lisa had lost her confidence from the bright young Irish button she was when they'd first met. She soon found out why.

"I met my husband at LSTM in Liverpool, where we studied together, but we divorced after eight years. He wanted children, and I was unable to have them. He started an affair after a few years, and he made it pretty obvious for me to find out. I put up with it for too long. He even tried to take the house that I'd bought before we married. Luckily, I was able to stop that with a good lawyer."

"Well, he sounds like a master manipulator," Patricia commented. She had met a few in her own life, but she never tolerated it for long, either in love or at work.

"I returned to Ireland, my parents' home, and settled in Waterford, as my sister lives nearby. I manage to do consultancies for companies in Ireland. I can't say I enjoy the work, and I'm bitter about my marriage, but I have a good life in Ireland and a few good friends. What about you, Marie Louise?" Lisa asked.

"That's sad, Lisa. I'm so sorry," Marie Louise replied. "I love our apartment in Paris. I always wanted to live in my favorite city, and most of the time, I'm out at restaurants, plays, ballets, and museums!"

Although Patricia was quite happy in Massachusetts, if she were going to live in Europe, Paris would be the place. She thought it was always the most cosmopolitan city in Europe and far more interesting than London.

"I retrained after Lesotho, a bit like you, Lisa! I recognized a significant need for expertise in climate change, so I pursued my master's degree at the Sorbonne and later worked at the World Bank. The problem with working there is that they have consultants or junior staff doing most of the work, and all the credit goes to their senior, permanent staff. I got married and had two children. They both work in France," Marie Louise continued.

"Ladies, your lives all sound more interesting than mine," Geeta moaned. "I gave up my job at the UN to follow Robert to Virginia. I felt guilty for a very long time since I'd wanted to stay with the UN. But the relationship wouldn't have worked. It was touch and go for a year or so since Robert continued to see his fiancée. We were involved under the radar until he ended things with her. Then we married, and I had Julia within a year."

"Did you go back to the UN? I thought you said you had?" Patricia asked.

"I worked with them as a consultant, but it's been difficult to find assignments at the same level of expertise as those I had before leaving the UN," Geeta responded. Patricia noticed that she was pretty tense.

"What was also so frustrating for me was that most of my work remained in water and sanitation, a sector dominated by men who have little consideration for women, despite the lip service they pay to it. It's fine if they hire women as long as the men hold the senior positions. That's been frustrating," Geeta said.

"I hear you", Patricia responded. "You were brave to step out of a senior position at the UN as you did in your forties. And I get what you're saying regarding male dominance. Although I was glad to leave the UN after the Philippines, I felt that once you hit your fifties, they made far less effort to place you and gave fewer options to women. And if you stood up to anyone in a position senior to your own, you were labeled as difficult. It's a different story for men who rarely retire before they are sixty-five, and even then, they are hired as consultants thereafter."

Geeta shuffled in her seat and rearranged her sari. Patricia noticed that she wasn't wearing her wedding ring.

"But the worst aspect is how little women at senior levels support other senior women. That was a rude awakening for me," Patricia commented.

"I agree," Geeta said. "It wasn't an issue when I started, but the older you get, the more women seem to become competitive with each other."

"Geeta, what about your husband?" Patricia asked.

"Robert spends most of his time in Hawaii on assignments. I hope he returns to Virginia and wants to retire there. Our daughter works in San Francisco, and loves it, so I don't get to see her much either. It's lonely in Virginia, so I go back to Delhi often to see my brothers and sisters."

Patricia wondered what she wasn't telling them about her marriage.

Rebecca blustered into the restaurant. Patricia observed that she was more rotund than the others, having put on quite a bit of weight since they last met, and was dressed far more bohemian. She squeezed herself into a chair and sighed heavily.

"Oh my god, it's so great to see you all after such a long time! I'm so sorry, guys. I had an urgent meeting in London with some American friends." Rebecca grabbed the wine bottle and poured herself a large glass.

No one knew what Rebecca did for work, as she was somewhat vague when they messaged and asked her. She had spent a few years in the United States after working in Nigeria and Mozambique with her lover. No one knew who he was, either, except all of them knew that he had died in the early 2000s.

"Where are you living now, Rebecca?" Patricia asked her.

"Well, at the moment, Costa Rica! I have a villa by the sea that I purchased cheaply in 2005. I spend a lot of time there and on assignments in Central America. After learning Portuguese, Spanish was easy, so after that, most of my work has been in Central and South America."

Patricia thought back to the shy, beautiful creature they had met in Brighton in 1979. She had found it the most difficult to articulate her needs or ambitions. Yet here she was in all her mysterious glory, overly confident and hiding a multitude of secrets. Whenever they asked Rebecca on WhatsApp anything about her life, she would respond in sweeping sentences that told them nothing.

"I go to the States often, so I should try to catch up with Geeta and you more frequently," Rebecca replied.

Patricia knew that wouldn't happen. It was a miracle that they had persuaded Rebecca to meet them here in Brighton.

"Well, it's sad Anna is not with us. It's tragic," Lisa commented.

"We should raise a glass to Anna. She would want us to celebrate her life," Patricia raised her glass in the air.

"I was so sad I couldn't attend the funeral," Geeta said.

"The funeral was small. It was held in North London, and I had a chance to talk to her parents and sister," Lisa explained.

"A few of the countries I visited were dangerous, but I always felt that the agencies provided good security. In Lesotho, though, at times, I did feel at risk, especially after a volunteer was killed in the same town where I lived," Marie Louise replied.

A waitress arrived and took food orders from Patricia for all the women while more bottles of wine were ordered. Most of the women were drinking quite conservatively, but Rebecca was guzzling down glasses at three times the speed of everyone else.

"So, friends, Patricia went the distance in terms of working with the UN and undertaking long-term assignments overseas. Was it worth it, Patricia?" Rebecca brought the conversation back to the person all of them considered the most successful career woman in the group. Patricia wondered if Rebecca was being sarcastic after all the wine she was knocking back.

"Don't forget I stepped out of the UN in 2012 and worked in the US for various NGOs," Patricia laughed as she responded. "But yes, it was worth it. I feel I made a difference in the countries where I worked. I was more cynical by the end, but that didn't affect the fact that I think I made a difference. I often wondered if I should have gone to the Philippines at all since I was following a man! For the first time in my life, I moved for a relationship!"

"It might have been better for my career if I'd remained longer with the UN. But then, I would have missed out on a completely different experience working with international NGOs, and, of course, I could write a book about that. How obsolete they're becoming in terms of international development," Patricia added.

"Interesting! Do tell us more! I tend to agree when I look at the larger NGOs working in South America. There are multitudes of excellent local civil societies that do a better job. There is a need for international emergency support, but really, that's about it now. And don't get me started on the UN!" Rebecca added.

"Geeta, are you glad you left the UN?" Patricia asked.

"No. I should have stayed. But I was in love, and I wanted a child with Robert. My hormones took over, and my work became secondary. I regret it. I don't regret the relationship, though," Geeta wistfully reflected.

"Oh, folks, you all should take a few lovers! One person is restricting! I have Jon in New Zealand, Pablo in Brazil, and my friend in Austin, whom I see at least three times a year." Rebecca reached again for the wine to replenish her glass. The others looked at Rebecca and wondered how she had changed so much from the painfully shy person they had met in Brighton all those decades ago.

"Well, what's next? Where do you think we'll be in another ten years when we're even older and greyer?" Marie Louise asked.

"At least it's warm where I live. I couldn't live in a cold climate anymore," Nancy said.

"To be honest, I got fed up with living in one season, like in the Philippines. Christmas was celebrated in 85 degrees! Nancy, did you regret following Martin?" Patricia asked.

"Yes. It was destined for failure. He was too young," Nancy explained.

"Eric was very similar to Martin," Patricia commented. "I think I told you all about him in emails. We were together in the Philippines, and I loved him deeply, but it was a strained relationship."

"What do you think Anna would have gone on to do?" Patricia asked the women as she lowered her glass soberly.

"She may have taken a headquarters position somewhere, or maybe even left development, like Lisa," Marie Louise said.

"And back to my earlier question of where we will all be in ten years: I envision myself living in a house by the sea, perhaps even on the West Coast of the United States. Geeta, I wouldn't mind Hawaii! I will have turned to writing novels and perhaps teaching yoga, with a few consultancies mixed in. I may even take Rebecca up on her idea, but one lover is enough! And plenty of dogs," Patricia told them.

The women laughed, drank, and ate a little longer until the restaurant was ready to close, and they were the last ones left. As they left the restaurant, they walked again over to the seafront, as they had done decades earlier, and walked on the sand barefoot, carrying their expensive shoes. It was difficult for them to say goodbye, as they were unsure if they would have any more opportunities to get together. All of them had busy agendas, and aside from the WhatsApp group, none of them had formed close friendships with each other. Patricia wondered why that was the case. Perhaps it was because, for most of them, they had each developed such deep independence over the years of living and working abroad. They'd learned to count on themselves so completely that trusting friends too much felt dangerous, as if the pain of being let down would be too much to bear. She couldn't say for sure, but in her heart, she knew she had lost many friends over the decades and only had a few she considered she could trust.

Patricia walked away alone, her step light as she made her way back to the hotel, taking the long route to walk by the sea. She felt a little happier than when she had arrived in Brighton. She might not have made all the right decisions, and maybe had taken quite a few wrong turns on her path. However, she was satisfied with where she was today and where she would be going tomorrow.

Acknowledgements

This is my first novel, and its journey began many years ago—specifically, in 2016—while I was slowly stepping away from a life in international development. It sat on the shelf for years as I navigated the complexities of retirement, explored new professional avenues, and finally embraced a sense of calm after a life shaped by upheaval, journeys, losses, and fresh beginnings.

I owe everything to my parents, Patrick and Anna, laid to rest in Tipperary, for my education, my stubborn streak, and the empathy they instilled in me for those less fortunate. To my family, I am forever grateful. To my dear friends, thank you for standing by me through all of life's trials. To Geraldine, Siobhan, and Niall, who guided me back to the land of my blood—thank you. To those who have passed who will never leave me, I am eternally grateful.

To my coach, Nicole Janz, and my editor, Rachel Bower, my deepest thanks. To Dawn, despite illness, your support in getting this to print was invaluable.

And to the many souls who touched my life along the way, you've given me more than words could ever capture.

Johanna Kirwan
August 2025

Johanna Kirwan draws on over three decades in international development, spanning the UN, NGOs, and the private sector. Her work has taken her across Asia, the Middle East, and Africa, shaping a deep understanding of the field's evolution. Seven Lives is her debut novel.

Printed in Dunstable, United Kingdom

68696269R10211